Exotic, passion
Greek go

Hot *Nights* with a
GREEK

Three exciting novels from Michelle Reid,
Sarah Morgan and Natalie Rivers

Hot nights with an AUSTRALIAN

EMMA DARCY · NICOLA MARSH · LINDSAY ARMSTRONG

Hot nights with a SPANIARD

CAROLE MORTIMER · INDIA GREY · LYNN RAYE HARRIS

Hot nights with a GREEK

MICHELLE REID · SARAH MORGAN · NATALIE RIVERS

Hot nights with an ITALIAN

SARA CRAVEN · HELEN BIANCHIN · LUCY GORDON

Hot nights with a GREEK

MICHELLE REID

SARAH MORGAN

NATALIE RIVERS

All the characters in this book have no existence outside the imagination of the author, and have no relation whatsoever to anyone bearing the same name or names. They are not even distantly inspired by any individual known or unknown to the author, and all the incidents are pure invention.

All Rights Reserved including the right of reproduction in whole or in part in any form. This edition is published by arrangement with Harlequin Enterprises II B.V./S.à.r.l. The text of this publication or any part thereof may not be reproduced or transmitted in any form or by any means, electronic or mechanical, including photocopying, recording, storage in an information retrieval system, or otherwise, without the written permission of the publisher.

This book is sold subject to the condition that it shall not, by way of trade or otherwise, be lent, resold, hired out or otherwise circulated without the prior consent of the publisher in any form of binding or cover other than that in which it is published and without a similar condition including this condition being imposed on the subsequent purchaser.

® and ™ are trademarks owned and used by the trademark owner and/or its licensee. Trademarks marked with ® are registered with the United Kingdom Patent Office and/or the Office for Harmonisation in the Internal Market and in other countries.

Mills & Boon, an imprint of Harlequin (UK) Limited,
Eton House, 18-24 Paradise Road, Richmond, Surrey TW9 1SR

HOT NIGHTS WITH A GREEK
© Harlequin Enterprises II B.V./S.à.r.l. 2012

The Greek's Forced Bride © Michelle Reid 2008
Powerful Greek, Unworldly Wife © Sarah Morgan 2009
The Diakos Baby Scandal © Natalie Rivers 2009

ISBN: 978 0 263 90209 9

25-0912

Harlequin (UK) policy is to use papers that are natural, renewable and recyclable products and made from wood grown in sustainable forests. The logging and manufacturing processes conform to the legal environmental regulations of the country of origin.

Printed and bound in Spain
by Blackprint CPI, Barcelona

The Greek's Forced Bride

MICHELLE REID

Michelle Reid grew up on the southern edges of Manchester, the youngest in a family of five lively children. But now she lives in the beautiful county of Cheshire, with her busy executive husband and two grown-up daughters. She loves reading, the ballet, and playing tennis when she gets the chance. She hates cooking, cleaning, and despises ironing! Sleep she can do without, and produces some of her best written work during the early hours of the morning.

CHAPTER ONE

LOUNGING in his chair at the head of the boardroom table, Leo Christakis, thirty-four-year old human dynamo and absolute head of the Christakis business empire, held the room in a state of near-rigid tension by the sheer power of his silence.

No one dared to move. All dossiers resting on the long polished table top remained firmly closed. Except for the folder flung open in front of Leo. And as five minutes edged with agonising slowness towards ten, even the act of breathing in and out became a difficult exercise and not one of those present had the nerve to utter so much as a sound.

For Leo's outwardly relaxed posture was dangerously deceptive, as was the gentle way he was tapping his neatly clipped fingernails on the polished surface as he continued to read. And anyone—anyone daring to think that the sensual shape of his mouth was relaxed in a smile needed a quick lesson in the difference between a smile and a sneer.

Leo knew the damn difference. He also knew that the nasty stuff was about to hit the fan. For someone around here had pulled a fast one with company money and what made him really angry was that the fiddle was so badly put together anyone with a rudimentary grasp of arithmetic could spot it a mile away. Leo did not employ incompetents. Therefore the list of employees who might just dare to believe they could get away with ripping him off like this could be shortlisted to one.

Rico, his vain and shallow, gut-selfish stepbrother, and the only person employed by this company to earn his place in it by favour alone.

Family, in other words.

Damn, Leo cursed within the depths of his own angry thinking. What the hell gave Rico the idea he could get away with this? It was well known throughout this global organisation that each branch was hit regularly by random internal audits for the specific purpose of deterring anyone from trying a stunt like this. It was the only way a multinational the size of this one could hope to maintain control!

The arrogant fool. Was it not enough that he was paid a handsome salary for doing almost nothing around here? Where did he get off believing he could dip his greedy fingers in the pot for more?

'Where is he?' Leo demanded, bringing half a dozen heads shooting up at the sudden sound of his voice.

'In his office,' Juno, his London based PA quickly responded. 'He was informed about this meeting, Leo,' the younger man added in case Leo was living with the mistaken belief that Rico had not been told to attend.

Leo did not doubt it, just as he did not doubt that everyone sitting around this table believed that Rico was about to receive his just desserts. His stepbrother was a freeloader. It went without saying that the people who worked hard for their living did not like freeloaders. And all it took was for him to lift his dark head with its hard, chiselled bone structure, which would have been stunningly perfect if it weren't for the bump in the middle of his slender nose—put there by a football boot when he was in his teens—and scan with his rich, dark velvet brown eyes half a dozen carefully guarded expressions to have that last thought confirmed.

Theos. There was little hope of him managing to pull off a cover-up with so many people in the know and silently baying for Rico's blood, he concluded as he hid his eyes again beneath the thick curl of his eyelashes.

Did he *want* to cover up for Rico? The question flicked at the muscle that lined his defined jawbone because Leo knew the answer was yes, he did prefer to affect a cover-up than to deal with the alternative.

A thief in the family.

Fresh anger surged. With it came a grim flick of one hand to shut the folder before he rose to his feet, long legs thrusting him up to his full and intimidating six feet four inches immaculately encased in a smooth dark pinstripe suit.

Juno also jumped up. 'I will go and—'

'No, you will not,' Leo said in tightly accented English. 'I will go and get him myself.'

Everyone else shifted tensely as Juno sank down in his seat again. If Leo had been in the mood to notice, he would have seen the wave of swift, telling glances that shifted around the table, but he was in no frame of mind to want to notice anything else as he stepped around his chair and strode out through the door without bothering to spare anyone another glance.

Just as he didn't bother to look sideways as he strode across the plush hushed executive foyer belonging to the Christakis London offices. If he had happened to glance to the side, then he would have seen the lift doors were about to open—but he didn't.

He was too busy cursing the sudden heart attack that took his beloved father from him two years ago, leaving him with the miserable task of babysitting the two most irritating people it had been his misfortune to know—his high-strung Italian stepmother, Angelina, and her precious son, Rico Giannetti.

Ah, someone save me from smooth, handsome playboys and hypersensitive stepmothers anxiously besotted with their beautiful sons, he thought heavily. Family loyalty was the pits, and the day that Rico's ever-looming marriage took place and he took his life and his gullible new wife back to his native Milan to live with Angelina, could not come soon enough for Leo.

If he could get Rico out of this mess without compromising his own reputation and standing in this company that was, or Rico would not be going anywhere but a prison cell.

A sigh hurt his chest as Leo chose to suppress it, the knowledge that he was already looking for a way out for Rico scraping the sides of his pride in contempt.

What was Natasha going to do if she found out she was about to marry a thief?

Though why the hell his stepbrother had chosen to marry Miss Cool and Prim Natasha Moyles was a mystery to Leo. She was not the nubile celebrity stick-like variety of female Rico usually turned on for. In fact, she lived inside a pretty much perfect long-legged and curvy hourglass shape she ruined by hiding it with her lousy dress sense. She was also cold and polite and irritatingly standoffish—around Leo anyway.

So why Natasha had fallen in love with a life-wasting playboy like Rico was just another puzzle Leo could not work out. The attraction of opposites? Did the cool and prim disguise fall apart around Rico?

Perhaps she became a bodice-ripping sex goddess in the bedroom, because she sure had the potential to be a raging sex goddess with her soft feminine features and her wide-spaced, too-blue eyes and that lush, sexy mouth she could not disguise, which just begged to be kissed out of its—

Theos, Leo cursed yet again as something familiarly hot gave a tug low down in his gut to remind how Natasha Moyles's mouth could affect him—while behind him the object of his thoughts walked out of the lift only to pull to a shuddering halt when she caught sight of his instantly recognisable, tall, dark suited shape striding into the corridor across the other side of the foyer.

Natasha's heart did a funny little squirm in her chest and for a moment she actually considered giving in to the sudden urge to leap back into the lift and come back to see Rico later when his stepbrother wasn't about.

She did not like Leo Christakis. He had an uncomfortable way of always making her feel tense and edgy with his hard-nosed, worldly arrogance and his soft, smooth sarcasms that always managed to make such accurate swipes at just about every insecurity she possessed.

Did he think she never noticed the sardonic little smile he always wore on his mouth whenever he was given an opportunity to run his eyes over her? Did he think it was great fun to make her freeze with agonising self-consciousness because she knew he was mocking the way she preferred to hide her curves rather than put them on show like the other women that circled his wonderful self?

Not that it mattered what Leo Christakis thought about her, Natasha then told herself quickly, while refusing to acknowledge the way her eyes continued to cling to him, or that one of her hands was nervously slotting a loose golden strand of hair back to her neatly pinned knot and the other hand clutched her little black purse to the front of her pale blue suit as if the purse acted like a piece of body armour meant to keep him at bay.

She wasn't here to see him. He was just the arrogant, self-important, overbearing stepbrother of the man she was supposed to be marrying in six weeks. And unless Rico had some very good answers to the accusations she was about to fire at him, then there wasn't going to be a wedding!

Natasha felt herself go pale as she recalled the scene some kind person had relayed to her mobile phone this morning. Why did some people take pleasure in sending another person images of their fiancé locked in the arms of another woman? Did they think that because she was attached to the pop-music industry she couldn't possibly have feelings to wound?

Well, look at me now, Natasha thought bleakly as she dragged her eyes away from Leo to stare at the way her trembling fingers were gripping her purse. *I'm not just wounded, I'm dying*! Or her love for Rico was dying, she revised bleakly. Because this was it, the final straw, the last time she was going to turn blind eyes and deaf ears to the rumours about his cheating on her.

It was time for a showdown.

Pale lips pressed together now, eyes fixed on the expanse of grey carpet spread out in front of her, Natasha set herself walking across the foyer and into the corridor that led the way to Rico's office in the now-forgotten wake of Leo Christakis.

The door was shut tight into its housing. Leo didn't bother to knock on it before he twisted the handles and threw it open wide, then took a long step forwards, ready to give Rico Giannetti hell—only to find himself freezing at the sight that met his flashing dark gaze.

For the next few numbing seconds Leo actually found himself wondering if he was dreaming what he was seeing. It was so difficult to believe that even Rico could be this crass! For standing there in front of his desk was his handsome stepbrother with his trousers pooled round his ankles and a pair of slender female legs wrapped around his waist. The very air in the room seethed with gasps as Rico's tight and tanned backside thrust forwards and backwards while soft groans emitted from the naked and not-so-prim female spread out on the top of the desk.

Clothes were scattered all over the place. The smell of sex was strong and thick. The very floor beneath Leo's feet vibrated to Rico's urgent gyrations.

'What the *hell*—?' Leo raked out in a blistering explosion of grinding disgust at the precise moment that an entirely separate sound hit him from behind and had him wheeling about.

He found himself staring into the shock-frozen face of Rico's fiancée. Confusion locked onto his hard golden features because he had believed the blonde ranging about on the desk must be her!

'Natasha?' he ground out in a surprise-driven rasp.

But Natasha didn't hear him. She was too busy seeing her worst nightmare confirmed by the two people who were beginning to realise they were no longer alone. As she watched as if from a strange place somewhere way off in the distance she saw Rico's handsome dark head lift up and turn. Sickness clawed at the walls of her stomach as his heavy-lidded, passion-glazed eyes connected with hers.

Then the woman moved, dragging Natasha's gaze sideways as a blonde head with a pair of blue eyes lifted up to peer around Rico's blocking frame. The two women looked at each other—that was all—just looked.

'*Who* the—?' Leo spun back the other way to discover that the two lovers were now aware of their presence.

The woman was trying to untangle herself, levering herself up on an elbow as she pushed at Rico's bared chest with a slender hand. Shifting his eyes to her, Leo felt true hell arrive as the full horror of what they were witnessing slammed like a truck into his face.

Cindy, Natasha's sister. Two blondes with blue eyes and an age gap that made Cindy seem still just a kid.

His stomach revolted. He swung back to Natasha, but Natasha was no longer standing behind him. Her tense long-legged curvy shape in its stiff pale blue suit was already half-way back down the corridor, making as fast as she could for the lift.

Anger on her behalf roaring up inside him, Leo twisted back to the two guilty lovers. The serious questions Rico should be answering suddenly flew right out of his head. 'You are finished with me, Rico,' he raked out at the younger man. 'Get your clothes on and get the hell out of my building before I have you thrown out—and take the slut with you!'

Then he walked out, pulling the door shut behind him before taking off after Natasha at a run and feeling an odd sense of disorientating empowerment now that Rico had given him just cause to kick him right out of his life.

The lift doors closed before he got there. Cursing through his clenched teeth, Leo turned and headed for the stairs. One flight down and the single lift up to the top floor became three lifts, which fed the whole building. Glancing up to note that Natasha was going down to the basement just before he strode inside another lift, he hit the button that would take him to the same place.

His insides were shaking. All of him was pumped up and pulsing because—*Theos*, sex did that to you. Even when what you'd seen sickened and disgusted, it still had a nasty way of playing its song in your blood.

Striding out of the lift, Leo paused to look around the basement car park. Natasha's Mini stood out like a shiny red stain in a murky world of fashionable silver and black. He saw her then. She was leaning heavily on the car and her shoulders were heaving. He thought she was weeping but as he approached her he realised that she was being violently sick.

'It's OK…' he muttered for some stupid reason because

nothing could be less *OK*, and he placed his hands on her shoulders.

'Don't touch me!' She jerked away from him.

Offence hit Leo full on his chiselled chin. 'I am not Rico!' he raked back in sheer reaction. 'Just as you are not your slut of a sister—!'

She turned and slapped him hard on the face.

The stinging slap rang around the basement as Leo rocked back on his heels in surprise. Natasha was quivering all over, nothing going on inside her burning brain but the remains of that searing surge of violence that had made her turn and lash out. She had never done anything like it before, not in her entire life!

Then she was suddenly having to reel away and double up to retch again, while sobbing and shaking and clutching at the car's bodywork with fingernails that scraped the shiny red paint.

Rico with Cindy—how could he?

How could *she*?

A pair of long fingered hands dared to take hold of her shoulders again. She didn't pull away, but just sagged like a quivering sack into his grasp as the final dregs of her stomach contents landed only inches away from her low-heeled black shoes. By the time it was over she could barely stand upright.

Grim lips pressed together, Leo continued to hold her while she found a tissue in her jacket pocket and used it to wipe her mouth. Beneath the grip of his fingers he could feel her trembling. Her head was bowed, exposing the long, slender whiteness of her nape. That hot sensation flicked at his insides again and he looked away from her, flashing an angry look around the car park like a man being hunted by an invisible quarry and wondering what the hell he was going to do next.

She was not his problem, one part of his brain tried telling him. He had a meeting to chair and a serious financial discrepancy to deal with, plus a dozen or so other points of business to get through before he flew back to Athens this evening and…

A man suddenly appeared from the lurking shadows where the security offices were situated in a corner of the basement. It was Rasmus, his security chief, eyeing them curiously. Leo dismissed him with a frowning shake of his dark head that sent the other man melting back into the shadows again.

His next thought was to coax Natasha back into the lift and take her up to his own office suite to recover. But he could not guarantee that he could get her in there without someone—Rico or her sister—seeing them and starting up another ugly scene.

'OK now?' he dared to question once her trembling started to ease a little.

She managed a single nod. 'Yes. Thank you,' she whispered.

'This is not a moment for polite manners, Natasha,' he responded impatiently.

Natasha jerked away from him, hating him like poison for being here and witnessing her complete downfall like this. Receiving picture evidence that Rico was cheating on her was one thing, but to actually see him doing it with her own sister was absolutely something else.

Just thinking about it had fresh nausea trying to take a grip on her stomach. Working desperately to control it, Natasha fumbled in her bag for her car keys, then turned to unlock the Mini so she could reach inside it for the bottle of water she always kept in there. She wanted to dive into the car and just drive away from it all, but she knew she didn't have it in her yet to drive herself anywhere. She was still too shaken up, too sick and dizzy with horror and shock.

As she straightened up again she had to step around the mess she had ejected onto the ground. *He* didn't move a single inch so she brushed against him in an effort to gain herself some space. It was like brushing against barbed wire, she likened as a hot-rod prickle scraped down through her body and forced her to wilt backwards with a tremor of flayed senses against the side of the car.

Keeping her eyes lowered and away from Leo, she twisted the cap off the bottle of water and put it to her unsteady lips so she could take a couple of careful sips. Her heart was pounding in her head and her throat felt so thick it struggled to swallow. And he continued to stand there like some looming dark shadow, killing her ability to think and making her feel the insignificance of her own diminutive five feet six inches next to his overpowering height.

But that was the great and gloriously important Leo Christakis, she mused dismally—a big, tough, overpowering entity with a repertoire in sardonic looks and blunt comments that could shrivel a lesser person to pulp, and a brain that functioned for only one thing—making money. Even as she stood here refusing to look at him she could feel him fighting the urge to glance at his watch, because he must have more important things to do with his time than to stand here wasting it on her.

'I'll be all r-right in a minute,' she managed. 'You can go back to work now.'

She'd said that as if she believed work was the only thing he lived for, Leo picked up. His chiselled chin jutted. Natasha Moyles always had a unique way of antagonising him with her polite, withdrawn manner or her swift, cool glances that dismissed him as if he were nothing worthy of her regard. She'd been doing it to him from the first time they were introduced at his stepbrother's London apartment.

Leo thrust his clenched hands into his trouser pockets, pushing back the flaps of his dark pinstripe jacket to reveal the pristine white front to his handmade shirt. She shifted jerkily as if the action threatened her somehow and he was suddenly made acutely aware of his own long, muscled torso and taut, bronzed skin. Even the layer of hair that covered his chest prickled.

'Take some more sips at the water and stop trying to out-guess what I might be thinking,' he advised coolly, not liking these sensations that kept on attacking him.

'I wasn't trying to—'

'You were,' he interrupted, adding curtly, 'You might dislike me intensely, Natasha, but allow me a bit more sensitivity than to desert you here after what you have just witnessed.'

But he did not possess quite enough sensitivity to hold back from reminding her of it! Natasha noted as the whole sickening horror of what she had seen sucked her right back in. Her inner world began to sway dizzily, the groan she must have uttered bringing his fingers back up to clasp her arms. She wanted to shrug him off, but she found that she couldn't. She needed his support because she had a horrible feeling that without it she was going to sink into a great dark hole in the ground.

An eerie-sounding beep suddenly echoed through the car park. It was the executive lift being called back up the building to pick up new passengers. Leo bit out a curse at the same time that Natasha's head shot up to stare at him, her wide, blue eyes clashing full on with his dark brown eyes. For a long moment neither of them moved as they stood trapped by a strange kind of energy that shimmered its way through Natasha's body right down to her toes.

Theos, she's beautiful, Leo heard himself think.

She made a sudden dive towards her open car door. Moving like lightning, Leo managed to get there before her, one set of fingers closing around her slender wrist to hold her back while he closed the car door, then took the keys from her hand.

'W-what—?'

Her stammered half-question was cut short by a man used

to making snap decisions. Leo turned and all but frogmarched her across the basement to where his own low sleek black car was parked.

'I can drive myself!' she protested when she realised what he was doing.

'No, you cannot.'

'But—'

'That could be Rico about to walk out of the lift,' he turned on her forcefully. 'So make your mind up, Natasha, which one of us would you prefer to be with right now!'

So very brutal in its delivery. Natasha's mind flooded yet again with what she had witnessed upstairs and she turned into a block of ice.

Opening the car door, Leo propelled her inside. She went without protest, accidentally dropping the water bottle as she did. Jaw set like a vice now, Leo closed the door as, like a man born with special mental powers, Rasmus reappeared not far away. Leo tossed her keys at him and didn't need to issue instructions. His security chief just slunk away again, knowing exactly what was expected of him.

Ignoring the fallen water bottle, Leo strode around the car and got in behind the wheel. She was huddled in the passenger seat, staring down at her two hands where they knotted together on the top of her little black purse and she was shivering like crazy now as the classic reaction to shock well and truly set in.

Pinning his lips together, Leo switched on the engine and thrust it into gear, then sent the car flying towards the exit on an ear-shattering screech of tires. They hit daylight and the early afternoon traffic in a seething atmosphere of emotional stress. A minute later his in-car telephone system burst into life, the screen on his dashboard flashing up Rico's name. A choice phrase locked in the back of his throat and he flicked a switch on the steering wheel that shut the phone down.

Ten seconds later and Natasha's phone started to ring inside her bag.

'Ignore it,' he gritted.

'Do you think I am stupid?' she choked out.

Then they both sat there in thick, throbbing silence, listening to her phone ring until her voicemail took over the call. Her phone kept on ringing repeatedly as they travelled across London with the two of them sitting there like waxwork dummies waiting for her voicemail to keep doing its thing while anger pumped adrenalin into Leo's bloodstream making his fingers grip the steering wheel too tight.

Neither spoke a word to each other. He didn't know what to say if it did not include a string of obscenities that would probably make this woman blanch.

Natasha, on the other hand, had closed herself off inside a cold little world filled with reruns of what she had witnessed. She knew that her sister's behaviour was out of control, but she'd never thought Cindy would sink so low as to…

She had to swallow to stop the bile from rising again as she replayed the moment when Cindy had seen her standing in the door. She saw the look of triumph hit her sister's face followed by the oh-so-familiar pout of defiance that revealed the truth as to why she was doing that with Rico.

Cindy didn't really want him. She did not even like him that much, but she could not stand the thought that Natasha had anything she hadn't first tried out for herself.

Selfish to the last drop of blood, Natasha thought painfully. Spoiled by two parents who liked to believe their youngest daughter was the most gifted creature living on this earth. She was prettier than Natasha, more outward-going than Natasha. Funnier and livelier and so much more talented than Natasha ever could or wanted to be.

Blessed, their parents called it, because Cindy could sing

like a bird and she was the latest pop discovery promising to set the UK alight. After a short stint on a national TV singing competition, Cindy's was the face that everyone recognised while Natasha stood in the background like a shadow. The quiet one, the invisible one whose job it was to make sure everything ran smoothly in her talented sister's wonderful life.

Why had she allowed it to happen? she asked herself now when it all felt so ugly. Why had she agreed to put her own life on hold and be drawn into playing babysitter to a self-seeking, spoiled brat who'd always resented having an older sister to share anything with?

Because she'd known their ageing parents couldn't cope with Cindy. Because from the moment that Cindy's singing talents had been discovered she'd realised that someone had to attempt to keep her from going right off the egotistic rails.

And, face it, Natasha. At first you were excited about being part of Cindy's fabulous life.

Cindy, of course, resented her being there. *Riding on her coat-tails*, she'd called it. Natasha was unaware that she'd said it out loud until Leo flicked a gruff-toned, 'Did you say something?'

'No,' she mumbled—but it was exactly what she'd let herself become: a pathetic hanger-on riding on the coat-tails of her sister's glorious popularity.

Meeting Rico had been like rediscovering that she was a real person in her own right. She'd stupidly let herself believe he had actually fallen in love with her in her own right and not just because of whom she was attached to.

What a joke, she thought now. What a sick, rotten joke.

Rico with Cindy…

Hurt tears scalded the back of her throat.

Rico doing with Cindy what he had always held back from doing with her…

'Oh,' a thick whimper escaped.

'OK?' the man beside her shot out.

Of course I'm not OK! Natasha wanted to screech at him. *I've just witnessed my fiancé bonking the brains out of my sister!*

'Yes,' she breathed out.

Leo brought his teeth together with a steel-edged slice. He flashed her a quick glance to find that she was still sitting there with her head dipped and her slender white fingers knotted together on top of her bag.

Had Rico ever taken this woman across his desk the way he'd been having her sister?

As if she could hear what he was thinking, her chin lifted upwards in an oddly proud gesture, her blue eyes staring directly in front. She possessed the flawless profile of a chaste Madonna, Leo found himself thinking. But when he dropped his eyes to her mouth, he was reminded that it was no chaste Madonna's mouth. It was a soft, very lush, very sexy mouth with a short, vulnerable upper lip and a fuller lower lip that just begged to be—

That sudden burn grabbed hold of him right where it shouldn't—residue from what had happened to him as he'd travelled down in the lift, he stubbornly informed himself.

But it wasn't, and he knew it. He had been fighting a hot sexual curiosity about Natasha Moyles from the first time he'd met her at her and Rico's betrothal party. Her sister had been there, claiming centre stage and wowing everyone with her shimmering star quality, wearing a flimsy flesh-coloured dress exclusively designed for her to show off her stem-like figure and her big hairstyle that floated all around her exquisite face, accentuating her sparkling baby-blue eyes.

This sister had worn classic black. It had shocked him at the time because it was supposed to be Natasha's party yet she'd chosen to wear the colour of mourning. He remembered remarking on it to her at the time.

One of his shoulders gave a small shrug. Maybe he should not have made the comment. Maybe he should have kept his sardonic opinion to himself, because if he had done it to get a rise out of her, then he'd certainly got one—of buttoned-lipped, cold-eyed ice.

They'd exchanged barely a civil word since then.

So, she'd taken an instant dislike to him, Leo acknowledged with a grimace that wavered towards wry. Natasha didn't like tall, dark Greeks with a blunt, outspoken manner. He didn't like loud pop-chicks with stick figures and big hair.

He preferred his woman with more softness and shape.

Rico didn't.

Natasha had both.

Leo frowned as he drove them across the river. So what the hell *had* Rico been doing with Natasha, then? Had the stupid fool started out by playing a game with one sister to get him access to the other one, only to find he'd got himself embroiled too deep? Natasha wasn't the type you messed around with. She just would not understand. Had his bone-selfish stepbrother discovered a conscience somewhere between hitting on Natasha and asking her to marry him within a few weeks?

If so, the bad conscience had not stretched far enough to make him leave the other sister alone, he mused grimly as he shot them through a set of lights on amber and spun the car into a screeching left turn.

'Where are you going?' Natasha burst out sharply.

'My place,' he answered.

'But I don't want—'

'You prefer it if I drop you off at your apartment?' Leo flicked at her. 'You prefer to sit nice and neat on a chair with the bag on your lap waiting for them to appear and beg you to forgive?'

His English was failing, Leo noticed—but not enough

to mask the sarcasm from his voice that managed to shock even him.

'No,' she quivered out.

'Because they will appear,' he persisted nonetheless. 'She needs you to keep her life running smoothly while she struts about playing the pop-chick with angst. And Rico needs you to keep his mama happy because Angelina likes you, and she sees you as her precious boy's saviour from a life of wild women and booze.'

Was that it? Had Rico been using her to appease his old-fashioned mother who'd taken a liking to her on sight? Natasha felt hot tears fill her eyes as she replayed the relieved smile Angelina had sent her when they'd happened to bump into her at a restaurant one night. 'Such a nice girl,' Angelina had said later.

Was that the moment when Rico decided that it might be a good idea to make her his wife? He'd asked her to marry him only a few days later. Like a fully paid-up idiot, she had jumped at the chance. They'd barely shared a proper kiss by then!

And no wonder. She wasn't Rico's type, she was *his mother's* type. Cindy was Rico's type.

Her heart hurt as she stared out of the car window. Beside her, Leo felt the truth hit him hard in the gut.

He had his answer as to what had made Rico want to marry this sister while lusting after the other one. He was keeping his mother happy because Angelina had been making stern warning noises about his lifestyle and Rico saw his loving mama as his main artery source to the Christakis coffers—next to Leo himself, of course.

Which made Natasha Rico's love stooge as much as Leo was his family stooge. From the day eight years ago when his father had brought Angelina home as his new bride with her eighteen-year-old son in tow, Leo's life had become round after round of making Rico feel part of the family because Angelina was so hypersensitive to the differences between the two sons. And his father would do anything to keep Angelina happy and content. When Lukas died so suddenly, Leo continued to keep Angelina, via Rico, happy because she'd been so clearly in love with his father and naturally devastated by his death.

Well, not any longer, he vowed heavily. It was time for both Angelina and Rico to take control of their own lives. He was sick and tired of sorting out their problems.

And that included the money Rico had stolen from him, Leo determined, a black frown bringing his eyebrows together across the top of his nose because he'd allowed himself to forget the reason he'd gone into Rico's office in the first place.

Natasha was yet another of Rico's problems, he recognised, winging another swift, frowning glance her way. She was sitting there with her face turned the colour of parchment, looking as if she might be going to throw up in his car.

What, *this* woman? he then cruelly mocked. This ultra-composed creature would rather choke on her own bile than to allow herself to do anything so crass as to throw up on his Moroccan tan leather.

Which then brought back the question—what had such a dignified thing seen in a shallow piece of manhood like Rico?

Fresh anger tried to rip a hole in his chest.

'Think about it,' he gritted, wishing he could keep his mouth shut, but finding out he could not. 'They are more suited to each other than you and Rico. He famously likes them like your sister—surely you must have known that, heard some of his history with women? He's been playing the high-rolling playboy right across fashionable Europe for long enough. Did you never stop to ask yourself what it was he actually saw in you that made you stand out from the flock?'

The hurt tears gathered all the stronger at his ruthless barrage. Feeling as if she'd just been knocked over by a bus then kicked for daring to let it happen, 'I thought he loved me,' Natasha managed to push out.

'Which is why he was enjoying your sister over his desk when he should have been attending my board meeting, defending himself.'

'Defending?' she picked up.

Leo didn't answer. Clamping his lips together, he climbed out of the car, annoyed with himself for wanting to beat her up for Rico's sins. Rounding the car bonnet, he opened her door, then reached in to take hold of one of her wrists so he could tug her out, even though he knew she didn't want to get out. Her phone started ringing again, distracting her long enough for him to get her into his house.

He pulled her into the living room and pushed her down into a chair then strode off to the drinks cabinet to pour her a stiff drink.

His hands were trembling, he noticed, and frowned as he splashed neat brandy into a glass. When he walked back to Natasha, he saw that she was sitting on the edge of the chair, all neat and prim with the bag on her lap as he'd predicted she would do.

Fresh anger ripped at him. 'Here.' He handed her the glass. 'Drink that, it might help to loosen you up a bit.'

What happened next came without any warning at all that he was about to receive his just desserts when Natasha shot to her feet and launched the full contents of the glass at his face.

'W-who do you think you are, Mr Christakis, to *dare* to think you can be this horrid to me?' she fired up. 'Listening to you, anyone would be f-forgiven for thinking that it had been *you* who'd been betrayed back there! Or is that it?' she then shot out. 'Are you being this downright nasty to me because you wished it *had* been you doing *that* with my sister instead of Rico—is that what your foul temper is about?'

Standing there with brandy dripping down his hard golden cheekbones, Leo Christakis, the dynamic and cut-throat head of one of the biggest companies in the world, heard himself utter…

'No. I wished it had been you with me.'

CHAPTER TWO

IN THE thick, thrumming silence that followed that mind-numbing declaration, Natasha stared up at Leo's liquor-drenched face—and wished that the brandy were still in the glass so she could toss it at him again!

'H-how dare you?' she shook out in tremulous indignation, eyes like sparkling blue diamonds darkening to sultry sapphires as the tears filled them up. 'Don't you think I've been h-humiliated enough without you poking fun at me as if it's all been just a jolly good joke?'

'No joke,' Leo heard himself utter, then grimaced at the full, raw truth in his answer. There was definitely no joke to find anywhere in the way he had been quietly lusting after Natasha for weeks.

No, the real joke here was in hearing himself actually admit to it.

Turning his back on her, Leo dug a hand into his jacket pocket to retrieve the never-used handkerchief his various housekeepers always insisted on placing in his suits. Wiping the brandy from his face, he flicked a glance at the way Natasha was standing there in her neat blue suit and her sensible heeled shoes but with her very expressive eyes now blackened by shock.

'You have a strange idea about men, Natasha, if you believe that the scraped-back hair and the buttoned-up clothes stop them from being curious about what it is you are attempting to hide.'

She blinked at him.

Leo laughed—oddly.

'We don't all go for anorexic pop-stars barely out of the schoolroom,' he explained helpfully. 'Some men even like a challenge in a woman instead of seeing it all hanging out and handed to us on a plate.'

His gaze dropped to the rounded shape of her breasts where they heaved up and down inside her jacket. It was pure self-defence that made her pull in her chest. His eyes darkened as he flicked them back to her face and Natasha knew then what it was he was talking about.

'You want to unwrap yourself and fulfil my curiosity?' he invited. 'I didn't think so.' He smiled at her drop-jaw gasp.

'Why are you doing this—*s-saying* these things to me?' she whispered in genuine bafflement. 'Do you think that because you witnessed what I witnessed it gives you the right to speak to me as if I am a slut?'

'You would not know how to play the slut if your life depended on it,' Leo grimly mocked. 'It is a major part of your fascination to me that with a sister like yours, you are like you are.'

Natasha just continued to stare at him, trying to work out what it was she must have done to deserve any of this. 'Well, you are being loathsome,' she murmured finally. 'And there is nothing in the least bit fascinating about being that, Mr Christakis.'

Her bag had fallen to the floor when she'd jumped to her feet. Natasha bent to recover it, then with as much dignity as she could muster, she turned to leave.

'You're right,' he responded.

'I know I am.' She nodded, taking a shaky step towards the door, and heard him suck in his breath.

'All right,' he growled. 'I'm sorry. OK?'

For mocking her situation just to get the clever quips in?

Straightening her trembling shoulders, 'I didn't ask you to bring me here,' Natasha pushed out in a thick voice. 'I have never asked you to do anything for me. So my sister is a slut. Your stepbrother is a slut. Other than that you and I have nothing in common or to say to each other.'

With that she took another couple of steps towards the door, just wanting to get out of here as quickly as she could do now and willing her legs to continue to hold her up while she made her escape.

Her mobile phone started ringing.

It was like chaos arriving to further agitate havoc because yet another telephone started ringing somewhere else in the house and Natasha's feet pulled her to a confused standstill, the sound of those two phones ringing shrilly in her head.

Behind her *he* wasn't moving a muscle. Was he—was Leo Christakis really as attracted to her as he'd just made out? Her jangling brain flipped out.

Then a knock sounded on the door and the handle was turning. Like a switch that kept on flicking her brain from one thing to another, Natasha envisaged Rico about to walk in the room and her feet were taking a stumbling step back. Maybe she swayed, she didn't know, but a pair of hands arrived to clasp her upper arms and the next thing she knew she was being turned around and pressed against Leo Christakis's shirt front.

'Steady,' his low voice murmured.

Natasha felt the sound resonate across the tips of her breasts and she quivered.

'Oh, I'm sorry, Mr Christakis,' a female voice exclaimed in surprise. 'I heard you come in and assumed you were alone.'

'As you see, Agnes, I am not,' Leo responded.

Blunt as always. His half-Greek housekeeper was used to it, though her eyes flicked curiously to his stepbrother's fiancée standing here held against his chest. When Agnes looked back at his face, not a single hint showed in her expression to say that what she was seeing was a shock.

'Mr Rico keeps ringing, demanding to speak to Miss Moyles,' the housekeeper informed him.

Natasha quivered again. This time he soothed the quiver by tracking a hand down the length of her spine and settling it in the curvy hollow of her lower back. 'We are not here,' Leo instructed. 'And no one gets into this house.'

'Yes, sir.'

The housekeeper left the room again, leaving a silence behind along with a tension that grabbed a tight hold on Natasha's chest. Just totally unable to understand what it was she was feeling any more, she took a shaky step away from him, confused heat warming her cheeks.

'Sh-she's going to think w-we—'

'Agnes is not paid to think,' Leo cut in arrogantly and moved off to pour another brandy while Natasha sank weakly back down into the chair.

'Here, take this...' Coming to squat down in front of her, he handed her another glass. 'Only this time try drinking it instead of throwing it at me,' he suggested. 'It is supposed to be better for you that way.'

His dry attempt at humour made Natasha flick him a brief guilty glance. 'I'm sorry I did that. I don't even know why I did.'

'Don't worry about it.' Leo's smile was sardonic. 'I am used to having my face slapped in car parks and drinks thrown at me. Loathsome guys expect it.'

He added a grimace.

Natasha lowered her eyes to watch his mouth take on that grimacing tilt. It was only as she watched it settle back into a straight line again that she realised it was actually a quite beautifully shaped mouth, slender and firm but—nice.

And his eyes were nice, too, she noticed when, as if drawn by a magnet, she looked back at them. The rich, dark brown colour was framed by the most gorgeous thick, curling black eyelashes that managed to add an unexpected appeal to his face she would never have allowed him before. That pronounced bump in the middle of his nose saved his face from being a bit too perfect. A strong face, she decided, hard hewn and chiselled yet very good-looking—if you didn't count the inbuilt cynicism that was there without her actually knowing *how* it was there.

OK, so he was a lot older than her. Older than Rico by eight years, which made him older than her by a very big ten. And those extra years showed in the blunt opinions he had no problem tossing at people—her especially.

But as for his looks, they weren't old. His skin was a warm honey colour that lay smooth against the bones in his face. No age lines, no smile lines, not even any frown lines, though he did a lot of frowning—around her anyway.

Unaware that she was taking short sips at the brandy as she studied him, Natasha let her eyes track the width of his muscled shoulders trapped inside the smooth fit of his jacket, then let them absorb the fact that his torso was very long and lean and tight. When standing up, he was taller than Rico by several inches and his dark hair was shorter, cut to suit the stronger shape of his face.

She was asking for trouble, Leo thought severely as he watched that lush, pink, generous mouth adopt a musing pout while she looked him over as if he were a prime piece of meat laid out on a butcher's slab.

'How old are you, Natasha?' he asked curiously. 'Twenty-six—twenty-seven?'

Her spine went stiff. 'I'm twenty-four!' she iced out. 'And that is just one more insult you've hit me with!'

'And you're counting.' His eyes narrowed.

'Yes!' she heaved out.

With her blue eyes flashing indignation at him she looked pretty damn fantastic, Leo observed as he knelt there, trying to decide what to do next.

He could leap on her and kiss her—strangely enough she seemed to need him to do that. Or he could gently remove the glass she was crushing between her slender fingers, ease her down on her knees in front of him, then encourage her to just get it over with and use his shoulder to have a good weep.

Something twisted inside him—not sexual this time, but an ache of a different kind. Did she know how badly she was trembling? Did she know her slender white throat had to work like crazy each time to swallow some of the brandy and that her hair was threatening to fall free from its knot?

'I th-think I w-want to go home now,' she mumbled distractedly.

To the apartment she shared with her sister? 'Drink the rest of your brandy first,' Leo advised quietly.

Natasha glanced down at the glass she was holding so tightly between her fingers, then just stared at it as if she was shocked to find it there. As she lifted it to her mouth Leo watched her soft lips take on the warm bloom of brandy and the ache inside him shifted back to a sexual ache.

The doorbell rang.

Rico called her name out.

Natasha's head shot up, the brandy glass falling from her fingers to land with a thunk on the carpet, sending brandy fumes wafting up.

'Natasha—' Leo reached out to her, thinking she was going to keel over into a faint.

But once again Natasha Moyles surprised him. He did not need to pull her to her knees because she arrived there right between his spread thighs with her arms going up and over his shoulders to cling to his neck, those vulnerable blue eyes staring up at him with a helpless mix of pleading and dismay.

'Don't let him in,' she begged tensely.

'I won't,' Leo promised.

'I h-hate him. I never want to see him again.'

'I will not let him in,' he repeated gently.

But Rico called out her name again hoarse with emotion and Leo felt her fingernails dig into the back of his neck while the two of them listened to his housekeeper make some stern response.

'My heart's beating so fast I can't breathe properly,' Natasha whispered breathlessly.

A spark of challenge lit Leo's eyes. He should have contained it—he knew that even as he murmured the challenging, 'I can make it beat faster.'

If he'd said it to distract her attention away from Rico, it certainly worked when her mouth parted on a surprised little gasp. Leo raised a ruefully mocking eyebrow, feeling the buzz, the loin heating, sex-charging, *challenging* buzz.

And he leant in and claimed her mouth.

It was like falling into an electrified pit, Natasha likened dizzily as not a single part or inch of her missed out on the high-voltage rush. She'd never experienced anything like it. He crushed her lips to keep them parted, then slid his tongue into her mouth. The sheer shock feel of that alien wet contact stroking across her own tongue made her shiver with pleasure, then stiffen in shock. He did it again and this time she whimpered.

Leo murmured something, then slid his arms around her

so he could draw her closer to him and deepen the kiss. The next few seconds went by in a fevered hot rush. She felt plastered against his muscled torso. She could hear Rico shouting. Something hard and ridged was pushing against her front. The wildly disturbing recognition of what that something was sent her deaf to everything else as her own senses bloomed with an excited sparkle in response.

It was crazy, she tried telling herself. She didn't even *like* Leo Christakis yet here she was *drowning* in the full on power of his heated kiss! In all of her life she had never kissed anyone like this—never felt even remotely like this! It was like throwing herself against a rock only to discover that the rock had magical powers. His hand skated the length of her spine to her waist, then pressed her even closer, at the same time that he increased the pressure on her mouth, sending her neck arching backwards as he used his tongue to create a warm, thick chain reaction that poured through her entire body like silk.

Natasha heard herself groan something. He muttered a very low, sensual rasp in response. Then Rico called out to her again, harsh and angry enough to pierce into her foggy consciousness, and she wrenched her mouth free.

Trembling and panting with her heart pounding wildly, she stared up at this man while her mind fed her an image of the way Rico had been enjoying Cindy across his desk.

As if her sister knew what she was thinking, her phone began to ring in her purse.

The scald of betrayal burned her up on the inside.

'For God's sake, Natasha, let me *talk* to you!' Rico's rasping voice ground out.

Revenge lit her up.

Leo saw it happen and knew exactly where it was coming from. Sanity returned to him with a gut-crushing whoosh. She was going to offer herself to him, but did he want her like this, bruised and heartbroken and throbbing with a desire for revenge on Rico, who could easily charge in here and catch them?

As they had walked into Rico's office and caught him.

Natasha leant away from Leo and began unbuttoning her jacket with shakily fumbling, feverish fingers.

Leo released a sigh. 'You don't want to do this, Natasha,' he said heavily.

'Don't tell me what I don't want,' she shook out.

The two pieces of fabric were wrenched apart to reveal a white top made of some stretchy fabric that crossed over and moulded the thrusting fullness of her two tight breasts.

Leo looked down at them, then up into her fever-bright eyes, and wanted to bite out a filthy black curse. As she wrenched the jacket off altogether, he reached out to try and stop her, only to freeze when he read the helpless plea that had etched itself on her paper-white face.

If he turned her down now, the rejection was going to shatter her.

Her smooth white throat moved as she swallowed, those kiss-warmed lips parting so she could whisper out a husky little, 'Please…'

And he was lost, Leo knew it. Even as she took the initiative away from him by winding her arms around his neck again, he knew he was not going to stop this. Lifting his hands up to mould her ribcage, he stroked them down the tight white fabric to the sexy indentation of her waist in an exploring act that rolled back the denials still beating an urgent tattoo in his head.

Her mouth was a hungry invite. Leo raked his hands back up her body again and this time covered the full perfect globes of her breasts. She fell apart on a series of gasps and quivers that sent her body into an acute sensual arch, fingernails digging into his neck again, hair suddenly tumbling free in a glorious roll of fine silken waves down her back. She was amazing, a stunningly complicated mix of prim, straight-lace and pure untrammelled passion with her lily-white skin and her lush parted mouth, and her breasts two sensational mounds that filled his hands and…

The front door slammed.

Rico had gone.

If Natasha recognised what the sound meant she did not make a response. Her eyes still burned into him with the fevered invitation she was offering.

Time to make a decision, Leo accepted grimly. Continue this or put a stop to it?

Then her fingernails dug deeper to pull his mouth back down onto hers and the decision was made for him.

Natasha felt his surrender and took it with a leap of triumph that bordered on the mad. She became aware of the power of his erection pressing against her again, instinct made her move against it. He muttered a low, throaty response and he was suddenly tightening his hold of her and drawing her to her feet. Next he was swinging her up into his arms and carrying her, the kiss still a seething hot fuse that frazzled her brain and had her heart pounding to the beat of his footsteps echoing on oak flooring as he headed across the hall and began climbing the stairs.

It was the moment that Natasha saw a small chink of sanity. Her head went back, rending the kiss apart as she opened her eyes to look deep into Leo Christakis's heavily lidded dark eyes before she glanced around her as if she'd been woken up suddenly from a dream.

It was only then that she realised that the hallway was empty. No one was there. No Rico witnessing his betrayed fiancée being carried to bed by her soon-to-be new lover. No housekeeper containing her disapproval and shock.

'Changed your mind now you don't have a witness?' Leo's hard voice swung her eyes back to him again.

He'd gone still on one of the stairs and the look of cold cynicism was back, lashing his skin to the bones in his face.

'No,' Natasha breathed, and she discovered that she meant it. She wanted to do this. She wanted to be carried to bed and made love to by a man who genuinely wanted her—she wanted to lose every single old-fashioned and disgustingly outmoded inhibition she possessed!

'Please,' she breathed softly as she leant in to brush a kiss across the hard line of his mouth. 'Make love to me, Leo.'

There was another moment of hesitation, a glimpse of fury in the depths of his eyes. Then he was moving again, allowing her to breathe again though she had not been aware of holding her breath. He finished the climb up the stairs and carried her into a sultry summer-warmed bedroom with pale walls and big dark pieces of furniture. A red Persian rug covered most of the polished oak floor.

Then he really shocked her by dumping her unceremoniously on the top of a huge soft bed.

As Natasha lay there blinking up at him Leo stood looking down at her, his expression as hard and cynical as hell. 'Stay there and pull yourself together,' was all he uttered before he turned around to walk back to the door.

'Why?' Natasha shook out.

'I will not play substitute to any man,' the cold brute answered.

Natasha sat up. 'Y-you said you wanted me.'

'Strange—' he turned, his kiss-heated mouth taking on a scornful twist '—but seeing you getting off on the possibility of Rico witnessing us together was a real turn off for me.'

Natasha sat up with a jolt. 'I was not getting off on it—!'

'Liar,' he lashed back, then really startled her by striding back to the bed to come and lean over her—close enough to make her blink warily because she just didn't know what was going to come next.

'To keep things clear between us, Natasha,' he murmured silkily, 'if you loved what we were doing downstairs so much you forgot all about Rico, then ask yourself what that tells me about Miss Betrayed and Broken-hearted, hmm—?'

It was as good as a cold, hard slap in the face. Natasha just stared up at him because the worst thing of all was that he had only told it how it was! She *had* been thinking about Rico when she'd invited what she had downstairs. And she had *no* excuse for the way she had begged him to bring her up here!

But had he behaved any better? 'You cruel, h-hateful swine,' she breathed, and pulled up her knees so she could bury her face.

Leo agreed. He was behaving like an absolute beast feeding her all the blame for whatever had erupted in *both* of them downstairs. It was still erupting inside him, he admitted as he turned away again and strode back to the door, wishing that he had stayed in Athens this morning instead of...

Telephones started ringing again, piercing through the high-octane atmosphere—his phone in his jacket pocket and another phone ringing somewhere else in the house. Retrieving his mobile, Leo glared at the display screen, expecting it to show Rico's name.

But it was Juno, his PA. Leo sanctioned the connection. 'This had better be important,' he warned as he stepped out of the bedroom and pulled the door shut.

Natasha lifted her head at the sound of the door snapping into its housing. He'd gone. He'd left her sitting here in a huddle on his bed and just walked away from her—because he could.

On a sudden pummelling punch of self-hatred she scrambled up off the bed, hurt beyond sense that yet another man had humiliated her in the space of one horrible day.

Oh, she had to get out of here! Natasha almost screeched that need at herself as she looked around the floor for her shoes and couldn't find them. Then she remembered the vague echo of them falling off her feet and hitting the floor when Leo had picked her up. Her hair fell forward, tumbling in long waves around her face as if to taunt how she'd been so wrapped up in what she'd been doing with him that she hadn't even noticed before now how her hair had sprung free of its restraints!

Like herself. She shuddered, turning like a drunk not knowing where she was going and heading for the door. She made it out onto the landing and even found her way back down the stairs without coming face to face with anyone else. The door to the living room still hung wide-open and the wretched tears almost broke free when she saw the way her jacket lay in a pale blue swish of fabric on the floor by the chair she had been sitting on before she...

Swallowing, she hurried forward to snatch up the offending garment, pulling it on and fastening it up while she scrambled her feet into her shoes.

He arrived in the doorway, lounging there and filling it with his lean, dark, overbearing presence and...

Her phone started to ring in her purse.

With what tiny bit of control she had left, Natasha bent down to scoop up the purse, then dragged the phone out with trembling fingers and just slammed the wafer-thin piece of shiny black plastic forcefully down on the floor.

It stopped ringing.

The sudden rush of silence throbbed like the beat of a drum in her head, and the tears were really threatening now like hot, sharp shards of flaming glass hitting the backs of her eyes and her throat. She spun towards the door to find Leo was still there, blocking her only exit.

Her mouth began to work, fighting—fighting the tears. 'Please,' she pushed out at him on a thick broken whisper. 'I need you to move out of my way so I can leave.'

Silence. He said nothing. He did not attempt to move. His eyes were half hooded, his lips straight and tight. And there was just enough narrow-eyed insolence in the way he was casually standing there with his arms folded across his front like that to make Natasha realise that something about him had altered dramatically.

'W-what—?' she shook out.

Leo wondered how she would react if he accused her of being a play-acting little thief?

'I am just curious,' he posed very levelly. 'Leave here for where?'

But inside he didn't feel level in any other way. Inside he was feeling so conned he didn't know how he was managing to hold it all in!

Rico's little accomplice—who would have thought it? Apparently Miss Cool and Prim was not so prim when it came to letting her greedy, grasping, slender fingers scoop up the cash Rico had stolen from him!

'To find Rico, perhaps?' he suggested when she didn't say anything.

'No!' She even managed to shudder. 'H-home,' she said, 'to my apartment.'

'You don't have your keys.'

'I'll get the janitor to let me in.'

'Or your loving sister,' Leo provided. 'I predict she is already there, waiting to pounce on you the moment that you arrive.'

Was the other sister in on the scam, too?

And look at this one, he thought as he shuttered his eyes that bit more before running them down her front. She was back to being buttoned up to the throat as if the passionate interlude they'd just shared had never taken place—if you didn't count the flowing hair and the flush on her cheeks and the kiss-swollen bloom on her lips that he had put there.

'What does it matter to you if she is?' Natasha asked. 'This was never your problem,' she informed him stiffly. 'You should not have become involved. I don't even know why you did *or* why you had to bring me here at all!'

'You needed a safe place to recover,' Leo said dryly.

'Safe?' Natasha choked out. 'You'd barely dragged me through your front door before you were coming on to me!'

His careless shrug shot Natasha into movement, wanting, *needing* to get away from the insufferable devil so badly now she was prepared to risk the feeble strength in her shaky legs to walk towards him—aware of the way his eyes followed her every footstep—aware that at any second now she was going to fall down in a screaming hot puddle of tears on the floor.

And *still* he did not move out of her way so she could get out of here, so the closer she came to him, the more her senses went wild, fluttering in protest in case he dared to touch her again—and at the same time fizzing with excitement in the hope that he did!

I don't know myself any more, Natasha thought helplessly. 'Move,' she demanded, resorting to a bit of his own blunt way of speech.

The slight tug his mouth gave was an acknowledgement of it, but he didn't shift. 'You cannot leave,' he coolly informed her.

Was he mad? 'Of course I can go.' Shoulders tense, Natasha tried to push him out of her way by placing her hands on his chest. It didn't happen. It was like trying to move a fully grown tree, and in the end Leo caught up her fingers to lift them away from his chest.

'When I said you cannot leave, Natasha, I meant it,' he informed her very seriously. 'At least not until the police arrive to take you away, that is...'

CHAPTER THREE

NATASHA froze for a second. Then, 'The police?' she edged out blankly.

'The Fraud Squad, to be more accurate,' Leo confirmed.

'Fraud...?'

His mouth gave a twitch at the way she kept on echoing him. 'As in swindler and charlatan,' he provided, driving his gaze down her body as if to say the crime was that she looked the way she did yet could turn on so hotly the way she had.

Natasha quivered, her cheeks turning pink with shamed embarrassment. 'I don't usually...'

'Turn on for a man just to pull the wool over his eyes...?'

Untangling her fingers from his, she fell back a couple of steps and really looked at him, catching on at last that he was leading somewhere with this that she was not going to like.

'Since I don't have a single clue what it is you're trying to get at, I think you had better explain,' Natasha prompted finally.

'Does that mean you *do* want to go to bed with me and it is not a sham act?'

Natasha tensed, lips parting then closing again, because the true answer to that taunt was just not going to happen. 'I was in shock when I—'

'In a state of fright, more like,' he interrupted, 'as to what

Rico had done to all your plans, with his crass bit on the desk today.'

'Plans for what?' Lifting a hand into her hair, she pushed the tumbling mass back from her angrily bewildered face. 'I was planning to marry him—well, there's one plan gone down the tubes,' she choked out. 'And as you've just kindly pointed out to me, I caught him having sex with my own sister—so there's my pride gone the same way along with any love for my sister!' The hand dropped to fold along with the other hand tight across her front. 'Then I surrendered to some mad desire to be wanted by *anybody* and you happened to be in the right place at the right time,' she pushed on, 'but that was just another plan sent off down the tubes when you changed your mind about w-wanting me!'

'And now your carefully creamed nest egg is about to go the same way,' Leo added without a hint of sympathy. 'So I would say that you are having a very bad day, today, Natasha. A very bad day indeed.'

'Nest egg?' Natasha picked up. 'What is it you are talking about now?'

Wearing that smile on his lips that she didn't like, Leo levered himself away from the doorframe and moved away, leaving her to turn and watch as he headed for the drinks cabinet.

He needed something strong, Leo decided as he poured neat whisky into a glass. He took a good slug, then turned back to look at her, 'I have just been talking to my PA,' he enlightened. 'Juno has been very busy investigating where Rico stashed the money he stole from me and has managed to trace it to an offshore bank account in your name, so lose the bemused expression, Natasha. I'm on to you....'

Nothing happened. She didn't gasp, she didn't faint, she didn't jump in with a flood of denials or excuses aimed to defend what it was he was talking about now. Instead, Leo stood there and watched while something cold struck into him because there it was, the dawning of *honesty* taking over her lying, cheating, paling face.

That mouth was still a killer though, he observed—and slammed the glass down, suddenly blisteringly angry with himself for being so easily duped by her *challengingly* prim disguise!

'I think you had better sit down before you fall down,' he advised her flatly.

And she did, which only helped to feed his anger all the more. The flowing-haired witch dropped like a stone into the nearest chair, then covered her guilty face with her light-fingered thieving hands!

Rico had *stolen* the money, Natasha was busily replaying over and over. He'd placed *stolen* money in an offshore bank account in *her* name! One of her hands twisted down to cover her mouth as the nausea returned with a vengeance. In the dragging silence blanketing the space separating them she could feel Leo Christakis's ice-cold anger and blistering contempt beating over her in waves.

If he'd made this declaration yesterday, she would not have believed him. But now, with everything else she'd been forced to look at today, Natasha didn't even see a chink of a question glimmering in the nightmare her mind had become as to whether there had been some kind of mistake.

Everything about Rico had been a lie from start to finish. The way he'd used his looks and his charm and his fabulous blinding-white smile to lure her to him, the way he'd poured soft words of love over her too-susceptible head and refused to make love to her because he wanted to protect her innocence, while all the time he'd been cynically planning to turn her into a thief!

Pulling her fingers away from her mouth, 'I'll give you the money back just as soon as I can access it,' she promised.

'Sure you will,' Leo confirmed. 'Once you have recovered your composure, we will go and see to it straight away.'

That brought her face up, whiter than white now so her eyes stood out bluer than blue. 'But you don't understand. I can't touch it yet.'

'Don't play the broken doll with me next, Natasha,' Leo bit out impatiently. 'It won't alter the fact that you are going to give me my money back now—today.'

'But I can't!' Anxiety shot her quivering to her feet. 'I can't touch it until the day before I was supposed to be marrying Rico! He said it was a tax loophole he'd discovered— that *you* had told him about! He said we had to lock the money up under my name in an offshore account until end of business the day before we marry, then transfer it to another account in our m-married name!'

Leo suddenly exploded spectacularly. 'I do not appreciate you trying to involve my name in your filthy scam!' he bit out at her furiously, 'and telling me stupid lies about access to the money is *not* going to get you out of trouble, Miss Moyles! So cough up the cash or watch me call the damn police!'

In a state of nerve-numbing terror, Natasha backed away as he took two long strides towards her with a murderous expression clamped to his face. The backs of her legs hit the chair she'd just vacated and she toppled back into it. He came to stand over her as he'd done in the bedroom, only this time Natasha put up her hands in an instinctive need to keep him at bay.

Watching her cower in front of him sent Leo into an even bigger rage. 'I don't hit women,' he rasped, then turned on his heel and walked away—right out of the room.

The police—he's going to call the police! Out of her mind with fear now, Natasha scrambled upright and chased after him, terrified of going anywhere near him but even more terrified of what would happen if she didn't stop him from carrying out his threat! He'd crossed the hall and entered a room opposite, which turned out to be a book-lined study.

Coming to a jerky halt in the doorway, she stared as he strode up to the desk and picked up the phone.

Panic sent her heart into overdrive. 'Leo, please...' The pleading quaver in her voice made him go still, wide shoulders taut. 'You have got to believe me,' she begged him. 'I didn't know the money was stolen! Rico conned me into banking it for him as much as he conned you out of it in the first place!'

The last part didn't go down too well because he began stabbing numbers into the telephone with a grim resolve that sent Natasha flying across the room to grab hold of his arm.

Warm, hard muscles bunched beneath her clutching fingers, anger and rejection pouring into his muscular frame. 'He s-said it was to ensure our f-future,' she rushed on unsteadily, 'He said it was a bequeath to him from your father *you* had been holding in trust! He s-said you...'

'Wanted to see the back of him so badly I was prepared to break the law to do it?' Leo suggested when her scramble of words dried up.

'Something like that,' Natasha admitted. Then— Oh, dear God, what had she let Rico do to her? 'Now you are telling me he lied, which means he lied to me about absolutely everything and I—'

The phone went down. Leo turned on her so suddenly Natasha was given no chance to react before she found herself trapped in his arms. His mouth arrived. It took hers with an angry heat that offered nothing but punishment yet she responded—responded to him like a crazy person, clinging and kissing him back as if she'd die if she didn't! When he pulled away again she was limp with shock at her own dizzying loss of control!

'Take my advice,' he rasped. 'Keep with the seduction

theme; it works on me a whole lot better than the innocent pleading does.'

Then his fingers gripped her arms like pincers, which he used to thrust her right away from him, and he was re-establishing his connection with the phone.

Natasha's heart lodged like a throbbing lump of fear in her throat. 'Please,' she begged him, yet again having to swallow to be able to speak at all. 'I did not know that Rico had stolen your money, Leo! I can give you back every penny in six weeks if you'll only wait, but, please—*please* don't ring the police—think of the effect it will have on Rico's mother if you have him arrested! She will—'

'You love the bastard,' Leo bit out roughly. Cutting into what she had been trying to say and making Natasha blink.

'At first, y-yes,' she admitted it. 'He flattered me and...' she swallowed again '...and I know it sounds pathetic but I fell for it because...'

Oh, because she'd been a blind fool! She knew it—probably *everyone* knew it!

'Because things were becoming really bad between me and Cindy and I think I was unconsciously searching for a way out.'

Rico had provided it. It was easier to believe she'd fallen in love with him than to admit to herself that she was so unhappy with her life that she'd grabbed the first opportunity handed to her to get out of it without having to cause ructions within her family. It had been so easy to turn blind eyes to what Rico was really like.

She was a coward, in other words, unwilling to take control of her own life without a nice acceptable prop with which to lean upon as she did.

'I'd already realised Rico wasn't w-what I wanted,' she forced herself to go on. 'I was on my way to tell him so today when we—when we caught him with Cindy. It was—'

'Juno…'

Natasha blinked as Leo's voice cut right through what she had been trying to tell him.

'Put a stop on your investigation of Miss Moyles,' he instructed. 'There has been a—mistake. Have my plane for Athens put on standby and add Miss Moyles's name to the passenger list.'

The phone went down. Natasha tugged in a tense breath. 'Why did you say that?'

'Why do you think?' He turned a hard look on her. 'I want my money back and since you've just told me it will be six weeks before you can give it back to me, I am not letting you out of my sight until you do.'

'But I don't want to go to Athens!' Natasha shrilled out. 'I don't want to go anywhere with you!'

'In your present situation that was not the cleverest thing you could say to me right now, Natasha,' Leo said dryly.

'W-what did you mean by that?'

'Sex,' Leo drawled as if that one shocking word were the answer to everything. 'It is your only bargaining chip, so telling me you don't want me is not going to get you out of this sticky situation, is it?'

A sudden dawning as to where he was going with this shot Natasha's trembling shoulders back, sending her loosened hair flying around her face. 'I am not paying you back with sex!' she protested.

'I should think not,' the cold devil answered. 'No woman, no matter how appealingly she presents herself to me, is worth a cool two million to bed.'

'No…' Yet again Natasha found herself sinking into a thick morass of confusion, the intended insult floating right over her as this new revelation struck a blow to her head. 'F-Five hundred thousand pounds,' she insisted through lips so paper dry now it stung to move them. 'Rico opened the account w-with...'

Her voice trailed away when she saw the expression of mocking contempt that carved itself into this man's face. 'Four separate instalments of five hundred thousand adds up to a cool two million—your arithmetic is letting you down,' Leo spelled out the full ugly truth for her.

'Are you sure?' she breathed.

'Grow up, Natasha,' Leo derided the question. 'You are dealing with a real man now, not the weak excuse for a man you fell in love with—'

'I *don't* love him!'

'So here is the deal.' He kept going as if she hadn't made that denial. 'Wherever I go from now on, you will come with me. And to make the pill sweeter for me to take, you will also share my bed as I wait out the six long weeks until you can access *my* money, when you will then hand it back to me before you get the hell out of my life!'

Real skin-crawling panic had to erupt some time because Natasha had been struggling for so long to keep it in. But now the wild need to get away from this ruthless man and the whole situation sent her spinning around and racing out of the room and back across the hall.

Once again she found herself searching for her bag.

'Going somewhere?' that cruel voice mocked her—again.

'Yes.' She dived on the offending article that kept getting away from her without her knowing it had. 'I'm going to find Rico. He's the only person who can tell you the truth.'

'You think I would believe anything he said to me?'

Swinging around, Natasha almost threw her bag at him! 'I will give you back—every single penny of your rotten two million pounds if it kills me trying!' she choked out.

'Euros...'

Leo's smooth drawl sent her still with her blue eyes relaying her next complete daze as to what he was talking about!

'The money will have been converted into Euros,' he pointed out helpfully, then he named the new figure in Euros, freezing Natasha where she stood. 'Of course it means the same when converted back into pounds sterling so long as the exchange rate remains sound, but...' His shrug said the rest for him—that the figure was growing and growing by the minute in the present financial climate. 'And then there is the interest I will charge you for the—loan.'

'I hate you,' was all she could manage to whisper.

'Fortunate for you, then, that you fall apart so excitingly when I kiss you.'

'I need to speak to Rico,' Natasha insisted.

'Still hoping the two of you can escape from this?'

'No!' She shot up her chin, eyes flashing, hair fascinatingly wild around her tense face. 'I need him to tell you the truth even if you do refuse to believe it!'

Leo observed her from an outwardly calm exterior that did not reflect what was crawling around his insides. He was blisteringly angry—with himself more than anyone because he would have been willing to swear that the prim, cool and dignified Natasha Moyles he'd believed he knew had been the genuine article.

No sign of her now, he observed.

'You will have to catch him first,' he told her dryly. 'Juno tells me that Rico has already left the country. He hitched a ride on a friend's private plane out of London airport. He was quicker than you were at realising what was going to come out of his fevered love fest today, you see. A one-minute telephone conversation with Juno after he left here and he knew he'd been sussed. He's left you to carry the can for him, Natasha.' He spelled it out for her in case she had not worked that out for herself.

Feeling as if the whole weight of the world had just dropped onto her shoulders, 'Then you might as well shop me to the Fraud Squad,' she murmured helplessly.

Leo grimaced. 'That is still one way for me to go, certainly,' he agreed, and watched the telling little flinch that she gave up. 'However, you do still have the other way to pull this around, Miss Moyles...' She even flinched at the formal Miss Moyles now. 'You could still try utilising the only asset you have as far as I am concerned and make me an offer I won't want to refuse?'

He was talking sex again. Natasha went icy. 'The money is peanuts to you, isn't it?'

He offered a shrug. 'The difference between the two of us being that I am wealthy enough to call it peanuts, whereas you are not.'

That was so very true that Natasha did not even bother to argue the point. Instead she made herself look at him. 'So you want me to pay the money back with—favours—' for the life of her she could not bring herself to call it *sex* '—and in return you will promise me you will not take this to the police?'

Leo smiled at the careful omission of the word *sex* and for once the smile actually hit the dark of his eyes. 'You do the prim stuff exceptionally well, Natasha,' he informed her lazily as he began to walk towards her, putting just about every defence mechanism she possessed on stinging alert. 'Shame that your hair is floating around your face like a siren's promise and your lips are still pumped up and hot from my kisses, because it forces me to remember the real you.'

Fighting not to flinch when he reached out to touch her, 'I want your promise that if I do what you w-want me to do, you won't go to the police,' she insisted.

His fingers were drifting up her arms. 'You do know you don't have anything left to bargain with, don't you?'

Pressing her lips together, Natasha nodded, her heart pounding in her chest when his fingers reached her shoulders and gripped. 'I'm relying on your sense of honour.'

'You believe I have one?' He sounded genuinely curious.

She nodded again. 'Yes,' she delivered on a stifled breath. She had to believe it because it was the only way she was going to cope with all of this.

He drifted those light caressing fingers along her shoulders until they reached her smooth skin at her nape, making her jump as a long thumb arrived beneath her chin to tilt up her face. His warm, whisky-scented breath had her lips parting like traitors because they knew what was coming next.

'Then you have my promise,' he said softly.

It was the most soul-shrivelling thing Natasha had ever experienced when she fell into that deal-sealing kiss.

Then her mobile phone started ringing, shocking them apart with Natasha turning to stare down at the phone in surprise because she thought she'd killed it when she'd thrown it to the floor.

Leo went to pick it up, since she didn't seem able to move a single muscle, stepping around her and reminding her of a big, sleek giant cat, the way he moved with such loose-limbed grace. Without asking her permission, he sanctioned the call and put her phone to his ear.

It was some fashion designer wanting to know why Cindy had not turned up for a fitting. 'Natasha Moyles is no longer responsible for her sister's movements,' Leo announced before cutting the connection.

Natasha stared up at him in disbelief. 'What did you say that for?'

He turned a mocking look on her. 'Because it is the truth?'

She went to take her phone back. He snatched it out of her way, then slid it into his jacket pocket. 'Think about it,' he insisted. 'You cannot continue play your sister's doormat while you are in Athens with me.'

And just like that he brought the scene in Rico's office pouring back in. Rico hadn't only involved her in his thieving scam, but he'd been treating her like his doormat, too! Natasha turned away, despising herself for being so gullible—despising Rico for making her see herself like this! And then there was Cindy, her loving sister Cindy playing the selfish, spoiled brat who took anything she felt like because she always had done and been allowed to get away with it!

Then another thought arrived, one that hit her like a brick in the chest. Cindy didn't even need Natasha to keep her life running smoothly because arrangements were already in place to hand her singing career over to a professional agency. One of those big, flashy firms with the kind of high profile Cindy had loved the moment its name was mentioned to her. From as early as next week, Natasha would no longer be responsible for Cindy at all, in effect, to free her up to concentrate on her wedding preparations and her move to Milan!

And she'd just found the reason why Cindy had been doing *that* with Rico. Cindy was about to get everything she'd always wanted—a high-profile management team that was going to fast-track her career and more significantly her absolute freedom from the restraints the sister she resented imposed.

She lifted a hand up to cover her mouth. Her fingers were trembling and she felt cold through to the bone.

'What now?' Leo Christakis shot at her.

She just shook her head because she couldn't speak. Cindy being Cindy, she just could not let Natasha walk off into the sunset with her handsome Italian without going all out to spoil it. *I've had your man, Natasha. Now you can trip off and marry him.* She could hear Cindy's voice trilling those words even though they had not yet been said!

Cindy's little swansong. Her wonderful farewell.

'She set me up,' she managed to whisper. 'She knew I was going to meet Rico today so she made sure she got to his office before I did and set me up to witness her doing—that with him.'

'Why would your own sister want to set you up for a scene like that?'

'Because I'm not her real sister.' Natasha slid her fingers away from her mouth. 'I was adopted...' By two people who'd believed their chances of having a child of their own had long passed them by. Five years later and their real daughter had arrived in their arms like a precious gift from heaven. Everyone had adored Cindy—*Natasha* had adored her!

A firm hand arrived on her arm to guide her down into the chair again, then disappeared to collect a second brandy. 'Here,' he murmured, 'take this...'

Natasha frowned down at the glass, then shook her head. 'No.' She felt too sick to drink anything. 'Take it away.'

Leo put the glass down, but remained squatting in front of her as he'd done once before. Strong thighs spread, forearms resting on his knees. His suit, she saw as if for the first time, was made of some fabulously smooth fabric, expensive and creaseless—like the man himself.

And his mouth might look grim, but it was still a mouth she could taste; she felt as if she already knew it far more intimately than any other man's mouth—and that included Rico.

'Stop looking at me as if you *care* what's happening inside my head!' she snapped at the way he was squatting there studying her as if he were really concerned!

He had the grace to offer an acknowledging grimace and climbed back to his full height. So did Natasha, making herself do it, feeling cold—frozen right through, because it had also just hit her that she was on her own now. No sister. No fiancé. Not even a pair of loving parents to turn to because, although they'd loved her in their own way, they had never loved her in the way they loved Cindy. Cindy was always going to come first with them.

'So what is it you want me to do?' she murmured finally in a voice that sounded as cold as she felt.

Leo threw her a frowning dark look. 'I told you what I want.'

'Sex.' This time she managed to name it.

'Don't knock it, Natasha,' Leo drawled. 'The fact that we find we desire each other is about to keep you out of a whole lot of trouble.'

He turned away then, leaving her to stare at his long, broad back. He was so hard she had to wonder who it was that had made him like that.

Then she remembered Rico telling her that Leo had been married once. From what Rico had said, his wife had been an exquisite black-haired, black-eyed pure Latin sex bomb who used to turn men on with a single look. The marriage had lasted a short year before Leo had grown tired of hauling her out of other men's beds and he'd kicked her out of his life for good.

But he must have really loved her to last a whole year with a faithless woman like that. Had his ex-wife mangled up his feelings so badly she'd turned him into the ruthless cynic she was looking at now?

As if he could tell what she was thinking he glanced round at her, catching the expression on her face. Their eyes maintained contact for a few nerve-trapping seconds as something very close to understanding stirred between them, as if he knew what she was thinking and his steady regard was acknowledging it.

'OK, let's go.' Just that quickly he switched from seeming almost human to the man willing to use her for sex until he could get his precious money back. 'Take it or leave it, Natasha,' he cut into the thrumming thick nub of her silence—

there because she was finding the switch much harder to make. 'But make your mind up, because we have a flight to catch.'

A flight to catch. A life to get on with while she put her own on hold—again.

Natasha answered with a curt nod of her head.

It was all he required to have him reach out and pull her back into his arms. The heat flared between them. She uttered a helpless protest as his mouth arrived to claim hers. And worst thing of all was how the whole heady, hot pleasure of it caught hold of her as fast as it took him to make that sensual stroking movement with his tongue along the centre of hers. By the time he drew back, she was barely focusing. Her lips felt swollen and thick—but deep inside, in the core element where the real Natasha lay hidden, she still felt as cold as death.

Leo thought about just saying to hell with it and taking her back upstairs to bed and forgetting about the rest of this. She had no idea—*none* whatsoever—what that hopeless look on her face teamed with the buttoned-up suit was doing to him.

He turned away from temptation, frowning at his own bewildering inclinations. How had he gone from being a tough business-focused tycoon to a guy with his brains fixed on sex?

More than his brains, he was forced to acknowledge when he had to stand still for a moment and work hard to bring much more demanding body parts under control.

Then she moved, swinging him back round to look at her, and he knew then exactly why he was putting this woman before his cool business sense. She had been driving him quietly crazy for weeks now, though he had refused to look at the reason why until Rico had ruined his chances with her.

Rico's loss, his gain. Natasha Moyles was going to come so alive with his tutelage she was not going to be able to hide anything from him. And he was going to enjoy every minute of making that exposure take place. Then once their six weeks were over he would get his money back and walk away so he could get on with his life without having her as a distraction that constantly crept into his head.

Maybe it was worth the cool two million to achieve it.

'I need to speak to m-my parents...'

'You can ring them—from Athens. Hit them with a situation they cannot argue with.'

'That wouldn't be—'

'You prefer to relay the full ugly details to their faces?' he cut in on her. 'You prefer to explain to them that you and Rico have been caught thieving and that their other daughter is a man-thieving tramp?'

The tough words were back. The sigh that wrenched from Natasha was loaded down with defeat. 'I will need to get my passport from the apartment,' was all she said.

'Then let's go and get it.' Leo held out his hand to her in an invitation that was demanding yet another surrender—one that sizzled in the short stillness that followed it.

A step on the road to ruin, Natasha recognised bleakly as she lifted her hand and settled her palm against his. His long tanned fingers closed around her slender cold fingers, she felt his warmth strike through her icy skin and his strength convey itself to her as he turned and trailed her behind him into the hallway, then out of the house.

CHAPTER FOUR

OUTSIDE the afternoon sunlight was soft on Natasha's face. The short journey to her apartment was achieved in silence. The first thing she saw when they arrived there was Cindy's silver sports car and her aching heart withered, then sank.

Leo must have recognised the car, too, because, 'I'm coming in with you,' he insisted grimly.

It had not been a request. And anyway Natasha was glad she was not going to have to face Cindy on her own.

Feeling dread crawling across her flesh, she walked into the foyer with Leo at her side. The janitor looked up and smiled. It was all she could do to smile politely back by return.

'I've mislaid my keys,' she told him. 'Do you think I could borrow the spare?'

'Your sister is home, Miss Moyles,' the janitor informed her. 'I can call up and she will let you—'

'No.' It was Leo who put in the curt interruption. The janitor looked up at him and it didn't take a second for him to recognise that he was in the presence of a superior power. 'We will take the spare key, if you please.'

And the key changed hands without another word uttered.

In the lift, Natasha began to feel sick again. She didn't want this confrontation. She would have preferred not to look into Cindy's face ever again.

'Do you want me to go in for you?'

The dark timbre of his voice made her draw in a breath before she straightened her shoulders, pressed her tense lips together and shook her head. The moment she stepped into the hi-tech, ultra-trendy living room, her sister jumped up from one of the black leather chairs.

Cindy's eyes were red as if she'd been crying and her hair was all over the place. 'Where have you been?' she shrilled at Natasha. 'I've been trying to reach you! Why didn't you answer your damn phone?'

'Where I've been isn't any of your business,' Natasha said quietly.

Cindy's fingers coiled into fists. 'Of course it's my business. I employ you! When I say jump you're paid to jump! When I say—'

'Get what you came for, *agape mou*,' a deep voice quietly intruded.

Leo's dark, looming presence appeared in the doorway. Cindy just froze where she stood, her baby-blue eyes standing out as hot embarrassment flooded up her neck and into her face. 'M-Mr Christakis,' she stammered out uncomfortably.

Ah, respect for an elder, Natasha noted, smiling thinly as she walked across the room to open the concealed wall safe where she kept her personal papers.

'I didn't expect you to come here....'

Nor had Cindy expected Leo Christakis to catch her with Rico, thought Natasha, and that was why she was embarrassed to see him again.

Leo said nothing, and Natasha winced at the dismissive contempt she could feel emanating from that suffocating silence. Cindy just wasn't used to being looked at like that. She wasn't used to being ignored. Embarrassment and respect changed to a sulky pout and flashing insolence, which she turned on Natasha.

'I don't know what you think you are doing in my safe, Natasha, but you—'

'Be quiet, you little tramp,' Leo said.

Cindy flushed to the roots of her hair. 'You can't speak to me like that!'

Natasha turned in time to watch the way Leo looked her sister over as if she were a piece of trash before diverting his steady gaze to her. 'Got what you need?' he asked gently.

Gentle almost crucified her, though she was way beyond the point of being able to work out why. Fighting the never-far-away-tears, she nodded and made her shaking legs take her back across the room towards him.

Cindy sent her a frightened look. 'You aren't leaving,' she shot out. 'You *can't* leave. That idiot Rico panicked and phoned the parents looking for you—now they're on their way here!'

Natasha ignored her, her concentration glued to the door Leo was presently filling up. *I just need to get away from her, she told herself. I just need to...*

'You're such a blind, silly, stupid thing, Natasha!' Cindy went back on the attack. 'Do you think I'm the only woman Rico has had while he's been engaged to you? Did you really believe that someone like him was going to fall in love with someone like you—?'

Natasha hid her eyes and just kept on walking.

'What are you but the right kind of stuffed-blouse type his silly mother likes? I did you a favour today. You could have married him still blind to what he's really like! It was time someone opened your eyes to reality. You should be thanking me for doing it!'

Natasha had reached Leo. 'Anything else before we get out of here?' he asked.

'S-some clothes and—things,' she whispered.

'Don't you *dare* ignore me!' Cindy screeched. 'The parents will be here in a minute. I want you to tell them that this was all your own fault! I've got a gig tonight and I just can't perform with all of this angst going on. And you need to get busy with some damage control because you won't like it if I have to do it myself!'

Leo stepped to one side to let Natasha pass by him. The moment she closed her bedroom door, he reacted, stepping right up to Cindy. 'Now listen to me, you spoiled little tart,' he said. 'One false word from you about what took place today and you're finished. I will see to it.'

Cindy's head shot up, scorn pouring out of her bright baby blue eyes. 'You don't have the power—'

'Oh, yes, I do,' Leo said. 'Money talks. Jumped-up little starlets like you come off a conveyer belt. Give me half an hour with a telephone and I can ruin you so quickly you won't see oblivion until you find yourself sunk in it up to your scrawny neck. Pending records deals can be withdrawn. Gigs cancelled. Careers murdered by a few words fed into the right ears.'

Cindy went white.

'I see that you get my drift.' Leo nodded. 'You are not looking into the eyes of a devoted fan now, sweet face, you're looking into the eyes of a very powerful man who can see right through the shiny packaging to the ugly person that lurks beneath.'

'Natasha won't let you do anything to h-hurt me,' Cindy whispered.

'Yes, she will,' Natasha said. She was standing just inside the door with a hastily packed bag at her feet.

As Cindy looked at her Natasha twisted something out of her fingers, sending it spiralling through the air. It landed with a clink on the pale wood floor at Cindy's feet. Looking down, even Leo went still when he saw what it was.

Her ring—her shiny diamond engagement ring. 'That's just something else of mine you haven't tried,' she explained. 'Why don't you put it on and see if it fits you as well as my fiancé did?'

Cindy's appalled face was a picture. 'I didn't want him, and I don't want—that!'

'Well, what's new there?' Natasha laughed, though where the laugh came from she did not have a single clue. 'When have you ever wanted anything once you've possessed it?'

Pandemonium broke out then as their parents arrived, rushing in through the flat door Leo must have left on the latch.

They looked straight at Cindy. They had barely registered that Natasha was even there.

Cindy burst into a flood of tears.

'Oh, my poor baby,' Natasha heard her mother cry out. 'What did that Rico do to you?'

Natasha began to feel very sick again. She stared at the way her two parents had gathered comfortingly around Cindy and felt as if she were standing alone somewhere in outer space.

Then her gaze shifted to Leo standing on the periphery of it all with his steady dark eyes fixed on her painfully expressive face. 'Can we leave now?' she whispered.

'Of course.'

And he was stooping to pick her bag up. As he straightened again his hand made a proprietary curl of her arm and Natasha heard Cindy quaver, 'He's been stalking m-me for weeks, Mummy. I went to see him to tell him to stop it or I would tell Natasha. The next thing I knew he…'

Leo closed the door on the rest. Neither said a single word to each other as they walked out of the apartment and headed for the lift. All the way down to the foyer they kept their silence, all the way out to his car. He drove them away in that same tense silence until Leo clearly could not stand it any longer and flicked a button on his steering wheel to activate his phone.

Natasha recognised the name 'Juno', then nothing as he proceeded to share a terse conversation in Greek.

She kept her eyes fixed on the side window and just let his deep, firm, yet strangely melodious voice wash over her as they drove out of the city and into lush green, rural England. The ugliness of her situation was crawling round her insides, the spin of once-loved faces turning into strangers as they flipped like a rolling film through her head. She didn't know them and, she realised painfully, they did not really know her—or care.

'Do you think they've noticed that you are no longer there yet?'

Realising Leo had finished his telephone conversation and had now turned his attention on her, Natasha lifted a shoulder in an empty shrug. Had they even noticed she was there in the first place? Pressing her pale lips together she said nothing.

A minute later they were turning in through a pair of gates leading to a private airport where, she presumed, Leo must keep his company jet. It took no time at all to get through the official stuff. All the way through it she stood quietly at his side.

So this is it, Natasha told herself as they walked towards a sleek white jet with its famous Christakis logo shining Ionian blue on its side. I'm going to fly off into the sunset to become this man's sole possession.

She almost—almost managed a dry little smile.

'What?' Leo just never missed anything—not even the smallest flicker of a smile.

'Nothing,' she murmured.

'Forget about Rico and your family,' he said harshly. 'You are better off without them. I am the only one you need to think about now.'

'Of course,' Natasha mocked. 'I'm about to become a very rich man's sexual doormat, which has to be quite a hike up from being my family's wimpish doormat and Rico Giannetti's thieving one.'

Leo said nothing, but she could sense his exasperation as he placed his hand on the small of her back to urge her up the flight steps.

The plane's interior gave Natasha an insight into a whole new way of travelling. Breaking free from his touch, she took a couple of steps away from him, then stopped, tension springing along her nerve-ends when she heard the cabin door hiss as someone sealed it into its housing and the low murmur of Leo's voice speaking to someone, though she did not turn around to find out who it was.

This wasn't right. None of it was right, a sensible voice in her head tried to tell her. She should not be on this plane or tripping off to Athens with Leo Christakis—she should be staying in England and fighting to clear her name!

'Here, let me take your jacket.' He arrived right behind her again, making her whole body jerk to attention when his hands landed lightly on her shoulders.

'I would rather keep it on,' she insisted tautly.

'No, you would not.' Sliding his fingers beneath the jacket collar, he followed it around her slender white throat until he located the top button holding her jacket fastened. 'You will be more comfortable without it.' He twisted the button free.

'Then I can do it.' Snapping up her hands, Natasha grabbed his wrists with the intention of pulling his hands away. He didn't let her.

'My pleasure,' he murmured smoothly as the next button gave.

Her two breasts thrust forward, driving a shaken gasp from her throat. 'I wish you would go and f-find someone else to torment,' she breathed out sharply when his knuckles grazed her nipples on their way to locate the next button, and felt her stomach muscles contract as he brushed across them, too.

He just laughed, low and huskily. 'When did you find the time to stick your hair up again?'

'At the flat,' she mumbled, then went as taut as piano wire when the last button gave way to his working fingers.

'You're too skittish,' he chided.

'And you're too sure of yourself!' Natasha flicked out.

'That's me,' he admitted casually, moving his hands down her sleeves to locate her handbag still clutched in one tense set of fingers. He gently prised it free to toss it aside.

Why the loss of her purse should make her feel even more exposed and under threat, Natasha did not have a clue, but by the time he'd eased the jacket from her shoulders she was more than ready to dissolve into panic. And the worst part about it was that she could not even say for sure any more what it was she was panicking about—Leo and his relentless determination to keep her balanced on the edge of reason, or herself because her senses persisted in responding to him even when her head told them to stop!

His hands arrived at the curve of her slender ribcage over the stretchy white fabric that moulded her so honestly it felt as if he were touching her skin. Natasha closed her eyes and prayed for deliverance when he eased her back against him and she felt his heat and his hard masculine contours.

'Leo, please…' It came out somewhere between a protest and a breathless plea.

It made no difference. He lowered his mouth and brushed his lips across the exposed skin at her nape and for Natasha it was like stepping off a cliff, she fell that easily. She murmured a pathetic little stifled groan and her head tipped downwards, inviting the gentle bite of his teeth. As he began kissing his way round her neck, she rolled it sideways on a slow and pleasurable, sensual stretch to give him greater access. She so loved what he was making her feel.

'Mmm, you feel good, like warm, living silk to touch,' he murmured. 'You have a beautiful body, Natasha,' he added huskily, gliding his hands upwards until he cupped her breasts and gently pressed his palms against their tightly budded peaks. 'I need you to turn your head and kiss me, *agape mou*,' he told her huskily.

And she did. She moved on a restless sigh of surrender when he reached for her hands and lifted them upwards, then clasped them around the back of his neck. The sheer sensual stretch of her body felt unbelievably erotic. She whispered something—even she didn't know what it was—then she was giving in and twisting her head and going in search of his waiting mouth.

Leo gave it to her in a hot, deep, stabbing delivery. Her fingers curled into the black silk of his hair. It was shocking. She didn't know herself like this, all soft and pliable and terribly needy.

'We are cleared for take-off, Mr Christakis,' a disembodied voice suddenly announced.

Leo drew his head back and the whole wild episode just went up in a single puff of smoke. Natasha opened her eyes and found that she couldn't focus. Passion coins of heat burned her cheeks. She became aware of her hands still clinging to his head and slid them away from him, her still-parted mouth closing with a soft burning crush of her warm lips.

'You are quite a bundle of delightful surprises,' she heard Leo mock. 'Once unbuttoned you just let it all flood out.'

And the real horror of it was that he was, oh, so right! Each time he touched her it was the same as losing touch with her common sense and dignity. Acknowledging that had Natasha breaking free of him to wrap her arms tightly around her body, then she just stood there, shaking and fighting to get a grip on herself.

An engine purred into life.

'Take a seat, strap yourself in, relax,' his hatefully sardonic tone invited, and he was stepping around her to stride down the cabin.

Watching him go, Natasha thought she glimpsed a flick of irritation in the way that he moved and kind of understood it. To a man like Leo Christakis the deal had been done, so to have her continue to play it coy annoyed him. From the little she'd heard about his private life, he liked his women with the experience and sophistication to know how to respond positively to his seduction routine, not blow hot then tense and skittish each time he attempted to act naturally with her.

The gap in their ages suddenly loomed. The fact that there was nothing natural at all in the two of them being together picked at her nerves as she chose a seat at random and sat down.

The plane slid into movement. Natasha watched Leo remove his suit jacket to reveal wide, muscled shoulders hugging the white fabric of his shirt. He draped the jacket over the back of the chair in front of the desk, then folded his long body into the seat placed at an angle to her, those muscled shoulders flexed as he locked in his seat belt, then reached out to pull a large stack of papers towards him and sat back to read.

Dragging her eyes away from him, she hunted down her seat belt with the intention of fastening it, but she spied her discarded jacket lying on the seat opposite and on sheer impulse she snatched it up and put it back on, buttoning it shut all the way up to her throat, though she had no idea what, by doing it, she was hoping to prove.

Unless it had something to do with the tight bubble of anger she could feel simmering away inside at the way he was lounging there already steeped in paperwork and putting on a good impression that he had already forgotten she was here, which hit too closely at the way her family had behaved at the apartment.

Ten minutes later they were in the air and his laptop computer was open, his voice that same melodic drone in her ears. A gentle-voiced stewardess appeared at Natasha's side to ask her if she would like something to eat and drink. She knew she wouldn't be able to eat anything right now, but she asked if it was possible for her to have a cup of tea, and the stewardess smiled an, 'of course,' and went away to see to it.

Leo swivelled around in his chair.

He looked at her, narrowing his eyes on the buttoned-up jacket. A new rush of stinging awareness spun through the air.

'It will have to stay off at some point,' he murmured slowly.

Natasha pushed her chin up and just glared.

It was a challenge that made his dark eyes spark and sent Natasha breathless. Then he was forced to turn his attention back to his satellite link, leaving her feeling hot and skittish for a different reason.

For the next three hours he worked at the desk and she sat sipping her tea or reading one of the magazines the stewardess had kindly brought for her. Throughout the journey Leo kept on swinging his chair around to look at her, waiting until she felt compelled to look back at him, then holding her gaze with disturbing dark promises of what lay ahead. Once he even got up and came to lean over her, capturing her mouth with a deep, probing kiss. As he drew away again the top button to her jacket sprang open.

He did it to challenge her challenge, Natasha knew that, but her body still tightened and her breasts tingled and peaked. The next time he turned his chair to look at her the button was neatly fastened again and she refused point blank this time to lift her head up from the magazine.

They arrived in Athens to oven heat and humid darkness. It was a real culture shock to witness how their passage through the usual formalities was so carefully smoothed. And Leo felt different, like a remote tall, dark stranger walking at her side. His expression was so much harder and there was a clipped formality in the way he spoke to anyone. A quiet coolness if he was obliged to speak to her.

Natasha put his changed mood down to the way people constantly stopped to stare at them. When she saw the cavalcade of three heavy black limousines waiting to sweep them away from the airport, it really came down hard on her to realise just how much power and importance Leo Christakis carried here in his own capital city to warrant such an escort.

'Quite a show,' she murmured as she sat beside him in the rear of the car surrounded by plush dark leather while the other two cars crouched close to their front and rear bumpers. Seated in the front passenger seat of this car and shut away behind a plate of thick, tinted glass sat a man Leo had introduced to her as, 'Rasmus, my security chief'. It was only as he made the introduction that Natasha realised how often she'd seen the other man lurking on the shadowy periphery of wherever Leo was.

'Money and power make their own enemies,' he responded as if all of this was an accepted part of his life.

'You mean, you always have to live like this?'

'Here in Athens, and in other major cities.' He nodded.

It was no wonder then that he was so cynical about anyone he came into contact with, it dawned on her. He flies everywhere in his private jet aeroplane, he drives around in private limousines and he has the kind of bank balance most people could not conjure up even in their wildest dreams. And he has so much power at his fingertips he probably genuinely believes he exists on a higher plane than most other beings.

'I never saw it in London,' she said after a moment, remembering that while he'd been in London he had driven himself.

He turned his head to look at her, dark eyes glowing through the dimness of the car's interior. 'It was there. You just did not bother to look for it.'

Maybe she didn't, but... 'It can't have been as obvious there,' Natasha insisted. 'I was used to some measure of security when Cindy was performing but never anything like this—and none at all with Rico.' She then added with a frown, 'Though that seems odd now when I think about who Rico is and—'

He moved, it was barely a shift of his body but it brought Natasha's face around to catch the flash to hit his eyes.

'What?' she demanded.

'Don't ever compare me with him,' he iced out.

Her blue eyes widened. 'But I wasn't—'

'You were about to,' he cut in. 'I am Leo Christakis, and this is *my* life you are entering into with all its restrictions and privileges. Rico was nothing.' He flicked a long-fingered hand as if swatting his stepbrother away. 'Merely a freeloader who liked to ride on my coat-tails—'

Natasha went perfectly pale. 'Don't say that,' she whispered.

'Why not when it is the truth?' he declared with no idea how he had just devastated her by using the same withering words to describe Rico as her sister had used to describe her. 'His name is Rico Giannetti, though he prefers to think of himself as a Christakis, but he has no Christakis blood to back it up and no Christakis money to call his own,' he laid out with contempt. 'He held an office in every Christakis building because it was good for his image to appear as if he was worthy of his place there, but he never worked in it—not in the true meaning of the word anyway.' The cynical bite to his voice sent Natasha even paler as his implication hit home. 'He drew a salary he did little to earn and spent it on whatever took his fancy while robbing me blind behind my back as I picked up the real tabs on his extravagant tastes,' he continued on. 'He is a hard-drinking, hard-playing liar to himself and to everyone connected to him, including you, his betrayed, play-acting betrothed.'

Shaken by his contemptuous barrage, 'Ex-betrothed,' Natasha husked out unsteadily.

'Ex-everything as far as you are concerned,' he pronounced. 'From this day on he is out of the picture and I am the only man that matters to you.'

He had demanded that she put her family out of her head, now he was insisting she put Rico out of her head. 'Yes, sir,' she snapped out impulsively, wishing she could put him out of her head, too!

A black frown scored his hard features at her mocking tone. 'I thought a few home truths at this point will help to keep this relationship honest.'

'Honest?' Natasha almost hyperventilated on the breath she took. 'What you're really doing here is letting me know that you expect to control even my thoughts!'

Impatience hit his eyes. 'I do not expect that—'

'You do expect that!'

Leo raked out an angry sigh. 'I will not have Rico's name thrown in my face by you every five minutes!'

Natasha swung round on him in full choking fury. 'I did not throw his name at you—*you* battered *me* with it!'

'That was not my intention,' he returned stiffly.

Twisting on the seat, she glared at the glazed partition. 'You're no better than Rico, just different than Rico in the way you treat people—women!' she shook out with a withering glance across the width of the seat. 'Since we are driving along here like a presidential cavalcade, your loathsome arrogance is one fault I will let you have, but your—'

'Loathsome—again?' he mocked lazily.

It blew the lid off what was left of her temper. 'And utterly, pathetically jealous of Rico!'

Silence clattered down all around them with the same effect as crashing cymbals hitting the crescendo note and making Natasha's heart begin to race. She could not believe she had just said that. Daring another glance at Leo, she could see him looking back at her like a man-eating shark about to go on the attack, and now she couldn't even breathe because the tension between them was sucking what was left of the oxygen out of the luxury confines of the car.

He reacted with a lightning strike. For such a big man he moved with a lithe, silent stealth and the next thing she knew she was being hauled through the space separating them to land in an inelegant sprawl of body and limbs across his lap. Their eyes clashed, his glittering with golden sparks of anger she hadn't seen in them before. Hers were too wide and too blue and—scared of what was suddenly fizzing in her blood.

She had to lick her suddenly very dry lips just to manage a husky, 'I didn't really m-mean—'

Then came the kiss—the hot and passionate ambush that silenced her attempt to retract what she'd said, and flung her instead into fight with lips and tongues and hands that did not know how to stay still. His breath seared her mouth and a set of long fingers was clamped to the rounded shape of her hip, her own fingers applying digging pressure to whatever part of his anatomy they could reach as their mouths strained and fought. The motion of the car and the fact that they were even *in* one became lost in the uneven fight. She wriggled against him. His hand maintained its controlling clamp. She felt her fingernails clawing at his nape and the rock-solid moulding of his chest so firmly imprinted against his shirt.

He loved it. She caught his tense hiss of pleasure in her

mouth and felt a tight, pleasurable shudder attack his front, the powerful surge of his response making itself felt against the thigh he held pressed into his lap. Then his hand was sliding beneath her skirt and stroking the pale skin at the top of her thigh where her stockings did not reach. If he stroked any higher, he was going to discover that she was wearing a thong and she increased her struggle to get free before he reached there, lost the fight, and a quiver of agonising embarrassment sent her kiss-fighting mouth very still.

'Well, what do we have here?' he paused to murmur slowly, long fingers stroking over a smoothly rounded, satin-skinned buttock and crippling Natasha's ability to breathe. 'The prim disguise is really beginning to wear very thin the more I dig beneath it.'

'Shut up,' she choked, eyes squeezed tight shut now. She was never going to wear a thong ever again, she vowed hectically.

He removed his hand and her eyes shot open because she needed to know what he was going to do next, and found herself staring into his mockingly smiling face. The anger had gone and his lazily, sensual male confidence was firmly back in place.

'Any more hidden treasures left for me to discover?' He arched a sleek, dark, quizzing eyebrow.

'No,' Natasha mumbled, which made him release a dark, husky laugh that shimmered right through her as potently as everything else about him did.

Then he wasn't smiling. 'OK, so I am jealous of Rico where you are concerned.' He really shocked her by admitting it. 'So take my advice and don't bring him into our bed or I will not be responsible for the way I react.'

Before she could respond to that totally unexpected backdown, he was lowering his head again and crushing her mouth. How long this kiss went on Natasha had no idea, because she just lost herself in the warm, slow, heady promise it was offering.

The car began to slow.

Both felt the change in speed but it was Leo who broke away and with a sigh lifted her from him to place her back on the seat. Lounging back into the corner of the car, he then watched the way she concentrated on trying to tidy herself, shaky fingers checking buttons and pulling her skirt into place across her knees.

'Miss Prim.' He laughed softly.

Lifting her fingers to smooth her hair, Natasha said nothing, a troubled frown toying with her brow now because she just could not understand how she could fall victim to his kisses as thoroughly as she did.

'It's called sexual attraction, *pethi mou*,' Leo explained, reading her thoughts as if he owned them now.

Her profile held Leo's attention as it turned a gentle pink. If he did not know otherwise, he would swear that Natasha Moyles was an absolute novice when it came to sexual foreplay. She ran from cold to hot to shy and dignified. She was not coquettish. She did not flirt or invite. She appeared to have no idea what she did to him yet she was so acutely receptive to anything that he did to her.

And she made him ache just to sit here looking at her. It was not an unpleasant condition; in fact, it had been so many years since he'd felt this sexually switched on to a woman, he'd believed he had lost the capacity to feel anything quite this intense.

Gianna had done that to him, scraped him dry of so many feelings and turned him into an emotional cynic. But his ex-wife was not someone he wanted to be thinking of right now, he told himself as he focused his attention back on this woman who was keeping his senses on edge just by sitting here next to him.

'We have arrived,' he murmured, using the information like yet another sexual promise to taunt her with, then watched her slender spine grow tense as she glanced beyond the car's tinted glass to catch sight of the twin iron gates that guarded the entrance to his property.

Natasha stared at the gates as they slid apart to their approach. All three cars swept smoothly through them, then two cars veered off to the left almost immediately while theirs made a direct line for the front of his white-painted, three-storey villa.

Rasmus was out of the car and opening Leo's door the moment the car pulled to a stop at the bottom of the curving front steps. Leo climbed out, ruefully aware that his legs didn't feel like holding him up. Desire was a gnawing, debilitating ache once it buried its teeth in you, he mused ruefully as he turned to watch his driver open the other passenger door so the object of his desire could step out of the car.

She gazed across the top of the car up at his villa with its modern curving frontage built to follow the shape of the white marbled steps. Light spilled out of curving-glass windows offset in three tiers framed by white terrace rails.

'I live at the top,' he said. 'The guest suites cover the middle floor. My staff have the run of the ground floor...what do you think?'

'Very ocean-going liner,' Natasha murmured.

Leo smiled. 'That was the idea.'

Rasmus shifted his bulk beside him then, reminding Leo that he was there. Leo glanced at him, that was all, and both Rasmus and the driver climbed back in the car and firmly shut the doors. Then the car moved away, leaving Leo and Natasha facing each other across its now-empty space. It was hot and it was dark but the light from the building lit up the two of them and the exotic scent of summer jasmine hung heavy in the air.

Natasha watched as Leo ran his eyes over her suit and the bag she once again clutched to her front. He didn't even need to say what he was thinking any more, he just smiled and she knew exactly what was going through his head. He was letting her know how much he was looking forward to stripping her of everything she liked to hide behind.

And the worst part about it was that her insides feathered soft rushes of excitement across intimate muscles in expectant response.

When he held out his hand in a silent command that she go to him, Natasha found herself closing the gap between them as if pulled across it by strings.

CHAPTER FIVE

No MAN had a right to be as overwhelmingly masculine as Leo did, Natasha thought as the feathering sensation increased as she walked. With his superior height, the undeniable power locked into his long, muscled body and that bump on his nose, which announced without apology that there was a real tough guy hiding inside his expensively sleek billionaire's clothes.

He turned towards the house as she reached him, the outstretched hand becoming a strong, muscled arm he placed across her back, long fingers curling lightly against her ribcage just below the thrust of her breasts.

Antagonism at his confident manner began dancing through her bloodstream—fed by a fizzing sense of anticipation that held her breath tight in her lungs. Walking beside him made Natasha feel very small suddenly, fragile, so intensely aware of each curve, each small nuance of her own body that it was as close as she'd ever come to experiencing the truly erogenous side of desire.

Inside, the villa was a spectacular example of modern architecture, but Natasha didn't see it. She was too busy absorbing the tingling sensations created by each step she took as they walked towards a waiting lift.

Once she stepped into it she would be lost and she knew it.

So that first step into the lift's confines felt the same to her as stepping off the edge of a cliff. The doors closed behind them. She watched one of Leo's hands reach out to touch a button that sent the lift gliding smoothly up. He still kept her close to him, and she kept her eyes carefully lowered, unwilling to let him see what was going on inside her head. The lift doors slid open giving them access into a vast reception hallway filled with soft light.

The very last thing Natasha wanted to see was another human being standing there waiting to greet them. It interfered with the vibrations passing between the two of them and brought her sinking back to a saner sense of self.

'*Kalispera*, Bernice,' Leo greeted smoothly, his hand arriving at Natasha's elbow to steady her shocked little backwards step.

'Good evening, *kirios—thespinis*,' the stocky, dark housekeeper turned to greet Natasha in heavy, accented English. 'You have the pleasant flight?'

'I—yes, thank you,' Natasha murmured politely, surprised that she seemed to be expected, then blushing when she realised just what that meant.

Bernice turned back to Leo. 'Kiria Christakis has been ringing,' she informed him.

'Kiria Angelina?' Leo questioned.

'*Okhi...*' Bernice switched languages, leaving Natasha to surmise that her ex-future mother-in-law had left a long message to relay her shock and distress, going by the urgency of Bernice's tone.

'My apologies, *agape mou*, but I need a few minutes to deal with this.' Leo turned to Natasha. 'Bernice will show you where you can freshen up.'

His expression was grim and impatient. And despite his

apology he did not hang around long enough for Natasha to answer before he was turning to stride across the foyer, leaving her staring after him.

'Leo...?' Calling his name brought him to an abrupt standstill.

'Yes?' He did not turn around.

Natasha was tensely aware of Bernice standing beside her. 'W-will you tell your stepmother for me, please, that I am truly sorry ab-about the way that—things have worked out?'

His silent hesitation lasted longer than Natasha's instincts wanted to allow for. Beside her, Bernice shifted slightly and lowered her head to stare down at the floor.

'I l-like Angelina,' she rushed on, wondering if she'd made some terrible faux pas in Greek family custom by speaking out about personal matters in front of the paid staff. 'None of what happened was her fault and I know she m-must be disappointed and upset.'

Still, he hesitated, and this time Natasha felt that hesitation prickle right down to her toes.

Then he gave a curt nod. 'I will pass on your message.' He strode on, leaving her standing there feeling...

'This way, *thespinis*...'

Feeling what? she asked herself helplessly as Bernice claimed her attention, indicating that she follow her into a wide, softly lit hallway that led off the foyer.

Bernice showed her into beautiful bedroom suite with yet more soft light spilling over a huge divan bed made up with crisp white linen. Dragging her eyes away from it, Natasha stared instead at a spectacular curving wall of glass backdropped by an endless satin dark sky.

Bernice was talking to her in her stilted English, telling her where the bathroom was and that her luggage would arrive very soon.

Luggage, Natasha thought as the housekeeper finally left her alone. Did one hastily packed canvas holdall classify as luggage?

Dear God, how did I get to be standing here in a virtual stranger's bedroom, waiting for my luggage? she then mocked herself, and wasn't surprised when her gaze slid back to that huge divan bed, then flicked quickly away again before her imagination could conjure up an image of what they were going to be doing there soon.

Heart thumping too heavily in her chest, Natasha sent her restless eyes on a scan of the remainder of her spacious surroundings, which bore no resemblance at all to Leo's very traditional Victorian London home. Here, cool white dominated with bold splashes of colour in the bright modern abstracts hanging from the walls and the jewel-blue cover she'd spied draped across the end of the bed.

Needing to do something—anything—to occupy her attention if she didn't want to suffer a mad panic attack, she walked over to the curved wall of glass with the intention of checking out the view beyond it, but the glass took her by surprise when it started to open, parting in the middle with a smooth silent glide—activated, she guessed, by her body moving in line with a hidden sensor.

Stepping out of air-controlled coolness into stifling heat caught her breath for a second, then she was dropping her purse onto the nearest surface, which happened to be one of the several white rattan tables and chairs spread around out there, and she was being drawn across the floor's varnished wood surface towards the twinkle of lights she could see beyond the white terrace railing, while still trying to push back the nervous flutters attacking her insides along with the deep sinking knowledge that she really should not be doing this.

A city of lights suddenly lay spread out beneath her, looking so glitteringly spectacular Natasha momentarily forgot her worries as she caught her breath once more. She'd been aware that they'd climbed up out of the city on the journey here from the airport, but she had not realised they'd climbed as high as this.

'Welcome to Athens,' a smooth, dark, warm velvet voice murmured lightly from somewhere behind her.

She hadn't heard him come into the bedroom, and now tension locked her slender shoulders as she listened to his footsteps bring him towards her.

'So, what do you think?'

His hands slid around her waist to draw her against him. 'Fabulous,' she offered, trying hard to sound calm when they both knew she wasn't by the way she grew taut at his closeness. 'Is—is that the Acropolis I can see lit up over there?'

A slender hand pointed out across the city. When she lowered it again, she found it caught by one of his.

'With the told quarters of Monastiraki and the Plaka below it,' he confirmed, taking her hand and laying it against her fluttering stomach, then keeping it there with the warm clasp of his. 'Over there you can see Zappeion Megaron lit up, which stands in our National Gardens, and that way—' he pointed with his other hand '—Syntagma Square...'

The whole thing turned a bit surreal from then on as Natasha stood listening to his quietly melodic voice describing the night view of Athens as if there were no sexual undercurrents busily at work. But those undercurrents *were* at work, like the tingling warmth of his body heat and the power of his masculine physicality as he pressed her back against him. She felt wrapped in him, trapped, surrounded and overwhelmed by a pulse-chasing vibration of intimacy that danced along her nerve-ends and fought with her need to breathe.

'It is very dark with no moon tonight but can you see the

Aegean in the distance lit by the lights from the port of Piraeus.' She had to fight with herself to keep tuned into what he was saying. 'After Bernice has served our dinner I will show you the view from the other terrace, but first I would like to explain to me, *pethi mou*, what has changed in the last five minutes to scare you into the shakes?'

'Leo...' Impulsive, she seized the moment. 'I can't go through with this. I thought I could but I can't.' Slipping her hand out from beneath his, she turned to face him, 'I need you to understand that this...'

Her words dried up when she found herself staring at his white-shirted front. He'd taken off his jacket and his tie had gone, the top couple of buttons on his shirt tugged open to reveal a bronzed V of warm skin and a deeply unsettling hint of curling black chest hair.

The air snagged in her chest, the important words—this will be my first time—lost in the new struggle she had with herself as her senses clamoured inside her like hungry beasts. She wanted him. She did not understand why or how she had become this attracted or so susceptible to him but it was there, dragging down on her stomach muscles and coiling around never before awakened erogenous zones.

'We have a deal, Natasha,' his level voice reminded her.

A deal. Pressing her trembling lips together, she nodded. 'I know and I'm s-sorry but—' Oh, God. She had to look away from him so she could finish. 'This is too m-much, too quickly and I...'

'And you believe I am about show my lack of finesse by jumping all over you and carrying you off to bed?'

'Yes—n-no.' His sardonic tone locked a frown to her brow.

'Then what do you expect will happen next?'

'Do you have to sound so casual about it?' she snapped out, taking a step back so her lower spine hit the terrace rail. Discomforted and disturbed by the whole situation, she wrapped her arms across her front. 'You might prefer to believe that I do this kind of thing on a regular basis, but I don't.'

'Ah,' he drawled. 'But you think that I do.'

'No!' she denied, flashing a glare up at him, then wished she hadn't when she saw the cynically amused cut to his mouth. 'I don't think that.'

'Good. Thank you,' he added dryly.

'I don't know enough about you to know how you run your private life!'

'Just as I know little about your private life,' he pointed out. 'So we will agree to agree that neither of us is without sexual experience and therefore can be sophisticated enough to acknowledge that we desire each other—with or without the deal we have struck.'

'But I haven't,' she mumbled.

'Haven't—what?' he sighed out.

Too embarrassed to look at him, cheeks flushed, Natasha stared at her feet. 'Any sexual experience.'

There was one of those short, sharp silences, in which Natasha sucked on her lower lip. Then Leo released another sigh and this one kept on going until it had wrung itself out.

'Enough, Natasha,' he censured wearily. 'I did not come out of the womb a week ago so let's leave the play-acting behind us from now on.'

'I'm not play-acting!' Her head shot up on the force of her insistence. All she saw was the flashing glint of his impatience as he reached out and pulled her towards him. Her own arms unfolded so she could use her hands to push him away again, but by then his mouth was on hers, hot, hard and angrily determined. Her fists flailing uselessly, he drew her into his arms and once again she was feeling the full powerful length of him against her body. Without even knowing it happened she went from fighting to clinging to his shoulders as her parted mouth absorbed the full passionate onslaught of his kiss.

There was no in-between, no pause to decide whether or not she wanted to give in to him, it just happened, making an absolute mockery of her agitation and her protests because Leo was right, and she did want him—badly.

This badly, Natasha extended helplessly as he deepened the kiss with that oh-so-clever stroke of his tongue, and she felt her body responding by stretching and arching in sensuous invitation up against the hardening heat of his.

And she knew she was lost even before he put his hands to her hips and tugged her into even closer contact with what was happening to him. When he suddenly pulled his head back, she released a protesting whimper—it shocked even Natasha at the depth of throaty protest it contained.

He said something terse, his eyes so incredibly dark now they held her hypnotised. 'You want me,' he rasped softly. 'Stop playing games with me.'

Before she could answer or even try to form an answer, he was claiming her mouth again and deepening the whole wildly hot episode with a kiss that sealed his declaration like a brand burned into her skin. Her arms clung and he held her tightly against him—nothing, she realised dizzily, was now going to stop this.

And she didn't want it to stop. She wanted to lose herself in his power and his fierce sensuality and the heat of the body she was now touching with greedily restless fingers. She felt the thumping pound of his heartbeat and each pleasurable flinch of his taut muscles as her fingers ran over them. His shirt was in her way—he knew it was in her way and, with a growl of frustration, he stepped back from her, caught hold of her hand and led her back inside.

The bed stood out like a glaring statement of intent. He

stopped beside it, then turned to look at her, catching her uncertain blue stare and leaning in to kiss it away before stepping back again. If there was a chink of sanity left to be had out of this second break in contact, it was lost again by a man blessed with all the right moves to keep a woman mesmerised by him.

He began removing his shirt, his fingers slowly working buttons free to reveal, inch by tantalising inch, his long, bronzed torso with his black haze of body hair and beautifully formed, rippling muscles, which Natasha's concentration became solely fixed on. She had never been so absorbed by anything. Sexual tension stung in the air, quickening her frail breathing as he began to pull the shirt free from the waistband of his trousers. When the shirt came off altogether, she felt bathed in the heady thrill of his clean male scent. He was so intensely masculine, so magnificently built—she just couldn't hold back from reaching out to place her hands on him.

And he let her. He let her explore him as if she was on some magical mystery journey into the unknown, his arms, the glossy skin covering his shoulders, the springy black hair covering his chest. As her hands drifted over him, her tongue snaked out to taste her upper lip, but she knew that really it wanted to taste him.

Leo reached up and gently popped the top button of her jacket and she gasped as if it was some major development, her eyes flicking up to catch his wry smile sent to remind her that this undressing part was a two-way thing. He leant in to kiss her parted lips as he popped the next button, and the whole battle they'd been waging with her jacket took on a power of its own as she just stood there and let him pop buttons between slow, deep, sensuous kisses, until there were no buttons left to pop.

He discarded her jacket in the same way he had discarded it once already that day, without letting up on his slow seduction by making her shiver as he trailed his fingers up her bare arms and over her shoulders, then down the full length of her back, making her arch towards him, making her whisper out a sigh of pleasure, making her eyes drift shut in response. Then he just peeled her stretchy white top up her body and right over her head. Cool air hit her skin and the shock of it made her open her eyes again. He was looking down at her breasts cupped in plain white satin, the fullness of their creamy slopes pushing against the bra's balcony edge. When the bra clasp sprang open and he trailed that flimsy garment away, her hands leapt up to cover her bared breasts. Leo caught her wrists and pulled them away again, his ebony eyelashes low over the intense glow in his eyes now as he watched her nipples form into pink, tight, tingling peaks.

Nothing prepared her for the shot of pleasure she experienced when he drew her against him and her breasts met with his hair-roughened chest.

No turning back now, Natasha told herself hazily as the wriggle of doubts faded away to let in the rich, drugging beauty of being deeply kissed. She felt her skirt give, felt it slither on its smooth satin lining down her legs to pool at her feet. Her bra was gone. The thong was nothing. The fine denier stocking clung to her slender white thighs. Her hair came loose next, unfurling down her naked back like an unbelievably sexy caress.

Leo had all but unwrapped her and she'd never felt so exquisitely aware of herself as a desirable woman. When he drew back from her, she reached for him to pull his mouth back to hers. He murmured something—a soft curse, she suspected—then picked her up and placed her down on the bed. Natasha held on to him by linking her hands around his neck to make sure that the kiss did not break. She wanted him—all of him.

'Greedy,' he murmured softly against her mouth as he stretched out beside her, and she was! Greedy and hungry and caught in the sexual spell he'd been weaving around her for most of the day.

Then one of his hands cupped the fullness of her breast and her breath stalled in her throat as he left her mouth to capture the tightly presented peak. Sensation made her writhe as he sucked gently, her fingers clawing into the thick silk of his hair with the intention of pulling him away—only it didn't happen because his teeth lightly grazed her, and soon she was groaning and clinging as the smooth, sharp feel of his tongue and his teeth and his measured suck drew pleasure on the edge of tight, stinging pain downward until it centred between her thighs.

Maybe he knew, maybe she groaned again, but his mouth was suddenly hot and urgently covering hers. And she could feel the hunger in him, the urgent intent of his desire demanding the same from her and getting it when he kissed her so deeply she felt immersed in its power.

Then he was leaving her, snaking upright and trailing the thong away as he did so. Eyes hooded again, dark features severe now, he removed her stockings, then straightened up to unzip his trousers and heel off his shoes while running his eyes over her possessively.

'You're beautiful,' he murmured huskily. 'Tell me you want me.'

There was no denying it when she couldn't take her eyes off him, no pretending that she was a victim here when her body responded wildly to the sight of his naked power.

'I want you,' she whispered.

It was Natasha who reached for him when he came down beside her again. It was she that turned to press the full length of her eager body into his.

Then he was taking control again, pushing her gently onto her back and rolling half across her. What came next was a lesson in slow seduction. He laid hot, delicate kisses across her mouth, touched her with gentle fingers, caressed her breasts and her slender ribcage, stroking feather-light fingertips over her skin to the indentation of her waist and across the rounded curves of her hips. It was an exploration of the most intense, stimulating agony; her flesh came alive as she moved and breathed and arched to his bidding. When he finally let his hand probe the warm, moist centre between her thighs, she was lost, writhing like a demented thing, clinging to his head and begging for his kiss. And he was hot, he was tense, he was clever with those deft fingers. The new shock sensation of what he was doing to her dropped her like a stone into a whirlpool of hot, rushing uproar.

'Leo,' she groaned out.

Saying his name was like giving him permission to turn up the heat. He appeared above her, big and dark—fierce with burning eyes and sexual tension striking across his lean cheeks. He recaptured her mouth with a burning urgency, shuddering when her fingers clawed into his nape. And still, he kept up the unremitting caresses with his fingers, driving her on while each desperate breath she managed to take made the roughness of his chest rasp torturously against the tight, stinging tips of her breasts.

She could feel the powerful nudge of his erection against her. Her tongue quivered with knowledge against his. A flimsy, rippling spasm was trying to catch hold of her and she whimpered because she couldn't quite seize it.

Leo muttered something thick in his throat, then rose above her like some mighty warrior, so powerfully, darkly, passionately Greek that if she had not felt the pounding thunder of his heartbeat when she sent her hands sliding up the wall of his chest, Natasha could have convinced herself that he just wasn't real.

He eased between her parted thighs with the firm, nude tautness of his narrow hips and the rounded tip of his desire made that first probing push against her flesh. Feeling him there, understanding what was coming and so naïvely eager to receive it, Natasha threw her head back onto the bed, ready, wanting this so very badly she was breathless, riddled by needs so new to her that they held her on the very edge of screaming-pitch.

So the sudden, fierce thrust of his invasion followed by a sharp, burning pain that ripped through her body had her clenching her muscles on a cry of protest.

Leo froze. Her eyes shot to his face. She found herself staring into passion-soaked, burning brown eyes turned black with shock. 'You were a virgin. You—'

Natasha closed her eyes and refused to say anything, while his deriding denial that this would be her first time replayed its cruel taunt across her tense body, and the muscles inside her that were already contracting around him.

'Natasha—'

'No!' she cried out. 'Don't talk about it!'

He seemed shocked by her agonised outburst. 'But you—'

'Please get off me,' she squeezed out in desperation and pushed at his shoulders with her tightly clenched fists. 'You're hurting me.'

'Because you are new to this...' His voice had roughened, the hand he used to gently push her hair away from her face trembling against her hot skin.

But he made no attempt to withdraw from her, his big shoulders bunched and glossed with a fine layer of perspiration, forearms braced on either side of her, and his face was so grave now Natasha knew what was coming before he said it.

'I'm sorry, *agape mou*...'

'Just get off!' She didn't want his apology. Balling her

hands into fists, she pushed at his shoulders, writhing beneath him in an effort to get free, only to flatten out again on a shivering quiver of shock when her inner muscles leapt on his intrusion with an excited clamour that made her eyes widen.

Reading her expression with an ease that pushed a hot flush through her body, 'You are not hurting any more,' he husked out, and lowered his head to adorn her face with soft, light, coaxing kisses—her eyes, her nose, her temples, her delicate ear lobes—that made her quiver and squirm and in the end dig fingers into his bunched shoulders and send her mouth on a restless search for his.

'Oh, kiss me properly!' she ended up begging.

Her helpless plea was all it took to tip a carefully contained, sexually aroused man over the edge. On a very explicit curse, he moulded her mouth to his. A second later and Natasha was lost—flung into a strange new world filled with sensation, piling in on top of sensation, unaware that the whole wild beauty of it was being carefully built upon by a master lover until she felt the first rippling spasm wash through her. She knew that he felt it, too, because he whispered something hot against her cheek, slid his powerful arms beneath her so he could hold her close, then angled his mouth to hers and began to thrust really deep, increasing the pace while maintaining a ferocious grip on his own thundering needs.

The grinding drag of fierce pleasure began to flow through her body. Natasha whimpered helplessly against his mouth. Knotting his fingers into her hair, he muttered tensely, 'Let go, *agape mou*.'

And like a fledgling bird being encouraged to fly, Natasha just opened her sensory wings and dropped off the edge of the world into an acutely bright, scintillating dive straight into the frenzied path of an emotional storm. A moment later she felt him shudder as he made the same mind-shredding leap, while urging her on and on until two became one in a wildly delirious, spiralling spin.

It was as if afterwards didn't exist for Natasha; pure shock dropped her like a rock through a deep, dark hole into an exhausted sleep.

Maybe she did it because she did not want to face what she'd done, Leo mused sombrely as he sat sprawled in a chair by the bed, watching her—watching this woman he'd just bedded like some raving sex maniac while giving himself every excuse he could come up with to help him to justify his behavior.

A virgin.

His conscience gave him a stark, piercing pinch.

And the guilty truth of it was, he could still feel the sense of stinging, hot pleasurable pressure he'd experienced when the barrier gave. A muscle low down in his abdomen gave a tug in direct response to the memory and he lifted the glass of whisky he held and grimly took a large sip.

The prim persona had been no lie.

She even slept the sleep of an innocent, he observed as he ran his eyes over her. No hint of sensual abandon in the modest curve of her body outlined against the white sheet.

Another slug at the whisky and he was studying her face next. Perfect, beautiful, softened by slumber and washed pale by the strain of the day she'd been put through when she should look…

He took another pull of the whisky, and as he lifted the glass to his mouth, her eyelids fluttered upwards and her sleep-darkened blue eyes looked directly at him.

The nagging tug on his loins became a pulsing burn that made him feel like a sinner.

He lowered the glass, and half hiding his eyes, watched her catch her breath, then freeze for a second before he said sombrely, 'We will get married.'

Natasha almost jolted right out of her skin. 'Are you mad?' she gasped, pulling the covering sheet tightly up against her chin. 'We have a deal—'

'You were a virgin.'

As she dragged herself into a sitting position her hair tumbled forwards in a shining, loose tangle of waves around her face and she pushed it out of her way impatiently. 'What the heck difference should that make to anything?'

'It means everything,' Leo insisted. 'Therefore we will be married as soon as I can arrange it. I am honour-bound to offer you this.'

'Stuff your honour.' Heaving in a deep breath, Natasha climbed out of the bed on the other side from where he was sitting, trailing the sheet around her as she went. 'Having just escaped one sleazy marriage by the skin of my teeth, I am *not* going to fall into another one!'

'It will not be a sleazy marriage.'

'Everything about you and your terrible family is sleazy!' she turned on him angrily. 'You're all so obsessed with the value of money, you've lost touch with what's really valuable in life! Well, I haven't.' Tossing her chin up, eyes like blue glass on fire with contempt, she drew the sheet around her. 'We made a deal in which I give you sex for six weeks until I can give you back your precious money. Show a bit of your so-called honour by keeping to that deal!'

With that she turned and strode off to the bathroom, needing to escape—needing some respite from Leo Christakis and his long, sexy body stretched out in that chair by the bed. So he'd pulled a robe on—what difference did that make? She could still see him naked, still visualise every honed muscle and bone, each single inch of his taut, bronzed flesh! And she could still feel the power of his kisses and the weight of him on top of her and the...

'You were innocent,' he fed after her.

Was he talking about her sexual innocence or her being innocent of all of the other rotten charges he had laid against her?

Did she care? No.

'Stick to your first impression of me,' she flung at him over her shoulder. 'Your instincts were working better then!'

On that scathing slice, she slammed into the bathroom.

Leo grimaced into his glass. His first impression of Natasha Moyles had been deadly accurate, he acknowledged. It was only the stuff with Rico that had fouled up that impression.

He heard the shower running. He visualised her dropping the sheet and walking that smooth, curvy body into his custom-built wet room. The vision pushed him to his feet with the grim intention of giving into his nagging desires and going in there to join her. This war they were having was not over yet and would not be over until he won it.

Then something red caught the corner of his eye and he glanced down at the bed.

'Theos,' he breathed as his insides flipped into a near-crippling squirm in recognition.

Proof that he had just taken his first virgin was staring him in the face like a splash of outrage.

Leo flexed his taut shoulders, glanced over at the closed door to the bathroom, then back at the bed. 'Damn,' he cursed, trying to visualise what she was going to feel like when she saw the evidence of her lost virginity, and added a few more oaths in much more satisfying Greek.

Instead of going to join her, he discarded his robe to snatch up his trousers and shirt and pulled them back on. He had no idea where Bernice kept the fresh bedlinen, but he was going to have to find out for himself because the hell if he was going to ask…

CHAPTER SIX

WRAPPED in a spare bathrobe she'd found hanging behind the door, Natasha tugged in a deep breath, then opened the bathroom door and stepped out. Her heart was thumping. It had taken her ages to build up enough courage to leave the sanctuary of the bathroom and her muscles ached, she was so locked on the defensive, ready for her first glimpse of Leo sprawled in the chair by the bed.

It took a few moments for her to realise that she'd agonised over nothing because he wasn't even in the room. And the bed had been straightened so perfectly it looked as if it had never been used. Even her clothes had been picked up and neatly draped over the chair he had been sitting in.

Had Bernice come in here and tidied up after them? The very idea pushed a flush of mortified heat into her cheeks. Natasha dragged her eyes away from the bed and began scanning the room for her holdall, while wishing that someone had bothered to tell her that she was going to feel like this—all tense and edgy and horribly uncertain as to what happened after you jumped into bed with a man you hardly knew!

Then the bedroom door flew open and she spun to face it with a jerk. Half expecting to find Bernice or one of the maids walking in, she was really thrown into a wild flutter when it was Leo standing there.

He was dressed and she definitely wasn't. The way his eyes moved over her turned the flush of mortification into something else.

He swung the door shut behind him, then began striding towards her like some mighty warlord coming to claim his woman for a second round of mind-blowing sex and making her more uptight the closer he came. How could he wear that relaxed smile on his face as if everything in his world was absolutely perfect? Had he never felt awkward or nervous or just plain shy about anything?

Not this man, she concluded with a deep inner quiver when he pulled to a stop right in front of her. He gave off the kind of masculine vitality that made her fingers clutch the collar of the bathrobe close to her throat.

'Your hair is wet,' he observed, lifting a hand up to stroke it across the slicked back top of her head.

'Your state-of-the-art wet room has a w-will of its own,' she answered, still feeling the tingling shock she'd experienced when jets of water had hit her from every angle the moment she'd touched the start button in there.

'I'll find you a hairdryer,' he murmured as he moved his hand to stroke the hectic burn in her cheek. 'But in truth, I think you look adorable just as you are and if I thought you could take more of me right now I would be picking you up and taking you back to bed.'

Natasha shook his hand away. 'I wouldn't let you.'

'Maybe,' he goaded softly, 'you would find yourself with little choice?'

Natasha's startled gaze clashed with his smiling dark eyes. 'You would make me, you mean?'

'Seduce you into changing your mind, beautiful one,' he corrected, then lowered his head to steal a kiss.

And it wasn't just a quick steal. He let his lips linger long enough to extract a response from her before he drew back again.

'Fortunately for you, right now I am starving for real food,' he mocked her smitten expression. 'Find yourself something comfortable to put on while I shower, then we will go and eat.'

With that he strode into the bathroom. Arrogant—arrogant—*arrogant!* Natasha thought as she wiped the taste of his mouth from her lips.

Thoroughly out of sorts with herself for being so susceptible to him, she hunted down her holdall and used up some of her irritation by hauling it up onto the bed and yanking open the zip. For the next few seconds she just stood looking down into the bag with absolutely no clue whatsoever as to what the heck she had packed inside it. She only had this very vague memory of grabbing clothes at random, then dropping them into the bag. Tense fingers clutching the gaping robe to her throat again, she let the other hand rummage inside the bag and pulled out an old pair of jeans and a pale green T-shirt.

Great, she thought as she discarded those two unappealing garments onto the bed. A pair of ordinary briefs—not a thong, thank goodness—appeared next, and she tossed those onto the bed, too. She found another suit styled like the pale blue suit she'd been wearing all day, only this one was in a dull cream colour that made her frown because she could not imagine herself buying it, never mind wearing such an awful shade against her fair skin. Yet she must have bought it or it wouldn't be here.

Or perhaps this new Natasha—the one clutching a robe to her throat after losing her virginity to an arrogant Greek—had developed different tastes. She certainly felt different, kind of aching and alive in intimate places and so aware of her own body it started to tingle even as she thought about it.

No make-up, she discovered. She'd forgotten to pack her make-up bag or even a brush or comb. A couple of boring skirts appeared from the bag, followed by a couple of really boring tops. Frowning now with an itchy sense of dissatisfaction that irritated her all the more simply because she was feeling it, she finally unearthed a floaty black skirt made of the kind of fabric that didn't crease when she pulled it free of the bag. A black silk crocheted top appeared next, which was going to have to go with the skirt whether she liked it or not since she did not seem to have anything else like it in the bag.

Only one spare pair of shoes—and *no* spare bra! she discovered. Sighing heavily, she turned towards the chair where her other clothes were neatly folded, and was about to walk over there to recover her white bra—when Leo strode out of the bathroom.

It was as if she'd been thrown into an instant freeze the way she stood there between the bed and the chair, pinned to the polished wood floor while her busy mind full of what to wear came to a sudden halt.

Other than for the towel he had slung low around his lean waist, he was naked. Beads of water clung to the dark hairs on his chest. Her heart began to race as her eyes dropped lower, over the taut golden brown muscles encasing his stomach that shone warm and glossy and sinewy tight. The towel covered him from narrow hips and long powerful thighs to his knees, and the strength she could see structuring his calf muscles held her totally, utterly breath-shot as she felt the undiluted wash of what true desire really meant suffuse heat into each fine layer of her skin.

Oh, dear God, I want him badly, she acknowledged as those legs came to a sudden standstill and brought her eyes fluttering up to clash with his. It was like being suffocated, she likened dizzily, because she knew by the way he narrowed his eyes that he was reading her responses to him.

'I've forgotten to pack any m-make-up.' The words jumped from her in a panic-stricken leap.

He continued to stand there for a few more seconds just studying her, then he started walking again. 'You will not need make-up for dinner here alone with me,' he responded evenly.

Natasha pulled her eyes away from him to glance at the scramble of clothes she'd thrown onto the bed. 'I don't even have anything here fit to wear for dinner,' she said, trying desperately to sound as calm as he had when calm was the last thing she was feeling.

He came to a stop beside her. 'Wear the cream thing,' he suggested with only the vaguest hint of distaste showing in his voice.

It was enough. Natasha shook her head. 'I hate it.'

Beginning to frown now, he turned to look down at her. 'Natasha, what—'

'W-what are you going to wear?' she heard herself blurt out, then grabbed in a tense breath because—in all her life she had never asked a man such a gauche, stupid question! And his frown was darkening by the second. She could actually *feel* him mulling over what to say next! She wanted to call back her silly question. She *wished* she weren't even here!

She turned to face him. 'Listen Leo, I...'

Then it came—his shockingly unexpected answer to her problem: he dropped the towel from around his waist. 'Let's wear nothing,' he said.

The sheer outrageousness of the gesture completely robbed Natasha of speech. Heat flowed through her body, soaking her groin like hot pins and needles before spreading everywhere else. She tried to breathe. She tried to swallow. She tried to stop staring at him but she couldn't. She tried to back off when he reached across the gap between them, but her legs had turned to liquid and were refusing to move.

He reached for the hand she was using to clutch the bathrobe to her throat and gently prized her fingers free.

'Leo, no...' She mouthed the husky protest with her heart clattering wildly against her ribs because she knew what was coming next.

'Leo—yes,' he interpreted softly.

Two seconds later the bathrobe fell to the floor at her feet and his hands were taking its place. Freshly showered skin met with freshly showered skin and her naked breasts swelled and peaked. Her shaken gasp was captured by the sensual crush of his mouth and her troubled world tilted right out of kilter as the whole sexual merry-go-round spun off again. She didn't even want to stop it, she just threw herself into the dizzying pleasure of the kiss with her hands clutching at his solid biceps and her hips swaying closer to the burgeoning evidence of his desire and its formidable promise. Within seconds she was a quivering mass of nerve-endings, moving against him and kissing him back, her heart racing, her breathing reduced to fevered little tugs at oxygen filled with his intoxicating clean scent.

The sound of the bedroom door being thrown open with enough force to send it slamming back into something solid almost blew the top off her head. She flicked her eyes open. Leo was already lifting up his head. Way too dazed to think for herself, Natasha watched him shift the burning darkness of his eyes away from her to look towards the bedroom door, then copied him to look in that direction, too.

A woman stood there. A tall, reed-slender, staggeringly beautiful woman, wearing a dramatically short and slinky red satin dress. Her flashing black eyes were fixed on Leo, her exquisite face turning perfectly white.

'Gianna,' he greeted smoothly. 'Nice of you to drop in, but, as you can see, we are busy....'

As cool as that, he turned Natasha into a block of ice as his wife—his *ex*-wife—threw herself into a rage of shrill spitting Greek. Leo said absolutely nothing while the tirade poured out. His heart wasn't thundering. His breathing was steady. He just stood holding Natasha close as if trying to shield her nakedness with his own naked length, and let the other woman screech herself out.

It was awful. Natasha wished she could just sink into a hole in the ground. It was so humiliatingly obvious that Gianna felt she had a right to yell at Leo like this or why would she do it? Likening this situation to the one she'd witnessed between Cindy and Rico made her shiver in shame.

Feeling her shiver, Leo flicked a glance at her, then frowned as with a smooth grace he bent and scooped up the robe she had been wearing and draped it around her shoulders. 'Shut up now, Gianna,' he commanded grimly. 'You sound like a shrieking cat.'

To Natasha's surprise the shouting stopped. 'You were supposed to be at Boschetto's tonight,' Gianna switched to condemning English. 'I waited and waited for you to arrive and I felt the fool when you did not turn up!'

'I made no arrangement to meet up with you,' Leo said, bending a second time to pick up his towel, which wrapped back around his hips. 'So if you made a fool of yourself, you did it of your own volition.'

'You were expected—'

'Not by you,' Leo stated. 'Here, let me help you...'

Trying to push her arms into the robe sleeves, Natasha found Leo taking over the task, but, 'I'll do it myself,' she breathed tautly, and pushed his hands away.

She couldn't look at him—did not want to look at his ex-wife. Embarrassment was crawling around her insides and she felt so humiliated she was trembling with it.

Speaking earned Natasha Gianna's attention; she felt the other woman scythe a skin-peeling look over her. 'So you like them short and fat now?' she said to Leo.

Fat? Natasha burned up inside with indignation, huddling her size-ten figure into the all-encompassing bathrobe.

'Much better than a rake-thin whore with a sluttish heart,' Leo responded, reaching out to stroke one of his hands down Natasha's burning cheek as if in an apology for his witch of an ex-wife's insult. 'Now behave, Gianna, or I will have Rasmus throw you out of here. In fact,' he then drawled curiously, 'I will be very interested to hear how you got in here at all?'

Daring a glance at the other woman, Natasha saw that she was standing there with her slender arms folded across her slender ribs. She had to be six feet tall and the way she'd been poured into that red satin dress said everything there was to say about the differences between the two of them.

No wonder she still claimed super-model status, she concluded, flicking her eyes up to Gianna's fabulous bone-structure to see that her almond-shaped, Latin black eyes were gleaming defiance at Leo, her lush red mouth set in a provoking pout.

Leo released a soft, very cynical laugh as if he understood exactly what the look was conveying.

'So, who is she?' Gianna flicked another snide look at Natasha. 'Yet another attempt you make to find a substitute for me?'

Natasha flinched. Leo drew her back into his arms again and ignored her when she tried to pull back. 'Never in a thousand years could anyone substitute you, my sweet-tongued angel,' he mocked dryly. Then he looked down at Natasha and, with the silken tone of a man about to rock her world off its axis, 'In the form of a heartfelt apology to you, *agape mou,*' he murmured soft to Natasha, 'I must introduce you to Gianna, my ex-wife.'

'I am your ex-nothing!' Gianna erupted.

'Gianna.' He spoke right across the shrill protest. 'Nothing in this world has ever given me greater pleasure than to introduce you to Natasha, my very beautiful *future* wife.'

As a cool, slick way of dropping a bombshell, it was truly impressive. Staring up at his totally implacable face, Natasha almost fell backwards in shock.

The beautiful Gianna turned deathly white. 'No,' she whispered.

'You wish,' Leo responded.

'But you love *me*!' Gianna cried out in pained anguish.

'Once upon a time you were worth loving, Gianna. Now...?' He gave a shrug that said the rest, then apparently committed the ultimate sin in Gianna's eyes and leant down to capture Natasha's shock-parted lips with a kiss.

Without any warning it was about to happen, fresh pandemonium broke out with a keening wail that spliced up the atmosphere, then Gianna was coming at Natasha like a woman with murder in mind. Natasha jumped like a terrified rabbit. Leo spat out a curse and stepped right in front of her, taking the brunt of Gianna's fury upon himself.

It was horrible, the whole thing. Natasha could only stand there behind him, shocked into shaking while Leo contained his ex-wife's wrists to stop her long nails from clawing his face.

Then he bit out a terse, 'Excuse us...' to Natasha, and he was manhandling the screaming woman out of the bedroom.

The door thudded shut in his wake. Natasha found that her legs couldn't hold her up a moment longer and she sank in a whooshing loss of energy down onto the edge of the bed.

Beyond the door, Rasmus was just stepping out of the lift.

Leo sent him a glancing blow of a look and his security chief paled. 'I'm sorry, Leo,' he jerked out. 'I don't know—'

'Get her out of here,' Leo gritted. 'Take her home and sober her up.'

Gianna had stopped fighting and screeching now and was sobbing into his chest and clinging instead. Disgust flayed Leo's insides when it took the controlled strength of both men to transfer her from himself to Rasmus and get her into the lift.

'I don't know how she got in here,' Rasmus said helplessly.

'But you will do,' Leo lanced out. 'Then see to it that whoever it was on your staff she laid in return for the favour is gone from here,' he instructed, then stabbed the button that shut the lift doors.

Alone in the hallway, he spun round in a full circle, then grabbed the back of his neck. Anger was pumping away inside him, contempt—repugnance. Having taken a telephone call from Gianna when he first arrived here, he'd told her that she had to get the hell off his back!

Her barging in here had been deliberate. Even the angry shrieking had been a put-up job. And the fact that she would not think twice about seducing one of his staff to get what she wanted was just another side to her twisted personality that filled him with disgust!

'Theos,' he muttered, long legs driving him through the apartment and pulling him to a halt outside the closed bedroom door, the knowledge that he'd lost the towel again having no effect on him at all.

He wasn't stupid. He knew that Gianna's nicely timed interruption had been a set-up, just as he knew the comparison Natasha had drawn from the moment it all kicked off.

Rico with her sister.

A curse ripped from him, followed by another. He paced out the width of the hall trying to clamp down on the anger still erupting inside him because—how the hell did he explain a sex-obsessed feline like Gianna, who only functioned this side of sane while she knew that he was always going to be around to help pick her up when she fell apart?

You didn't explain it. It was too damn complicated, he recognised as he took in a grim breath of air, then threw open the bedroom door.

Natasha was back in the blue suit, and she was stuffing her things back into her bag.

'Don't you pull a hysterical scene on me,' he rasped, closing the door with a barely controlled thud.

His voice sent a quiver down Natasha's tense spinal cord. 'I'm not hysterical,' she responded quietly.

'Then *what* do you call the way you are packing that bag?'

The searing thrust of his anger shocked even Leo as Natasha swung round to stare at him. Miss Cold and Prim was back with a vengeance, Leo saw, and she was stirring him up like...

She saw *it* happen, and lifted a pair of frosty blue eyes to his. 'Is that response due to her by any chance?' And her voice dripped disdain.

Hell, Leo cursed. 'Sorry,' he muttered, not sure exactly what it was he was apologising for—the snarling way he had spoken to her or his uncontrolled...

She spun her back to him again. Snapping his lips together, he strode over to the bank of glossy white wardrobes and tugged open one of the doors. A second later he was pulling a pair of jeans up his legs.

'She's mad,' he muttered.

'Enter the beautiful mad wife—exit the short, fat other woman.' Natasha pushed a pair of shoes into the bag.

'*Ex*-wife,' he corrected, tugging his zip up.

'Try telling her that.'

'I do tell her—constantly. As you saw for yourself, she does not listen—and you are not going anywhere, Natasha, so you can stop packing that bag.'

Straightening up, Natasha meant to spear him with another crushing look, only to find herself lose touch with what they were saying when she saw him standing there with his long legs encased in faded denim and looking like a whole new kind of man. Her heart gave a telling stuttering thud. Her breathing faltered. He was so blatantly, beautifully masculine it took a fight to drag her covetous mind back on track.

'S-so you thought you might as well make her listen by hitting her with that lie about a future wife?'

A frown darkened his lean features and made the bump on his nose stand out. 'It was not a lie, Natasha,' he declared like a warning.

'Oh, yes, it was,' she countered that. 'I wouldn't marry you if my life depended on it.'

'You mean, you are here merely to use me for sex?'

The sardonic quip was out before Leo could stop it.

'Substitute!' she tossed right back at him like the hot sting from a whip. 'And not even that again,' she added, yanking her eyes away from him altogether and zipping up the hastily packed bag with enough violence to threaten the teeth on the zip.

Easing his shoulders back against the wardrobe door, Leo folded his arms across his hair-roughened chest. 'So I was a tacky one-night substitute, then,' he prodded.

'Very tacky.' Pressing her lips together, she nodded in confirmation, then parted her lips to add bitterly, 'God save me from the super-rich class. Everything they do is so tacky it constantly makes me want to be sick.'

'Was that aimed at me, Gianna or Rico?'

'All three,' she said, frowning as she sent her eyes hunting the room for her purse. She couldn't see it anywhere and she couldn't recall when she had last had it in her hand.

'Lost something valuable?' his hatefully smooth voice questioned. 'Like your virginity, perhaps?'

It was as good as a hard slap in the face. Natasha tugged in a hot breath. 'I've just remembered why I dislike you so much.'

His wide shoulders gave a deeply bronzed shrug against the white wardrobe. He looked like some brooding dark male model posing for one of the big fashion magazines, Natasha thought, feebly aware that her eyes refused to stay away from him for more than ten seconds before they dragged themselves back again because he was so bone-tinglingly good to look at. Sexuality oozed out of every exposed manly pore and those jeans should be X-rated. How had she ever thought that he was nothing to look at next to Rico? If Rico dared to stride in here right now and stand next to this man, Natasha knew she wouldn't even see him. Leo won hands down in each single aspect of his dominant masculine make-up—even the bump in his nose yelled sexually exciting unreconstructed male at her!

Oh, what's happening to me? On that helplessly bewildered inward groan, she yanked her eyes away from him—yet again—and *made* them search the room for her purse! In less than a day it felt as if everything she'd ever held firm about herself had been corkscrewed out of her then mixed around violently before being shoved back inside her to form this entirely new perspective on everything!

And the way he was standing there looking at her with his eyes thoughtfully narrowed just wasn't right, either—as if he was considering striding over here and *showing* her the tough way in which this new order of things worked.

A sensation Natasha just did not want to feel spread itself right down her front. Tense upper lip quivering—she just *had* to get out of here.

'Have you seen my purse?'

'What do you need it for?'

Straightening her tense shoulders, she said, 'I'm ready to leave now.'

'By what form of transport?'

'Taxi!' she spat out.

'You have the Euros to pay for a taxi?' her cool tormentor quizzed. 'And a mobile phone handy to call one up? Do you speak any Greek, *agape mou*? Do you even know this address so you can tell the taxi driver where to come to collect you?'

He was deliberately beating her up with blunt logic. 'Y-you have my mobile phone,' she reminded him, hating that revealing quiver in her voice.

He responded to that with yet another of those irritatingly expressive shrugs against the glossy white wardrobe door. 'I must have mislaid it, as you have your purse.'

Deciding the only way to deal with the infuriatingly impossible brute was to ignore him, Natasha started hunting the bedroom.

While Leo watched her do it, his narrowed gaze ran over the way she looked all neat and tidy in every which way she could be—except for the wet hair which lay in a heavy silk pelt down her back. A man could not find a bigger contrast between Natasha's cool dignity and Gianna's reckless abandon, Leo observed grimly. Where Gianna clung to him like a weeping vine, this aggravating woman was preparing to walk out on him!

'Tell me, Natasha,' he asked grimly, 'why are you so eager to leave when only ten minutes ago you were ready to fall back into bed with me?'

'Your wife got in here somehow,' she muttered, checking beneath one of the cushions on the chair to see if her purse had slid behind it.

'Ex-wife—and...?'

'Maybe her claim on you has some justification,' Natasha said with a shrug.

'Like...?' he prompted, and there was no hint whatsoever left of the provoking mockery with which he had started this conversation. He was deadly curious to hear where she was going with this.

'The way you run your life is your own business.' Chickening out at the last second from stating outright the real question that was beating a hole in her head, she gave up on the chair and tossed the cushion back onto it.

But—did he still sleep with his ex-wife when he felt like it? Did Gianna have a genuine right to her grievances when she'd barged in on them as she had? If so, then it made him no better than Rico in the way that he treated women!

Tacky, as she'd already said. She returned to her search with his brooding silence twitching at her nerve-ends as she moved about the room.

'I do not have a relationship with my ex-wife,' he spoke finally. 'I do not sleep with her and I have no wish to sleep with her, though Gianna prefers to tell herself I will change my mind if she pushes long and hard enough... In case you did not notice,' he continued as Natasha turned to look him, 'Gianna is not quite—stable.'

It was the polite way to call it, but Natasha could see by the flick of a muscle at the corner of his mouth that he was holding back from voicing his real thoughts about Gianna's mental health. And what did she do? She stood here eating up every single word like some lovelorn teenager in need of his reassurance.

'In some ways I still feel responsible for her because she *was* my wife and I *did* care for her once—until she pressed the self-destruct button on our marriage for reasons not up for discussion here.' And the tough way he said that warned her not to try to push him on it. 'I apologise that she barged in here and embarrassed you,' he expressed curtly. 'I apologise that she found a way to enter this property at all!' A fresh burst of anger straightened him away from the wardrobe. 'But that's it—that is as far as I am prepared to go to make you feel better about the situation, Natasha. So stop behaving like a tragic bride on her wedding night and take the damn jacket off before *I* take it off!'

'W-what—?' Not quite making the cross-over from his grim explanation about Gianna to the sudden attack on herself, Natasha blinked at him.

Which seemed to infuriate him all the more. 'While you stand here playing the poor, abused victim, you seem to have conveniently forgotten about the money you stole from me!'

The money.

Natasha tensed up, then froze as if he'd reached out and hit her. Leo smothered a filthy curse because her hesitation told him that she *had* forgotten all about the money. Though the curse was aimed at himself for reminding her about it when he would have preferred it to remain forgotten about! Now she was looking so pale and appalled he grimly wondered if she was going to pass out on him.

A tensely gritted sigh had him striding over to her. Lips pinned together, he reached out and began unbuttoning her jacket with tight movements that bore no resemblance whatsoever to the other times he had taken it upon himself to do this.

She didn't even put up a fight, but just stood there like a waxen dummy and let him strip the garment from her body, which only helped to infuriate him all the more! With the muscles across his shoulders bunching, he tossed the jacket aside, then turned to walk back across the room to the wardrobes. Hunting out a white T-shirt, he dragged it on over his head.

When he turned back to Natasha, he found her still standing where he'd left her, giving a good impression of a perfectly pale ghost.

Theos, he thought, wondering why seeing her looking so beaten was making his senses nag the hell out of him to just go over there and apologise yet again—for being such a brute.

'Dinner,' he said, taking another option, keeping up the tough tone of voice because—well, she was a cheating thief even if he wanted to forget that she was!

At last she moved—or her pale lips did. 'I'm not hungry—'

'You are eating,' he stated. 'You have had nothing since you threw up in my London basement.'

And reminding her of that was Leo Christakis well and truly back as the blunt-speaking insensitive brute, Natasha noted.

Even in the T-shirt and chinos.

And his feet bare...

She felt like crying again, though why the sight of his long, bronzed bare feet moving him so gracefully across the room to the door made her want to do that Natasha did not have a clue, but suddenly she just wanted to sit in a huddle in a very dark corner somewhere and...

He pulled the bedroom door open, then stood there pointedly waiting for her to join him. Head lowered, she went because there was no point in continuing to argue with him when all he had to do was to mention the money to devastate her every line of defence.

Hard, tough, unforgivably ruthless, she reminded herself, wondering how she had allowed herself to forget those things about him while she had been giving him free use of her body—as a part of their *deal*.

She didn't look at him as she walked past him and out into the hallway. She kept her head lowered when he stepped in front of her to lead the way through the apartment and into a room lit by flickering candle-light and another glass wall.

Bernice was there, arranging the last pieces of cutlery on a white linen tablecloth intimately set for two. Candles flickered. Beyond the table stood the night view of Athens, making the most romantic backdrop any woman could wish for.

Any romantically hopeful woman, that was.

Friction stung the atmosphere and the housekeeper smiled and said something in Greek to Leo. He replied in the same language as he held out a chair for Natasha to use. After that there was no privacy to speak of anything personal because a maid arrived to serve them. Natasha had a feeling Leo had arranged it that way so he didn't get into yet another dogfight with her, but the tension between them made it almost impossible to swallow anything, though she did try to eat. When she couldn't manage to swallow another beautifully presented morsel, she stared at the view beyond the glass window, or down at the leftover food on her plate, or at the crisp white wine he had poured into the glass she was fingering without drinking—anywhere so long as it wasn't at him.

Then he shattered it. Without any hint at all that one swift glance from his eyes had sent the maid disappearing out of the room, Leo suddenly leant forwards and stretched a hand out across the table and brazenly cupped her left breast.

'I knew it,' he husked. 'You are wearing no bra, you provoking witch.'

Pleasure senses went into overdrive. Natasha shot like a sizzling firework rocket to her feet. He rose up more slowly, face taut, his dark eyes flickering gold in the candle-light.

'Don't ever touch me like that without my permission again,' she shook out in a pressured whisper, then she turned to stumble around her chair and made a blind dash out of the room.

The lift stood there with its doors conveniently open. Natasha did not even have to think about it as she dashed inside and sent the lift sweeping down to the ground floor. Outside in the garden the thick, humid air was filled with the scent of oranges. Soft lighting drew her down winding pathways between carefully nurtured shrubs and beneath the orange laden trees. She didn't know where she was heading for, all she did know was that she needed to find that dark corner she could huddle in so she could finally—finally give in to the tears she'd held back too long.

She found it in the shape of a bench almost hidden beneath the dipping branches of a tree close to the high stuccoed wall that surrounded the whole property. Dropping down onto the bench, she pulled her knees up to her chin, leant her forehead on them, then let go and wept. She wept over everything. She just trawled it all out and took a good look at everything from the moment she'd opened the message on her mobile telephone that morning to the moment Leo had touched her breast across the dinner table—and she wept and she wept and she wept.

Leo leant against a trunk of the tree and listened. Inside he had never felt so bad in his life. The way he had been treating her all day had been nothing short of unforgivable. The way he'd made love to her when he'd known she should have been doing this instead was going to live on his conscience for a long time to come.

But the way he had reached across the dinner table and touched her just now was, without question, the lowest point to which he had stooped.

And listening to her weep her soul into shreds was his deserved punishment. Except that he couldn't stand to listen to it any longer and, with a sigh, he levered away from the tree trunk and went to sit down beside her, then lifted her onto his lap.

She tried to fight him for a second or two, but he just murmured, 'Shh, sorry,' and held her close until she stopped fighting him and let the tears flow again.

When it was finally over and she quietened, he stood up

with her in his arms and took her back inside. He did it without saying a single word, ignoring the dozen or so security cameras he knew would have been trained on them from the moment Natasha ran outside.

She was asleep, he realised when he lay her down on the bed. With the care of a man dealing with something fragile, he slipped off her shoes and her skirt, then covered her with the sheets.

Straightening up again, he continued to stand there for a few seconds looking down at her, then he turned and walked out of the bedroom and into his custom-built office.

A minute later, 'Juno,' he greeted. 'My apologies for the lateness of the hour, but I have something I need you to do….'

CHAPTER SEVEN

NATASHA drifted awake to soft daylight seeping in through the wall of curved glass and to instant recall that sent her head twisting round on her pillow to check out the other side of the bed.

The sudden pound her heart had taken up settled back to its normal pace when she discovered that she was alone, the only sign that she had shared the bed at all through the night revealed by the indent she could see in the other pillow and the way Leo had thrown back the sheets when he'd climbed out.

Then the whispering suggestion of a sound beyond the bedroom door told her what it was that had awoken her in the first place, and she was up, rolling off the bed and running for the bathroom, only becoming aware as she did so that she was still wearing the white top she'd spent most of the day yesterday in.

So he'd shown a bit of rare sensitivity by not stripping her naked, she acknowledged with absolutely no thought of gratitude stirring in her blood. Leo had taken her to pieces yesterday brick by brutal brick, so one small glimpse of humanity in him because he'd put her limp self to bed and had the grace to leave her with some dignity in place did not make her feel any better about him.

She stepped into the wet room, with her hair safely wrapped away inside a fluffy white towel, frowned and at the range of keypads and dials, trying to work out how she could take a shower without having to endure a thorough dousing at the same time. Leo Christakis was one of life's takers, she decided. He saw an opportunity and went for it. He'd wanted her so he just moved in on her like a bulldozer and scooped her up.

Water jets suddenly hit her from all angles, making mockery of the buttons she'd pushed to stop them from doing it. A gasping breath shot from her as the jets stung her flesh. The sensation was so acute it made her look down at her body, half expecting to see that it had altered physically somehow, but all she saw was her normal curvy shape with its pale skin, full breasts and rounded hips with a soft cluster of dusky curls shaping the junction with her thighs.

But she had changed inside where it really mattered, Natasha accepted. She'd become a woman in a single day. One stripped of her silly daydreams about love and romance, then made to face cold reality—that you didn't need love or romance to fall headlong into pleasures of the flesh.

You didn't need anything but the desire to reach out and take it when it was right there in front of you to take.

Rico was like that. So was her sister, Cindy. They saw, they desired, so they took. It was there to take, so why not? Now she might as well accept that she'd joined the ranks of takers because she could stand here letting the shower jets inflict their torture on her and try to convince herself that she'd been blackmailed and bullied into Leo's bed, but it was never going to be the truth.

She'd wanted, she'd let him see it, Leo had taken, now it was done. What a fabulous introduction to the reality of life.

Bernice was walking in from the terrace when Natasha came out of the bathroom back in the bathrobe once again. Feeling a hot wave of shyness wash over her, Natasha felt like diving back into the bathroom and hiding there until the housekeeper had gone but it was already too late.

Bernice had seen her. *'Kalemera, thespinis,'* the housekeeper greeted with a smile. 'It is a beautiful day to eat breakfast outside, is it not?'

'Perfect.' Natasha managed a return smile, 'Thank you, Bernice,' she added politely.

Walking towards the wall of glass as Bernice left the room, she pushed her hands into the deep pockets of her robe and stepped out into a crystal-clear morning bathed in sunlight and the inviting aroma of hot coffee and toast. By the sudden growl her stomach gave she was hungry, Natasha realised, which shouldn't surprise her when she'd barely eaten anything the day—

Her mind and her feet pulled to a sudden standstill. For some crazy reason she just had not expected to find Leo out here seated at the table set for breakfast. However, there he sat, calmly reading a newspaper with a cup of hot coffee hovering close to his mouth.

Her soft gasp of surprise brought his eyes up from the newspaper, his heavy eyelashes folding back from liquid-dark irises that swamped her in heated awareness as they stroked up the length of her from bare toes to the tangling tumble of her unbrushed hair.

'Kalemera,' he murmured softly, and he rose to his feet.

It was like being hit head on by all the things she had not allowed herself to think about since she'd woken up this morning—the man in the flesh. Even though he was wearing a conventional business suit a warm tug of remembered intimacy made itself felt between her thighs. She found her eyes doing much the same thing as his eyes had done, feathering up the length of his long legs encased in smooth-as-silk iron-grey fabric, then his torso covered by a pale blue shirt and dark tie. By the time she reached his clean-shaven face with its too-compellingly, strong golden features, she was blushing and annoyed enough by it to push up her chin.

'Good morning,' she returned in cool English.

A half-smile clipped at the corners of his mouth. 'You slept well, I trust?'

He met her challenge with mockery.

'Yes, thank you.' Natasha kept with cool.

Pulling her eyes off him, she dug her hands deeper into her robe pockets, curled them into tense fists, then made herself walk towards the table and slip into the chair opposite him, expecting Leo to return to his seat, but he didn't.

'Bernice was unsure what you preferred to eat for breakfast so she has provided a selection.' A long, lean hand indicated another table standing to one side of the terrace, which was spread with covered dishes. 'Tell me what you would like and I'll get it for you.'

Glancing at it, then away again, 'Thank you, I'm fine with just toast.'

'Juice?' he offered.

A small hesitation, then she nodded. 'Please.'

He went to pour the juice from the jug set on the other table. You couldn't get a more pleasantly generated scene of calm domesticity if you tried, Natasha noted—though there was nothing domesticated in the way her eyes had to follow him or the way they soaked in every inch of his powerful lean frame like greedy traitors.

Looking away quickly when he turned around, she pretended an interest in the daytime view of Athens glistening in a hazy sunlight. Then one of his hands appeared in front of her to set down the glass of juice. Ice chinked against freshly squeezed oranges. He did not move away and another of those hesitations erupted between them sending out vibrating signals Natasha just did not want to read. And he was standing so close she could smell the clean, tangy scent of him, could *feel* the sheer masculine force of his sexuality that to her buzzing mind was barely leashed.

Then he brought his other hand around her to settle a rack of toast next to the glass of juice.

'Thank you,' she murmured.

'My pleasure,' he drawled—and he moved away to return to his seat, leaving Natasha to pull in a breath she had not been aware she had been holding on to.

He picked up his coffee cup and his newspaper.

Tugging her hands out of her pockets, she picked up the glass and sipped the juice. The sun beat down on the gardens below them while the overhang from the roof suspended above the terrace kept them in much pleasanter shade.

She was about to help herself to a slice of toast when she saw her mobile telephone lying on the table and her fingers stilled in midair.

'Bernice found it in my jacket pocket. I had forgotten I had it.' He might give the appearance of being engrossed in his newspaper, but he clearly was not.

Having to work to stop yet another polite thank-you from developing, Natasha pressed her lips together and nodded, then picked the phone up, her fingers stroking the shiny black casing for a few seconds before she flipped the phone open and looked at the screen.

It filled up with voice and text messages from Rico or Cindy. Aware that Leo was watching her, aware of the silence thickening between the two of them, she began to delete each message in turn, gaining a cold kind of pleasure from watching each one disappear from the screen. As the final one disappeared she flipped the phone shut and placed it back on the table before reaching for the slice of toast.

'I need to shop for some clothes,' she said coolly.

Leo said nothing, though Natasha could feel his desire to say *something* about the way she had wiped her phone clean. Had *he* read her messages? Had he expected to find a volley of instructions from Rico instructing her on how to sneak away from here so she could hole up with him somewhere until the six weeks were up and they could get at their stolen stash?

What Leo did do was to reach inside his jacket pocket and come out with a soft leather wallet. 'I will arrange an account for you with my bank,' he said evenly, 'but for now…'

A thick wad of paper money landed on the table next to her phone. Cringing inside, Natasha just stared at it.

'Buy anything you want,' he invited casually. 'Rasmus will drive you into Athens—'

'I don't need a driver,' she whispered tautly. 'I can find my way to the shops by myself.'

'Rasmus will not be there merely to play chauffeur,' his smooth voice returned. 'He will escort you wherever you go while you are here.'

'For what purpose?' Natasha forced herself to look at him—forced herself to keep silent about the phone and the hateful money he'd tossed down next to it. 'To guard me in case I decide to run out on you? Well, I won't run,' she stated stiffly. 'I don't want to be thrown into jail if I get caught.'

'In that case think of Rasmus as protection,' he suggested.

'Which I need because…?'

The attractive black arc of his eyebrows lifted upwards. 'Because it is a necessary evil in this day and age?' he offered.

'For you perhaps.'

'You are an intimate part of me now, which means you must learn to take the bad with the good.'

So where was the good in being his woman? she wondered

furiously. 'People would have to know I'm with you to make a bodyguard necessary for me.'

'But they will know—from tonight,' he countered, calmly folding his newspaper on that earth-rocking announcement. 'We will be dining out with some friends of mine. So while you are shopping buy a dress—something befitting a black-tie event. Something—pretty.'

Pretty? 'I don't do pretty.' Reaching for the pot of marmalade, Natasha began spreading it liberally on the toast.

'Something—colourful, then to—complement your figure.'

'I am not—' the knife worked faster '—going to dress up like some floozy just to help you prove a point to your awful ex-wife!'

'Why? Don't you believe you have the power to compete?'

The challenge hit Natasha blindside, and she felt her breath stick in her throat.

'It seems to me, Natasha, that you're too easily intimidated by conceited bullies like your selfish sister and my ex-wife,' he went on grimly. 'Woman like them can pick a shrinking violet like you out from a hundred feet away as an easy target. But what really gets to me is that you let them. Grow up, *agape mou*,' he advised as he climbed to his feet. 'Toughen up. You are with me now and I have a reputation for high standards in my choice of women.'

Tense as piano wire now, 'Your standard must have slipped when you married Gianna, then,' she hit back at him.

To her further fury he just uttered a dry husky laugh! 'We are all allowed one mistake. Rico was your mistake, Gianna was mine, so now we are quits.'

With no quick answer ready to offset that one, 'Why don't you just go and do—whatever it is you do and leave me alone?' she muttered, and picked up her slice of toast to bite into it.

The next thing she knew he'd moved around the table and was swooping down to capture her marmalade sticky mouth.

'Mmm, nice,' he murmured as he drew away again. 'I think we will try that again…'

Dipping a fingertip into the marmalade pot, he smeared it across the hot cushion of her bottom lip, then bent his dark head to lick the marmalade off. Like a captivated cat Natasha couldn't stop the pink tip of her own tongue from tracing her lip the moment he withdrew again.

'Yes,' he said softly, and she was drowning in a completely new kind of sensual foreplay that made her want to squirm where she sat.

Then he was straightening up to his full height and moving away from her towards the wall of glass with the smooth stride of an arrogantly self-confident male, leaving the rich, low sound of his amused laughter behind in his wake.

'You forgot to add yourself to the list of bullies in my life!' she threw after him, angrily snatching up a napkin to rub the residue of sticky marmalade from her mouth.

'But Miss Cool and Prim quickly slipped her chains, did she not? Think about it, Natasha.'

The glass slid open to allow him to stride through. Natasha stared after him until she couldn't see him any longer and sizzled and simmered—because she knew he was right. She had lost her cool the moment he'd touched her. It just wasn't fair that he could affect her that easily—it wasn't!

Her eyes went back to the wad of money still lying on the table where he'd tossed it down beside her phone. She was not so dumb that she hadn't recognised his criticism of her clothes and her uncompetitive nature for the challenge it was, but it had hurt to hear him say it in that disparaging tone he'd used.

Mr Blunt, she mocked dully, and felt the hurt tremor attack her poor, abused bottom lip.

Her mobile phone started ringing as she sat in the isolated luxury of one of Leo's limousines. Opening her purse—which

Bernice had also found for her this morning languishing on a table out on the terrace—Natasha plucked out her mobile phone and stared at the screen warily, expecting the caller to be Cindy or Rico, but it wasn't.

'How did you get my number?' she demanded.

'I stole it,' Leo confessed. 'Listen,' he then continued briskly, 'I have had an extra meeting dropped on me today so I will not be finished here in time to get back home and change before we go out. I have arranged with a friend of mine to kit you out with everything you might need in the way of clothes. Her name is Persephone Karides. Rasmus is transporting you to her salon right now. Don't turn stiff on her, *agape mou*,' he cautioned smoothly as if he just couldn't stop himself from criticising her! 'Trust her because she has more sense of style in her little fingertip than anyone else I know.'

Natasha drew in a hurt breath. 'You're very insulting,' she said as she breathed out again. 'Do you always have to think with your mouth?'

There was a silence—a short, sharp shock of one that rang in her ears and made her bottom lip quiver again. 'My apologies,' he murmured—earnestly. 'I did not intend what I said to sound like a criticism of you.'

'Well, it did.' Natasha flipped her phone shut and pushed it back in her bag. It rang again almost immediately but she ignored it.

'Oh, goodness me,' Persephone Karides gasped the moment she saw Natasha. 'When Leo told me you were different, I did not think he meant so fabulously different!'

Standing here in her miserable cream suit eyeing the eye-catching, raven-haired, tall, slender model-type standing a good six inches higher than herself—Natasha had to ask herself if Leo had primed Persephone Karides to say that.

'He's desperate I don't show him up by appearing in a sack, so he sent me to you,' she responded—stiffly.

'Are you joking?' Persephone Karides burst out laughing. 'Leo is much more concerned with his own comfort! He instructed me that he wants modest. He wants quietly elegant and refined. He does not want other men climbing over each other to get a better look at your front! I have not had as much fun in a long time as I did listening to a jealously possessive Leo Christakis, of all men, dictate how he wanted me to protect him!'

Natasha flushed at his intervention. Was he throwing down yet another challenge to her here or was Persephone Karides simply telling it as it was?

Whichever, the fact that he'd dared to give out such arrogant orders to the fashion stylist was enough to put the glinting light of defiance in her blue eyes.

Long hours later Rasmus pulled the car to a stop next to a fabulous-looking private yacht tied up against the harbour wall. Natasha gaped at it because the last thing she'd expected was to be dining in a restaurant situated on a luxury yacht.

'The boss owns it,' Rasmus told her as he shut off the car engine. 'The yacht used to belong to his father. When he decided to sell it, the boss objected. His father let him have the boat so long as he turned it into a profit-making enterprise.'

So he came up with the idea of turning the yacht into a restaurant? 'How old was he?' Natasha questioned curiously.

'Nineteen. He gave her a complete refit, then chartered her out and turned in a profit in his first year,' Rasmus said with unmistaken pride in his voice. 'Two years ago, when she was ready for another refit, he decided her sailing days were over and brought her here. Now she's one of the most exclusive restaurants in Athens.'

Here was a pretty horseshoe-shaped harbour tucked away

from the busy main port, Natasha saw when she climbed out of the car into the hot evening air, cooled by the gentle breeze coming in off the sea. The yacht itself had an old-world grandeur about it that revealed a sentimental side to Leo she would never have given him in a thousand years.

Or it reveals his money-making genius, the cynical side to her brain suggested to her as she walked up the gangway. She felt butterflies take flight in her stomach the closer she came to putting on show her day of defiance aided and abetted by an eager Persephone Karides.

Though the way she had allowed the moment to become so important to her came to lie like a weight across her chest when she saw him. He was leaning against a white painted bulkhead waiting for her. Natasha stilled as her spindle-heeled shoes settled onto the deck itself. He looked breath-shatteringly gorgeous in the conventional black dinner suit he was wearing with a black silk bow tie and a shimmering bright white shirt.

Uncertainty went to war against defiance as she waited for him to say something—show smug triumph because he had manipulated her to do what he wanted her to do or reveal his disapproval at the look she had achieved.

He took his own sweet time showing anything at all as he slid his hooded gaze over her from the top of her loose blonde hair tamed into heavy silk waves around her face and her bare shoulders, then took in the creamy, smooth thrust of her breasts cupped in a misty soft violet crêpe fabric held in place by two flimsy straps, which tied together at the back of her neck. The rest of the dress moulded every curving shape of her figure and finished modestly at her knees—though there was nothing remotely modest about the flirty little back kick pleat that gave her slender thighs length and a truly eye-popping—to Natasha anyway—sensual shape.

Sexy... She knew she looked sexy because Persephone had

told her she did and, as she'd learned during the long day in the Greek woman's care, Persephone did not mess around with empty compliments. 'Leo is going to kill me if you wear that,' she'd said.

And, true to Persephone's warning, Natasha saw that Leo was not happy. His growing frown teased her stomach muscles with a tingling surge of triumph. His mouth was flat, his eyes hidden beneath those disgustingly thick, ebony eyelashes. When he lifted a hand to run an absent finger along his bumpy nose, for some unaccountable reason she wanted to breathe out a victorious laugh.

Then she didn't want to laugh because he was lowering the hand and coming towards her, crossing the space separating them without uttering a single word. The expanse of creamy flesh she had on show began to prickle as he came closer, her wide-spaced, carefully made-up eyes with their eyelashes darkened and lengthened by a heavy lick of mascara trying their very best to appear cool. He came to a stop a few inches away, glanced down at her mouth so sensually shaped by a deep rose gloss, then dropped his gaze even lower, to the misty violet framework of the dress where it formed a perfect heart shape across the generous curves of her breasts.

By the time he lifted his eyes back to hers, Natasha felt as if she were standing on pins. She'd stopped breathing, was barely even thinking much beyond the sizzling clash their eyes had made. Then instinct kicked in and she lifted her chin in an outright challenge.

He slid his hands around her nipped-in waist, tugged her hard up against him, then stole her lipstick with a very hot, aggressive kiss.

'Move an inch from my side tonight and you will find

yourself floating in the water.' His eyes burned the threat into her as he drew away.

'It was you that told me to stop playing the shrinking violet,' she reminded him coolly.

Taking a small step back, he took his time looking her over once again. 'The colour of the dress is right anyway,' he observed finally.

Natasha pulled in a breath., 'Do you find it so totally impossible to say anything nice to me?'

She had a point, Leo acknowledged, but if she thought he had not noticed how pleased she was that she'd annoyed him, then—

'Come on,' he sighed, giving up because he'd got exactly what he'd asked for, and to discover only when it was too late that he no longer wanted it was his problem, not Natasha's. 'Let's find out if we can spend a whole evening together without embarking on yet another fight.'

Walking beside him with one of his long fingered hands a possessive clamp around her waist, Natasha wished she knew if it was triumph or annoyance that was sending sparking electrodes swimming in her blood. The moment they stepped inside the main salon she was immediately struggling with a different set of new conflicts when she found herself the instant centre of attention for twenty or so curious looks.

She moved a bit closer to Leo. Her hand slid up beneath his jacket to clutch tensely at his shirt against his fleshless waist. He liked it, she realised as she sensed a kind of quickening inside him as if his flesh had woken up to her presence. She went to snatch her hand back again, shocked that she'd even dared to put it there in the first place.

'Leave it where it is,' Leo instructed.

Her fingers quivered a little before they settled back against his shirt again. He responded with a delicate caress of her waist. Quickly the sensual charge that had been sparking between them from the moment they first kissed at his home in London was relaying its message again.

He began introducing her around his guests as 'Natasha', that was all, because to add the Moyles was bound to give rise to speculation about Rico, since half the people she was being introduced to were also on the wedding invitation list Rico's mother had emailed to her only last week.

And thinking about Rico did not make her feel comfortable about being here. It began to bother her that Leo had brought her into these people's midst at all. In fact, the more she thought about it, the more sure she became that, once these people found out the truth about exactly who she was, they were going to stop treating her with respect. At the moment they were only doing so because she was with Leo Christakis.

It also began to bother her that she needed to stick this close to Leo—touching, feeling his body warmth and his possessive arm across her back, his hand fixed like a clamp to her waist. Putting herself on show had never been her thing and it took only half an hour of being the centre of attention before she was certain she was never going to want to do it again.

Dinner took place in another salon, presided over by one of Athens's top chefs, she was reliably informed by a friend of Leo's seated opposite her. 'Leo likes only the best in everything,' Dion Angelis told her, grinning at the man in question who occupied the place next to Natasha.

Dion Angelis was about Leo's age and wore the same cloak of wealth about him—as all these people did. The beautiful creature sitting beside him was Marina, his very Greek wife.

Greek wives didn't speak to other men's lovers—at least not in this circle of people, Natasha had discovered tonight. And now she knew why as she watched Dion Angelis drift a lazy look over her with his eyelids lowered in a way she would have to be blind to miss what it meant.

Tensing slightly in her seat, Natasha flicked a glance at Marina who tried her best to hide her anger at her husband's blatant interest—but not before she had sent Natasha a scathing look of contempt. Then she slid her dark gaze to Leo.

'Leonadis...' it made Natasha start in surprise because she had not heard anyone call Leo that before '...Gianna expected you at Boschetto's last night. She was really quite upset when you failed to appear.'

Sitting further back into her chair, Natasha turned her expression blank. So even ex-wives rated higher than lovers, she gleaned from Marina's attempt to put her in her place.

'Gianna has already voiced her objection,' Leo returned smoothly. 'Dion, kindly remove your eyes from my future wife's breasts...'

As a softly spoken show-stopper it silenced a room full of chattering voices. The sophisticated Dion turned a dull shade of red. His wife snapped her lips together and turned her widening stare onto Natasha along with everyone else. Natasha was the only one to turn her shocked stare onto Leo while he, the cool, implacable devil, stared down at his wineglass and remained perfectly calm and relaxed with the kind of smile playing with his lips that turned Natasha's flesh to ice.

'Congratulations,' someone murmured, setting off a rippling effect of similar sentiments while Natasha continued to stare at Leo until he lifted his head and looked back at her, his steady, dark gaze silently challenging her to deny what he'd said.

It was on the tip of her tongue to do it. It was right there hovering on that tingling tip that she should just get it all over with and announce to everyone exactly who she was!

With an ease that belied the speed with which he did it and the strength that he used, Leo's hand caught hold of hers and squeezed. 'Don't,' he warned softly.

He was back to reading her mind again—back to playing it tough! Natasha turned to look at Marina, the light of fury like a crystal-blue haze she could barely manage to see through. 'Tacky, other people's relationships, don't you think?' she remarked with a wry smile that beat Leo's hands down in the chilly stakes. 'I can only hope that my marriage to Leo will come to a less volatile ending than his first marriage did and that I accept it with more—grace.'

With that she stood up, shaking inside now but knowing that she had made her point. She already knew about Gianna. She knew the ex-wife still chased her lost man. And she also knew that Leo had just said what he had because Marina's husband had been eyeing Natasha up and that Dion did it because other men's lovers were clearly fair game around here—which said what about Marina's place in her husband's life?

Leo also came to his feet, his hand still a crushing clamp around her fingers, which kept her pinned to his side. 'Excuse us,' he said dryly to their captive audience. 'It seems that Natasha and I need to find some privacy to discuss her desire to consign our marriage to the divorce courts before it has even begun.'

With that he turned and strode towards the exit, towing her behind him like some naughty child, while leaving a nervously uncertain shimmer of laughter to swim in their wake.

'You always planned to make that announcement, didn't you?' She leapt on the accusation the moment Rasmus closed them inside the car. 'It was the reason why you took me into their company, the reason why you sent me to Persephone to make sure I was suitably dressed for the part!'

'You chose your own style makeover, Natasha,' Leo imparted without a single hint of remorse for what he had just done. 'I recall warning Persephone that I wanted quietly elegant.'

The look she flicked him should have seared off a layer of his skin. 'Before or after you challenged me to put it all out on show?'

A muscle along his jaw flexed. 'I changed my mind about that.'

'Why?' she demanded.

Leo released an irritated sigh. 'Because I feel safer when you play it prim!'

The fact that he was actually admitting it was enough to stop Natasha's breath in her throat.

'Why does this surprise you?' he asked when he caught her expression. 'Your modest mystique was the first thing to attract me to you. Having come to know you a little better, I now realise that I prefer it if you remain mysterious—to everyone else but me.'

'That is just so arrogant I can't believe you even said it!'

All he offered was an indifferent shrug. 'Marina attacked you tonight because she believes you are merely my current lover. Now she knows that my intentions are honourable she will not dare to treat you like that again.'

'Until she finds out who I really am, then she will see the dangerous woman again—the kind that drops one brother to take up with the richer one!'

'Well, that puts Dion out of the frame,' Leo drawled with cool superiority. 'And as for Marina, she will make sure he keeps his wandering eyes to himself from now on.'

'I'm still not marrying you,' Natasha shook out, 'so it's up to you how you get out of the mess you made for yourself.'

Leo met that with silence. Natasha turned to look directly ahead and let the silence stretch. But she could feel his eyes on her, *feel* him trying to decide if she possessed enough determination against his relentless push to get her to agree to marry him, and she could feel the fizz in her insides—as if her newly awakened senses found it stimulating to be constantly sparring with him like this!

Leo was silent because he was considering whether to tell her that he never declared anything without a fault-free strategy already worked out. But he let that consideration slide away in favour of wondering what she would do if he leapt on her instead. She was already expecting it to happen, he could tell by the way she was sitting there tense, clutching her fingers together on her lap and with that invitingly curvy upper lip trembling in readiness of a full on sensual attack.

But it could wait—as *she* could wait until they were within reach of their bed. Though that did not mean he wasn't prepared to up the sensual ante a little. 'So you still only offer me the sex.'

'*Yes!*' Natasha insisted.

And only realised the trap she'd fallen into when he murmured softly, 'Good, because you look so beautiful tonight I ache to slide you out of that dress.'

His intentions declared, Leo left her to sizzle in her own strategic error as they arrived at his house. The heavy gates swung open. The car pulled to a stop at the bottom of the front steps. They both climbed out of it under their own steam, leaving Rasmus to slide the car out of their way so Natasha could cross the gap to Leo's side. He did not attempt to touch her as they walked up the steps and into the house. He let the stinging stitch of anticipation spin separate webs of expectation around both of them as they crossed the foyer and into the lift.

The moment they achieved the privacy of his floor Leo gave up on the waiting and reached for her—only Natasha took a swift step back.

'Tell me why you told everyone we are getting married,' she insisted.

His sigh was filled with irritation that she was persisting

with the subject. 'Because a formal announcement of our intention to marry will appear in all the relevant newspapers tomorrow, so I saw no reason to keep quiet about it,' he answered, and watched her delectable mouth drop.

'But you can't have done that without my say-so!'

'Well, I did.' He strode off, tugging impatiently at his bow tie.

Natasha hurried anxiously after him. 'But you can't have it both ways, Leo. You can't keep my relationship to Rico a secret to your friends *and* announce my name in the press at the same time!'

'You don't have a relationship with Rico.' The bow tie slid free of his shirt collar and was discarded onto a chair.

'Excuse me?' Natasha choked out. 'Aren't you the one who insists I'm Rico's thieving accomplice?'

He turned a steady look on her. 'Are you—his accomplice?'

Sheer angry cussedness made Natasha want to spit out a very satisfying *yes!* Then her innate honesty got the better of her. 'Not intentionally, no,' she answered wearily.

'Then do us both a favour and drop the subject.' As if he was bored with it, he shrugged out of his jacket. 'You were attacked tonight by a woman who cannot keep her husband in check and who is also a good friend of my ex-wife. I defended you. You should be feeling grateful, not screeching at me.'

It was the inference that she had been screeching that snapped Natasha's ready lips shut. Gianna was a screecher. Not in any way, shape or form did Natasha want to be compared with her!

It was only as she watched his hands move to the top button of his shirt that Natasha realised where they were standing in the bedroom and the need to keep fighting him withered right there.

She glanced at the bed, all neat and tidy with its corners turned down ready for them to slide between the cool white sheets. Her heart gave a flutter and she turned her gaze back onto Leo, who was calmly unbuttoning the rest of his shirt while he watched the telling expressions trip across her face.

'You led me in here deliberately,' she murmured.

His acknowledging smile was as lazily amused as hell. 'I am a natural tactician, *agape mou*. You should already know this.'

He was also the most sensuously beguiling man to watch undress. Natasha lost the thread of the conversation when her eyes fixed on the ribbon of hair-matted, bronzed flesh now on show down his front.

'You want to touch me?' The husky question in his voice made her lips tremble and part.

She couldn't even deny it with a shake of her head.

'Then come over here and touch me.' It was a soft-toned invitation—a darkly compelling masculine command.

And it tugged her towards him as if she were attached to him by invisible strings. She didn't even hate herself for giving in to it so easily, she just *wanted*—with a mind-blocking, sense-writhing need that brought her fingers up and reaching for him. He helped by taking hold of them and guiding them to his chest before he sank her into the warm, dark luxury of pleasure with the power of his kiss.

He peeled her out of her dress as promised. He stroked each satin curve of her body as if he were consigning each detail of her to memory, and eventually sank her down onto the bed.

'I shouldn't let you do this to me,' she groaned at one point when he made her feel as if she had molten liquid moving through her veins.

'You think I feel less than you do?' Catching one of her hands, he laid it against the pounding of his heart in his chest.

The rest of the night turned into long—long hours of slow loving. If Natasha had ever let herself wonder if there were really men out there that could sustain the flowing peaks of pleasure so often, then by the time they drifted into sleep she knew she need wonder no more.

Then the morning came, as bright and blue and glittering as the day before had been—only this morning Leo was tipping her unceremoniously out of the bed and pushing her into the bathrobe before dragging her out onto the terrace.

'What do you think you are doing?' Her sleep-hazed brain made her feel dizzy.

He made no answer, and there was no sign of the wonderfully warm and sensual man who'd loved her into oblivion the night before, just a cold, hard, angry male who pushed her down into a chair, then stabbed a finger at the newspaper he had folded open on the table in front of her.

'Read,' he said.

Read, Natasha repeated silently while still trying to get her muddy brain to work. He'd woken her up. He hadn't even let her use the bathroom. She could barely get her eyes to focus, never mind read a single thing!

Then she had no choice but to focus because the headline was typed in such bold black lettering it stabbed her with each soul-shattering, nerve-flaying word.

CHAPTER EIGHT

LOVE CHEAT CHOOSES RICHES OVER RAGS! it yelled at her.

In an intriguing love triangle, Natasha Moyles—sister of Cindy Moyles, the new singing sensation everyone is talking about—has dumped the man she was supposed to be marrying in six weeks to run off with his Greek billionaire stepbrother, Leo Christakis, in a riches over rags love scandal that leaves the poorer Italian playboy Rico Giannetti out in the cold.

Cindy Moyles claims that she didn't see it coming. 'I had no idea that Natasha was seeing Leo Christakis behind Rico's back. I'm as shocked as everyone,' she insisted today as she sat with her new management team, who are about to launch her career with a new single predicted to clean up when it's released.

Rico Giannetti was not available for comment. His mother is said to be very upset. The Christakis PR department is denying there is anything untoward between their employer and his stepbrother's fiancée. However the picture below tells it all...

There was more—lots of it—but Natasha's eyes had stuck on the photograph showing her standing in a heated clinch with Leo right here on the balcony of this house. She was wrapped around him like a sex-hungry feline. There wasn't a hope that anyone was going to call it an innocent clinch.

'The beauty of power-zoom lenses,' Leo mocked from his lounging posture in the chair on the other side of the table.

With her face going white with shock to horror then heart-clutching dismay, she asked, 'But—how did they find out I was here with you?'

'Your sister,' he provided grimly. 'This is a very good example of damage limitation. Cindy's new management team is clearly on the ball. She must have gone straight to them with what happened and they got their heads together and decided to take the initiative by getting in her side of the story first. Fortunately for her I managed to gag Rico before she did or your dear sister placed herself at risk of coming out of this looking like the manipulative little whore that she is.'

'Don't say that.' Natasha felt stifled by the ugly picture he was painting. The truth was bad enough, but this made it all so much worse!

'Look at the evidence, Natasha,' he advised harshly. 'Look at the free publicity she is getting from this. Even her new management team has made sure their company name is printed.'

His angry tone made her shiver. 'Is there anything you can do to—?'

'Plenty of things,' he clipped in. 'I could strangle your sister, but I suspect it is already too late to do that. Or I could kick you out and allow myself the small satisfaction of knowing I will be painted as one hell of a ruthless bastard to have stolen you from beneath Rico's nose for the pleasure of a two-night stand! Being seen as that ruthless is good for my business image—the rest I don't give a toss about.'

Stung right through by his angry barrage, 'Or I could walk away under my own steam,' Natasha retaliated. 'I could play the true slut by making it known that I've had *both* brothers and neither were worth it!'

Across the table Leo's eyes darkened dangerously. Natasha didn't care. 'Well, think of it from my point of view,' she suggested stiffly. 'Miss Cool and Prim isn't quite as cool and prim as people like to think! I could make a small fortune selling my story—a juicy kiss-and-tell about the sexual antics of a billionaire tycoon and the poor Italian playboy!'

'Not worth it?' He picked up on the only part of what she'd thrown at him that seemingly mattered.

'I hate you,' she breathed, hunching inside her bathrobe. 'This was always going to get nasty. You carried me away on a cloud of assurances, but when I think back, you needed only half a minute once you'd got me into your house in London before you were flipping my head by telling me that you wanted me for yourself! What kind of man does that to a woman who'd just witnessed what I had witnessed? What kind of man picks her up and takes her to bed? What kind of man, Leo,' she thrust out furiously, 'propositions a woman, then carries through, knowing she was in no fit state to know what she was doing?'

'What kind of woman falls in love with a useless piece of pampered flesh like Rico and is too blind to notice he's still putting it out there with every female he can lay his hands on?'

Strike for strike, Leo cut deeper than anything she'd stabbed him with. Natasha tugged in a shuddering breath. 'I suppose next you're going to remind me that Rico didn't even want me.'

'So you can accuse me of accepting his unwanted cast offs?'

Natasha pushed to her feet on a daze of trammelled feelings. 'Is that how you see me?' she choked as last night's long loving strangled itself to death.

'No,' his voice rasped like coarse sandpaper across her ragged senses. 'I do not see you like that.'

'They why say it?' she shrilled out. 'Do you think I am

proud of the way I jumped into bed with you? Do you think I hadn't already worked out for myself that I was going to be labelled gold-digging tart for doing it?'

'Then why did you do it?'

He just didn't know when to leave something alone! Natasha's whole body quivered on the deep breath she took. 'Because you wanted me and I needed to be wanted.' And the devil himself couldn't tempt her to add that she'd been lost to reason from the moment their mouths had first touched. 'You get what you ask for,' she then mocked with weak tears thickening it. 'So, thank you, Leo, for taking such great care to teach me I am a normal sexual woman. I really do appreciate it.'

'My absolute pleasure,' he grimly silked out. 'But—to bring this discussion back to its original problem—there is one other option open to me that would save my face and your face.'

'W-what?' she couldn't resist prompting.

He laughed, low and deep and as sardonic as hell. 'A wedding,' he said as he picked up another newspaper, then leant forwards to place it on top of the other one. Instead of a tabloid, this one was a respected UK broadsheet, also conveniently folded at the right place.

It was the announcement of their forthcoming marriage. Natasha had forgotten all about it. Pressing her tense lips together, she made herself sit down and read it.

'It feels quite good to know that my instincts were working so well when I placed that in the papers,' Leo's dry voice delivered.

'I will still always look like a gold-digging tart with or without this.'

'Everyone loves a passionate romance, *agape mou*—so long as we do marry and make ourselves respectable, that is. It convinces the doubters that we cannot live without each other, you see. Of course,' he then added, 'you will have to agree to a gagging clause written into the prenuptial contract you are going to sign once my lawyers have drawn it up.'

And that, Natasha heard, was payback because she had just threatened to involve him in a kiss-and-tell exposé.

'Did you *know* about this tabloid article last night when we were dining with your friends?' she flashed out suddenly, though why the suspicion entered her head was beyond her capability to understand right now.

The velvet dark set of his eyes gave a surprised flicker before he carefully hooded them away. 'I happened to hear of it,' he disclosed coolly.

So he put out a counter-announcement declaring their intention to marry in a bid to make himself look better? Natasha threw herself back into her seat. 'You're as sly and manipulating as Cindy,' she quivered out in shaken dislike. 'God help us all if the two of you ever join up to make a team!'

'Your sister isn't my type. *You* are my type.'

The gullible type that didn't look around corners to see what others were hiding from her? Unable to stop the cold little shiver from tracking her spine, she said, 'A marriage between you and me is never going to work.'

Those sexy, heavy eyelids lifted upwards. 'Did I say I expected it to work?' he silked out.

As an image of the manic Gianna flashed across her eyes Natasha began to understand why the other woman—*wife*— of this man had turned so manic. He just didn't know when to quit with the knives!

'Marriage to Rico is starting to look more appetising by the minute,' she attacked back in muttering derision. 'At least he possessed *some* charm to offset the low-down, sneaky side to his character, whereas you—'

Leo was up out of his chair and looming over her before she could let out a startled shriek. 'You believe so?' he thinned out.

It was then that Natasha caught the glittering gold sparks burning up his eyes and remembered too late what it conveyed. The last time she'd seen that look she'd just accused him of being jealous of Rico, and his reaction then had—

'I was just kidding!' she cried out as his hands arrived around her waist and he hauled her bodily off the chair.

She found herself clamped to his front by a pair of arms that threatened to stop her breathing, her eyes on a level with his.

'I w-was just kidding, Leo,' she repeated unsteadily, forced to push her arms over his shoulders because there was nowhere else she could put them, and it didn't help that she was feeling the buzz, feeling the deep and pulsing, sense-vibrating buzz slink over each separate nerve-end as he held her gaze prisoner with the fierce heat of his next intention, turned with her and started walking them towards the curving glass.

And he didn't say a single word, which made the whole macho exercise even more exciting. He just tumbled her down onto the bed and followed her there, lips flat, face taut, his hands already making light of the belts holding their robes shut.

'Y-you deserved to hear it, though.' Natasha just could not resist adding fire to his anger. 'If—if you think about it, Leo, you're as ruthless ab-about getting what you want as—'

'Say his name again if you dare,' he breathed.

Natasha had the sense to block her tongue behind her teeth and knew she should be feeling alarmed and intimidated by his angry intent, but she didn't. She just lay there and let him part the two robes and waited for him to stretch out on top of her.

Heat by burning heat, their skin melded together at the same moment that his mouth took fierce possession of hers. And like someone who just did not know any better she fell into it all to kiss with every bit of aroused excitement at work inside her, hungry for him, greedy for him, slipping her legs around his waist so she could invite his full driving thrust.

He filled her and she loved it. He still held her eyes total prisoner as he moved in her with the deep and driven plunge of his hips. She loved that, too. Loved it so much she lifted her head to capture his mouth with short, soft, encouraging kisses that pulled a groan from his throat and sent his fingers spearing into her hair so he could hold her back to maintain the electrifying eye contact.

Nothing in her admittedly small experience warned her that the climax she was about to hit would turn her into a trembling state of shimmering static. Or that the man creating it was going to tremble in her arms.

When it was over, he lay heavy on her, his face buried in the heat-dampened hollow of her throat. Her heart was hammering, she could barely draw in her breath. What had just taken place had been so fevered and physical she lay there shell-shocked by the power of it. Every inch of her flesh still trembled, she could feel the same tremors still attacking him. And their limbs were tangled, the white towelling bathrobes generating a cocoon of intimacy all of their own.

When eventually he lifted his head to look down at her, the deep and intense darkness in his eyes snagged her breath all the more.

'I was rough with you,' he murmured unsteadily.

'No.' Natasha drew her hand up to rest it against his mouth. 'Don't say that,' she whispered. 'I—liked it.' And because she simply had to do it, she removed her hand and replaced it with the warm, soft tremor of her mouth.

One kiss led to another. Their robes disappeared. No matter how much angry passion had brought them back to this bed in the first place, this climb back through the senses was slow and deep and breathtakingly intense. He kissed her everywhere and with complete disregard of any shyness she might have had left. She curled herself into him wherever she could do, she kissed and licked and bit his flesh and scored her hands over him, absorbing every pleasurable shudder he gave while whispering his name over and over again.

Afterwards was as if it weren't happening. They drifted with a silent sense of togetherness from the bed to the shower. In the husky deep voice of a man still in the power of what they'd created Leo showed her how to work the wet-room buttons and dials, then handed her a bar of soap and encouraged her to wash him while he stood, big shoulders pressed back against the white tiles with his eyes closed and his lean face stripped of its usual arrogance.

Natasha knew that something crucial had altered between them, though she could not put a name to what that something was.

Then—yes, she could, she thought as she leant in closer and moulded her lips around one of his tightly budded nipples. Somewhere during all of that intense loving, they had both dropped their guard.

Ages later, Leo dressed and went off to work and she—well, Natasha crawled back between the rumpled bedding, curled up on his side of the bed and whispered, 'I love him,' into his pillow.

It was shockingly, horribly that simple. She fell asleep wondering how she could have let it happen—and what the heck she was going to do about it….

That evening he took her out to dinner again. She chose to wear a little black dress that skimmed her curves rather than moulded them. As he ran his eyes over her, he lifted a hand up to absently stroke the bump in his nose and it struck

Natasha that he did that when he was unhappy about something—this time probably the little black dress.

Still, he chose to say nothing. He chose not to comment on the way she had pinned her hair up, leaving her neck and her shoulders bare. He wore a casual, taupe, linen suit and a black T-shirt that made her fingers want to stroke his front. He took her to a small, very select place in the hills outside the city away from the main tourist haunts. They ate food off a tiny candlelit table and drank perfectly chilled white wine. And each time she moved, the luxurious thickness of his eyelashes flowed down low over his eyes and she knew—just knew he was making love to her in his mind.

It was all so heady to be the total centre of his concentration like this. And the knowledge now that she was in love with him tugged and ached inside her so badly she was sure he must be able to tell in the husky quality of her voice and in her body language. Self-awareness became an irresistible drug that made her hold his attention with soft small talk and dark blue, tempting looks she didn't even realize she knew how to do.

Leo was captivated. She was so hooked on what was passing between them she was unaware how she'd drawn an invisible circle around the two of them. People he knew came up to speak to him. Natasha barely noticed. She barely heard the congratulations they were receiving or noticed the interested looks of speculation they sent her way. Whenever his attention was demanded elsewhere, he claimed her slender hand across the table and she even used this contact to keep his senses locked on her with the light brush of her fingers against his.

It was intoxicating to know that this beautiful and tantalising creature revealed herself only for him. To anyone else her responses were quiet and polite, but cool and reserved like the old Natasha. Rico had no idea what it was he had missed out on.

Rico. Leo flicked a hooded, dark glance at her and wondered how often his stepbrother's name crept into her head. Would she prefer to be sitting here with Rico? When she looked at him like this, was she secretly wishing that his face were Rico's face?

On a flick of tension he stood up suddenly and pulled her to her feet. 'Let's go,' he said.

He needed to be alone with her—in his bed.

'What's wrong?' Natasha asked him as Rasmus drove them down the hillside.

Leo didn't even turn his head to look at her, his long body sprawled in the seat beside her so taut she could almost feel the tension plucking at him.

'You are going to marry me whether you want to or not,' he announced coolly.

Silence clattered down around them, increasing the tension holding Leo, while he waited for her to shoot him down with a refusal as she usually did. When nothing came back at him he turned his head. She was sitting beside him with her spine a gentle curve into the leather seat and her eyes were fixed straight ahead. Everything about her was calm and still.

'Did you hear what I said?' he flicked out.

Lips forming the kind of lush, vulnerable profile that made him want to leap on them, she nodded her head.

'Then answer me,' he instructed impatiently.

'I was not aware that you had asked a question,' she responded dryly, 'more a statement of intent.'

'It will still require a *yes* from you when I drag you in front of a priest.'

So it will, Natasha thought with a wry kind of smile altering the contours of her mouth. Yesterday he'd made that shocking announcement to his friends and followed it up this morning with the printed version, tossed at her like a challenge, before coolly informing her that he did not expect a marriage between them to last. Then he'd taken her back to bed and seduced her into falling in love with him. He'd *made love* to her throughout the whole evening. Now the tough-talking man with a marriage ultimatum was back.

'Look at me, Natasha,' he commanded grimly.

She didn't want to look at him—but she still turned her head. It was like drowning in her own newly discovered feelings. Everything about him had become so overwhelmingly important to her in such a short space of time, she'd never felt so hopelessly helpless in her entire life.

'Marry me,' he repeated quietly.

'To help you save face?'

'No,' he denied. 'Because I want you to.'

It was like the final nail in the coffin of her resistance—not just the words he'd spoken, but the deep, dark, husky seriousness with which he had said them—and fed her with an oh-so-weak injection of hope.

'OK—yes,' she said.

OK—yes, he had to live with because, Leo acknowledged frustratingly, OK—yes, was all he was going to get. But he punished her for it later when they hit the bed.

He possessed her body and obsessed her senses, and Natasha let him. She had to because once she'd surrendered the marriage war she found she had no control left over with which to fight him about anything else.

And if this was real love, then it made her hurt like crazy, because, no matter how profoundly she knew she affected him, she also knew deep down inside her that the mind-blowing sex was as deep as it went for him.

Yet he rarely let her leave his side during the next couple of weeks leading up to their marriage. He took her with him wherever he went—even into his office sometimes, where she would stand by the window or sit in a chair and let him throw his weight around with the deeply resonant tone of his voice.

People got to know them as a couple so quickly, it came as no surprise that within days they were being talked about in Athens gossip press. Her betrothal to Rico came out for an airing and the 'riches over rags' label was just too good not to keeping using when they referred to her.

'Do you mind?' Leo asked her when one newspaper in particular did a real character assassination on her.

'It should be me asking you that question, since you don't come out of this any better than I do.'

'How can I mind? You did drop Rico, and you are here with me, and I am most definitely wealthier than Rico will ever be.'

And that was Leo, telling it as it was. Even Natasha couldn't argue with such simplicity and she knew the full truth.

There was no word from Rico. Natasha could find no photograph of him in any newspaper, and no one had tracked him down to get his comments on his broken engagement. He seemed to have dropped off the face of the earth.

Two weeks exactly from the day she had walked onto the Christakis private plane with Leo, Natasha married him in a quiet civil ceremony that took place in a closely guarded, secret location. She wore white—at his insistence—a strapless, French silk, tulle dress with a rouched bodice Persephone had found for her. When she stood beside Leo as they took their vows, he looked so much the tall, dark, sober-faced groom that she almost—almost lost courage and changed her mind.

The announcement of their marriage appeared in the next day's papers. By then they were already in New York. It was being called a honeymoon, but what it actually turned out to be was the beginning of a tour of Leo's business interests, which took them around the world. By day Leo played the powerful and cut-throat businessman, by night he played the suave sophisticate, socialising with business associates, and Natasha learnt to play the game at his side. While in the privacy of their bedroom, whichever country they were in, she played the lover to a man with an insatiably passionate desire for her.

From New York to Hong Kong to Tokyo then Sydney. By the time they landed back on Greek soil two more weeks had gone by and Natasha was such a different person she could barely remember the one she used to be.

But, more than that, she had allowed herself to forget the real reasons why they had embarked on this marriage in the first place.

She received her first jolting reminder as they walked through the airport and passed an English newspaper stand. She saw Cindy's name and face splashed across every magazine, celebrating her first UK number-one hit.

'So she got her dearest wish,' Leo remarked dryly.

'Yes,' Natasha answered, staring at the way Cindy looked so different, more like a beautiful and youthful, blue-eyed blonde with no hint of her old angst or petulance in sight.

Cindy had pulled on a new persona—just as she had, Natasha likened. Whether it went further than skin-deep with her sister was a question she was not likely to find the answer to because Cindy belonged in her past now.

The next stark reminder as to what she'd left behind in England came amongst the stack of congratulation cards they found waiting for them at the house. This particular one stood out from the rest because she recognised the writing and it was addressed only to her. Inside was a traditionally standard greeting card with silver embossed wedding bells on the front and a simple message of congratulations printed inside. It was from her parents, with a brief note written in her mother's hand.

'We wish you every happiness in your marriage,' was all that it said. No loving endearments, no sign that she had ever been their daughter at all.

'Perhaps they know they treated you badly and don't know how to say so,' Leo suggested quietly.

'And perhaps they're just relieved to bring closure to a twenty-four-year-old mistake.' Turning the envelope over, she frowned at it. 'I wonder how they managed to get hold of this address?'

'Angelina,' Leo provided the answer. 'They have been—keeping in touch.'

That brought Natasha's attention up to his face. 'And you knew this but didn't think to tell me?'

'What was there to tell?' he answered with a shrug. 'Angelina needed to ensure her son was not pilloried in the press by an enterprising Cindy. Your parents needed to ensure that Cindy was not pilloried by a bitter Rico out to get his revenge.'

'You mean, Cindy *did* set him up?'

'Whoever made the first move, *agape mou*, it happened.'

And that was Leo at his tell-it-as-it-is best.

Natasha slipped the card back in its envelope and did not look at it again.

Another week went by and Leo was busy with a major takeover he'd been working on while they'd travelled the world. Now they were back in Athens, he was devoting his whole time to it, busy, preoccupied, some nights not coming home at all because he had to fly off to one place or another to meet with people, which meant an overnight stay.

The fact that he didn't take her with him on these occasions didn't worry Natasha at all. She had other things to think about. She might have let Leo pay for all the expensive designer stuff she now wore with such ease and indifference, but she paid for everything else herself. Now her small nest of savings had shrunk so small she needed to find a job.

Anything would do, she wasn't picky. She soon discovered, though, that without even a smattering of Greek in her vocabulary she was pretty much unemployable in a formal office environment. So she started trawling the tourist spots hoping someone would like to employ an Englishwoman with reasonable intelligence and a pleasant speaking voice.

Leo found out about what she was doing. They had their first major row in weeks. He had the overbearing nerve to prohibit *his wife* from working in such menial employment as a tourist shop. He would increase her allowance if she was so strapped for cash, he said.

'Don't you think I *know* I owe you enough money already without letting you shell out even more?'

Saying it out loud like that hit both of them harder than either of them expected. In one week she would have been marrying Rico. In one short week she could access the money locked up in the offshore account.

Leo just stared at her coldly, then spun on his heel and walked away. Natasha felt as if she'd just murdered something special, but the truth was the truth and she had to face up to that.

By telling it as it is, she thought heavily. She'd been taught by a master at it, after all.

The long, swooping dive down into reality began from that moment on. For the next few days they lived in a state of unarmed combat, in which Leo made himself scarce—being busy—and Natasha job-hunted with a grim determination not to let him dictate to her, by working her way along the tourist shops in the Plaka through the stifling heat of a melting July, perfectly aware of the minder Leo had put on her to track her every move.

It had to be the worst luck in the world when she literally bumped right into his ex-wife, Gianna, as she was coming out of one shop, still unemployed, hot, tired and miserable with it. Maybe the meeting had been contrived. How was she to know? But the way Gianna stopped her from walking right past her by clipping her long fingernails to Natasha's arm was enough to make her wonder if the dark beauty had been waiting to pounce.

'I want to talk to you,' Gianna said thinly.

'I don't think so.' Natasha tried to move on, but the nails dug in deeper to keep her still.

'Leo is mine!' Gianna spat at her. 'You think you have him caught with that ring on your finger, but you do not. You think with your cool blonde looks you are the perfect antidote to me, but Leo has always and will always belong to me!'

'Not so anyone would notice,' Natasha responded, refusing to be shaken by the venom in Gianna's voice. 'As you say, I wear his ring now. *I* sleep in his bed. And I *don't* pass myself around his friends!'

Even Natasha could not believe she'd said that. Gianna responded with a laugh that went with the wildly hysterical look in her eyes. She unclipped her fingernails and for a second Natasha thought she was going to score them down her face. She even took a jerky step back, sensed her minder step in closer to her and watched Gianna's top lip curl in scorn.

'You little fool,' she said. 'Where do you think he spends his nights when he is not with you?'

'That's a lie,' Natasha breathed, not even giving the suggestion room to apply its poison and sending Gianna a pitying look. 'Get some help, Gianna,' she advised coldly. 'You desperately need it.'

Then she beat a hasty retreat, with her minder tracking in her shadow as she disappeared into the crowds, angrily refusing to rub her arm where the other woman's fingernails had bit.

Leo was waiting for her when she got back to the house. Grim as anything, he didn't say a single word, but just took possession of her arm and turned it to inspect the angry red crescents embedded in her smooth white skin.

'How did you find out?' Natasha asked as she watched his fingertips lightly stroke the red marks.

'Does it matter?'

'No.' Natasha sighed, remembering the minder by then anyway. 'I think she's stark staring mad and I actually feel very sorry for her.'

'Well, don't,' he said. 'Believe me, it is dangerous to feel sorry for Gianna.'

'Thanks for the warning.' She took her arm back. 'Now you've checked I'm not bleeding to death, you can go back to work.'

It was the way she said it that rang a familiar bell inside Leo's head. He took a step back to look at her. She was *not* looking at him. And if he had been wondering lately if the old Natasha had gone for ever, with that cool remark he discovered that she had not.

He heaved out a sigh. He'd had a lousy week. Several times the takeover had threatened to go stale and he'd had to fly off somewhere at the last minute to affect a recovery. Normally he thrived on the cut-and-thrust challenge of testing deals like this. It was what made his hunter's instincts tick. But it was only now as he stood here listening to Natasha's cool attempt to dismiss him that he realised how much he had missed using his hunter's instinct on her.

'You want to indulge in another argument?' he prompted smoothly.

'No.' She turned her back as if meaning to walk away from him.

'You want to come to bed with me, then, and spend the afternoon showing me how much you wish I did not have to fly to Paris tonight?'

'Paris?' That swung her back to face him. 'But you've only just got back from there yesterday!'

'And now I must go back there tonight.' His elegant shrug made light of the constant travelling his job demanded, but the look in his eyes did not make light of what was now going on in his head.

Natasha folded her arms across her front. 'Is that why you're here—to pack a bag?'

Playing the provoking innocent just flew right over Leo's head because he could read her body language and those folded arms were no protection at all from what he was generating here. 'I was thinking more on the lines of—something different,' he silked out, closing the gap between them like a big, dark and hungry, stalking cat. 'I have this bottle of champagne on ice, you see, no glasses and several novel ways of enjoying it, if you are interested, that is…'

Natasha couldn't help it, she laughed. 'You're shocking—'

'You love me to be shocking.' He took hold of her wrists and gently unlinked her arms. 'It's what makes you give in so easily when I do this…'

And she did give in. She let him possess her mouth and take her to bed and she let him spend the afternoon shocking her, because she wanted him and she'd missed making love with him and…

The power of a poisoned barb, she heard herself think heavily at one point within the sensual haze he'd wrapped her in and knowing that there was a small part of her that let him do this to her because Gianna's comments made her want to send him away to Paris so totally satiated he wouldn't need to look elsewhere for this.

They stayed hidden in the bedroom throughout the afternoon and she could tell that he did not want to go when it was time for him to leave.

'Will you do me a big favour, and take a day off from job-hunting tomorrow?' he requested.

Her stubborn pout was the beginning of a refusal, which he kissed away.

'Please?' he added when he lifted his head again.

'One good reason,' she bargained, slender white fingertips toying with his smoothly shaved face.

Did he remind her that tomorrow was the day she would have been marrying Rico? Leo brooded. And knew it wasn't really a question because the last thing he wanted to do was to leave her here in his bed thinking about his stepbrother instead of him.

'Because I will be back by lunch with a surprise for you…' catching hold of her caressing fingers, he kissed them '…but only if you are right here waiting for me when I get back.'

'Ah,' said Natasha. 'Blackmail is much more your style. It had better be a good surprise, then.'

Leo just smiled as he rose to his impressive six feet four inches of pure arrogant male in a suit. His gaze lingered, though, on the way she was lying there like a fully-fledged siren stretched out on his bed with her tumbled hair and provoking blue eyes and sumptuously kissed, reddened mouth.

'Where did I get the impression that you were a prude?' he mocked as his gaze slid lower over the creamy fullness of her breasts with their tempting pink centres, and the cluster of dusky blonde curls delineating the heart-shaped juncture with her slender white thighs.

Impulse made him lean down again and place a kiss on that cluster, his tongue darting down in a claim of possession that caused one of those delicious quivers of pleasure she was so free with him.

'See you tomorrow,' he murmured, and left the room before he changed his mind about going anywhere, taking with him the confidence that his woman would be thinking only of him until they came together again.

Natasha slept fitfully that night because she missed him beside her. And awoke the next morning with a thick headache that made her decide to take the day off from job hunting as Leo wanted her to do, which should please him—she thought with a smile.

She was lingering over a solitary breakfast when her mobile phone started to ring. So sure it was going to be Leo calling her, she snatched it up and answered it without checking who it was.

So it came as a shock when it was Cindy's voice that jarred her eardrum.

CHAPTER NINE

'WHAT do you want?' Natasha demanded coldly.

She heard her sister's sigh of relief. 'I wasn't sure you still used this mobile number,' Cindy explained the relieved sigh.

Natasha said nothing, just lowered her eyes to watch the way her fingers stroked the frosted dampness from her glass of orange juice and let the silence stretch.

'OK, so you don't want to speak to me,' Cindy acknowledged. 'But I need to talk to you, Natasha, ab-about the parents.'

Natasha's fingers went still. 'Why—what's wrong with them?'

'Nothing—*everything*,' Cindy sighed out. 'Look…I'm in Athens. I flew in this morning without telling anyone I was coming here, and I have to be back in London this afternoon before I'm missed. Will you meet with me to—talk about them? Trust me, Tasha, it's important or I would not be here.'

Which told her that Cindy wanted this contact no more than she did. But if she'd flown all the way just to speak to her, then whatever she needed to say had to be serious.

Her parents—her parents…that weakness called love gave an aching squeeze. 'OK,' she agreed. 'Do you want to come here so we can—'

'Good grief, no,' Cindy shuddered out. 'I have no desire

to bump into Leo, thank you very much. He gives me the heebie-jeebies.'

'He isn't here.'

'I still won't take the risk. I hired a limo at the airport. Just name a location away from your place and I will get my driver to take me there.'

Natasha glanced at her watch, then named a café in Koloniki Square, and heard Cindy consulting with her driver before she said, 'OK. We can be there in an hour.'

It did not occur to Natasha to question the *we* part. It did not occur to her to question why her totally selfish-seeking sister would come all the way here from England to discuss their parents when it would have been so much quicker and easier for her to just say it on the phone. It was only when she sat waiting at a café table beneath the shade of a leafy tree and watched a silver limo pull up at the edge of the square, then a man climb out of it instead of her sister, that she realised just how thoroughly she had allowed herself to be duped.

Natasha stood up, her first instinct being to just walk away! Then curiosity made her go still as she watched Rico pause to look around him, his eyes hidden behind a pair of silver-framed sunglasses as he scanned the whole square until he located Natasha's minder, then took a quick glance at his watch before he continued towards her.

Dressed in a designer casual pale linen suit and a plane white T-shirt, he looked his usual fashion-plate self. His black hair shone like silk in the sunlight and there wasn't a female in the vicinity from the age of nine to ninety that didn't turn and stare.

But then that was Rico, Natasha thought as she watched him. She, too, had fallen instant victim to his amazing good looks and that special aura he carried everywhere with him, so it was no use her pretending it wasn't there. Except—as she looked at him now she felt absolutely nothing. It was like looking at a stranger—a great-looking stranger, she still had to allow, but a total stranger nonetheless.

When he reached her table, Natasha sat back down in her chair and waited for him to take the seat.

'Still hating me, *cara*?' he drawled as his opening volley.

'Isn't Cindy going to join us?' was all she said in return.

'No.' Leaning back in the chair, Rico glanced at Natasha's minder, who was already talking into his mobile phone.

'I would say you have about five minutes to say what you've set me up to say,' Natasha offered up helpfully.

Looking back at her, Rico pulled off his sunglasses and something strange appeared in the dark brown depths of his eyes. 'You look different,' he murmured. 'That dress suits you.'

'Thank you.' Natasha was not in the least bit impressed by the compliment since the dress was a simple coffee-coloured shift thing she had chosen at random and with no intent to impress anyone.

'I think I should…'

'Get straight to the point,' she suggested. 'Since neither of us want to watch Leo appear in his three-car cavalcade.'

Rico grimaced, clearly understanding exactly what it was she was referring to. One of his hands went into his inside jacket pocket and came out with a folded set of documents.

'All I need you to do, Natasha, is put your signature on these, then I will be out of here.'

He laid a set of papers down on the table in front of her, then followed them with a pen. Natasha looked down, understanding instantly what it was he was expecting her to sign.

She looked back at him. 'Would you like to explain to me why you think I should sign these?'

He shifted his wide shoulders. 'Because the money does not belong to you,' he replied with the absolute truth. 'I want it now that it's accessible.'

He didn't know that she knew where the money had come from, Natasha realised. Leo could not have told him, which left her wondering why he hadn't, and what she was supposed to do next.

Her eyes flickered over to where the silver limo was still parked with its tinted windows denying her a glimpse inside. 'Did you convince Cindy to get you this meeting by threatening to give the true story about her involvement with you to the press?'

Rico offered another shrug. 'I lost everything while she gained everything. You tell me if that was fair? Your sister got her record contract and her number-one hit. I got to be laughed at for losing my woman to my big-shot stepbrother.'

'I was never yours in the true sense, Rico,' Natasha reminded him.

He ignored that. 'Leo put me out of a job with no damn reference and I am suddenly persona non grata in every social circle that counts. Even my own mother doesn't like me right now and you sit here looking like a million dollars because Leo likes his women to look worthy of him. But I hope you are happy with him, *cara*, while you share him with his sex-mad ex-wife.'

With a flip of a long, graceful hand, Rico dropped his flashy, state-of-the-art phone down on the table in front of her. 'Take a look,' he invited.

Natasha's eyelashes quivered as she dropped her gaze to the phone. She didn't want to pick it up. She didn't want to look. A cold chill was beginning to freeze her heart muscles because she knew Rico wasn't inviting her to check out his phone for fun, just as he hadn't mentioned Gianna without a reason for doing it.

Even her fingers felt chilled by the time they made a trembling crawl towards the phone and hit the key that would light the screen up. Leo appeared in stark digital clarity with the beautiful Gianna plastered to his front. They were standing outside what looked like a hotel. 'Leo, please,' she heard Gianna's pleading voice arrive in her ears in a near-perfect English speaking voice. 'She does not have to know!'

In full gut-churning colour, she watched Leo smile, watched him run a finger along the lush red contours of Gianna's beautiful mouth. 'OK.' He leant down to kiss that pleading mouth. 'I will come in with you.'

Then they walked up the steps and into the hotel.

'Paris,' Rico answered the question Natasha was trying so hard not to let herself think. 'Last night, to be exact. You can check the date and time if you like,' he indicated to the phone. 'I hung around for two hours waiting for him to come out again, but he didn't. You tell me, *cara*, what you think they were doing with those two hours?'

Natasha didn't answer. She was recalling another scene weeks ago, when she had stood in Rico's office doorway watching *his* betrayal of her drag the blind scales from her eyes. In this case it was Rico's telephone that formed the doorway from which she watched this new betrayal.

Without saying a word she put down the mobile and picked up Rico's pen.

Natasha just scrawled her name on the document, then she got up and walked away.

If she'd looked back she would have seen her minder pausing beside Rico's chair—but she didn't look back. She didn't even offer a sideways glance at the silver limo as she walked past it.

Leo arrived home as she was packing her bag. He came in through the bedroom door like a bullet, a seething mass of barely controlled fury trapped inside a sleek dark business suit.

'What the hell were you doing with Rico?' he bit out.

Natasha didn't answer; she just turned back to her bag.

'I asked you a question!' He arrived at her side and caught hold of her arm to swing her around. It was only as he did so that his eyes dropped to the bag she was packing. Cold fury suddenly lit him up. 'If you think you are leaving me for him you can think it through again,' he raked out.

Natasha just smiled.

The smile hit him as good as a hard slap. 'You bitch,' he choked, tossing her arm aside and reeling away from her. 'I can't believe you could do this to me.'

'Why not?' Natasha let herself speak at last—and the hell if she was going to tell him what she knew about him and Gianna. Let him know what it feels like to have his pride shredded!

It was like watching a mighty rock turn into an earthquake. The shudder that shook him almost shook her, too. 'You signed the money over to him,' he stated hoarsely.

'Yes, I did, didn't I?' she said smoothly. 'Are you going to inform the police?'

His bunched shoulders tensed. 'You're my wife.'

'So I am.'

He swung back, his angry eyes sharpened by the dry tone in her voice. 'What the *hell* is that supposed to imply?'

Natasha offered a shrug. 'Our marriage was just a form of blackmail you used to bring darling Gianna into line, so I don't think it counts as anything much.'

'Don't change the subject. Gianna has nothing to do with this.'

'She has everything to do with it!' Natasha cried out, then took a deep breath and pulled herself together again because she was close to telling him what she knew and she didn't want to do that. She *never* wanted him to know how much he had hurt her today! 'I was there, if you recall. Until she turned up, I was just the little thief you took to your bed to enjoy for six weeks until you got your precious money back. The marriage thing came up as one of your smart-mouthed quips aimed to punish your silly ex-wife for barging in while you were busy with me!'

'That's not true.'

'It is true,' she insisted. 'What was it you said to me before we left London, Leo? Six weeks keeping you sweet in your bed until I could access your money, then I was gone? Well, the six weeks are up. I've accessed the money and now I'm leaving.'

With that she turned back to pick up her holdall. He was at her side before she had touched the strap. The packed bag went flying to the floor. Natasha barely managed a quivering gasp of protest before he was spinning her round to face him again. Black fury was firing from his every skin cell. She had never seen his eyes so hard. He was white—ghost white. He was even shaking as he held her.

'To go back to him?' he shot out.

Eyes like iced-blue glass, she gave him his answer. 'Well, you of all people must know what they say about the devil you know,' she provoked.

She was referring to Gianna and he knew that she was. His eyes gave a blinding bitter flash of instant understanding. 'You know about Paris.'

He was that quick-thinking, the rotten, cruel, heartless swine! 'I hate you, Leo,' she shook out thickly. 'You're a cold and hard, calculating devil. For all his faults, Rico is worth ten of you!'

'You think so?'

'I know so!' Natasha tried to pull free of him.

His fingers tightened. 'Say hello to this devil, then,' he gritted, then his mouth landed on hers like a crushing blow.

They'd kissed in anger before and turned the whole thing into a glorious fight, but this was different. Natasha didn't want this, but her body was not listening. She hated him with every spinning atom of her being but one touch from him lit her up like a torch. And her thin dress was no barrier to help shield her. He dealt with it by the simple method of wrenching the back zip apart so the dress fell in a slither to the ground.

'Get off me!' she choked at him.

'When you stop wanting me so desperately,' he rasped back.

Then he was kissing and touching and caressing and *goading* her to reject what he knew she could not! He knew every weak inch of her. He stripped away her clothes and aroused her with a grim ruthlessness that had her whimpering against his possessing mouth. And when that wasn't enough for him, he lifted her up against him, making her straddle his hips while his mouth maintained the deep, driving possession of her mouth.

Next thing she knew she was being dropped on the bed while he stood over her, holding her still by the sheer power of his angry desire-blackened gaze as he stripped off his clothes. The jacket, the shirt—shoes heeled off and flicked out of his way. When he stripped the last garments away, he was like a menacing threat that completely dominated her every thought and sense, and tingling tight fear cloaked her in sizzling excitement.

'Leo—please…' she begged in an appeal for sanity.

'Leo—please…' he mimicked tautly. 'You have no idea what it does to me when you say that.'

Then he came over her, arriving on the bed. With a bewilderingly slick show of controlled strength Natasha found her thighs smoothly parted and he was lowering his angry dark head. 'Make sure you tell Rico all about this later,' he muttered.

What took place next cast her into an agony of skin-tingling pleasure. She moved and groaned and sobbed and shuddered and he just went on doing it, keeping her finely balanced on the edge of frantic hysterics and a clamouring, desperate need for release. If she tried to protest he snaked up and kissed her. If she tried to get away, he stayed her with the clamp of his hands to her hips. When he finally decided it was time to join them, his first driving thrust made her cry out in soul-crushing relief. Then he was lifting her up and tipping her head back so he could devour her mouth while he rode her like that, with her hair flowing behind her and her fingers clinging to the sinew-tight tension in his neck. The angry glare in his eyes would have been frightening if it weren't for the glaze of hot, urgent desire that matched the quick, deep, thrusting drive of his hips as he brought them both rushing towards the pinnacle of a nerve-screeching release.

When it came, she arched like a slender bow strung so tight she couldn't relax again. The stinging whip-crack of her orgasm played through her in a series of violent, electric shocks as Leo let go with a single powerful quake of his body. The whole wild seduction with its total breakdown of control had taken just a few short dizzying minutes, yet when it was over, Natasha felt as if she'd been scraped clean of energy, exhausted of the strength to even move.

Not so Leo. On a thick growl of contempt he withdrew from her and climbed off the bed. Whether the contempt had been aimed at her or at himself didn't matter. The way he picked up his clothes and left her lying there in a weak, quivering huddle and just strode out of the room riddled her with contempt for herself.

Natasha continued to lie there for ages, trying to come to terms with what had happened—trying to come to terms with the whole barbaric crescendo ending to their relationship. She hated herself for falling victim too easily. She despised him for encouraging it. When she could find the strength to move, she just got off the bed, got dressed in the first clothes that came to hand, then repacked her bag with only the clothes she'd brought with her to Greece.

Then she left. Nobody tried to stop her from going. She didn't even bother to ring for a taxi before she stepped outside and walked down the drive towards the pair of gates. The guard on the gate said absolutely nothing, but just opened them and let her into the street.

Leo stood in front of the curving glass wall and watched her do it. She hadn't even stopped long enough to tidy her hair, he saw, and she was wearing that damn pale blue suit.

He turned away from the window, bitterness warring with an agony that was tightening the muscles lining his throat. He looked at the tangle of sheets on the bed.

Then he saw the manila envelope lying there on top of the bedding. As he walked over to it and saw *'Leo'* scrawled on it he felt his legs turn hollow with dread as he picked the envelope up.

A cruising taxi picked Natasha up and a few minutes later she was heading for the airport without allowing herself a single glance back. It was only when she sat back in the seat that she noticed she was wearing the pale blue suit.

Fitting, she thought bleakly. Maybe the suit should be preserved in a glass case to remind her that she was a fool and all men were lying cheats.

The airport was busy. Trying to get a seat on a flight back to England was impossible, she discovered, beginning to wilt now as that first rush of adrenalin that had carried her this far began to ebb.

'You can only hope for a cancellation, Kyria Christakis,' the booking agent told her. 'Otherwise we have no seat available for the next two days.'

'W-what about a different airport?' Her voice was beginning to shake, Natasha noticed. She could feel a bubble of hysteria fighting to burst free from her throat. 'M-Manchester, perhaps, or Glasgow. I don't really care where I land so long as it is on UK soil.'

What was there in London for her to go back to anyway? she was just asking herself when a hand arrived on her shoulder.

Natasha jumped like a scalded cat as her mind threw up a terrifying image of the hand belonging to the police.

He wouldn't—he *wouldn't*! her mind screamed at her.

Then the voice came. 'That will not be necessary.'

CHAPTER TEN

As Natasha trembled in recognition, Leo's hand became an arm clamping around her shoulders that contained her tense tremor within the power of his grasp. She was engulfed within seconds, by his height, by his strength, by his grim determination and by the cool use of his native language as he spoke to the curious booking agent while Rasmus appeared beside her and calmly bent to claim her bag.

'No...' She tried to stop him. 'I don't w-want—'

'Don't make a fuss, *agape mou*,' Leo murmured levelly. 'We are under surveillance from the Press.'

She was suddenly surrounded by his security men. Before she'd grasped what was happening they were hustling her through the airport like a human bulldozer, which gave her no view as to where they were going, and the tight grip Leo maintained on her kept her clamped against his side.

Gates magically opened for them. Having thought he was taking her back to his apartment, it came as a hard shock to find herself walking across tarmac towards what looked like a helicopter from the brief glimpse she caught of the rotor-blades already beginning to turn as they approached.

Panic erupted. 'I am not getting on that with you!' She pulled to a shuddering halt, causing men to struggle not to bump into her.

Breaking free of his grip, she spun back the way they had come. Leo bit out a command that sent burly men scattering. He hauled her up off her feet and into his arms, then completed the rest of the distance between them and the helicopter with the grim surefootedness of a man happy to dice with death by rotor-blade.

Natasha ducked her head into his shoulder in sheer fright and did not lift it up again until he'd put her down on a seat. The moment he let go of her she hit out at him with her fists.

He chose not to notice as he grimly fastened her into the seat while her angry blows just glanced off him. 'I hate you, *I hate you!*' she kept choking out.

'Save it until later,' he responded, and she'd never seen his face look so tough.

'But why are you doing this?'

He didn't answer, just stepped back to allow six men to pile in the helicopter, swarming like black-suited rats into the seats in front of her and behind. Natasha felt so wretchedly deserted and so terrified that Leo was going to send her off somewhere with his men so that they could deal with her, she couldn't stop herself from crying out, 'Leo—*please* don't leave me with them!'

By then he had his back to her. His wide shoulders gave a tense flex, but he did not turn around. Without offering her a single word of reassurance he just strode round the helicopter and climbed in the seat beside the pilot. In what felt like no time at all they were up in the air and shooting forwards towards the glinting blue of the Aegean. Natasha closed her eyes and tried hard not to let the panic inside her develop any more than it had done already. At least he was in here with her, she told herself fiercely. Whatever else that was happening, *at least* he wasn't leaving her to the care of his horrible men!

Leo dared a brief glance at her via the mirror positioned above the cockpit controls. Her eyes were shut tight, her lips parted and trembling and pale, and she had gone back to clutching her damn purse to her lap as if it were her only lifeline. The blue suit, the purse, the expression—all of them reminded him of the last time he'd virtually abducted her like this.

Except for the hair. The hair was free and tumbling around her stark white beautiful—*beautiful* face!

Hell, damn it. *Theos* help me! he thought angrily as his insides creased up, and he had to look away from her.

His pilot said something. He didn't hear what it was. He was so locked into one purpose it left no room in his head for anything else.

It did not take long to reach their destination. They touched down as the sun was turning everything a warm golden red. Even as they settled onto the ground he could see Natasha struggling to unlock her seat belt and—*hell*, maybe he should just let her escape because he knew he was in no fit state of mind to be safe around her right now.

Rasmus undid the seat belt for her because she couldn't seem to do it. It was from within a dazed state that Natasha stared at her fingers, which seemed to have turned to trembling jelly with no hope of control left. All of her felt that way, when she thought about it.

Rasmus also helped her down onto solid ground with an unusual gentleness for such a tough man. When she glanced up at him to whisper a shaky, 'Thank you,' he sent her the strangest apologetic look.

For some reason that look almost finished her. The tears were suddenly flooding upwards in a hot, raging gush. She turned away from him, not wanting Rasmus to see the tears—not wanting to see his apology! Leo appeared around the nose of the helicopter looking exactly like the tall, dark, tough stranger she used to see him as.

He needed a shave, she noticed hazily. And he was wearing the same clothes he had picked up off the bedroom floor. They looked creased and dishevelled. *He* looked creased and dishevelled.

Her stomach dipped and squirmed but she refused to analyse why.

And she dragged her eyes away from Leo, too.

He didn't touch her.

'Shall we go?' he said, and took an oddly formal step to one side in a silent invitation for her to precede him.

Where to, though? Natasha wondered anxiously as her reluctant feet moved her ahead of him, hating him like poison for doing this to her, and despising him further for bringing her down to the point that she had cried out to him in fear.

They rounded a tall hedge and suddenly she was faced with a rambling two-storey villa with sun-blushed white walls. No housekeeper waited to greet them. Everyone else seemed to have just melted away. Leo stepped in front of her to open the front door, then he led the way across a soft eggshell-blue and cream hallway and into the kind of living room you only usually saw in glossy magazines.

'Wh-what is this place?' Natasha could not stop herself from asking, looking round her new surroundings that were as different again from the two other places Leo taken her to. Not a hint of the old-fashioned heaviness of the London house here, and it was certainly no ultra-modern, urban dwelling aimed to please the eye of the wealthy male.

No, this place was pure classical luxury with stunning artwork hanging on the walls and pieces of handmade furniture that must have cost the earth.

'My island retreat,' Leo answered, removing the jacket to his suit and slinging it over the back of a chair.

His *island* retreat, as in his *whole* island retreat?

In other circumstances Natasha would have been willing to be impressed by that, but she refused to be impressed by anything he said or did from now on—other than to give some answers to the real questions running round in her head.

Standing still just inside the doorway, she clutched her purse in her fingers and lifted up her chin. 'So is this to be my new luxury prison?' she iced out.

'No.' He moved across the room to pour himself a drink.

'You mean, I get to leave it whenever I want to, then?'

She saw his grim mouth flex at her sarcasm. 'No,' he said again.

'Then it's a prison.' She looked away from him.

To her absolute shock, he slammed the glass down and turned to stride back across the room to pull her into his arms and kiss her—hard.

There had never been a kiss like it. This one seemed to rise up from some deep place inside him and flow with a throbbing heat of pure feeling aimed to pour directly into her. It shook Natasha, really shook her. When he put her from him, she could only stare up at him in a bewildered daze.

He turned his back on her. 'Sorry,' he muttered. 'It was not my intention to—'

Like a woman living in some kind a surreal alternative life, Natasha could only stumble into the nearest chair.

'I don't understand what's going on here,' she whispered when he just stood there like a stone pillar. 'You kidnap me from the airport and hustle me like a piece of cattle onto your helicopter and scare me out of my w-wits. Then you bring me in here and *dare* to kiss me like that!'

He didn't speak. He didn't turn. His hands clenched into

fists, then disappeared into his trouser pockets. She noticed that his shirt cuffs were hanging open around his wrists.

'What else do you want from me, Leo?' she cried out in a thick voice.

'Nothing,' he said, his big shoulders flexing. 'I don't want anything else from you. I just don't want you to leave me.'

Then he really bewildered her by striding towards a pair of French windows and throwing them open so he could go outside.

Natasha stared after him and wished she understood him. Then on a sudden rush of angry hot blood she decided that she didn't *want* to understand a man like Leo, she just wanted him to explain that last remark!

Getting up on legs that did not want to carry her anywhere, she followed him outside and found herself stepping onto a deep terrace. The sun was hanging so low in the sky now it blinded her eyes. But she could see enough to know that Leo wasn't here. Casting her gaze out wider, she caught sight of his white shirt moving down through a garden towards the ocean gleaming a deep silken blue not far away.

By the time she reached a low wall that kept the beach back from the gardens, he was standing at the water's edge, hands still pushed into his pockets, staring out to sea.

'What is it with you?' she demanded. 'Why are you doing this to me? If it's because of the money, you only—'

'I don't want the money.'

Natasha paused several feet away from him. 'You found the envelope, then?' He just nodded. She let out a sigh. 'Then what do you want?' she asked helplessly.

Still he made no answer and the tears started coming again. Any second now he was going to succeed in completely breaking her control. Maybe that was what he wanted, she thought as she sank down on the low wall because her legs had finally given in.

'You're so arrogant, Leo,' she said unsteadily. 'You're so cynical about everyone and everything. You see no good in anyone. You believe everyone out there is trying to fleece you in one way or another. Y-your ex-wife wants your body, I want your money, Rico wants to stand in your shoes and *be* you. If you want my opinion, you would be better off poor and downright ugly—then at least you could be happy knowing no one liked you for just being you!'

He laughed when he wasn't meant to. Natasha had to swallow on the lump her throbbing heart had become in her throat. 'You just love it when you think s-someone has proved your every cynical suspicion about them true.'

'Are you referring to what happened this afternoon?'

So he speaks! Natasha glared at him but couldn't see him through the bank of tears misting up her eyes. 'Yes,' she said, though that wasn't all of it. 'You came into our bedroom today expecting to see a cheating wife so you treated m-me like a cheating wife.'

'I thought you had signed the money over to Rico. It—hurt me.'

'Not enough to make you demand a proper explanation before you drew your own conclusions, though.'

Then she tensed warily as he spun on his heel, crunching gravelly sand beneath his shoes as he did.

'What did you sign for Rico?' he asked curiously.

'Permission to access an empty offshore account,' she answered with a shrug. 'I'd already transferred the money over to my private bank account yesterday. I meant to give you the envelope with the banker's draft in it yesterday but we were—sidetracked.'

By Gianna first, she remembered bleakly, then by an afternoon of—

Something dropped onto her lap and made her blink. 'W-what's this?' Warily she picked up the narrow white envelope.

'Take a look.'

Natasha looked at the envelope for what felt like ages before she could get her fingers to slip the seal. Her lips felt so dry she had to moisten them with her tongue as she removed the contents. It was getting really dark out here now, but still light enough for her to recognise what it was she was looking at.

'I d-don't understand,' she murmured eventually.

'Rasmus took it from Rico,' Leo explained. 'You know, Natasha,' he said dryly then, 'you possess more honour than I do. Even when he showed you evidence of my meeting with Gianna in Paris, you still could not take your revenge on me by signing your money over to him.'

She did not want to talk about his betrayal with Gianna. In fact, she began to feel sick just by recalling it. 'I signed for an empty account,' she pointed out.

'But you still signed Natasha *Christakis* instead of Natasha *Moyles*, which meant that Rico could not touch the account, even an empty one.'

'So what are you accusing me of now?' she demanded helplessly.

'Nothing.' Leo sighed.

'So, how did you get Rico to hand this over?' she asked him next.

'Rasmus—persuaded him.'

'Ah, good old Rasmus,' she mocked, recalling the way her minder had had his phone to his ear from the moment that Rico had put in an appearance. It was a shame that Rasmus did not extend his loyalty to her or maybe he would have felt duty-bound to tell her about his employer's night spent in Paris.

And remembering *that* brought Natasha to her feet. 'Does this prison have a bedroom to which I can escape?' she asked stiffly.

'My bedroom,' he confirmed.

'Not this side of hell, Leo,' Natasha informed him coldly. 'I come too expensive even for you from now on.'

'Then name your price....'

Turning on him, Natasha almost threw some obscene figure at him just to see how he would react! But she didn't. In the end she went for blunt honesty. 'A speedy way off this island and an even speedier divorce!' she flicked out, then turned to walk back to the house.

'Deal,' Leo said, bringing her to a taut-shouldered standstill after only two steps. 'For one more night in my bed,' he extended, 'I will arrange your transport away from here.'

'I can't believe even you dared to say that,' she whispered.

'Why not? I am the world's worst cynic who believes everyone has their price. If escape from here and divorce is your price, *agape mou*, then I am willing to pay it—for my own price.'

Natasha walked on, stiff-backed and quivering with offence. Leo followed, feeling suddenly rejuvenated and—more importantly—hungry for the fight. What he had done that afternoon had been pretty much unforgivable. He'd accepted that even before he had watched her take that long walk down his drive. What his beautiful, proud, icy wife had just unwittingly done was to hand him his weapon of salvation and his last chance to put this right between them.

'You just s-stay away from me!' she shrilled when she heard his footsteps closing in on her.

'I'm wildly in love with you—how can I stay away?'

'How *dare* you say that?' Natasha swung around on him,

eyes like glistening blue chips of hurt. 'What do you know about love, Leo? You would not know how to recognise it!'

'And you do?' he threw back. 'You were supposed to be in love with Rico, but where is that broken-hearted love now?'

Pulling in a deep breath, Natasha snapped her lips together. A tense spin of her body and she was continuing up the path and into the house.

Leo followed, more relaxed the more tense that she became. 'You know I'm madly jealous of Rico,' he offered up from the open French windows. 'I have been jealous of him since I first saw you with him. But I refused to recognise what was wrong with me each time I attacked you—'

'With your nasty sarcasms aimed to make me feel small?'

'I wanted you to notice me— What are you looking for?'

'I noticed you, Leo. My purse.'

'On the floor marking the spot where I last kissed you,' he indicated. 'You have to drop the purse, you see, so you can dig your nails into my neck in case I decide to stop.'

Face burning fire now, Natasha went and picked the purse up then walked out of the room.

'Ask yourself, *agape mou*, did you ever see me with another woman from the first night we met?'

She swung around. 'Gianna, in your bedroom, calling me her whoring substitute?' she offered up. 'Gianna, in Paris, coaxing you into a hotel for a cosy—chat?'

Leo sighed. 'I can explain about Gianna. She—'

'Do I look like I *want* an explanation?' Natasha flicked out.

The stairs drew her. She hadn't a clue where she was going, but it suited Leo that she'd taken that direction.

'Middle door on the right,' he offered helpfully. 'My room. My bed. My offer still in place. I will even throw in a candlelit dinner for two on the beach— Damn.'

He should have seen it coming. He had, after all, been

goading her towards some kind of reaction since he'd decided to go on the offensive. But to watch her drop down on one of the stairs and bury her face in her hands, then start weeping, was more than he'd bargained for.

He was up there and squatting in front of her and pulling her into his chest before she had a chance to let out the second sob. 'No,' he roughed out. 'Not the tears, Natasha. You were supposed to fly at me with your fists so I could catch you and kiss you out of your head.'

'I hate you,' she sobbed. 'You're so—'

'Loathsome, I know,' he sighed out. 'I'm sorry.'

'You think I'm a thief.'

'I have never, for one second, believed you were a thief,' he denied. 'I have a split personality. I can go wild with jealousy over Rico and can still recognise that you're the most honest person I know.'

The sobs stopped coming; she replaced them with a forlorn sniff. 'That wasn't what you said when you made me come to Greece with you.'

'I was fighting for my woman. I was prepared to say or do anything.'

'You were *ruthless* this afternoon.'

'Unforgivably so,' he agreed. 'Give me one night in our bed and I will make it up to you.'

'Then let me go tomorrow?'

'Ah.' That was all, just that rueful *Ah*, and Natasha knew she had caught him out.

'And I always believed you spoke only the truth,' she denounced, frowning when she caught the way her fingers were toying with the buttons on his shirt and wondering why she was letting them do that. 'It was your only saving grace as far as I could tell.'

'I thought the fantastic sex was.'

She shook her head, still watching as a section of hair-roughened, bronzed skin appeared close enough for her to kiss. He smelled warm—of Leo, masculine and tempting.

'I need a shower….'

Natasha shook her head as another button gave on the shirt. His hands moved on her back. 'Dangerous, Natasha,' he warned her gently.

Too late. Her tongue snaked out and she licked.

That's it! he might as well have announced as he rose up to his full height, pulling her up with him, then clamping her hard against his body before mounting the rest of the stairs. 'You know what you are,' he bit out at her. 'You are a man-teaser.'

'I am not!' Natasha denied.

'You tell me you hate me then you lick me as if I am the sweetest-tasting thing in your world! If that is not man-teasing, then I don't know what is.'

'I am still not going to bed with you!'

'No?' He opened up his arms and dropped her like a discarded bundle on a bed and was right there with her before she could recover from the drop, his fingers already busy with the buttons on her jacket. 'You pull this blue thing on like a suit of armour…' he muttered.

The jacket flew open to reveal a skimpy lilac silk camisole, then he was reaching round beneath her so he could unzip her skirt. 'When I think of the years I indulged in classy, sophisticated sex with classy, sophisticated women—' he gritted.

'I don't want to hear about your other women,' Natasha protested, trying to stop him from undressing her by wriggling her hips.

'Were you listening to anything I have already said?' he husked out. 'There have been no other women since I met you! Before you is none of your business.'

'Then don't *talk* about them!'

'I was trying to make a point—that sex without all of this mad, wild, crazily emotional stuff is rubbish sex! Not that you are ever going to find that out.'

'I might do—after tonight.'

About to remove her skirt altogether, Leo went still. 'So you are staying here with me tonight?'

'I might do,' she repeated coolly. 'I suppose it depends on what you're going to tell me you were doing with Gianna in Paris and if I decide to believe you.'

'Ah.' There it was again, the *Ah* sound that said— Caught me out again, Natasha. And he rolled away from her to stretch out beside her on the bed. 'It was not a hotel in Paris,' he stated flatly. 'It was at a very exclusive private clinic made to look like a hotel, and Rico knew that when he showed you what he did because Gianna has been there countless times before....'

'A clinic that looks like a hotel? Very convenient,' Natasha said dryly. 'Next thing you will be telling me you accidentally bumped into her on the steps.'

'No. I took her there,' Leo sighed out. 'The way she put her nails into you made me decide that it was time for me to get tough. You have to know something about her past to understand Gianna,' he went on heavily. 'Things I did not know about until after we were married and had to find out the hard way,' he admitted. 'She is not a bad person just a— very sad product of a sick upbringing in the centre of a wealthy but corrupt family who taught her that sex equalled love.'

'Oh, that's awful,' Natasha murmured, catching on to what he meant.

'And it is her story, not mine to tell. So let me just say that we had been lovers for a couple of months when she told me she was pregnant. Of course I married her, why not?' He was almost asking himself. 'She was beautiful, great company and about to become the mother of my first child. I saw no problem being faithful to her. Then two weeks after we married I caught her in bed with another man. She tried to tell me it didn't mean anything—but it meant a hell of a lot to me.'

'So you threw her out?'

'Walked out,' he amended. 'A week later she lost the baby and I've never felt so bad or so guilty about anything in my entire life because I had allowed myself to forget the fragile life growing inside her when I walked out. She suffered her first breakdown, which placed her in the Paris clinic for the first time. It was while she was in there that the truth about her past came out. Because I felt sorry for her and she needed someone to care about her, I took her back into my life.'

'Because you loved her,' Natasha murmured.

He turned his head to look at her, dark eyes glowing in the darkening sunset. 'I am not going to lie to you, Natasha, and say she no longer means anything to me,' he stated flatly. 'I did not go into my marriage with her, expecting it to turn out the way that it did. But as for loving her? No, I never did love her the way that you mean. But I did and do still care for her, and, believe me, she really does not have anyone else that does.'

Moving onto her side so she could watch his expression, 'So you—look out for her?' she questioned carefully.

His chiselled jaw tightened. 'I do not sleep with her.'

'That was not what I asked.'

'But you are still thinking it,' he said, reading her face the same as she was reading his. 'I have not slept with Gianna since I took her back into my life. She had another lover within days of arriving back in Athens anyway.' He shrugged. 'The unpalatable fact that she can't help using sex as a substitute for love and affection is not her fault, but I couldn't live with it, though we struggled on for several months before I finally walked out.'

'OK…' It was crazy of her to think that he needed her to touch him, but that was what Natasha sensed in him while he lay there talking himself out. But not yet. 'So you still care for her. You look out for her. You do not sleep with her,' she listed. 'Are you expecting me to accept her as a part of my life, too?'

'Hell, no.' He was suddenly rising up to lean over her and crushing her mouth with a hot kiss. 'That part is over,' he vowed as he drew away again. 'She finally killed my lingering guilt and my sympathy for her when it hit me that it was very fortuitous that Rico happened to catch me with her on the clinic steps.'

Natasha frowned. 'I don't follow—'

'Gianna is good at seducing people to do what she wants them to do—so is Rico, come to that. She wanted you out of my life and he wanted his money. Put the two together, plus the fact that Rico knows what Gianna is like about me, and you have a great conspiracy plot to get you to sign over the money and have you walk out of my life at the same time.'

'Oh, that is so—sick.'

'That's Gianna and Rico,' Leo acknowledged ruefully. 'Now can we talk about you and me? What do *you* want, Natasha?' he questioned her.

Natasha lowered her eyes to look at his mouth. It wasn't smiling. It wasn't even thinking about smiling, his question was that serious.

So what did she want?

She felt his fingers come to rest lightly on her cheekbones, felt the weight of his thighs pressing hers into the bed. She lifted her hands up to his chest and watched her fingertips curl into dark coils of hair and felt, heard—saw him take a slow and careful intake of breath. She saw the wedding band he'd placed on her finger glow as the last of the sun caught hold of it and set the gold on fire.

Then she looked up at him, into his eyes, his dark—dark,

serious eyes. 'You,' she breathed out whisperingly. 'I just want you.'

Vulnerable, Leo saw, so vulnerable her lips had to tremble as she made herself say it as if she was still scared to open up to him with the truth.

He pulled in a deep breath. 'I've changed my mind about this suit,' he said, not looking into her eyes any more. 'I love it. It reminds me of the woman I first fell in love with—'

'M-miss Buttoned Up, you mean?'

'Miss *Sexily* Buttoned Up,' he extended, then pushed himself away from her so he could button her back up again before he rose up off the bed, pulling her up so he could turn her around and do up her skirt zip.

'Why are you doing that?'

'I had forgotten about something.' Transferring his fingers to his shirt buttons, he fastened those, too. Natasha watched as he hid his bronze, muscled body away from her and felt the sting of disappointment.

Then he was taking possession of one of her hands and trailing her out of the bedroom, back down the stairs, back through the living room and back through the French doors, where Natasha pulled to a breathless stop in surprise.

The darkened terrace had been transformed while they'd been upstairs in the bedroom, and was now a flickering wonderland of soft candle-light.

A table had been laid for two and Bernice was just turning away from it. '*Kalispera*.' She smiled at the two of them. 'You ready to eat now?'

Leo answered in his own language, while trailing a silenced Natasha over to the table, then politely held out her chair.

'What's going on?' she managed in bewilderment.

'When I plan something this carefully, I usually follow through with it,' this unusual, hard-crusted, soft-centred man standing there drawled. 'The surprise I promised you,' he explained. 'You had forgotten about it, I see.'

'Oh,' she murmured, because she had forgotten.

Leo smiled as he sat down. 'I was not expecting to do this with us both dressed like this. However…' He reached across the table to take hold of her hands. 'Natasha, this is my home. My real home. The others are just convenient places I use when I need a place to stay. But this island will always be the place I come home to.'

'Well, that's—very nice,' she said, wondering where this was leading.

'More than nice, it's special.' His dark eyes were focused intently on her face. 'I am madly, wildly, jealously in love with you, *agape mou*. I spoiled that part too by telling you so earlier,' he then acknowledged with a rueful tilt to his mouth. 'But I do—love you. If it was not already too late, I would be sitting here now asking you to marry me. Since I've already done that part, too, all I can ask you is, will you live here with me, Natasha? Share my home with me, have my children and bring them up here with me, and make this cynical Greek a very happy man…?'

Natasha didn't know what to say. She hadn't come here expecting him to say any of this. In fact, she'd come here believing that she hated him and that he hated her.

'And this is your surprise?' she asked finally.

His fingers twitched on her fingers because she clearly was not giving him the response he desired. 'Until I tried my best to murder my chances this afternoon.' He nodded. 'Did I murder them?'

The outright challenge from the blunt speaker, Natasha noticed distractedly.

She shook her head.

'Then say something a bit more—positive,' he prompted impatiently, 'because I feel like I am sinking very fast here….'

Sinking fast...she was sinking fast...beneath his spell.
'Yes, please,' she said.

Leo muttered something she didn't catch, then sat back in his seat. 'It must be the suit.' He laughed, though it wasn't a real laugh. 'Would you like to explain to me what the polite *yes, please* covers exactly?'

Now he was cross. Natasha frowned. 'You're sitting there just *expecting* me to say it back to you, aren't you?'

'*Theos*, if you don't love me, then I've caught myself yet another little liar for a wife because every damn thing you do around me *tells* me you love me!'

'All right—I love you!' she announced on a rush of heat. 'I love you,' she repeated. 'But I'm still angry with you, Leo, so words like that don't come easily!'

'Angry about what?' His eyes flickered red with annoyance in the candle-light. 'I've already apologised for—'

'You scared me half to death when you hustled me at the airport!'

'I scared myself more when I thought I wasn't going to catch you before you flew away.'

'Oh,' she said.

'Oh,' he repeated, then climbed back to his feet. 'We are going back to bed.'

He already had hold of her hand again and was pulling her to her feet. 'We can't,' she quavered. 'Bernice—'

'Bernice!' Leo called out as they hit the hallway. 'Hold the dinner. We are going back to bed!'

'God, why do you have to be so openly *blunt?*' Natasha gasped in hot embarrassment.

'OK...you make the nice babies now...' the calm answer came drifting back towards them.

'Even Bernice knows blunt is best.' Leo turned on the stairs to grin down at her.

'All right!' Natasha pulled to a stop, eyes flashing blue flames of anger and brimming defiance. 'So I love you!' she repeated at the top of her voice. 'I don't understand *why* I should love you because, quite *bluntly*, Leo, you drive me up the wall! But—'

He pulled her towards him and kissed her right there on the stairs. Her fingers shot around his neck to stop her tumbling backwards—and because they couldn't help themselves.

'That is why you love me,' he insisted when he eventually pulled back.

'You could be right,' Natasha conceded with her eyes fixed on his oh-so-kissable mouth before she lifted them up to clash with his eyes. 'Do you think we could check it out some more, please…?'

Powerful Greek, Unworldly Wife

SARAH MORGAN

Sarah Morgan trained as a nurse, and has since worked in a variety of health-related jobs. Married to a gorgeous businessman, who still makes her knees knock, she spends most of her time trying to keep up with their two little boys, but manages to sneak off occasionally to indulge her passion for writing romance. Sarah loves outdoor life and is an enthusiastic skier and walker. Whatever she is doing, her head is always full of new characters and she is addicted to happy endings.

CHAPTER ONE

LEANDRO DEMETRIOS, billionaire banker and the subject of a million hopeful female fantasies, dragged the 'A' list Hollywood actress through the doorway of his exclusive London townhouse and slammed the door shut on the rain and the bank of waiting photographers.

The woman was laughing, her eyes wide with feminine appreciation. 'Did you see their faces? You scared them half to death! I feel safer with you than I do with my bodyguards. *And* you have bigger muscles.' She slid her hand up his arm, her manicured fingernails lingering on the solid curve of his biceps. 'Why didn't we just use the back entrance?'

'Because I refuse to creep around my own house. And because you like to be seen.'

'Well, we've certainly been seen.' The fact evidently pleased her. 'You'll be all over the papers tomorrow for terrorising the paparazzi.'

Leandro frowned. 'I only read the financial pages.'

'And that's the bit I *don't* read,' she sighed. 'The only thing I know about money is how to spend it. You, on the other hand, know how to make it by the bucketload, and that makes you my type of guy. Now, *stop* looking all moody and dangerous and smile! I'm only in town for twenty-four hours and we need to make the most of the time.' Her lashes lowered provocatively. 'So, Leandro Demetrios, my very own sexy Greek billionaire. *Finally* we're alone. What are we going to do with our evening?'

Leandro removed his jacket and threw it carelessly over the back of a chair. 'If that's a serious question, you can leave right now.' His remark drew a gurgle of delighted laughter from the woman clinging to his arm.

'No one else dares to speak to me the way you do. It's one of the things I love most about you. You're not starstruck and that's so refreshing for someone like me.' The tip of her tongue traced the curve of her glossy lips. 'If I told you I was going to kiss you goodnight and go back to my hotel, what would you do?'

'Dump you.' Leandro's bow-tie landed on top of the jacket. 'But we both know that isn't going to happen. You want what I want, so stop playing games and get up those stairs. My bedroom is on the first floor. Last door on the left.'

'*So-o* macho.' Laughing, she smouldered in his direction. 'According to a poll just last week, you're now officially the world's sexiest man.'

Bored by the conversation, Leandro's only response was to close his fingers around her tiny wrist and pull her towards the staircase.

She gave a gasp of shocked delight. 'You honestly don't care what anyone thinks about you, do you? Indifference is *such* a turn-on. And when it comes to indifference, you wrote the manual.' She walked with a slow, swaying motion that she'd perfected for the cameras. 'There's a special chemistry between us. I can feel it.'

'It's called lust,' Leandro drawled, and she shot him a challenging look.

'Haven't you ever had a serious relationship with a woman? I heard you were married for a short time.'

Leandro stilled. *A very short time.* 'These days I prefer variety.'

'Honey, I can give you variety.' She used the soft, smoky voice that earned her millions of dollars per movie. 'And I'm just dying to know whether everything they say about you is true. I know you're super-bright and that you drive your fancy cars *way* too fast, but what I want to know is just how much of a bad boy you really are when it comes to women.'

'As bad as they come,' Leandro said smoothly, his hand locked around her slender wrist as he led her up the stairs. 'Which makes this your lucky night.'

'Then lead on, handsome.' She kept pace with him, a smile on her full, glossy mouth. 'You have a lot of art on your walls. Great investment. Are they original? I hate anything fake.'

'Of course you do.' Leandro focused on her surgically enhanced breasts with wry amusement. At a rough estimate he guessed that ninety per cent of her was fake. The short time he'd spent with her had been enough to prove to him that she was so used to playing other people, she'd forgotten how to be herself.

And that was fine by him.

As far as he was concerned, the shallower the better. At least you knew what you were dealing with and you adjusted your expectations accordingly.

'Oh, my! Only you would have a picture of a naked woman at the head of your staircase.' Stopping dead, she gazed up at the huge canvas and wrinkled her nose with disapproval. 'Strange choice for a man who surrounds himself with beauty. Isn't she rather fat for your tastes?'

Leandro's gaze lingered on the celebrated Renaissance masterpiece that had only recently returned from being on loan to a major gallery. 'When she was alive, it was fashionable to be curvy.'

The girl stared blankly at the exquisite brush strokes. 'I guess they didn't know about low carbs.'

'Curves were a sign of wealth,' Leandro murmured. 'It meant you had enough to eat.'

Throwing him a look of blank incomprehension, the actress stepped closer to the painting and Leandro's fingers tightened like a vice around her wrist.

'Touch it and we'll have half the Metropolitan police force keeping us company tonight.'

'It's that valuable?' Her knowing gaze turned to his and she licked her lips. 'You are one rich, powerful guy. Now, why is that such a turn-on, I wonder? It isn't as if I care about your money.'

'Of course you don't,' Leandro said, his tone dry because he knew full well that her lovers were expected to pay handsomely for the privilege of escorting her. 'We both know you're interested in me because I'm kind to old ladies and animals.'

'You like animals?'

Looking down into those famous blue eyes, Leandro's own eyes gleamed. 'I've always had a soft spot for dumb creatures.'

'That's so attractive. I love a tough man with a gentle side.' She slid her arms round his neck like bindweed around a plant. 'Do you realise we've had dinner three times and you haven't told me a single thing about yourself?'

'Do you realise that we've had dinner three times and you haven't eaten a single thing?' Skilfully steering the conversation away from the personal, Leandro smoothly released the zip on her dress and she sucked in a breath.

'You don't mess around, do you?'

'Let's just say I've had enough of verbal foreplay,' Leandro purred, sliding the dress over her shoulders in a practised movement. He frowned slightly as his fingers brushed hard bones rather than soft flesh.

'People pay good money to see this body of mine up on the screen.' She scraped her nails gently down his arm. 'And you, Leandro Demetrios, are getting it for free.'

Hardly, he thought, looking at the earrings she was wearing. *Earrings he'd given her at the beginning of the evening.* 'Shame you're not sold by the kilogram,' he said idly, 'because then you wouldn't cost me anything.'

'Thank you.' Assuming his remark was a compliment, she smiled. 'You, on the other hand, would cost a woman a fortune because muscle is heavier than fat and you have to be the most impressively built man I've ever met. And you're so damned confident. Is that because you're Greek?'

'No. It's because I'm me. I take what I want.' He took her chin in his fingers, his eyes steely. 'And when I've finished with it, I drop it.'

She shuddered deliciously. 'With no apology to anyone. Cold, ruthless, single-minded...'

'Are we talking about me or you?' Leandro removed the diamond clip securing her hair. 'I'm confused.'

'I'm willing to bet you've never been confused about a single thing in your life, you wicked boy.' Smiling, she dragged her finger over his lower lip. 'Tell me something personal about yourself. Just one thing. This latest story about you being the father of that baby—is it true? The papers are full of it.'

Not by the flicker of an eyelid did Leandro reveal his sudden tension. 'Are those the same papers that accused you of being a lesbian?'

'The difference is that my people issued a stern denial—you've said nothing.'

'I've never felt the need to explain my life to anyone.'

'So does that mean it isn't your child?' She lowered her lashes. 'Or are you such a stud you don't even *know?* You're not giving anything away, are you? Tell me something about *you.*'

'You want to know something about me?' Leandro eased her dress down her painfully thin body and lowered his mouth to the base of her throat. 'If you give me your heart, I'll break it. Remember that, *agape mou*. And I won't do it gently.' The warmth of his tongue brought a soft gasp to her lips and she tipped her head back with a shiver.

'If you're trying to scare me, you're not succeeding.' Her eyes were dark with arousal. 'I love a man who knows how to be a man. Especially when that man has a sensitive side.'

'I don't have a sensitive side.' Leandro's voice was hard as he lowered his forehead to hers. For a moment he stared into her wild, excited eyes, his breath mingling with hers. 'I don't care about anyone or anything. Lie down in my bed and I'll guarantee you fantastic sex, but nothing else. So if you're looking for happy ever after, you've taken a wrong turning.'

'Happy ever after is for movies. It's my day job. At night, I prefer to live for the moment.' Squirming against him, she lifted her hand and stroked his rough jaw. 'I should make you shave before you touch me, but I like the way it makes you look. You are so damn handsome, Leandro, it shouldn't be allowed,' she breathed, lifting her mouth to his. 'My last leading man needed satellite navigation to find his way round a woman's body. I have a feeling you won't suffer from the same problem.'

'I've always had a very good sense of direction.' Leandro backed her against the door and the actress gasped her approval.

'Oh, yes...' Panting, she wrenched at his shirt, sending buttons flying. With a low moan of desire she pushed the shirt off his shoulders and let it fall to the floor. 'Your body is incredible. I'm *definitely* going to get you a part in my next movie. I want you *now.*'

Having reached the part of the evening that interested him, Leandro scooped her up, strode purposefully towards the bed and then froze because his bed was already occupied.

The woman sat glaring at him, her eyes a fierce blue in a face as pale as his dress shirt. She'd obviously been caught in the rain because her thin cardigan clung to her body and her long hair curled damply past her shoulders like tongues of red fire.

Given the state she was in, she should have looked pathetic, but she didn't. She looked angry—the blaze of her eyes and the angle of her chin warning him that this wasn't going to be a gentle reunion.

It was as if a small, unexploded firework had landed in his bedroom and Leandro felt a dart of surprise because he'd never seen her angry before—*hadn't known she was capable of anger.*

He'd been on the receiving end of her injured dignity, her silent reproach and her agonised pain. He'd witnessed her disappointment and contempt. But a good healthy dose of old-fashioned anger had been missing from their relationship.

She hadn't thought that what they had was worth fighting for.

His own anger bubbled up from nowhere, threatening his usual control, and the emotion caught him by surprise because he'd thought he had himself well in hand.

Unfinished business, he thought grimly, and was about to speak when the actress gave a shocked squeak and tightened her grip on his neck.

'Who's *she?* You bastard! When you said you were going

to hurt me, I didn't expect it to be that quick,' she snarled. 'How *dare* you see someone else while you're with me? I expect my relationships to be exclusive.'

Surprised to realise that he'd forgotten he had the actress in his arms, Leandro lowered her unceremoniously to the floor. 'I don't do relationships.' *Not any more.*

'What about her?' Balancing on her vertiginous heels, the actress shot him a poisonous look. 'Does *she* know that?'

'Oh, yes.' Leandro was watching the girl on the bed and his humourless smile was entirely at his own expense. 'She wouldn't trust me as far as she could throw me, isn't that right, Millie?'

Her eyes were two hot pools of blame and he ground his teeth. *Fight me,* he urged silently. *If that's really what you think of me, stand up and scratch my eyes out. Don't just sit there. And don't walk out like you did the first time.*

But she didn't move. She sat in frozen silence, her eyes telling him that nothing had changed.

The actress made an outraged noise. 'So you *do* know her! Surprising. She doesn't look your type,' she said spitefully. 'She needs to fire her stylist. That natural look is *so* yesterday. This season is all about grooming.' She snatched her dress from the floor and held it against her. 'How did she get in here, anyway? Your security is really tight. I suppose no one noticed her.'

Nothing killed sexual arousal faster than female bitchiness, Leandro thought idly, regretting the impulse that had driven him to invite the actress home. The woman's tongue was as sharp as the bones poking out through her almost transparent flesh.

'Well? Are you going to throw her out?' The actress's voice turned from sultry to shrill and Leandro studied the girl sitting on his bed, noting the flush on her cheeks and the accusation in her eyes.

He met that gaze full on, with accusation of his own.

Silent communication raged between them and the atmosphere was so thick with tension that both of them forgot about the third person in the room until she stamped her foot.

'Leandro?'

'No,' he said harshly. 'I'm not going to throw her out.' The timing wasn't what he would have chosen but now she was here, he had no intention of letting her go. *Not until they'd had the conversation she'd walked away from a year earlier.*

The actress gave a gasp of disbelief. 'You're choosing that plain, bedraggled, badly dressed nobody over me?'

Leandro sent his date a cold, assessing glance that would have triggered shivers of trepidation through any one of the people who worked for him or knew him well. 'Yes. At least that way I'm guaranteed a soft landing when we tumble onto that mattress. No bones. No claws.'

The actress gasped. 'I won't be treated like this!' Delivering a performance worthy of an Oscar, she wriggled back into her dress and tossed her head in anger. 'You told me you weren't involved with anyone and I believed you! I'm obviously more of a fool than I look.'

Deciding that it was wisest not to respond to that particular statement, Leandro stayed silent, his gaze returned to the girl sitting on his bed. In that single, hotly charged moment he felt the blaze of raw sexual chemistry erupt between them. It was elemental, basic and primitive—the connection so powerful that it was beyond control or understanding. Recognising that fact, she gave a murmur of denial, her expression one of sick contempt as she dragged her gaze from his.

Vibrating with desperation, the actress sent a look of

longing towards Leandro's bare, bronzed torso. 'I know you didn't expect to see her here. I know women throw themselves at you. Just get rid of her and we can start again. I forgive you.'

Propelled by a need to ensure that forgiveness would never be forthcoming, Leandro urged her towards the door. 'You need to learn to play nicely with the other girls. I don't mind knives in my boardroom but I do find them shockingly uncomfortable in my bedroom.'

Her face scarlet, the actress snatched her phone out of her tiny jewelled handbag. 'All the rumours about you are true, Leandro Demetrios. You *are* cold and heartless and just missed your chance to have the one thing every man in the world wants.'

'And that would be?' Leandro raised an eyebrow, deliberately provocative. 'Peace and quiet?'

The actress simmered like milk coming to the boil. 'Me! And next time you're in LA, don't bother calling. And you.' She glared at the girl on the bed. 'If you think he'll ever be faithful to you, you're crazy.' Checking that the diamond earrings were still in place, she stormed from the room and several moments later Leandro heard a distant thud as the front door slammed closed.

Silence closed in on them.

'If you're going to cry, you can leave now,' Leandro drawled softly. 'If you choose to wait in my bedroom, you deserve to get hurt.'

'I'm not going to cry over you. And I'm not hurt,' she said stiffly. 'I'm past being hurt.'

Then she'd done better than him, Leandro reflected grimly. 'Why are you here?'

'You know why I'm here. I—I've come to take the baby.'

Of course, the baby. He'd been a fool to think anything else, and yet for a moment…

Leandro curled one hand into a fist, surprised to discover that his thick protective layer of cynicism could still be breached.

'I was asking what you're doing in my bedroom at midnight.' Strolling across to the bedroom door, he pushed it shut. He trusted his staff, but he was also sharp enough to know that this story was the juiciest morsel the media had savoured for a long time. They were slavering outside his house, waiting for something to feast on.

And everyone had their price.

He'd learned that unpalatable truth in the harshest way possible, and at an age when most children were still playing with toys.

'I'm intrigued as to how you got past my security.'

'I'm still your wife, Leandro. Even if you've forgotten that fact.'

'I haven't forgotten.' Keeping his gaze neutral, he looked at her. 'You really pick your moments. Thanks to you, my night of hot sex just walked through that door.'

Her slender shoulders stiffened, her back rigid. 'I'm sure you'll find a replacement fast enough. You always do.' Her chest rose and fell as she breathed rapidly and then her eyes flew to his, bright with accusation and pain. 'You *are* a complete and utter bastard, she's right about that.'

'I've never heard you use bad language before. It doesn't suit you.' Leandro strolled across the bedroom and lifted a bottle of whisky from a small table. *Funny,* he thought, *that his hand was so steady.* 'And I don't understand why you're angry. You walked out on our marriage, not me. I was in it for the long haul.'

'Only you could make it sound like an endurance test. It's nice to know you had such a positive view of our relationship. No wonder it didn't last five minutes. You're even more unfeeling than I thought you were—' She broke off, as if she was trying to control herself. 'You're horribly, *horribly* insensitive.'

'I'm living my life. What's insensitive about that?' Leandro's hand remained steady as he poured. 'There was a vacancy in my bed and I filled it. In the circumstances, you can hardly blame me for that. Drink?'

'No, thank you.'

'Such perfect English manners.' Leandro gave a humourless laugh as he lifted the glass. 'Don't tell me—alcohol is fattening and you're watching your weight.'

'No. I'm watching my tongue. If I drink, I'll tell you exactly what I think of you and right now that might not be a good idea because what I think of you isn't very flattering.'

His hand stilled on the glass. 'Don't hold back on my account. It's interesting to know you're capable of expressing what you're feeling providing you're sufficiently provoked. Just for the record, I actually prefer confrontation to retreat.'

She closed her eyes, misery visible in every angle of her pretty face. 'I *hate* confrontation. I didn't come here to argue with you.'

'I'm sure you didn't.' Leandro examined the golden liquid in his glass. 'You don't talk about problems, do you, Millie? And you were certainly never interested in fixing the problems in our relationship. It's so much easier to just walk away when things become awkward.'

'How *dare* you say that to me when *you're* the one who—?' She broke off as if she couldn't even bear to say it, and his mouth tightened.

'I'm the one who what?' His silky soft voice was in direct contrast to the passion in hers. 'Spell it out, Millie. Come on—let's hear what I'm guilty of.'

'You *know* what! And I didn't come here to talk about that. 'You're a—a...' She appeared to struggle with her breath and he gave her a long look.

'You really must learn to finish your sentences, *agape mou.*' His tone bored, he offered no sympathy. As far as he was concerned, she deserved none. He'd given her a chance. He'd given her something he'd never offered a woman before. And she'd thrown it back in his face. 'I'm cold and heartless, isn't that right, Millie? Wasn't that what you were going to say?'

'I wish I'd never met you.'

'Now, that's just childish.' Leandro suppressed a yawn and she looked away.

'Our relationship was a disaster.'

'I wouldn't say that. For a short time you were a revelation in bed, and I was reasonably entertained by your gift for saying the wrong thing at the wrong time.'

'It's called telling the truth.' She glared at him through lashes spiked with rain. 'Where I come from, that's what people do. They tell it like it is and that way there's no confusion. When someone says, "Lovely to see you," they mean it. In *your* world when someone says, "Lovely to see you," they certainly *don't* mean it. They kiss you even though they hate you.'

Leandro added ice to his glass. 'It's a standard social greeting.'

'It's superficial—everything about your world is!' She sprang off the bed and walked towards him, her eyes flashing fire. 'And that included our relationship.'

'I'm not the one who called time on our marriage.'

'Yes, you did!' Angry and hurt, she faced him. 'You blame me for walking out, but what did you think I'd do, Leandro?

Did you think I'd say, "Don't worry, that's fine by me"?' Her voice rose, trembling and thickened by pain. 'Did you think I'd turn a blind eye? Maybe that's what women do in your world, but that isn't the sort of marriage I want. You slept with another woman and not just any woman.' Her breathing was jagged. 'My sister. *My own sister.*' Her distress was so obvious that Leandro gave a frown.

'You're working yourself up into a state.'

'Please don't pretend you care about my feelings because you've already amply demonstrated that you don't.' Holding herself together by a thread, she wrapped her arms around her body and met his gaze.

Brave, he thought absently, part of him intrigued by the sudden strength he saw in her. Yes, she was upset. But she wasn't caving in, was she? He hadn't known that she possessed a layer of steel. By the end of their relationship he'd come to the conclusion that she was so lightweight that the only thing preventing her from being blown away was the weight of his money in her handbag.

Leandro's hand tightened on his glass and then he lifted it to his lips and drained it. Then he placed the glass carefully on the table in front of him.

'Given the circumstances of your departure, I'm surprised you chose to come back.'

Sinking back onto the side of the bed, the fight seemed to go out of her and she suddenly looked incredibly tired. Tired, wet, beaten. 'If you thought I wouldn't then you know even less about me than I thought you did.'

'I never knew you.' It had been a fantasy. An illusion. *Or maybe a delusion?*

'And whose fault is that? You didn't *want* to know me, did you? You weren't interested in *me*—just in sex, and when that—' She broke off and took a breath, clearly searching for the words she wanted. 'I wasn't right for you. To start with you liked the fact that I was "different". I was just an ordinary girl, living in the country, working on her parents' farm. Unsophisticated. But the novelty wore off, didn't it, Leandro? You wanted me to fit into your life. Your world. And I didn't.'

Watching her so closely, he was able to detect the exact moment when anger turned to awareness.

Her eyes slid to his bare, bronzed shoulders and then back to his. It was like putting a match to kerosene. The chemistry that had been simmering exploded to dangerous levels and she turned away with a murmur of frustration, although whether it was with herself or him, he wasn't sure. 'Don't you dare, Leandro! Don't you *dare* look at me like that—as if everything hasn't changed between us.'

'You were looking at me.'

'Because you're standing there half-naked!'

'Does that bother you?'

'No, it doesn't.' She rubbed her hands up and down her arms, trying to warm them. 'I don't feel anything for you any more.'

'Oh, you feel plenty for me, Millie,' Leandro said grimly, 'and that's the problem, isn't it? You hate the fact that you can feel that way. A woman like you shouldn't find herself hopelessly attracted to a bad boy like me. It's not quite decent, is it?'

'I'm not here because of you.'

'Of course you're not.' His tone caustic, he watched as she flinched away from his words. 'You wouldn't have made the journey for something as trivial as the survival of our marriage, would you? That was never important to you.' Filled with contempt, Leandro lifted the glass, wondering how much whisky it was going to take to dull what he was feeling.

'Are you drunk?'

'Unfortunately, no, not yet.' He eyed the glass. 'But I'm working on it.'

'You're totally irresponsible.'

'I'm working on that, too.' He was about to lift the glass to his lips when he noticed that the sole of her boot was starting to come away. Remembering how obsessive she'd been about her appearance, he frowned. 'You look awful.'

'Most people would look awful compared with the cream of Hollywood,' she said tartly. She lifted her hand and he thought she was going to smooth her damp hair, but then she let her hand drop as if she'd decided it wasn't worth the effort. 'She's very beautiful.'

He heard the pain in her voice and gritted his teeth. 'Jealousy was the one aspect of our relationship at which you consistently excelled.'

'You're *so* unkind.'

Leandro discovered that his fingers had curled themselves into a fist. 'Unkind?' His mouth tightened. 'Yes, I'm unkind.'

'Do you love her?'

'Now you're getting personal.'

'Of course I'm getting personal! Did my sis—?' Her voice cracked and she cleared her throat. 'Did...Becca know you were seeing the actress?'

The mention of that name made Leandro want to drain the bottle of whisky, as did the unspoken accusation behind her words. 'Are you blaming me for the fact that your sister crashed the car while under the influence of drink and drugs?'

'She drank because you rejected her! She was suffering from depression.'

Thinking about what he knew, Leandro gave a humourless smile. 'I'll just bet she was.'

She sprang to her feet and crossed the room with the grace of a dancer. 'Don't you *dare* speak about the dead like that! If anyone was responsible for my sister's fragile mental state, it's you. You broke her heart.'

And Leandro committed the unpardonable sin. He laughed. And that grim humour cost him.

She slapped him.

Then she put her hand against her throat and stepped backwards, as if she couldn't believe what she'd done. Her skin was so pale she reminded him of something conjured from a child's fairy story.

'I should probably apologise but I'm not going to,' she whispered, her fingers pressed against her slender neck. 'Do you know the most hurtful part of all this? You don't even care. You destroyed our marriage for sex. It didn't even *mean* anything. If you'd loved her maybe, just maybe, I would have been able to understand all this, but for you it was just physical.'

'As a matter of interest, did you say any of this to her?'

'Yes. Actually, I did. I went to see her just after she was admitted to that clinic in Arizona. I…' She rubbed her fingers across her forehead. 'I needed to try and understand. She confessed that she was so madly in love with you that she wasn't thinking clearly.'

'She knew exactly what she was doing,' Leandro said flatly. 'The only person your sister ever loved was herself. That was probably the only thing we ever had in common.'

'That's a very cynical attitude.'

'I'm a cynical guy.'

'So you wrecked our marriage for a woman you don't even care about.'

'I didn't wreck our marriage, *agape mou*,' Leandro spoke

softly, his eyes fixing on her white face, as he hammered home his barb. 'You did that. All by yourself.'

If he'd hit her, she couldn't have looked more shocked. 'How can you say that? What did you expect? I'm not the sort of woman who can turn a blind eye while her husband has an affair. Especially when the woman involved was his wife's sister. You made her pregnant, Leandro! How was I supposed to overlook that?' Visibly distressed, she turned away. 'What I don't understand is why, if you wanted my sister, did you bother with me at all?'

Leandro let that question hover in the air. 'And does the fact that you don't understand help you draw any conclusions?'

His question drew a confused frown and he realised that she was too upset to focus on the facts.

She'd seen. She'd believed. She hadn't questioned. Hadn't cared enough to question and the knowledge that she hadn't cared left the bitter taste of failure in his mouth.

In a life gilded by success, she'd been his only failure.

Leandro flexed his shoulders to relieve the tension and the movement caught her attention, her eyes drifting to the swell of hard muscle. Her gaze was feather light and yet he felt the responding sizzle of sexual heat and almost laughed at his own weakness.

It seemed his body was nowhere near as choosy as his mind.

Millie stared at him for a long moment and then sank her teeth into her lower lip. 'Leandro, do me a favour.' Her voice was strained. 'Put your shirt on. We can't have a proper conversation with you standing there half-naked.'

'This may surprise you, but I've been known to conduct a conversation even when naked.' His sardonic tone masked his own anger and brought a flush to her cheeks.

'I'm sure. But if it's all the same with you, I'd like you to get dressed.'

'Why? Is the sight of my body bothering you, Millie?' His tone silky smooth, Leandro strolled across the bedroom and retrieved his shirt from the floor. 'Are you finding it hard to concentrate?' He shrugged the shirt back on, discovered that there were no buttons and spread his arms in an exaggerated gesture of apology. 'She was a bit over-eager, I'm afraid. This is the best I can do.'

'It's fine.' She averted her eyes, but not before both of them had shared a memory they would rather have forgotten. 'The media have been running the story for days now, and it's *awful*. Somehow they know about you and my sister, and they know the baby's been brought here.' Her voice wobbled. 'Where…?'

'Asleep on the next floor.' His voice terse, Leandro strolled over to the window that overlooked the garden. 'Someone from the clinic brought the baby to me. Your sister left him alone and uncared for while she went for her little drive. He was found crying and neglected.' The anger in him was like a roaring beast and he was shocked by the strength required to hold it back. Control was a skill he'd mastered at an impossibly young age, but when he thought of the baby his thoughts raced into the dark. 'Evidently she didn't have a maternal bone in her body.' *Another woman, another place.*

'She was sick.'

'Well, that's one thing we agree on.' *Infested with greed.* Aware that the past and the present had become dangerously tangled and the conversation was taking a dangerous turn, Leandro changed direction. 'Why do you think they brought the baby here, Millie?'

'The clinic said she left a note saying that you were the father. She wanted the baby to be with family.'

He made an impatient sound, marvelling at her naivety. 'Or perhaps she just wanted to make sure there was no chance of reconciliation between us. Her last, generous gift to you.' His carefully planted seed of suggestion landed on barren ground.

'There never was any chance of reconciliation.' She didn't look at him. 'Where's the baby? I should be going.'

Leandro stilled. 'Where, exactly, are you planning to go?'

'It's already past midnight. I've booked into a small bed and breakfast near here.'

'A bed and breakfast?' Leandro looked at her with a mixture of disbelief and fascination, realising just how little he knew about this woman. 'Are you suggesting what I think you are?'

'I'm taking the baby, of course. What did you think?'

'So you're planning to take in your sister's baby and care for it—this is the same baby that is supposedly the result of an affair between your own sister and your husband. Whether you think your sister was lying or telling the truth—'

'Telling the truth.'

Leandro's jaw tightened. 'Whichever. Your sister wrecked your marriage. She hurt you. And you're willing to take her baby? What are you, a doormat?'

Her narrow shoulders were rigid. 'No, I'm responsible. And principled. Qualities that you probably don't recognise. Am I angry with my sister? Yes, I'm angry. And that feels really horrible because even while I'm grieving I'm hurt that she could have done that to me.' Her voice shook. 'She behaved terribly. Some people wouldn't forgive that. If I'm honest I'm not sure that I'll ever forgive that. She betrayed my trust. But at least she was in love with you. And I think at the end she was truly sorry.'

Leandro raised an eyebrow but she ploughed on.

'It was the guilt that pushed her into depression. And whatever had happened, I would never have wanted her to...' Her voice trembled. 'We were sisters. And as for the baby—well, I don't believe that a child should be held responsible for the sins of his parents. My sister is dead. You can't bring up a baby, so I will have him. He will have a loving home with me as long as he needs one.'

'So you're proposing to love and care for your husband's bastard, is that right?'

'Don't *ever* call him that.' Her eyes blazed. 'And, yes, I'm intending to care for him. He's three months old. He's helpless.'

Curiously detached, Leandro looked at her. She wasn't classically beautiful, he mused, but there was something about her face that was captivating. 'So you have forgiven your sister.'

'I'm working on it.' She caught her lip between her teeth. 'I understand the effect you have on a woman. Even that Hollywood actress was willing to humiliate herself to spend a night with you. Tell me one thing—why, when you have a reputation for not committing to a woman, did you marry me?'

'Frankly?' Leandro lifted his eyes from his scrutiny of her soft lips. 'At this moment I have absolutely no idea.'

'You *really* know how to hurt. You treated our marriage lightly.'

'On the contrary, *you're* the one who walked out at the first obstacle.'

Her shoulders sagged, as if she was bearing an enormous weight. 'If you've said everything you wanted to say, I'd like to take the baby.'

'As usual you are being quite breathtakingly naïve. For a start there is a pack of journalists on my doorstep. How do you think they're going to react if you leave here clutching the baby?'

'I think it would reflect very badly on you. But you don't care about that, do you? You never care what people think about you. If you did, you wouldn't behave so badly.'

Leandro pressed the tips of his long fingers to his forehead, his control at breaking point. 'We'll talk about this in a minute,' he snapped. 'For goodness' sake, go and use the bathroom. You're soaking wet. And next time use the front door, like my wife, instead of creeping through the garden like a burglar.'

'Whatever you say, you wouldn't have wanted those headlines any more than I did.'

Leandro sent her a brooding glance, marvelling that the male libido could be such a self-destructive force. 'The headlines will stop when they realise there is no story.'

She didn't appear to register his words. Certainly she didn't question his meaning. 'As soon as I'm dry, I'll take him away. We'll both be out of your life.'

Leandro watched in silence, allowing her to delude herself for a short time.

His wife was back.

And he had no intention of letting her walk out again.

CHAPTER TWO

NUMB with misery, Millie stood in front of the mirror in the huge, luxurious bathroom. She didn't reach for a towel. She did nothing to improve her appearance. She simply stared at herself.

No wonder, she thought numbly. *No wonder he'd strayed.*

Leandro Demetrios was six feet two inches of devastatingly handsome, vibrant masculinity and she was—she was, what?

Ordinary.

She was just so *ordinary.*

Staring at her wild, curling hair, she reflected on how long it had taken her each day to straighten it into the tame, sleek sheet that everyone expected. And even with the weight she'd lost during the misery of the last year, her breasts were still large, and her hips curvy.

No wonder he'd chosen her sister.

Trying not to think about that, Millie ran the tap and splashed cold water on her face. One thing about already having lost your husband to another woman, she thought, was that you no longer had to pretend to be someone different. She could just be herself. What did she have to lose?

Nothing.

She'd already lost it all.

But life kept throwing boulders at her, and she had a whole new challenge ahead of her. She had to put aside all her dreams of having her own baby, and instead love and nurture the baby that had been the result of her husband's affair with her sister.

Caught in a sudden rush of panic, Millie covered her mouth with her hand. It was all very well to say she was going to do this, but what if she looked at the baby and hated it? That would make her an awful person, wouldn't it?

She wanted to do the right thing, she really did, but what if doing the right thing proved too hard?

Her encounter with Leandro had been a million times harder than she'd anticipated and she'd always known it was going to be awful.

Even though their marriage was over, nothing had prepared her for the agonising pain of seeing Leandro with another woman. And worse still was the realisation that she hadn't healed at all. She wasn't over him and she never would be.

She'd learned to survive, that was all. But life without him was flat and colourless.

'Millie?' Leandro's harsh tones penetrated the closed door and she stilled, fastened to the spot like a rabbit caught in headlights. Then her eyes slid to the bolt on the door. Even Leandro in a black temper couldn't break his way through a solid bolt, could he?

She didn't understand his anger. Surely he should have been grateful to her for solving a problem for him. The last thing he needed in his life was a baby.

An image of the actress slid into her brain and paralysed her. For a moment she couldn't move or think.

What had she expected? That he was sitting in alone at night, thinking of her?

'Wait a minute!' Hands shaking, she looked at herself in the mirror, hoping that she'd turn out to be the person she hoped she was. She didn't want to be a pathetic, jealous wimp, did she? She wanted to have the strength to walk away from this marriage with her head held high and her dignity intact. She wanted to be mature enough to care for the baby and give him the love he deserved, regardless of how much his parents had hurt her.

That was the person she wanted to be.

Gritting her teeth, Millie turned away from the mirror, walked across the bathroom and opened the door.

Leandro was leaning against the doorframe, dark lights in his eyes warning her of just how short his fuse was. 'What have you been doing for the last half an hour? You look exactly the same as you did when you went in. I assumed you were going to shower and change. Or at least use a towel.'

Up until that point she hadn't realised that she'd forgotten to dry herself. 'I...didn't have anything to change into.'

Leandro reached out a hand and touched her damp hair with a frown of exasperation. 'You didn't bring any clothes.'

'I left my suitcase on the train,' she muttered. 'I was...upset. And I'm only staying in London for one night. It will be fine.' She wished she could feel angry again. The anger had given her energy to cope with the difficult situation. Without it, she felt nothing but exhaustion.

His hand dropped to his side. 'You still have clothes here. Wear them.'

'You kept my clothes?' Shocked, Millie stared up at him and his cold, unemotional appraisal chilled her.

'I hate waste and I find them useful for overnight guests.'

The barb sank deep, the pain resting alongside the earlier

wounds he'd inflicted, and she wondered why it was that emotional agony could be so much more traumatic than physical wounds.

He'd dismissed her from his life so easily.

Millie thought about all the bleak, lonely hours she'd spent agonising over whether or not she was right to have walked out—*about the tears she'd shed*. The times she'd wondered whether he was thinking about her. Whether he cared about their break-up.

Well, she had her answer now.

He was just fine. He'd moved on—apparently with effortless ease. Which just proved that he'd never loved her. He'd married her on impulse. He'd seen her as a novelty. Unfortunately it hadn't taken long for her novelty value to wear off. When they'd been living in their own little world everything had been fine. It had been when they'd returned to *his* world that the problems had started.

Did you really think you'd be able to hold him? Her sister's sympathetic question was embedded in her brain, like a soundtrack that refused to stop playing.

'The baby.' Knowing that the only way she was going to be able to hold it together was if she didn't dwell on how she felt, Millie forced herself to ask the question. 'Who has been looking after him?'

'Two nannies. Change your clothes,' Leandro said roughly. 'The last thing I need is you with pneumonia.'

'I'm not cold.'

'Then why are you shivering?'

Did he honestly not know? She wanted to hit him for not understanding her feelings. He possessed confidence by the barrel-load and that natural self-assurance seemed to prevent him understanding those to whom life didn't come quite so easily. What did a man like Leandro Demetrios know about insecurity? He didn't have a clue.

Neither had he shown any remorse for the way their relationship had ended. In fact, he'd made it obvious that he thought she'd been in the wrong.

Maybe other women would have turned a blind eye, but she wasn't like that.

'I'm shivering because I'm finding this situation...' She struggled to find a suitably neutral word. 'Difficult.'

'Difficult?' His sensual mouth formed a grim, taut line in his handsome face. 'You haven't begun to experience difficult yet, *agape mou*. But you will.'

What did he mean by that?

What could possibly be worse than being forced into the company of the man she adored and hadn't been able to satisfy, and forced to care for the child he'd had with another woman? At the moment that challenge felt like the very essence of difficulty.

Feeling as though she was balancing precariously on the edge of a deep, dark pit, Millie took a deep breath. 'I'd like to see my nephew.' She drew the edges of her damp cardigan around her. She was shivering so hard she might have been in the Arctic, rather than his warm bedroom. 'Where's the baby?'

'Sleeping. What else did you expect at this hour?' His mouth grim, he strode across the bedroom and into the dressing room, emerging moments later with some clothes in his hands. 'Put these on. At least they're dry.'

'They're my old jeans.' She frowned down at them. 'The ones I wore when I first met you.'

'This isn't a trip down memory lane,' he gritted. 'It's an attempt to get you out of wet clothes. Get back in that bathroom. And this time when you come out, make sure you're dry.'

With a sigh, Millie turned back into the bathroom. The lights came on automatically and she stopped, remembering how that had amused her when he'd first brought her to this house. She'd walked in and out of all the rooms, feeling as though she'd walked into a vision of the future. Lights that came on when someone walked into a room, heating sensors, a house that vacuumed itself—Leandro exploited cutting-edge technology in every aspect of his life, and for her it had been like walking into a fantasy.

Trying not to think how the fantasy had ended, Millie stripped off her wet clothes, rubbed her cold skin with a warm towel and pulled on the jeans and silky green jumper he'd handed her.

She glanced in the enormous mirror and decided that the lighting had been designed specifically to highlight her imperfections. She looked nothing like a billionaire's wife.

Emerging from the bathroom, her eyes clashed with his. 'Now can I see the baby? I just…' She swallowed. 'I just want to look at him, that's all.' *To get it over with. Part of her was so afraid she wouldn't be able to do it.*

This was a test, and she wasn't sure whether she was going to pass or fail.

Leandro yanked a towel from the rail and starting rubbing her hair. 'You've been in that bathroom twice and your hair is still soaking.'

'You need to invest in a device that automatically dries someone's hair if it's wet.'

Something flickered in his eyes and she knew he was thinking of the time when he'd first brought her here and she'd played with the technology like a child with a new toy. 'What were you doing all that time?'

Thinking about him. About her life.

Trying to find the strength to do this.

'I was playing hide and seek with the lights. They're a bit bright for me.' Millie winced as his methodical rubbing became a little too brisk and tried not to think about the fact that he was turning her hair into a tangled mess.

What did it matter? What did smooth, perfect hair matter at this point in their relationship? They were way past the point where her appearance was an issue.

Leandro slung the towel over the heated rail. 'That will do.'

'Yes, there's no point in working on something that's never going to come up to scratch,' Millie muttered, and he frowned sharply.

'What's that supposed to mean?'

'Nothing.' Trying to forget her appearance, Millie lifted her chin. 'I want to see the baby.' At least the baby wouldn't care whether her hair was blow-dried or not.

She felt inadequate and out of place in this man's life, but she was here because the baby needed her. It was abandoned. Unloved. *Like her...*

For a whole year she'd locked herself away—*protected herself from the outside world.* And if it hadn't been for the baby she would have stayed in her hiding place. Not that she'd needed to hide. *Leandro hadn't come to look for her, had he?* She'd left, but he hadn't followed.

Leandro gave her a long, hard look, as if asking himself a question.

Knowing with absolute certainty what that question was, Millie walked towards the bedroom door.

'You can see the baby,' he drawled as they walked out of the room. 'But don't wake him up.'

The comment surprised her. Why would he care whether

she woke the baby or not? She'd thought he would have been only too anxious for her to remove the child and get out of his life.

Millie glanced at the paintings, reflecting that most normal people had to go to art galleries to see pieces like this. Leandro could admire them on his way to the bathroom.

Following him up a flight of stairs, she frowned. 'You've put him as far away from you as possible.'

'You think he should sleep in my bedroom, perhaps?' His silken enquiry brought a flush to her cheeks.

'No. I don't think that. I can't think of a less suitable environment for a baby than your bedroom.'

Millie leaned against the wall for support, unable to dispel the image of his hard, muscular body entwined with the sylph-like actress.

Of course he'd had relationships since they'd broken up. What had she expected? Leandro was an intensely virile man with a dark, restless sex appeal that women found irresistible. Just as she had. And her sister.

Millie gave a low moan, wondering how she'd ever found the arrogance to think their marriage could work. How naïve had she been, thinking that they shared something special. When they'd first met he'd been so good at making her feel beautiful that for a while she'd actually believed that she was.

Leandro opened a door and stood there, allowing her to go first.

Her arm brushed against the hard muscle of his abdomen and her stomach reacted instantly.

A uniformed nanny rose quickly to her feet. 'He's been very unsettled, Mr Demetrios,' she said in a low voice. 'Crying, refusing his bottle. He's asleep now, but I don't know how long it will last.'

Leandro dismissed her with a single imperious movement of his head and the girl scurried out of the room.

Had he always been that scary? Millie wondered. *Had he been cold and intimidating when she'd met him?*

The answer was yes, probably, but never with her. With her he'd always been gentle and good humoured. That was one of the things that had made her feel special. The power and influence he wielded made others stutter and stumble around him, but when they'd met, she hadn't known who he was. And that had amused him. And she'd continued to amuse him. With *her,* the tiger had sheathed his claws and played gently, but she'd never been under any illusions. She hadn't tamed the tiger and she doubted any woman ever would.

As the door closed behind the girl, Millie wondered how on earth she'd ever had the courage to talk to this man.

'Your nephew.' He spoke the words in a low tone and Millie forced aside all other feelings and tiptoed towards the cot. Her palms were clammy and she felt ever so slightly sick because she'd pictured this scene in her head so many times, but now it was twisted in a cruel parody of her dream.

Yes, she and Leandro were leaning over a cot. But her dream had never included a baby who wasn't hers, fathered by the man she loved with the woman who was closest to her.

Agony ripped through her, stealing her breath and her strength. She thought she gave a moan of denial, but the baby didn't stir, his perfect features immobile in sleep.

Innocent of the tense atmosphere in the room, he was so still that Millie felt a rush of panic and instinctively reached out a hand to touch him.

Strong fingers closed over hers and drew her away from the cot.

'He's fine.' Leandro's low, masculine voice brushed

against her nerve endings. 'He always sleeps like that. *When* he sleeps, which isn't that often.'

'He looks—'

'As though he isn't breathing. I know.' He gave a grim smile. 'I've made that mistake several times myself. Once I even woke him up just to check he was alive. Believe me, I don't advise it. He's very much alive and if you poke him just to check, he'll confirm it in the loudest possible way. He has lungs that an opera singer would envy and, once woken up, he doesn't like going back to sleep. I had to walk him round the house for three hours.'

Leandro worried about the baby so much he'd woken him? And then he'd carried him around the house? It didn't fit with what she knew of him.

'What did you do with your BlackBerry?' She asked the question without thinking and he gave a faint smile.

'You think I spoke into the baby and tucked my mobile phone into the cot?' His eyes were mocking and Millie looked away, flustered.

'I didn't think you'd want anything to do with the baby.' In a way her question was a challenge. Would he care for a baby that wasn't his?

For a moment—*just for a moment*—something shimmered between them and then she dragged her eyes away from his and focused on the baby. Her heart was thumping, her stomach was tumbling over and over. But he'd always had this effect on her, hadn't he? He could turn her legs to jelly with just one glance. Everything else became irrelevant.

Except that it wasn't irrelevant and she had this baby to remind her of that fact.

He lay quietly. Even in sleep Millie could see the dark feathering of his eyelashes against his cheek and the shock of dark hair. And her heart melted. To her intense relief, the baby softened everything inside her. 'You poor thing,' she whispered, gently touching his head with her hand. 'You must be missing your mummy—wondering what you're doing in this strange place.' Aware that Leandro was looking at her oddly, she flushed. 'Sorry. I suppose it's a bit crazy speaking to a baby who's asleep.'

Her eyes met his and in that single instant she knew he was thinking about the child they could have made together. The image was too painful and she looked away, determined not to torture herself with what she would never have. *If she'd produced a child quickly, perhaps this would never have happened.* But that had been another failure on her part. Another failure to add to the list. 'He's sweet. He has your hair.'

'Then the child is a miracle of conception,' Leandro snapped. 'But I can assure you that your sister was definitely the mother.'

Millie struggled not to react. 'Becca was always confident. I think that's why she was so successful. It just didn't enter her head that she couldn't do something or have something.' *Even her sister's husband.* 'Like you, she never questioned herself or doubted herself. You had that in common.'

'Alpha woman.'

Millie looked at him. 'Yes. She was.' And she'd always felt insecure around her big sister. There had been just no way she could ever measure up. Even as a very young child, she'd been aware that she was walking in her sister's shadow.

And even in death Becca had left that shadow—a dark cloud that had stolen the light from Millie's marriage. *From her life.*

'Let's leave the baby to sleep.' Taking control, Leandro put a hand in the centre of her back and urged her out of the room. 'Have you eaten?'

'No.' Millie wondered how he could be thinking about food. 'It's past midnight. I was going to go straight to the bed and breakfast.'

'You're not going to any bed and breakfast. We need to talk—and I need coffee, so we'll have the conversation in the kitchen.'

Too drained to argue, Millie followed him downstairs. The kitchen was another room that had surprised her when she'd first seen the house. It was a clever combination of modern and traditional, a large range cooker giving warmth and comfort, while the maximal use of glass ensured light poured into every available space. As a result the lush garden appeared to be part of the room and the table was positioned in such a way that, whatever the season, it felt as though you were sitting outdoors.

'Sit down before you fall down.' Leandro strolled to the espresso machine and ground some beans.

The sound pounded her throbbing head and Millie winced. 'You still make it all from scratch, then?' It had been one of the many things that she'd learned about him early on. He wanted the best. Whether it was art, coffee or women—Leandro demanded perfection. *Which made it even more surprising that he'd picked her.*

He made the coffee—as competent in the kitchen as he was everywhere else. Leandro used staff because his life was so maniacally busy, not because he was deficient in skills. And sometimes, she knew, he just preferred to be on his own.

He'd rolled back his shirtsleeves and the muscles of his forearm flexed as he worked.

Strong, Millie thought as she looked at him. He was strong; physically, emotionally—and that inherent strength was part of his devastating appeal. He was a man who led while others followed. A man women were drawn to.

'Why didn't you tell me that the baby had been brought here?' To distract herself, she asked the question that was on her mind. 'Why did I have to read about it in the newspapers?'

'You walked out on me.' His voice terse, he reached for a cup. 'I had no reason to think you'd be interested.'

Absorbing that blow, Millie curled her fingers over the back of the chair. 'Why are you so angry with me? I would have thought you'd be apologetic or at least a little uncomfortable but you're not. You're…'

'I'm what, Millie?'

'You're…' She hesitated. 'Boiling with rage. And I just don't get it.'

He didn't reply, but she knew he'd heard her because his hand stilled for a moment. And then he lifted an empty cup. 'Do you want one?'

'No, thank you. You make it so strong it will keep me awake.' Not that she'd sleep anyway. The adrenaline was pumping round her bloodstream like a drug. She wanted to walk. Pace. *Sob?*

Leandro waited while the thick dark brew filled the small cup. Then he walked across to the table. 'Right, let's talk.' He put the cup on the table and sprawled in the nearest chair. The edges of his torn dress shirt slid apart, revealing his flat, bronzed abdomen.

Millie kept her eyes fixed straight ahead. 'What is there to talk about?'

'This is going to be a tiring conversation for you if you stand all the way through it. And you already look ready to drop.'

She sat, too emotionally wrung out to think for herself. 'I'm fine.'

'You look wrecked. You should have told me you were coming. I would have sent my private jet.'

'I wouldn't have felt comfortable.'

'You're still my wife. You're entitled to the perks of the job.'

'I don't want anything from you.' Millie sat very upright. 'Except maybe the stuff you've bought for the baby. It's a waste to buy a second pram and things. Tomorrow I'll remove Costas from your life. You can get back to your BlackBerry and your—' She almost said 'actress' but thought better of it. 'And your undisturbed nights.' From the corner of her eye she saw his fingers close round his coffee cup.

'I don't want to talk about Costas.' He let that hover in the air while he drank his coffee. 'I want to talk about us.'

Her heart started to thump faster because she could feel him watching her and his scrutiny made her squirm. 'How is that relevant?'

'It's relevant.'

'How? There is no "us". There's nothing to talk about.' Why would he want to go back over old ground? Millie wasn't sure she could stand reliving the whole thing again.

'You made promises, Millie. You stood up in that little village church and made those vows.' Leandro put his cup down slowly. 'And then you just walked away. *For richer for poorer, in sickness and in health*—remember that?'

Her chin lifted. *'Forsaking all others…'*

'I might have known you'd throw that one at me.' He inhaled deeply, his eyes holding hers. 'You asked me how it's relevant—let me tell you. You're my wife, Millie. And to a Greek man, marriage is binding. It isn't something you opt in and out of depending on the mood. It's forever.'

'Leandro—'

'You chose to come back, Millie.' His mouth tightened and his eyes glinted hard and dangerous. 'And now you're going to stay.'

CHAPTER THREE

MILLIE sat in frozen silence, so stunned by his unexpected declaration that she could barely breathe, let alone speak. It took several uncomfortable moments for the full implications of his words to sink into her shocked brain.

Then she sprang to her feet and paced to the far side of the kitchen, so agitated that it was impossible to stay still. 'You expect me to come back to you? You're blaming me for walking away?'

'Yes.' His tone was hard. 'I am.'

Millie stared at the row of shiny saucepans on the wall. 'The fact that you won't let me take the baby tells me only one thing.'

Leandro gave a humourless laugh. 'I always insist that my employees are capable of thinking laterally. For some reason I didn't apply the same standards to my wife. Take a word of advice from me—when you study a picture, there is almost always more going on than first meets the eye.'

'I can see only one reason why you'd be so protective of this baby.'

'Then remind me not to set you up in business. Tunnel vision is a guaranteed path to failure.' He was a tough adversary—intelligent, articulate and able to counter every word spoken with the effortless ease of a practised negotiator. 'Did you really think I'd let you walk out with him? A baby is a massive responsibility, requiring the ultimate commitment. Given your track record, I'm hardly likely to hand him over.'

'*My* track record?'

'When you met an obstacle in life, you walked away.'

His accusation was so unfair that her breath hitched. 'You were with my sister. What did you expect? My blessing?'

'You are my wife. I expected your trust.' He was on his feet, too. And determined to halt her retreat. 'Answer me a question.' His handsome face taut and grim, he closed his hands over her shoulders. 'After everything we shared—after those vows you made—why were you so quick to believe the worst of me? You stalked out that night and you never contacted me again. You didn't ask me about it.'

Her eyes level with his bare chest, Millie's heart was pounding uncomfortably. 'I saw what I saw.'

'You saw what your sister wanted you to see.'

'I know that some of the blame lay with her, but—'

'Not some of it,' his tone was harsh, 'all of it. She set you up, Millie, and you believed all the lies she fed you. And I was so angry that you believed her, I let you go. And that was a mistake, I admit that. One of many I've made where you're concerned. I should have run after you, pinned you to our bed and made you see the truth.'

'Don't do this!' Millie covered her ears with her hands. 'Why are you doing this now when it's all too late?'

'Because this is a conversation we need to have. What about those feelings you claimed you had for me, Millie? Or was it all a damn lie because you wanted the lifestyle?'

She almost laughed at that. The lifestyle had been the

problem, but he'd never understand that, would he? 'I didn't care about the lifestyle.'

'Really? For a woman who didn't care, you certainly spent enough time on your appearance.'

It was such an unexpected interpretation of the facts that for a moment Millie just gaped at him. *He had no idea.* 'What you said just now,' she croaked, 'about a picture sometimes having another meaning—'

'Shopping is shopping.' There was an acid bite to his tone. 'It's hard to find another meaning for that. Unless you convinced yourself that it was an act of charity to prop up the world economy single-handed.'

Millie was so shocked and stung by that all she managed by way of response was a little shake of her head. 'I was trying to be the woman you wanted me to be.'

'What the hell is that supposed to mean?'

Wasn't it obvious? She was standing in front of him in her oldest jeans with bubbling hair and no make-up. The shiny surface of his large American fridge reflected her deficiencies back at her. Even in the kitchen there was no escape. 'I'm not your type. We met and married in less than a month. It was just too quick. We didn't know each other. It was a mistake.'

'Which part, exactly, was the mistake?' He made a rough sound in his throat and stepped towards her, trapping her against the wall with the sheer force of his presence. 'The part when you lay underneath me, sobbing my name?'

She felt the hard muscle of his thighs against her. 'Leandro—'

He slid his hand into her hair, tilting her face so that she was forced to look at him. 'Or the part when you came again and again without any break in between—was that when you thought, This is a mistake?'

'Don't do this—please don't do this.' Millie pushed at his chest and immediately regretted it because her hands encountered sleek muscle and it took every fibre of her being not to slide her greedy fingers over the deliciously masculine contours of his chest.

'When you fell asleep with your head on my shoulder, were you dreaming of mistakes?'

He'd conjured up one of her most precious memories and she closed her eyes against the tears and felt them scald the backs of her eyelids. The sex had always been incredible but also a little bit overwhelming because she could never quite let go of the thought that a man like him couldn't possibly want a girl like her. But in those moments afterwards—*those moments when he'd held her and murmured soft words against her hair*—that had been her favourite time. The time she'd actually let herself believe that the fairy-tale might be happening.

'When you told me that you loved me, Millie…' His voice was hoarse and his fingers tightened in her hair. 'Were you thinking that it was a mistake? Was it all a lie?'

'No.'

Her eyes flew to his and for one desperate moment she thought he might actually kiss her. His mouth hovered, a muscle flickered in his lean, dark jaw and his eyes glittered black and dangerous. He looked like a man on the edge.

And then he stepped back from the edge, displaying that formidable control that raised him apart from other men. 'I don't think you know what you want, Millie. And that's why I'm not letting you take this baby.' With a searing glance in her direction, he closed his hand over her wrist and propelled her back to the table. 'Sit down.'

'Leandro, you can't—'

'I said *sit down*. I haven't finished.' His harsh tone was all the more shocking because she'd never heard it before. Always, with her, he'd been gentle. She'd never been on the receiving end of his biting sarcasm or his brutal frankness.

'If you yell, I won't listen.'

'I'm *not* yelling.' But he drew in a breath to calm himself and Millie sat, wondering again why he was so angry.

'Leandro—'

'You walked out without even giving me a hearing,' he said thickly, 'and at the time I was so angry with you that I let you go. Your lack of trust diminished what we shared to nothing. But I can see how skilfully your sister manipulated you. I can almost understand why you might have believed what you believed. You're right. We didn't know each other well enough or you wouldn't have run so fast. You wouldn't have looked at me with that accusation in your eyes. You wouldn't have been so quick to doubt me. You would have known me better.'

'I saw you,' she whispered, but his gaze didn't waver.

'What did you see, Millie? You saw your sister naked in the pool with me. Isn't that what you saw?'

The reminder was like the sting of a whip. 'You're trying to tell me I was imagining things.'

'No. I'm trying to make you see the rest of the picture. Was *I* naked?' His tone demanded an answer. 'Was I having sex with her?'

'Not then, no, but—'

'Can you think of any other reasons why Becca might have been naked in my pool?'

'Frankly, no.' Millie wished he'd sit down too. Staring up at six feet two of muscle-packed male wasn't an experience designed to induce relaxation.

Her answer drew a frustrated growl from him and he

muttered something under his breath in Greek. 'Perhaps your sister wasn't quite the person you thought she was.'

'It isn't fair to talk about her like this when she's not here to defend herself!'

'Fair?' His voice exploded with passion. 'Don't talk to me about fair!'

'You blame my sister, but you're no saint, Leandro.'

He gave a twisted smile. 'I have never laid claim to that title.'

'You have a dangerous reputation. Before me you'd dated all those beautiful women and you hadn't committed to any of them.' Millie bit her lip, wondering how she could have been such a fool.

'And what does that tell you?'

'It tells me that you're not good at sticking with one person.'

Tension vibrating through his powerful frame, Leandro stared up at the ceiling, apparently trying to control his response. When he finally looked at her again, his eyes glinted volcanic black and his body language was forceful and menacing as he loomed over her.

'Given that you can only see one image, I am going to have to show you the rest of the picture. But I'm only going to say this once,' he said softly, 'so make sure you are listening.'

'*Stop* trying to intimidate me.'

Shock shimmered in his eyes and his head jerked back as if she'd slapped him. 'I am *not* intimidating you.'

'That depends on where you're sitting.' Her voice was strong and steady and Millie had the satisfaction of seeing him take a deep breath.

Inclining his head by way of apology, he modulated the tone of his voice. 'Understand that the only reason I'm prepared to give you this explanation is because you're my wife and that allows you a degree of leeway that I would *never* grant to another person.'

Millie wanted to point out that she didn't inhabit that role any more but she couldn't push the words past her dry throat.

'Millie—look at me.'

She looked.

'I did *not* have sex with your sister.' Leandro spoke the words with deadly emphasis. 'At no time in our short, ill-fated marriage was I ever unfaithful to you. The baby is not mine.'

Millie's heart jumped. *She wanted to believe*—and then she remembered her sister. 'Why would Becca lie?' She breathed in and out. 'That would make her…'

Leandro straightened, his expression cold. 'Yes,' he said flatly, 'it would.'

'I know what I saw.'

'I've given you the facts. You decide. I have never doubted your intelligence, just your ability to use it.'

Millie stared at him in confusion, thinking of what he'd just said. *What she'd seen.* Everything she knew, everything she'd believed was suddenly thrown in the air. It was as if someone had dropped a giant jigsaw puzzle and the picture was no longer visible. 'One of you is—was—lying,' she said hoarsely, and he gave a grim smile.

'And your sister is no longer able to tell you the truth. An interesting dilemma, *agape mou*. Who are you going to believe? Live husband, or dead sister?'

Faced with that choice, her head started to throb. 'Let me tell you about my sister, Leandro. Let me tell you what my sister was to me. It was Becca who held my hand on my first day at school. It was Becca who helped me with my maths homework. It was Becca who taught me how to do my hair and make-up. Every step of my life, she was there, *helping* me. She encouraged me when my parents barely noticed I existed. It's bad enough to think she'd have an affair with my husband, but now you're suggesting she made up this entire thing just to hurt me?'

His silence said more than a thousand words would have done and Millie gave a distressed sigh.

'Obviously that *is* what you're suggesting. That's madness. What could she have possibly gained by that? And why would you expect me to believe you without question? I've known you a fraction of the time I knew my sister.'

'I expect you to believe me,' he said acidly, 'because you're my wife and that role should bring with it trust and commitment, two qualities that appear to be sadly lacking in your make-up. The truth is that our marriage started to go wrong long before you saw me with your sister.' Leandro straightened. 'I presume that's why you started avoiding sex.'

Her face flamed. 'I wasn't...avoiding sex.'

'Night after night you turned your back on me. You pretended to be asleep. And if I arrived home too early for you to play that trick, then you threw excuse after excuse at me—"headache", "tired", "wrong time of the month"—and I let you hold back because I was only too aware that you'd had absolutely no sexual experience before I came into your life. I was extremely patient with you. I had no idea what was going on in your head and you gave me no clues. You just lay there and hoped it would go away.'

The fact that he'd seen through her pitiful attempts to keep him at a distance increased her humiliation. 'I'm sure you really regretted marrying me.' *In fact, she knew he did. Wasn't that why he'd slept with her sister?*

'Do you want to know what I regret, Millie?' His voice was suddenly weary and he ran his hand over the back of his neck to relieve the tension. 'I regret that I didn't tie you to that damn bed and force you to tell me what was going on in that pretty head of yours. I backed off when I should have pushed you for answers, and I regret that more deeply than you'll ever know.'

'There was nothing in my head,' she lied. 'I was tired, that was all. When you weren't away on business trips, we were always out—every night there was something you wanted me to go to.' *Another event designed to highlight the differences between them and sap her confidence.*

'Tired?' His gaze was sardonic. 'On our honeymoon you had no sleep at all. We had sex virtually every hour of every day. You were as insatiable as I was. Fatigue wasn't the reason you had your back to me when I came to bed.'

'Leandro—'

'The honeymoon was perfect. The problems started when we arrived home. Suddenly you couldn't bear me to touch you. In fact, you went to the most extraordinary lengths to make sure that I didn't touch you.' His lips tightened. 'I even wondered whether the reason you invited your sister to stay with us was because you wanted something else to keep us apart.'

Appalled by the gulf in their mutual understanding, she dug her fingers into her hair and shook her head. 'You think I *wanted* you to have an affair with my sister?'

'I've said all I'm going to say on that particular subject.'

Millie was shaking so much she was relieved she was sitting down. 'I invited my sister to stay because I trusted her. And because I needed her help—she was always the one I turned to when I was in trouble.'

His brows met in a frown. 'How were you in trouble?'

Millie sat in silence, wishing she'd phrased it differently. Talking to him wasn't easy, was it? They didn't have that depth of understanding in their relationship. They'd shared scalding passion and nothing more. And Leandro was so confident, he wouldn't be able to understand anyone who wasn't. 'This is very hard for me,' she muttered, emotion swamping her. 'I didn't just lose my husband, I lost my sister. She was my best friend. And I lost her long before she died on that dusty, lonely road.'

'I want to know why you were so quick to assume that I'd have an affair. We'd been married three months, Millie! *Three months*. Hardly enough time for disillusionment to set in.'

'I knew your reputation.'

'Which was earned *before* I met you.'

Millie smiled through tears that refused to be contained. 'Oh, sure.' Her voice was choked. 'Beautiful me. So vastly superior in every way to those skinny models and actresses who knew how to dress, how to walk—I can quite see how it would have been impossible to notice them with me in the room. You should have reprogrammed the lights in this house so that they went *off* when I walked into a room. That might have helped our marriage.'

'Sarcasm doesn't suit you. It was your sweet nature and your gentleness that drew me to you.' Leandro's eyes narrowed, his gaze suddenly intent and focused. 'You always put yourself down. Why didn't I notice that before?'

'I don't know. At the beginning we didn't do much talking and after that you were too busy being exasperated with me for getting everything wrong, I suppose.' Millie thought about all those tense hours she'd spent trying to be who he wanted her to be. What an utter waste of time. Obviously she hadn't even come close. Which just proved that even eight hours in a beauty salon couldn't make a billionaire's wife out of a farm girl. 'You were partly to blame—you just dumped me in that situation and left me.'

'What situation?' He looked genuinely perplexed and she decided that there was no reason not to talk about it now.

It wasn't as if she was trying to impress him. She'd given up on that. 'You dumped me at all those really glitzy parties.'

'I did *not* "dump" you. I was by your side.'

'You were either talking business with someone in a suit— or you were smiling your smile at some beauty who was determined to grab your attention even though you were with me. And they all looked at me as though I'd crawled out from under a rock.'

'You were my wife.'

'Yes. That was the problem.'

Leandro gave her a look of exasperation. 'You are making no sense at all! Being my wife gave you status—'

'It was hugely stressful.'

He rubbed his fingers over his forehead. 'If this is a problem you expect me to discuss rationally, you're going to have to be a little more specific. In what way was being my wife "stressful"?'

Millie rubbed her hands over her legs, staring down at nails that had been bitten to nothing over the past year. 'I didn't have the necessary qualifications. I don't know why you married me, but you made a mistake.'

'Yes, you're right. I did make a mistake.' His fingers drummed a slow, deadly rhythm on the table. 'And I'm putting that mistake right and we're ending this mess.'

His words crushed her. For a horrible moment she thought she might make a fool of herself and slide to the floor and beg, *No, no, no*. The pride was stripped from her, leaving her vulnerable and exposed. She felt like a mortally wounded animal waiting for the final blow.

Oddly enough, the desire to cry suddenly ceased. It was as if her body had shut down.

'You want a divorce.' Somehow she managed to say the words, her eyes fixed on the wooden table, studying the grain of the wood. Anything, rather than look at him and fall apart. It was illogical, she knew, but she'd rather be married to him and never see him than cut the ties forever. 'Of course you do. Just let me take the baby, and I'll give you a divorce.'

'*Theos mou*, haven't you been listening to a word I've said?' His voice was rough and angry. 'I do *not* want a divorce.'

'You said you made a mistake.'

'It seems that whatever one of us says, the other misinterprets it.' Clearly struggling with his own volatile emotions, Leandro paused for a moment, his hand to his forehead. The he looked at her. 'The mistake I made,' he said harshly, 'was letting you walk out that day. I should have dragged you back and made you look at the truth. But I was furious that you doubted me. I was furious that you didn't stand your ground and fight for what we had.'

'If something isn't right, sometimes it's better just to let it go.'

Leandro threw her a fulminating glare and then paced to the far side of the kitchen, his broad shoulders rigid with tension.

Millie watched him—*this man she loved*—wondering what was going through his mind. As if reading her thoughts, he turned. The ever-present chemistry flickered across the room, resurrecting a connection that had never died.

'When I said that I'm ending this mess, I meant that we're ending this ridiculous separation. I want you back by my side where you belong. When the going gets tough, I want you to stay and fight instead of running. Those are the qualities I expect in the woman I've chosen to be my wife and the mother of my children.'

Millie pressed the palm of her hand against her heart to relieve the almost intolerable ache. 'Are you saying that you don't think I'd make a good mother?'

Something dark and dangerous shifted in his eyes. 'Let's just say that at the moment I'm not convinced.'

Appalled that he could possibly think that of her, Millie stared at him, seeing dark shadows in his eyes that she didn't understand. 'You don't know me at all.'

'No,' he said grimly. 'I don't. But I intend to rectify that.' He spoke the word with deadly emphasis. 'Let's see how powerful that commitment is this time around, shall we, Millie? If you want to be a mother to that child, you'll do it by my side, as my wife.'

The shock of his words silenced her and he lifted an eyebrow.

'It's a yes or no answer, Millie.'

She stood up, so agitated that she couldn't stay sitting. The fact that he intended to keep the baby suggested that he must be the father. Did he expect her to just ignore that fact? She wondered why he was so determined to continue the marriage. Was it a matter of pride? 'Why do you want this?' Her chair scraped on the floor, the sound grating against her jagged nerves. 'I don't understand you.'

'I know that. But you will have the whole of our marriage to understand me. And I'm going to understand you.' He strolled across to her and she stepped backwards, but he kept coming, backing her against the wall, planting his hands either side of her head. 'You and me, Millie.' His voice was suddenly dangerously masculine and she caught her breath because he was casting the same spell that had drawn her in right at the beginning.

'Leandro, don't—'

His hand caught her face, his gaze intense. 'I want you to stand by those promises you made to me in the church that day.'

His eyes darkened to a fierce black, as if her silence had somehow given him an answer to a question still unasked.

'Millie?'

Millie closed her eyes. She wanted to ask why he was so determined to keep the baby. Couldn't he see how that looked? Her mind was a mess—her thoughts so tangled and confused that she couldn't follow a single strand through to its conclusion. 'You can't just resurrect our marriage. We were a disaster.'

'Our communication was a disaster, that I agree.' Leandro shrugged. 'I rarely make mistakes and when I do, it's just once, so you can relax.'

She'd never felt less relaxed in her life. 'I can't be what you want me to be.'

Leandro gave a humourless laugh. 'Our communication has been so appalling up until this point, *agape mou,* I seriously doubt that you have any idea what I want from you. But this time around you will *not* be turning your back on me. And you will not be walking out when we hit a problem.'

Millie thought about what she had to offer him. *Even less than last time.* 'You want me to come back as your wife, but things have changed, Leandro. You don't know everything. Things have happened over the past year.'

'I don't want to know,' he said roughly, and she realised that he thought she was referring to another relationship.

'There are things I need to tell you.'

'Don't tell me. At least, not right now. I'm Greek, remember? I'm trying to be modern, but I have a long way to go.' With a low growl of frustration he lowered his head towards hers, the gesture an erotic reminder of everything they'd shared. For a moment his mouth hovered and he was obviously deciding whether to kiss her or not and then he lifted his head and stepped back. 'No. This time we're *not* going to let the sex do the talking. You look exhausted. Get some sleep. Just for tonight you can sleep in one of the spare bedrooms but after that you'll sleep where my wife is supposed to sleep. By my side.'

CHAPTER FOUR

'DON'T cry. Don't cry.' Crying herself, Millie held the baby against her, rocking gently as he gulped and sobbed.

She'd been lying fully dressed and wide awake on top of the bed in one of the rooms just down the corridor from the nursery when she'd heard the baby howling. Instantly she'd sprung from the bed, driven by a deep instinct that she hadn't felt before.

To begin with she'd stood back and allowed the nannies to comfort him, reminding herself that they were familiar to him, whereas she was a stranger. But after a few minutes she'd realised that they were getting nowhere and she'd taken over and dismissed them.

'Are you hungry? Is that what's wrong?' Wiping away her own tears on her sleeve, Millie lifted the baby out of the cot, feeling his sturdy body beneath her hands as she held him awkwardly. 'I haven't done this before so you'll have to tell me if I'm getting it wrong. Are you missing your mummy?' Although, from what the clinic had told her, Becca had spent precious little time with her baby.

The baby's yells increased and Millie settled herself in the chair and tentatively offered him the bottle that the nannies had left. 'Is this the right angle? I've never fed a baby before so you're going to have to yell a bit louder if I get it wrong.'

But the baby clamped his little mouth round the teat and sucked fiercely, gulping noisily as he greedily devoured the milk.

Millie gave an astonished laugh. 'You really are starving. You certainly don't take after your mother. She never ate anything.' As the baby fed, she stared down at him, examining his features with an agonising pang.

There was no escaping the fact that he had Leandro's hair. And his beautiful olive skin.

'Is he your daddy?' Speaking softly, she adjusted the angle of the bottle. 'And if he is, how do I live with that? I don't know. This is like one of those hypothetical dilemmas you talk about with your friends over a coffee. What would you do if your husband has an affair? Except maybe he didn't—I don't know. Should I really trust his word—or my sister's? Am I supposed to just overlook it? Is that what he means about being the wife of a Greek man? I'm supposed to be in the kitchen stirring a casserole while he's off having fun with his mistress?' The baby sucked rhythmically, his eyes fixed on her face. 'There's no way we can carry on where we left off, even if I wanted to. Everything has changed. Things happened to me—things he doesn't know about. He's assuming everything is the same as when I left, and it isn't.'

The baby sucked happily and Millie gave a watery smile. 'You're not giving me much help, are you? I don't know what to do. If I wasn't attractive enough to keep him the first time, it's going to be even worse this time. He doesn't know what he's taking on.' She thought about the last year and gave a despairing laugh. 'On the other hand, there's no way I'm leaving you here with him. You'll be corrupted in a month.'

One of the nannies appeared in the doorway. 'You persuaded him to take a bottle! We couldn't get him to feed. I'd really had it with him by the time I went off duty last night.' She yawned. 'I even woke Erica because she's been doing this job for twenty years and knows every trick in the book. But he wouldn't take it for her either. He's the most miserable baby we've ever looked after. Probably knows there's this big row about his parentage. His mum's dead, apparently. And sexy Leandro Demetrios is supposedly his father. Scandal, scandal, scandal.' She gave a conspiratorial giggle, and walked across the room. 'Of course, *he* won't say whether the baby is his or not, but he's taken it in, hasn't he? So that must say a lot.'

'It says that he's a responsible human being,' Millie said stiffly, concentrating on the baby and *hating* the thought that everyone was gossiping. 'Am I giving it to him too fast?'

'No. He's fine. He's not crying, is he? I much prefer toddlers. At least you have the option of sticking them in front of the television when you get fed up with them.' The nanny frowned. 'Thank goodness you've got the touch. I was expecting to get fired this morning.'

'Fired?'

The girl gave a fatalistic shrug. 'Well, Leandro Demetrios isn't exactly known as someone who accepts failure, is he? Erica and I decided in the night that if we hadn't got the baby to take the bottle by morning, both of us would be for the chop. Shame. The pay is good and the boss is gorgeous. We're trying to find excuses to be on his floor of the house in case he sleeps in the nude. So—who are you, exactly? I didn't know he was hiring anyone else.'

'I'm his wife.' The moment she'd said the words, Millie wished they could be unsaid because the girl gaped at her in astonished disbelief.

Then the drive for job security overtook her natural astonishment and she cleared her throat. 'I had no idea.' Her eyes slid from Millie's tumbling hair to her old jeans. 'God—sorry. I mean—And you're looking after his—' Her face turned scarlet but it was obvious from the look in her eyes that she thought Millie was a fool. 'We didn't know he was still married.'

'We've been apart for a while.'

'I see.' The girl's expression said, No wonder, and Millie wished she didn't mind so much. She *knew* she was an unlikely choice. Why did it still hurt so much to see the surprise in people's eyes? Why did she have to be so sensitive? Annoyed with herself for caring, she wished she were more like Leandro, who was always coolly indifferent to the opinions of everyone around him. Or failing that, she would have chosen to be more like Becca, who had been born assuming that the whole world adored her.

Would she have been more confident if she hadn't had Becca as an older sister? Or if she'd been born with Becca's blonde, perfect looks? Becca had appeared on the covers of all the high-class glossy magazines—her trademark slanting blue eyes and flirtatious expression guaranteeing the publication flew off the shelves.

'So…' The nanny looked at her curiously. 'Are the two of you back together, then?'

Were they?

The question was cheeky, but Millie had been asking herself the same thing all night. Instead of snatching some much-needed sleep, she'd locked herself in one of Leandro's many spare guest suites and lain on the bed, wondering whether she had the courage to face what was ahead of her if she agreed to his suggestion.

He'd reject her again, of course. Once he knew…

If she'd disappointed him then, how much more disappointed was he going to be this time?

But if she refused, she'd lose access to her sister's child. Her nephew.

As confused as ever, Millie carefully removed the teat from the baby's mouth. His stomach pleasantly full, he blinked his eyes and focused on her. And then he smiled. A lopsided, not very confident smile, but a smile nevertheless, and the nanny gave a short laugh.

'He's never done that before. He's never smiled at anyone. Can I have a cuddle?' She scooped the baby from Millie's arms and the baby's eyes flew wide and then his face crumpled. 'Oh, gosh, forget it.' Pulling an exasperated face, the nanny lowered the baby back into Millie's arms.

Costas immediately snuggled close and fell asleep.

The nanny rolled her eyes. 'Well, now you're stuck,' she said dryly. 'If you move, he'll wake up.'

'I don't need to move. I'll just stay here with him.'

'You're just going to sit holding him? That will get him into bad habits.'

'Since when is enjoying a cuddle a bad habit?'

'When it stops him wanting to sleep in his cot. You should put him in there and let him cry,' the nanny advised firmly. 'Let him know who's boss. It's five o'clock in the morning. Don't you want to go back to bed?'

To do what? Lie awake, thinking? Going over and over everything in her mind? She could do that here, cuddling the cause of her dilemma. 'I'm fine here.'

And she thought she *was* fine until the door opened and Leandro strode into the room.

'Oh!' The nanny flushed scarlet and gave an embarrassed laugh, the way women often did when they laid eyes on

Leandro Demetrios. Then she tweaked her uniform and smoothed her hair. Millie didn't blame her. Women did that too, didn't they? She'd tweaked her uniform and smoothed her hair every minute of every day they'd been together. The only difference being that her 'uniform' had been the designer clothes he'd bought her. Not that any of them had helped. The truth was that no amount of straightening and smoothing had transformed her into something that had looked good alongside his extraordinary looks.

Last night he'd been very much the dominant husband but this morning he was all billionaire tycoon. Smooth, sleek, expensive and indecently handsome. Everything about him shrieked of success in a realm above the reach of ordinary mortals, and Millie took one glance at the elegant dark grey suit and knew that he was off on one of his business trips.

'I need to talk to you before I leave for my meeting.' He turned and delivered a pointed glance at the nanny, who took the hint and melted away, closing the door behind her.

Millie was willing to bet she was standing outside it with her ear pressed to the wood. 'She has to go.'

In the process of looking at the baby, Leandro frowned. 'Go where?'

'Just go. The nanny. I don't want her looking after the baby.' Millie curved the baby against her and fiddled with the blanket that covered him. 'She's a gossip and her only interest in Costas is that his mother is dead and his father is a billionaire.'

'Whoever I appoint can't fail to be aware of the rumours surrounding this baby.'

'I agree, but she showed no warmth or care towards him. And she doesn't even *like* babies—she said she prefers them older. And even then she just sticks them in front of the television.'

'Fine.' He glanced at his watch. 'You want me to fire her, I'll fire her.'

'No. I'll do it,' Millie said firmly, and he lifted his eyebrows.

'*You?*'

'Yes.'

Leandro gave a disbelieving laugh. 'I'm seeing a totally different side to you today. I wouldn't have thought you were capable of firing someone.'

'It depends on the provocation. I'm thinking of Costas and what he needs. He doesn't need someone who is going to think about his parentage all the time. He needs someone who *likes* him.' She scanned Leandro's immaculate appearance. 'It's five in the morning. I can't believe you have a meeting at this hour.'

'I have a breakfast meeting at my offices in Paris. My pilot is waiting.'

'Of course he is.' Millie gave a weary smile. Other people queued for a bus. Leandro had a pilot waiting for his instructions. It was a reminder of how different their lives were. His house contained a pool, a spa, a media room and an underground garage complete with car lift, and *everything* was automated.

Millie thought of the tiny flat she'd been renting since she'd walked out a year earlier. If she wanted light, she had to press a switch, and even then it didn't always work because the electrics were so dodgy.

Leandro was frowning impatiently. 'Why was the baby crying?'

'I don't know. He hasn't had a good night. And neither of the nannies you appointed could get him to take the bottle. And having met one of them, I'm not surprised.'

'They have impressive references.'

'From whom?' Millie put the empty bottle down. 'Not the babies they looked after, I'm sure.'

His eyes narrowed. 'Delivering smart remarks seems to have become a new hobby of yours.'

Realising that for once she hadn't felt too intimidated to say what she thought, Millie gave a little smile. 'It wasn't a smart remark. It was the truth. I'm simply pointing out that what pleases a mother or an agency might not please a baby. This nursery is immaculate—everything in order—but they obviously haven't done anything to build a relationship with Costas.' She curved her nephew closer, lowering her voice. 'He was very upset. But he's settled down now. I think he was hungry.'

'The nannies weren't capable of giving him a bottle?'

'He wouldn't take it from them.'

'He seems to be taking it from you.'

'Perhaps he knows I'm on his side.'

'Perhaps.' He gave her a curious look, watching her with the baby, and she looked at him questioningly.

'Why are you staring? Do you want to hold him or something?'

'Not at the moment.'

'Of course. Sorry.' Millie flushed. 'I'm sure your suit cost a fortune. Baby sick on designer menswear isn't a good look.'

Leandro strolled over to her. 'I have more important things to worry about than the state of my suit. I do, however, care about disturbing an otherwise contented baby when I want a conversation. He's clearly comfortable with you at the moment and I'm wise enough to leave him where he is. If I take him, he'll protest, and neither of us will be able to talk.'

As if to signify his agreement, Costas nestled close to her, practised his smile again and then his eyes drifted shut.

Millie felt a warm feeling pass through her and a fierce stab of protectiveness.

'There's nothing to talk about. You're not the right man to look after a baby. You spent the first thirty-two years of your life avoiding babies. He needs someone who is going to forget the questions about his parentage and just love him.'

'And that's you?' Leandro studied her for a moment, incredulity lighting his dark eyes. 'Unless I'm misreading your extraordinarily expressive face, you still believe this baby to be the child of your husband and his lover.'

'That isn't relevant.'

'Most people would consider it relevant, Millie.' With a sardonic lift of his eyebrow, he studied her and then shrugged. 'Make whatever decisions you like about hiring and firing,' he said smoothly. 'Appoint whoever you want, but I do want him to have a nanny. You can care for him if you're willing to do that, but not at the expense of our relationship.'

Millie licked her lips. 'We still have to talk about that part.'

'Then talk. You had plenty to say for yourself a moment ago so don't expect me to believe you're suddenly short of opinions.' Leandro glanced at the Rolex on his wrist. 'Are you staying or going?'

It was her turn to look incredulous. 'How can you be so emotionally detached about the whole thing? This is our *marriage* you're talking about, not a corporate takeover. But I get the feeling I'm just another task on your ridiculously long "action" list! "Find out if Millie is staying or going."' She mimicked his voice. '"Tick that box."'

He gave a faint smile. 'You've changed.'

'Well, I'm sorry, but—'

'Don't apologise,' he drawled. 'I like it. If you're going to speak your mind, I might have a chance of knowing what's going on inside it. Why didn't you ever do this before?'

'Because you're scary.'

Leandro sucked in a breath and looked at her in genuine amazement. 'Scary? What do you mean, *scary?* I have never threatened you in any way.'

'It's not what you say or what you do, it's just who you are—' She broke off. 'I don't know. It isn't easy to describe. But next time you're being really scary I'll point it out.'

'Thank you.' The irony in his tone wasn't lost on her and she looked up at him, wishing he wasn't so insanely good-looking. Every time she looked at him she lost the thread of the conversation. It made it worse that she knew exactly what was underneath that sleek designer suit.

'All right. Let's get this over with. You want to know my decision, but it isn't that easy.' She glanced down at Costas, now sleeping quietly in her arms. 'I need some time to think about it.'

He leaned against the wall, tall handsome and breathtakingly confident. 'I've given you time.'

'I want *more* time.'

'You're my wife. What is there to think about?'

Millie adjusted the blanket. 'Whether or not it can work.'

'If you come back to this marriage expecting us to fall at the first fence, we'll fall.'

Millie thought about what he didn't know. 'Things have changed, Leandro.'

'Good. They needed to change.' He studied her thoughtfully, his gaze sharp. 'Did you find me scary in bed?'

'Sorry?' Her face burned but he refused to let her look away.

'You said you found me scary,' he said quietly, 'and I'm asking you if I scared you in bed. You weren't experienced, were you? And things grew pretty intense between us, pretty quickly. Was that part of the problem?'

Embarrassed by the images his words created, Millie looked down at the baby. 'We shouldn't be talking about this in front of him!'

'He's three months old,' Leandro said dryly. 'I don't feel the need to censor my conversation just yet. Answer my question. Did I scare you?'

'No.' What was it about him that made her body react like this? Her nipples were hard, pressing against her lace bra as if inviting his attention. 'You didn't scare me.'

'But you were shocked.'

Millie wished there was a drink nearby. Her mouth was suddenly as dry as the desert in a drought. 'I was a bit self-conscious.'

'Why?'

Because she hadn't been able to throw off the feeling that he must be comparing her to the beautiful women he usually dated. 'I don't know—you were just very bold and confident, I suppose. You didn't care if it was the middle of the day. And there was that time in your office—'

'Sex isn't restricted to the bedroom at night time.'

'I know—but in the dark I could have been anyone.'

'Which is why I like daylight.' Leandro let out a long breath, his exasperation obvious. 'This isn't good enough for me, Millie. You're saying that you'll think about it, but you obviously don't believe it's going to last. That doesn't work for me. I want your total commitment to making our marriage work.' His eyes were hard and she gave a sigh.

'All right, you told me to tell you when you were doing it and you're doing it now,' she croaked. 'You're being scary.'

He muttered something in Greek under his breath. 'Are

you sure "scary" isn't just a word you apply to a situation that isn't to your liking?'

'No. It's a word I apply to you. It's what you are when something doesn't meet with your approval. You're so used to getting your own way, you don't know how to compromise.'

Leandro looked startled. 'I am perfectly able to compromise.'

'What if you're the one who wants a divorce?'

'We weren't talking about divorce,' Leandro said silkily, 'we were talking about marriage.'

Millie stared down at the baby, finding the thought of marriage to Leandro quite impossibly daunting. Marriage meant bed and bed meant he'd find out…

How would he handle it? Would he turn away with revulsion? Or would he feel sorry for her and try and pretend he didn't care? Could men pretend? No, it was a physical thing—there would be no pretending.

'There will be no divorce,' he said firmly. 'Neither will there be any more turning your back on me. Or piling up resentment in your head and not telling me why you're glaring at me. This time, if something isn't working for you, I want to know why.' He was hard and uncompromising and she felt her heart lurch because she knew that he was going to be the one who stumbled this time.

And perhaps she wasn't being fair to him, not telling him the truth about what had happened since they'd last met.

But she just couldn't. Not yet.

He'd find out soon enough. And his reaction would decide the future of their marriage. And Costas's future.

Millie stared down at the baby, wishing she was young enough to have someone make her decisions for her. 'I'll think about it today.'

'I want my wife back, Millie. In every sense of the word.' His gaze was hard and direct. 'No more headaches, no more "too tired".'

'What if I *am* too tired?'

'I'll wake you up.' Leandro's eyes gleamed dark with sexual intent. 'I was very patient and gentle with you last time because I knew how inexperienced you were and I didn't want to rush you. It was a mistake. A woman is never too tired for good sex. There was something else going on and I should have pushed you to tell me what it was.'

Millie's stomach cramped and the rush of heat in her pelvis shocked her. 'What are you saying? That this time you're not going to be patient or gentle?'

'That's right,' he said silkily, 'I'm not. This time we're going to have an adult sexual relationship. I look forward to introducing you to the pleasures of truly uninhibited sex. In full daylight.'

Her face turned scarlet. 'You're trying to shock me.'

'No. But neither am I trying *not* to shock you, as I did before.' His eyes lingered on her mouth. 'You're a very sexual woman but we barely explored the surface the first time round. This time, it's going to be different.'

'It might not be! Perhaps I won't find you attractive any more!' The moment she said the words she realised how ridiculous they sounded and he obviously agreed because an ironic smile played around his mouth.

'Do you want me to explore that statement further?'

'No.' Millie was grateful that she was holding the baby. 'I don't. I don't want to talk about it at all.'

'Well, tough, because from now on no subject is off limits.' His mobile phone buzzed insistently and Leandro retrieved it from his pocket, registered the caller's name and then looked at her face. 'What?'

'If I come back, I want you to switch off your phone when you're with us,' she said stiffly, 'otherwise Costas will grow up feeling second best to a mobile network.'

Leandro gave her a long look and then rejected the call with an exaggerated stab of his finger. 'Satisfied?'

Millie nodded, although she had no expectations that it would last. She really didn't need to worry about saying yes to coming back, Millie thought bleakly, because he'd be working all the time. He always did. She'd barely see him.

'I have one rule for our relationship,' he purred, dropping the phone back into his pocket. 'Just one.'

'Go on.'

'No matter what happens—you don't run off. You don't walk away from this marriage. You stay, no matter what.'

Millie licked her lips. 'What if you're the one who wants to run?'

'That isn't going to happen.'

'It might do.' She thought about everything that had happened to her and felt a lurch of unease. If things had been bad before, how much worse were they going to be this time around?

She was dreading the moment when he discovered the truth about what had happened to her.

Leandro wasn't a man to couch his true feelings under a soft blanket of political correctness or sensitivity, was he? He'd say what he thought.

And she knew what he was going to think.

And it would be like hammering nails into raw flesh.

Millie rocked the baby, afraid that her emotional turbulence might somehow communicate itself to the sleeping child and disturb him.

'I'll allow you the rest of the day to think it over.' Having delivered what he obviously considered to be a considerable compromise, Leandro strolled towards the door. 'I have a meeting in Paris. Feel free to fire the nanny and choose someone else. I will be back by tonight and you will give me the answer I want to hear. And after that I will be switching off my mobile phone. And if you feel even a flicker of a headache, I suggest you take a painkiller because I won't be allowing that as a valid excuse.'

CHAPTER FIVE

Why had he allowed her time to think it over?

Surrounded by a room full of lawyers, Leandro drove the meeting at a furious pace, determined to close the deal that had been the main focus of his attention for six months. But he was aware that the timing was bad.

His mind on Millie, he was impatient to return to London. He didn't trust her not to vanish, taking the child with her.

What evidence did he have that she was committed to their marriage? To the baby?

None.

On edge and impatient, he pushed through the agenda with supersonic speed, issuing orders, obtaining clarification on points he considered important, and ignoring issues that he considered irrelevant.

Having condensed what should have been an all-day meeting into a few intense hours, he rose to his feet and paced over to the window that ran from floor to ceiling along one side of the spectacular boardroom that dominated his Paris office. 'We're done here. Finish off. If you have any questions, you can speak to my team in London.'

The lawyer in charge of the deal picked up the thick pile

of papers that had formed the focus of the discussion. 'I wish everyone was as decisive as you. Clearly the abysmal state of the markets isn't keeping you awake at night.'

'No.' Something else was responsible for that. *His personal life.*

The man snapped his briefcase closed. 'I must congratulate you, Mr Demetrios. You have a quite startling ability to predict and understand human behaviour. Somehow you have still managed to make quite extraordinary profits even though the markets are collapsing around you. You anticipated the shift in the market before there were any outward signs. Stock in the Demetrios Corporation actually rose yesterday and yet market conditions have never been more challenging.'

'One person's challenge is another person's opportunity.' Distracted, Leandro kept his eyes fixed on the Paris skyline, his mind on his fragile marriage. *Was he mad, trying to save it?* Or was it like rare china dropped onto concrete? Shattered beyond repair.

In the past twenty-four hours he'd learned how little he knew about Millie.

Either that, or she'd changed. She was more…assertive. Or maybe she'd always been like that and he hadn't looked closely enough. Certainly there were plenty of aspects to her personality that he hadn't seen.

Leandro frowned. Had she really found him scary?

'Speculation about the parentage of the baby doesn't seem to have had an adverse effect on the price of your stock.' The voice of the lawyer broke into his thoughts and Leandro stilled.

'Our business is concluded for the day,' he said coldly. 'My assistant will show you out.'

Aware that he'd committed a gross error of judgement in

mentioning something so personal, the man turned scarlet and stammered an apology but Leandro didn't turn.

Perhaps he couldn't blame Millie for believing the worst of him, he thought grimly, *when the rest of the world was thinking it alongside her.*

His reputation had always been a matter of supreme indifference to him, but he was starting to realise that it was now coming back to bite him.

The lawyers rose, like a room full of children drilled in classroom etiquette, almost comical in their desperation to absent themselves.

Once the room was empty Leandro rolled his shoulders, trying to relieve the tension. He prowled the length of the boardroom, gazing through the floor-to-ceiling plate-glass window that allowed him to enjoy a view of the Seine as it snaked through the city.

A sense of foreboding came over him. He really shouldn't have left her.

He ran his hand over the back of his neck and withdrew his phone from his pocket. He'd speak to her—tell her that he'd be home in the next few hours. They'd spend some time together.

Tapping his foot, he waited for someone to answer.

And it was a long wait.

When the housekeeper finally answered the phone and informed him that both his wife and the baby had gone out, his tension levels increased tenfold. When he was told they'd gone out without a driver or a member of his security staff, Leandro abandoned thoughts of work for the rest of the day and ordered his car to be brought round to the front of the building.

She'd left.

She'd run again.

What had he expected?

'An astonishing ability to predict and understand human behaviour'—wasn't that what the lawyer had said?

Leandro gave a humourless laugh. Where had that ability been when it had come to understanding his own wife? If he'd studied her as closely as he studied the stock markets and company portfolios, he would never have left London.

At every turn, she surprised him. He hadn't expected her to show up at the house, he certainly hadn't expected her to offer to care for her sister's baby. And as for their relationship, he'd made a number of assumptions—assumptions he was now beginning to question. Her humble confession that she was 'ordinary' had revealed a depth of insecurity that he'd been unaware of. And the fact that he'd been unaware of it made him realise just how little he knew of her.

But he intended to rectify that.

If he wasn't already too late.

'Do you like this one? Shake it and it plays a tune, touch this bit and it's soft and furry, this bit is rough.' Millie held the toy over the pram. 'And you can chew the rings on the end. The book says you're going to want to start chewing fairly soon.'

Baby Costas gurgled quietly to himself and Millie leaned over and gently tucked the blanket more firmly around him. 'I suppose we'd better be getting back. I need the rest of the afternoon to get ready. Believe me, it takes me that long to look even vaguely presentable. And even then I won't look good enough for Leandro. If I'm going to tell him that I'll stay married to him, I need to look the part. Don't pull that face at me.' She smiled down at him. 'You try being married to someone who looks like him. It's hard work, trust me. Especially when you start off with a face and body like mine.

Come on—I'll just pay for these and then we'll wander home.'

She put the toy down on top of the pram. On impulse she added a little outfit that caught her eye. Then she made her way across the shop to pay. Standing in the queue, she stared down at Costas, automatically searching for a resemblance to Leandro.

'Oh, my—just take a look at that.' The girl in front of her in the queue gave a wistful sigh. 'What are the chances of my losing ten kilos in the next five seconds?'

'Forget it. Your best bet is to hope he likes curvy women,' her friend said gloomily, pulling in her rounded tummy.

'His type always go for the skinny sort.'

'With blonde hair.'

'*Straight,* long blonde hair.'

'He is truly spectacular. If I had him in my bed I might actually decide that sex was a more attractive option than sleep.'

'He's coming this way.'

'I'd give a million pounds just to be kissed by him once.'

Sensing the shift in the atmosphere and interested to know what kind of man could induce such enthusiasm among the members of her sex, Millie glanced up idly and saw Leandro striding purposefully across the store. Like a lion wandering into the middle of a herd of gazelle, the women all stared at him, transfixed.

Millie gave a whimper of horror. What was he doing here? Wasn't he supposed to be in Paris? She hadn't expected him to return to the house until dinnertime at the earliest. When they'd been together before, he'd frequently missed dinner, working late into the evening. But here he was, in the middle of the afternoon, clearly looking for her.

How had he known she was here?

Aware that any moment now he was going to spot her and

even more aware that she'd spent absolutely *no* time on herself since he'd last seen her, Millie slid out of the queue, turned her back and walked quickly towards the door.

The thought of him seeing her when she wasn't prepared filled her with horror. Even the 'natural' look took her hours to achieve.

Furtively she glanced over her shoulder, taking a roundabout route via cots and prams so that he'd be less likely to notice her. She didn't want him to see her like this.

She'd planned to spend the rest of the afternoon getting ready to face him. *Ready to give him her answer.* True, her outward appearance wasn't going to make any difference at all to the eventual outcome of their relationship, but she knew she'd have more confidence with him if she was at least looking her best on the outside.

Another glance over her shoulder showed him frowning around the shop and Millie melted quietly out of the door, pondering on the fact that to be so ordinary as to be unnoticeable could be a blessing. In this instance, it had worked to her advantage, but once in a while it would be nice to be so beautiful that every man in the shop was staring at her.

Except that she didn't want every man in the shop, did she? She just wanted Leandro.

A hand closed over her shoulder. 'Excuse me, madam. I have reason to believe you're in possession of goods you haven't paid for.'

Millie froze. Several people passing turned to stare and she felt the hot singe of mortification darken her cheeks as she noticed the items she'd selected still sitting on top of the baby's pram. 'Oh, no.' She turned and looked at the uniformed security guard. 'I'm so sorry. I—I completely forgot that I'd picked them up.'

'Don't waste your time thinking up excuses.' The security guard's expression warned her that he was no soft touch. 'I've been watching you for a few minutes. You were behaving in an extremely suspicious manner. Instead of taking a direct route to the door, you took a roundabout route, ducking down and quite obviously trying not to be seen.'

'I *was* trying not to be seen,' Millie said quickly and saw his expression harden. 'I—I don't mean by you. I was...' Realising how much trouble she was in, she pressed her fingers to her forehead and the security guard's mouth tightened.

'We have a very strict policy about prosecuting shoplifters. I'd like you to come with me.'

'I'm not a shoplifter!' Her tone urgent, Millie put her hand on his arm, affronted that he'd think that of her. 'It was a genuine mistake.'

He withdrew his arm pointedly. 'If you just come back into the store, madam, you can explain it to the police.'

'No!' Millie was aware of the crowd gathering and wanted to disappear into a big hole in the ground. *Why was it,* she wondered desperately, *that people were so fascinated by other people's misfortunes?* What pleasure did they gain from standing around, staring? Not one of them had stepped in to support or defend her. She was on her own. 'You don't understand.' She licked her lips and tried one more time. 'This was an oversight, nothing more. I saw something—someone—'

'She saw me.' The deep masculine voice came from behind her and Millie suppressed a groan. She didn't need to look to know who it was. So much for not drawing attention to herself.

Great. Now her humiliation was complete. Not only was she looking a complete mess but she'd been behaving like a criminal.

'You know this lady?' The security guard squared his shoulders. 'She walked out without paying, sir.'

'And I'm afraid I take the blame for that.' Leandro's tone was a mixture of apology and smooth charm. 'She was up in the night with the baby. I'd given her strict instructions to rest today and not leave the house. Do you have children…' his gaze flickered to the man's identity badge '…Peter?'

'Two,' the man said stiffly. 'Boys.'

Leandro smiled his most charismatic smile. 'And I'm sure they've given you a few sleepless nights in their time.'

'You could say that.' Under Leandro's warm, encouraging gaze, the man relaxed slightly. 'There were days when the wife walked around in a coma. I remember she left the bath running one morning and flooded the entire house.'

'It's unbelievable that something as apparently small and innocent as a baby can cause so much disruption,' Leandro purred sympathetically. 'And unbelievable what sleep deprivation can do, Peter.' Having personalised the conversation, he put a hand on Millie's shoulder and kissed the top of her head. 'This is *all* my fault. Tonight, *agape mou,* I will take my turn with the baby and you will catch up on some sleep.'

There was a collective sigh among the crowd and the security guard looked undecided.

'I still have to take her back inside and call the police. That's my job.'

Millie opened her mouth to defend herself again but Leandro brought his mouth down on hers in a gentle but determined kiss that effectively silenced her. It only lasted seconds but when he lifted his head she was too flustered to do anything except gape at him.

He gave her a smile and pulled her into the protective circle of his arm, taking control of the situation. 'I understand that it isn't part of your job description to make individual judgements so I'm more than happy to be the one to present the details to the manager of the store and the police. I'm sure they'll understand. And perhaps we could talk to the local paper.' Leandro's voice was smooth as polished marble. 'It's ridiculous that you aren't allowed to exercise judgement on individual cases like this one. You should be allowed to take responsibility for your decisions.'

The man straightened his shoulders. 'In some circumstances I can make my own decisions, of course, it's just that—'

'You can?' Leandro looked impressed. 'Then it's lucky for us that *you* were the one on duty today. Someone as experienced as yourself will be able to tell the difference between a genuine mistake committed in a state of exhaustion and an attempt to steal.'

The security man flushed under the attention and then gave a nod. 'If you'll just take your purchases to the till, sir, I'll report to my superiors that this was all a genuine misunderstanding.'

'You're more than generous,' Leandro murmured, lifting the items from the top of the pram and glancing at Millie. 'This is all that you wanted, *agape mou?*'

Swamped with humiliation, still stunned that the brief kiss had affected her so much, Millie nodded mutely and stood there, clutching the pram for support while Leandro strode back inside the store with the security guard.

'Don't worry, love,' one of the women said to her, 'I was the same when my Kevin was born. Didn't get a wink of sleep for two years. I was so tired that I once found my car keys in the washing machine. At least you've got a gorgeous man willing to chip in. Mine didn't lift a finger for the first seven years of their lives. Now, if I'm lucky, he'll kick a football with them.'

Millie moved her lips to reply but she could still feel Leandro's mouth on hers, the latent sensuality in that brief kiss enough to have reawakened something she'd tried desperately hard to bury.

Nothing had changed, she thought helplessly. He still had the ability to turn her to a quivering wreck. Only this time things were a thousand times worse, her insecurities a thousand times deeper.

Leandro appeared by her side. He shot her a questioning look and then gave a knowing smile that indicated that he knew exactly why she was looking so dazed. Without comment, he handed her a bag and then guided her down the paved street towards the main road.

Desperate to escape from what felt like a hundred pairs of eyes, Millie stared straight ahead and then saw a burly man standing next to a sleek black Mercedes.

He sprang to attention as Leandro strode towards him and opened the rear door with military efficiency. 'If you take the baby, sir, I'll deal with the pram.'

Reluctant to be trapped with Leandro in a confined space, Millie stopped dead on the pavement but the firm pressure of Leandro's hand urged her towards the car. 'Inside, now,' he ordered, 'before you draw any more attention to yourself.'

'Does everyone always do exactly as you tell them?' Arching her back to free herself of his lingering touch, she stumbled into the warm cocoon of leather and luxury, shockingly aware of him. He slid in after her, holding the baby safely in the crook of his arm.

Only then did Millie notice the baby car seat.

With surprising gentleness, Leandro laid the baby in the car seat and strapped him in carefully. Then he sat down next to her, the length of his hard thigh brushing against hers.

The driver slid into the car, locked the doors and then pulled into the stream of traffic.

Millie shifted sideways in her seat. 'I wasn't expecting you back so soon.'

'Is that a complaint?'

'More of an observation. Since when did you work half-days?'

His eyebrow lifted in mockery. 'Since you made the rules.'

'I said it would be nice if you were home at some point before the middle of the night,' Millie muttered, stifled by how near he was, 'not halfway through the afternoon.'

'Is this going to be one of those conversations that a man can't possibly win?'

She flushed, realising that she sounded completely unreasonable. 'You shouldn't have kissed me in front of all those people. Why did you do that?'

'To stop you saying something that would have landed you in even more trouble. Every time you opened that mouth of yours, you dug a deeper hole in which to fall.' Leandro's gaze cool and assessing. '*What* did you think you were doing?'

'I—I wasn't thinking. I'm sorry I embarrassed you. I just forgot to pay.'

'I'm not talking about the shoplifting episode, I'm talking about the fact that you were walking around central London on your own.'

'I was shopping for the baby.'

'You left the house without telling anyone.'

'I didn't know I was *supposed* to tell anyone. You told me I could go shopping.'

His jaw tensed. 'I assumed you would have called your driver.'

Millie blinked. 'I have a driver?'

'Of course.'

'But I didn't want to go in the car. I wanted to walk,' she muttered. 'All the books say that babies like fresh air. And I needed the fresh air too. I wanted to think.'

'You didn't appear to be doing much thinking when you walked out of the shop without paying,' he said caustically, and she flushed.

'I walked out because I saw you. You flustered me.'

'I *flustered* you?' His eyes gleamed with sardonic humour. 'Exactly what made you "flustered"?'

'You did. Flustering everyone around you is what you do best.'

Leandro removed his tie and leaned back in his seat, a faint smile touching his mouth. 'I can see that I have a grossly inflated opinion of myself. So far, in our new spirit of honesty, I've discovered that I'm scary, intimidating and that I fluster you. I'm beginning to understand why you left. Who in their right mind would stay married to such an ogre?'

Remembering the circumstances of her departure, Millie glanced sideways at him only to find him watching her— *reading her with almost embarrassing ease.*

'Our problems started before that day,' he observed softly, and she didn't deny it.

'Our problems started the day I married you.'

'No. Our honeymoon was wonderful. The day we returned from our honeymoon. And I'm still trying to work out why.' A muscle flickered in his jaw. 'Did I change?'

'Yes.' Millie frowned. 'Or perhaps you didn't. Perhaps you were just being you. I just didn't know you that well. Once you were back in working mode, our relationship took a back seat to your business.'

'Just for the record, were there any parts of my behaviour that met with your approval?'

'I like the fact that you're confident.'

'Confidence is acceptable?'

She ignored the irony in his tone. 'As long as you're not so confident you make me feel like a waste of space.' Seeing one of his eyebrows lift, she gave an awkward shrug. 'When I can see you grinding your teeth and thinking, idiot, just because someone isn't as quick or as decisive as you, I *don't* like it.' Millie hesitated, naturally honest. 'But I can see why I annoyed you. I had no idea how to behave in your world.'

'You make it sound as if we are occupying parallel universes.' Leandro's lazy drawl was in direct contrast to his sharp, assessing gaze. 'I was under the impression that my world, as you call it, comes something close to female nirvana. You had access to unlimited funds and a lifestyle most people dream about.'

'Well, that's the thing about dreams, isn't it? They don't always turn out so well in reality. All the money in the world didn't save our marriage, did it?' Millie found it hard to think about that time. She turned to stare out of the window, trying not to think of how ecstatically happy she'd been. 'It wasn't real, was it? Those early days when we first met—it was like living in a bubble. We got married in a hurry without thinking through what we both wanted.'

'I knew what I wanted. I thought you did, too.'

'I suppose I didn't know what it was all going to involve.'

'Did it occur to you to talk to me about how you were feeling?'

'When?' Millie looked at him. 'You were always working. And when you weren't—well, you weren't that approachable. You were stern—'

'And intimidating—yes, I got that message.' Leandro seemed unusually tense. 'Just for the record, I had no idea you found me intimidating,' he said gruffly. 'Is that why you scurried out of the shop like a fugitive when you saw me arrive?'

'Partly. I wasn't expecting to see you.'

'You need notice?'

Millie touched her jeans self-consciously. 'I would have dressed up.'

His gaze slid down her body. 'You have fantastic legs. You look sexy in those jeans.'

Her heart danced. 'I—I thought you'd prefer me in a dress.' *And she didn't wear dresses any more.*

'You look sexy in everything. And nothing.' His velvety remark brought a blush to her cheeks and she felt slightly sick because she knew something that he didn't.

'What were you doing in the shop, anyway?'

'Looking for you.'

'Why not just wait for me in the house?'

Leandro drew in a breath. 'I had no reason to believe you'd be returning to the house.'

'You thought I'd run?'

'Yes.' He was characteristically direct. 'Do you blame me? It's what you did the last time. It's understandable that I'd be concerned that you won't do it again. Maybe it's time I introduced a little gentle bondage into our relationship,' he said softly. 'You were so innocent when I met you, I never did introduce you to the possibilities of velvet handcuffs. They might come in useful.'

A disturbingly erotic vision played across her brain and Millie felt the slow burn of awareness inside her. Everything she knew about sex, she'd learned from him. *And he was a master.* 'I'm not innocent any more. You took care of that.'

'We'd barely begun, *agape mou*.' Leandro relaxed in his seat, a dangerous smile playing around his mouth. 'But things will be different this time. This time we're going to talk.' He studied her, his dark eyes resting on her curling hair and then sliding to her faded jeans and her scuffed trainers. 'Today you look exactly the way you looked when I first met you.'

That bad?

Millie opened her mouth to apologise and then stopped herself. She'd spent a year trying to accept the way she was and she wasn't going to let him undo all that good work. She wasn't going to let being with him hammer holes in her confidence.

Self-conscious, she lifted a hand to her hair and then let it drop because she knew that it was going to take far more than a few tweaks of her fingers to turn her into a svelte groomed version of herself. She didn't need a mirror to know that her hair was curling wildly, falling past her shoulders in ecstatic disarray, as if relieved to have been given a break from her endless attempts to tame it.

It was a good job he worked so hard, she thought, biting back a hysterical laugh. It had taken her almost an entire day to tame her hair into the sleek, groomed look, apply her make-up, choose the right outfit.

'I'm dressed like this because I was shopping with the baby,' she said defensively. 'I wasn't expecting to see you.'

'It's lucky for you I found you...' Leandro stroked his fingers down the back of her neck '...or you'd currently be trying to talk your way out of shoplifting charges.'

'How *did* you find me?'

'My security team have inserted a tracking device into Costas's pram.'

'They *what?*' Millie looked at him in astonishment. 'Are you mad?'

'No, I'm security conscious. Which is more than you are.' Leandro's mouth tightened. '*Maledizione,* do you ever *think,* Millie? You are my wife. And you're walking around the streets pushing this baby in his pram. This baby with whom the whole world appears obsessed.'

'They're waiting for you to admit or deny that you're the father.' Her gaze settled on his but he held that gaze, as if challenging her to doubt him.

'Then they're going to be waiting a long time because I will never feel obliged to explain myself to strangers. I'm surprised you left the house with him. Why weren't you mobbed by journalists?'

'Because I sent the new nanny out earlier with a decoy pram.'

'A *decoy* pram?'

'Yes. After you left I rang the agency and they sent someone round straight away. I really liked her. We talked about the problem and decided that it wasn't fair for Costas to be housebound because of these people. So I suggested she leave the house with a doll in a pram. That's what she did. And she walked fast and kept her head down, like someone with something to hide. And they all followed her. Poor girl.' Still feeling guilty about that, Millie pulled a face. 'But I think she'll be all right. She's very down-to-earth.'

Leandro leaned his head back and laughed. 'I've *definitely* underestimated you. Nevertheless, it has to stop. There are people out there who would use you and the baby to get to me.'

Millie felt as though her stomach had been dropped off the side of a cliff. 'They'd kidnap the baby?'

'I don't want to frighten you. I receive threats occasionally—it comes with the territory,' he said carefully, 'and it's the job of my security team to work with the police to assess the risk. From now on I want you to take basic precautions.'

Instinctively, Millie put a hand on Costas's car seat and looked nervously out of the window.

'He will be fine.' Leandro leaned his head against the seat and closed his eyes, apparently undisturbed by the serious topic of the discussion. 'The car is bulletproof and my chauffeur is an expert in defensive driving.'

'*What?* You think someone's going to shoot at us? This gets worse and worse.' Millie was rigid on the edge of her seat, wondering how he could relax there with his eyes shut. 'And you think we live in the same world? Where I come from I don't need an armed guard to go to the supermarket.'

He didn't open his eyes. 'If going to the supermarket forms a high point in your day, I will arrange for them to open early for you. That way you can shop without a security hassle.'

Millie gave a choked laugh. 'You mean I can have first pick of the food.'

'If that's what you want. I would have thought scouring the shelves of the supermarket is an overrated pastime,' he murmured, 'but I've never claimed to understand women. From now on I want you to discuss your itinerary with Angelo and he will do whatever needs to be done to ensure your safety.'

'Who is Angelo?'

'The security guard that my team has selected for you. He's ex-special forces.'

'So he's going to abseil down the side of the house every morning in a black ski mask and bring me breakfast in bed?' Her caustic remark drew a wolfish smile from him and his eyes finally opened, like a predator who has discovered that there is something worth waking up for.

'No, *agape mou*. If he goes anywhere near your bedroom, he's fired. When you're naked between the sheets, I'll do the protecting.'

Trapped by the molten sexuality in his dark eyes, Millie felt her heart pound and her stomach tumble. Breathless, she dragged her eyes from his, only to find her gaze trapped by the hint of dark body hair visible at the base of his bronzed throat. Looking away from that had her noticing the width of his shoulders and in the end she just closed her eyes because the only way not to want him was not to look. And even then the delicious curl of awareness that warmed her belly didn't fade. *Help,* she thought desperately. Leandro possessed monumental sex appeal, and he knew it.

'Leandro.' Her voice was a croak of denial. 'It's been a year…'

'I know exactly how long it's been,' he purred softly, and Millie glanced at him and then immediately looked away, shaken by the look of sexual intent in his eyes.

'I don't know why you want me back,' she muttered, and he gave a soft laugh.

'You're my wife, Millie. And I expect my wife to stand by my side, no matter what.'

No matter what.

What was that supposed to mean? That she was supposed to overlook his affairs? *Was that what he was saying?*

Her stomach churned and the sick feeling rushed towards her, the same feeling she'd had when she'd seen him with her sister.

He was expecting her to spend a lifetime overlooking the fact that he had other women. Looking the other way while he took another woman to his bed. And she knew that every time she thought he was with someone else, a little piece of her would die.

Millie stared straight ahead, her expression blank.

What self-respecting woman would say yes to those terms?

CHAPTER SIX

'I'M JUST not like that. He might be my husband, but that doesn't give him the right to walk all over me. I'm not going to let him hurt me a second time.' Millie stuffed baby clothes into a holdall. 'That would make me stupid, wouldn't it?'

The baby cooed and kicked his legs.

'We're just *wrong* for each other. Why can't he see that? There's no point in me trying to talk to him about this because he's good with words and I'm not. With any luck he won't follow me. He didn't follow me the first time and I can't believe he wants a baby cramping his lifestyle.' Millie thought about the actress and then wished she hadn't. 'It isn't easy being married to a man every woman in the world wants. Unless you're the woman every man in the world wants. And I'm not.' Dwelling on that dismal thought, she closed the bag.

'"*I expect my wife to stand by my side no matter what.*" Obviously I'm expected to watch while he smiles at models and actresses.' She stowed the bag under the cot out of sight. 'Well, I can't do that. I've spent a year trying to get over him. I'm not putting myself through that again.'

'What are you not putting yourself through again?' Leandro stood in the doorway and Millie jumped.

'B-being chased by j-journalists,' she stammered. Her heart thumping, smothered with guilt, she scooped Costas up in her arms and then faced Leandro.

He was dressed in black jeans and a casual shirt and he looked every bit as sexy as he did in a suit.

No wonder she hadn't been able to hold him, she thought miserably. He was stunning.

She'd be doing him a favour by leaving.

He didn't want her and he didn't want a baby.

He wanted a life.

Clearly undisturbed by her emotional turbulence, Costas fell asleep on her shoulder and Leandro gave a faint smile.

'Someone is tired. Put him to bed and come and eat. We need to make plans.'

It obviously hadn't occurred to him that she might refuse.

Faced with no alternative, Millie followed him to the dining room, but she was too nervous to eat and too nervous to talk. Pushing the food around her plate, her mind explored the safest route and means of transport.

Leandro lounged across from her, relaxed and watchful, as if he was trying to get inside her head.

Millie was frantically searching for reasons not to share his bed when a member of staff approached him and delivered a message.

His mouth tightening, Leandro stood up and dropped his napkin on the table. 'I apologise. This is one call I have to take. After this there will be no more, I promise.'

'Don't worry about it. I'll go and check on Costas.' Almost weak with relief, Millie seized on the excuse to go and hide away with the baby. Maybe she should leave now, except that it was too late in the day and the trains would soon stop running.

No, it had to be tomorrow. But early.

Exhausted after the events of the past few days, she lay down on the bed in Costas's room and immediately fell asleep.

Leandro opened the door of the baby's room, his mouth tightening as he saw Millie asleep on the bed. Her hair was loose and tangled, her cheeks prettily flushed and her body curled up, very much like the baby who slept in the cot next to her.

She was avoiding sex again, he thought grimly. The obvious reason was that she hadn't forgiven him for his 'affair' with her sister, but Leandro knew that their problems went much deeper than that. She'd been avoiding sex long before the 'pool incident' as he now called it.

But whatever the reason, in the end she'd walked out. To him, that was an unpardonable sin that nothing could excuse.

Cold fingers of the past slid over his shoulder and he shrugged them away, refusing to dwell anywhere other than the present. That was what he did, wasn't it? He moved forwards. Always, he moved forwards.

Was that why he was so angry with Millie? *Because her actions had forced him to remember a time that he'd tried to forget?*

His disappointment in her was as fresh today as it had been a year ago.

Disappointment in her, or himself?

Was it his pride that was damaged? Because he'd got her wrong? He'd seen something in her that hadn't been there. On the day of their wedding she'd told him how much she wanted babies and he'd congratulated himself on finding the perfect wife and mother.

He'd thought she was a woman who would stand and fight. Instead, she'd walked out at the first opportunity.

Acknowledging that failure in his judgement hadn't grown any easier over the past year, Leandro mused as he left the nursery and walked towards his own suite of rooms.

So why had he insisted that she stay? Was he a masochist?

No. But his expectations of his wife had been seriously modified.

He'd give the child a home, he'd promised himself that he'd do that.

And as for his wife—well, he'd long ago learned how to lust without love, so that shouldn't be a problem.

Swearing in Greek, he yanked his shirt off and strode into the bathroom. Given that Millie had chosen to sleep with the baby, a cold shower was the only solution.

'Life won't be as fancy with me,' Millie told Costas as she strapped him in the car seat inside the taxi. 'None of this mood-altering lighting system, comfort cooling and underfloor heating. If your feet are cold, you wear socks, OK? It's a simple life, but I *can* promise I won't ever leave you. I know I left him, but that was different. I'll explain it to you when you're older.' It was still dark outside and she'd slipped out through the garden, careful to avoid any journalists who might still be camped at the front of the house. 'I've been renting a little flat in a village near the coast. I think you'll like it.'

She saw the taxi driver glance in his mirror and coloured. He probably thought she was mad, talking to a baby.

Or maybe he'd recognised her.

That horrifying possibility had had her sliding down in her seat, but then she told herself that she was being paranoid.

Who was going to look twice at her?

She'd pushed the pram and carried her bag and the car seat

to the next street so that no one would see her emerging from Leandro's house and make the connection.

The driver pulled up outside the train station. He helped her with the pram and the car seat and Millie gave him a generous tip, trying not to think what that money would have bought her.

'There's another half an hour until our train leaves, so we'll find a coffee shop and see if they'll warm your bottle.'

Even this early in the morning, the station was busy, and Millie weaved her way through suited men and women, all of whom appeared to be in a hurry.

She found a quiet corner in a coffee shop, bought herself a cappuccino and lifted Costas out of his pram to give him his bottle.

She was so engrossed in the business of feeding him that she didn't notice anyone else in the coffee shop until a light almost blinded her.

With a murmur of shock, Millie glanced up and what felt like a million cameras flashed.

Horrified, Millie snatched Costas's blanket and threw it around him, concealing him from the cameras. 'Go away!' She recoiled from the intrusive lenses, all pointed in her direction. 'What are you doing here?'

'The whole world wants to know about the Demetrios baby.'

'Well, the whole world should just mind its own business,' Millie snapped, her eyes searching for an escape route. There was none. The row of journalists between her and the door was now three deep and she could see other people in the station glancing across in curiosity, wondering what was happening.

How could she not have noticed?

Because she hadn't been looking for it. She wasn't used to living her life looking over her shoulder.

'Are you happy to look after the kid? Can't be easy for you.' The rough male voice came from right next to her and Millie turned her head and saw a man in shabby clothes sitting at the table next to her, a tape recorder in his hand.

Had he been there when she'd arrived? No, he'd arrived soon afterwards—which meant he must have followed her.

Hands shaking, Millie started to put Costas back in the pram but the photographers pressed closer, determined to get a shot of his face.

As one particularly persistent journalist stretched out a hand to move the blanket, Millie shifted Costas safely to one side. Her protective instincts going into overdrive, she gave her coffee a small nudge.

The hot liquid spilled over his arm and he cursed fluently, hopping backwards and glaring at her.

'Don't you dare use bad language in front of my child,' Millie snarled, but she was shaking so badly she could hardly speak. And she had no idea what to do. The crowd was building by the minute and she was trapped.

Seeing the determination in their eyes, she did the only thing she could do.

Still holding Costas protectively, she dragged her phone out of her pocket and called Leandro.

She'd expected him to be furiously angry with her for leaving, but instead their interchange was brief and to the point as he demanded to know her exact location and then ordered her to stay where she was and not move.

Looking at the pack of journalists pressing in on her, Millie gave a strangled laugh. Move? How?

Leandro arrived shortly after, the fact that he was unshaven simply adding to the aura of menace that shimmered around his muscular frame as he strode into the small coffee shop.

Radiating power and authority, Leandro said something to the journalists that she didn't catch, but it clearly had an effect because they fell back and a few of them melted away into the station. Millie thought she even heard one of them mutter an apology, but she couldn't be sure.

Wishing she had a morsel of Leandro's presence, she stood up shakily and lowered Costas into the pram, still shielding him from the cameras with her body.

'Is this all you brought?' Leandro picked up her bag, his handsome face taut and unsmiling as he gathered her things.

'Bag, pram, car seat,' Millie muttered, wondering whether she should have just taken her chances with the journalists. 'I'm *not* coming home with you.'

'We're not discussing this here.' He scooped up the car seat in his other hand and stood aside to let her pass. 'Let's move, before we attract any more attention.'

'Is it possible to attract any more attention than this?'

Her remark drew a faint smile from him. 'Believe it or not, yes.'

'I didn't think they had much of a story,' she murmured, and Leandro looked at her with naked exasperation.

'You just gave them a story, Millie. Don't you know *anything* about the media?'

'No. Just as I don't know anything else about your life. Now do you see why our marriage won't work?' Angry with herself for doing something so stupid, humiliated and close to despair, she stalked towards the entrance. Only then did she see the four bulky men from Leandro's security team positioned there.

Wondering why he'd tackled the journalists himself instead of using the heavyweights he'd brought with him, Millie walked through them with as much dignity as she could muster. Which wasn't much.

For a woman who didn't want any attention, she wasn't doing very well, she thought miserably, her face flaming with embarrassment as, protected by a circle of male testosterone, she moved through the now crowded station.

People stopped walking and stared and she could almost hear them wondering why a woman who looked like her required an entourage to keep her safe.

As she walked through the front of the station she would have paused but Leandro's palm was in her back, urging her towards the sleek dark car parked in the no parking zone.

As she slipped inside, the doors locked and the driver pulled away, the security team following in a different vehicle.

Millie braced herself for confrontation, but Leandro said nothing. Instead he drew his phone out of his pocket and made a single call, speaking in rapid Greek.

Moments later the car sped through the gates of his drive, through the private courtyard and straight into the garage. From there they were able to walk into the house without being seen while Leandro's driver used the car lift to take the car down to the basement garage.

Millie stood in the stunning double-height entrance atrium, lit by the skylight far above. She felt small and insignificant and wondered how Costas could possibly still be asleep after so much drama.

Leandro put her bag down in the hallway, left his staff to deal with the pram and gave instructions for the nanny to take charge of the baby. Then he propelled Millie into the beautiful conservatory that wrapped itself around the back of his enormous house.

The room was full of exotic plants, but Millie was too despondent to derive any comfort from the beauty of her surroundings.

'You left again.' His tone was raw and she flinched, wondering why he even cared.

'I didn't leave the baby,' she muttered. 'I left *you*. You want me to overlook the fact that you're going to have affairs, but I won't do that, Leandro. I won't grow old and grey watching while you play around with other women. Maybe that's what other Greek wives do, but I couldn't live like that.'

'Play around with other women? When did I say I wanted to play around with other women?' He looked stunned by the suggestion and she lifted her chin defensively.

'You said I was supposed to stand by your side, no matter what,' she reminded him. 'I assume "no matter what" means "no matter who I go to bed with". I can't turn a blind eye. It's asking too much.'

'"No matter what" means you and I standing together, facing whatever life throws at us.' His tone rang with incredulity. 'I said nothing about affairs. I have no intention of having affairs. I want you in my bed. No one else.'

Her assumptions having exploded into the atmosphere, Millie stood uncertainly, knowing that he'd change his mind once she was undressed. 'What if you discover the chemistry isn't there any more?'

Leandro moved so quickly she didn't see it coming. One moment he was facing her, legs apart in a confrontational stance; the next he was right in front of her, his hand on the back of her neck and his mouth on hers. And he knew exactly how to kiss to ensure maximum response. With the erotic exploration of his mouth and tongue, Leandro turned a kiss into something indescribably good and as Millie felt her grip on reality sliding away, her last coherent thought was that if she died now, she'd die happy.

Only after several minutes during which she lost track of

time and place did he finally lift his head. 'I don't foresee a problem.' He stepped back with all the easy confidence of a man who has proved his point and Millie ran shaking hands over her jeans, not sure whether to slap him or slide her arms round his neck and beg him to kiss her again.

'You shouldn't have done that.'

'People have been saying that to me all my life. If I'd listened to them, I'd still be playing in the dust on a remote Greek island.' Maddeningly relaxed, he glanced at his watch. 'Make up your mind, Millie. I'm only going to ask this *once*. Are you staying or going?'

Knowing that he'd dump her soon enough when he found out what had happened to her, Millie nodded. 'Staying.' At least then she could spend time with Costas.

'Good. I'll instruct my people to put out a statement saying that we are adopting the baby. Hopefully that will kill the story.'

'If I come back to you, I'll be surrounded by media.'

'As my wife you'll have more protection than if you go it alone. This morning has proved that.'

'But Costas and I can't leave the house without a bodyguard and a driver! What sort of life is that?'

'A privileged one,' Leandro drawled, ignoring the buzz of his phone. 'But while they're hovering like hyenas, we'll stay elsewhere.'

'We're leaving London?'

'This media circus presents a risk to the baby. I don't want to have to go through the courts to keep his picture out of the papers.'

Millie bit her lip. 'Where are we going?' It was touching that he was so protective, but at the same time it was upsetting because she could only see one reason why he would care so much for the baby's welfare.

'We're flying to Spiraxos later this morning. I just have some important calls to make.'

'We're going to Greece?' Her heart dropped. He'd taken her to his island on their honeymoon and they'd had three weeks of sun, sea and sex. Three indulgent weeks during which she'd been so happy. At that point in their relationship none of their problems had surfaced. She'd been ecstatically happy and so wildly in love that she'd woken up every morning with a smile on her face. The thought of returning there now made her feel sick. It would be like a cruel taunt, reminding her of that magical time before her life had fallen apart. 'Why Greece?'

'Because the island will give us privacy. And because our relationship was perfect when we were in Greece.' His gaze was bold and direct. 'We had an incredible time there. And if we're going to put the pieces of our marriage together, I'd rather the details of our reconciliation weren't documented in the pages of sleazy celebrity magazines. We will be able to relax, away from the eyes of the world.'

Relax? How could she possibly relax, trapped with him on Spiraxos, where she'd once spent the happiest time of her life? How could she relax, knowing what was coming? 'I—I'm not ready to fly to Greece. I need some time.'

'My staff will make any necessary preparations. All you have to do is walk onto my plane. And if you're worried about clothes, I can tell you now that you're not going to need any. Last night you slept alone, but tonight, *agape mou*...' Leandro flashed her a dangerous smile '...well, let's just say you won't be dressing for dinner.'

Tonight?

It was tonight.

No more excuses.

Millie's stomach churned horribly.

He was going to fly her all that way, only to discover that he didn't want to be with her any more.

It was going to be the shortest reconciliation on record.

Millie checked Costas again, grateful for any excuse to delay joining Leandro on the sun-baked terrace that overlooked the sparkling blue Aegean sea.

The journey to Greece had been smooth. Costas had slept most of the way and Leandro had spent his time reading and deleting endless emails, which meant she'd had far too much time to brood on the evening ahead of her.

Now that it had arrived, she couldn't bring herself to walk down to the terrace.

She was dreading the inevitable rejection.

'Are you planning to eat dinner with the baby? You have a hidden passion for baby milk perhaps?' Leandro's smooth, masculine tones came from behind her and she jumped because she hadn't expected him to come looking for her.

'I was just making sure he's all right.'

'Of course he's all right. He slept for the entire journey and now he's asleep again, which means, *agape mou,* that you have no excuse for not joining me.'

'Why?' Millie heard the ring of desperation in her own voice. 'Why would you want my company?'

'Because that's what married couples do. They eat dinner together.'

'Perhaps I'd better stay with the baby, just for tonight,' she hedged, 'in case he's unsettled after the journey.'

'He's asleep.'

'He might wake up and realise he's in a new environment.'

'In which case he'll yell. One of Costas's qualities is that he isn't shy about letting you know he's unhappy,' Leandro said dryly, staring down at the baby with a faint smile on his handsome face. 'All the bedrooms open onto the terrace, you know that. If he cries, we'll hear him.'

'I don't like leaving him.'

'We have a team of eight staff here, including the nanny that you appointed yourself.'

'He doesn't know them yet!'

'Neither is he likely to, if you don't allow them near him. Enough, Millie. The baby is going to be asleep!' His tone held a note of exasperation. 'Why is it that you're afraid to spend an evening with me? I've made a particular effort to be approachable and thoughtful. Am I such an ogre?'

She shook her head. 'No.'

Leandro gave an impatient sigh and slid his fingers under her chin. 'I am *trying* to understand what is going on here,' he breathed, 'and you're not giving me any clues. I thought you loved Spiraxos. I thought you'd be pleased to be here.'

'It's very quiet.' She meant that she found the intimacy difficult, but he misinterpreted her words.

'I'll arrange a few shopping trips it that's what's bothering you.'

Preoccupied by what was to come, Millie barely heard him. 'Why would that help? I'm not interested in shopping.'

'Millie.' His tone was dry. 'You used to spend hours deciding what to wear, so don't tell me you're not interested in clothes. I've never known a woman spend so long staring into her wardrobe.'

Because she'd had no idea what to wear. She'd been desperately insecure and those insecurities had grown and grown, fed by his gradual withdrawal. The harder she'd tried, the more he'd backed off until it had become obvious to her that he'd deeply regretted the romantic impulse that had driven him to marry her. And how much more insecure was she now? If she'd found it hard being his wife a year ago, now it seemed a thousand times harder.

This was the perfect opportunity to tell him everything that had happened to her after she'd walked out that day, but Millie just couldn't get the words past her lips.

'Given that you're so dedicated to the baby's welfare,' Leandro drawled, 'I will watch him while you take a shower and change for dinner. Remembering how long it used to take you, I'll prepare myself for a long wait.'

Millie cast a last reluctant look into the cot, willing Costas to wake up and yell. *Willing him to give her an excuse to miss dinner.* But for once he lay quietly, sleeping with a contented smile on his tiny mouth, oblivious to her silent signals and growing distress.

Which meant that she'd run out of excuses.

Leandro glanced at his watch and sprawled in the nearest chair with a sigh of resignation. Previous experience told him that he was going to be in for a serious wait. The length of time Millie took to get ready had been one of the things that had driven him crazy about her.

Not at first, of course. When they'd first met he'd been startled and charmed by how unselfconscious and natural she was. She couldn't bear to be away from him, even for a moment. Any time spent in the bathroom had been together. Making love. Touching.

She'd been addicted to him, and so affectionate that it had astonished him. Accustomed to women who guarded their behaviour and protected themselves, he'd never met anyone as free and honest with their emotions as Millie. She'd been as straightforward and honest as the fruit that grew on her parents' farm.

Or so he'd thought.

It had all changed on the day they'd arrived in London after their honeymoon.

Suddenly she'd morphed into one of those women he'd spent his adult life mixing with. She'd become obsessed with her appearance. It was as if she'd become a different person. Leandro had given up surprising her at home for a few stolen hours of daytime passion because she'd never been there. She'd spent her days in beauty salons and her nights out partying with him. And she'd spent hours scouring the celebrity gossip, looking for pictures of herself.

Leandro, up to his ears in work as usual, had been unable to work out what had happened to the girl he'd married. Had it all been an act designed to trap him and then she'd shown her true self? Or had it been marriage to a billionaire that had changed her? After all, up until her marriage with him she hadn't had the funds to allow her to indulge her apparent obsession with clothes and beauty products.

And yet over the past two days she'd seemed almost oblivious to her appearance.

Whoever said that women were a mystery hadn't been exaggerating, Leandro mused, stretching out his legs and making himself comfortable.

He looked at the sleeping baby and felt a rush of emotion that shook his self-control.

Alone, abandoned, a mother who had used him as a pawn...

Determined not to continue down that path of thought, he dug his BlackBerry out of his pocket, intending to distract himself with work. Then he heard a noise and glanced up to find Millie standing in the door of the dressing room, which connected directly to both bathroom and bedroom.

Leandro slipped his phone back into his pocket. 'That was quick.' He scanned her appearance, noticing with surprise that she'd left her hair curling and loose in its natural state and that the only make-up she was wearing was a shimmer of clear gloss on the curve of her lips. She was wearing a simple green top over a pair of trousers. 'I was expecting to wait at least an hour while you picked your outfit.'

Colour touched her cheeks and she gave a wan smile. 'There didn't seem much point in that. I'm no longer trying to impress you.'

Leandro frowned. 'Is that what you used to do?'

'Obviously I wanted to look my best.' She stooped, sliding her slender feet into the pair of shoes she was carrying.

Still pondering on her comment, he noticed that the only concession to her old look was a pair of killer heels. 'You never used to wear trousers.'

There was something in her expression that he couldn't read. 'I find trousers comfortable. Is it a problem?'

'Not at all.' They had problems far deeper than her choice of wardrobe, he mused, watching as she walked across to the cot and checked the baby again. Something was very wrong with her, and he had no idea what. 'Are you ready? Alyssa has laid dinner on the terrace.'

Millie stared down at the baby as if willing him to wake up and save her, and Leandro stared at her frozen profile in mounting frustration, searching for clues.

Was she looking at the baby, wondering if it was his? Or was there something more going on here?

Reaching into the cot, she tucked the sheet tenderly

around the sleeping baby and then withdrew her hand slowly. 'I'm ready.'

She spoke the words like someone preparing to walk to their doom and her whole demeanour was such a dramatic contrast from the last time they'd stood in this villa that Leandro wanted to close his hands around her shoulders and demand answers.

But his years in business had taught him when to speak and when to stay silent and he chose to stay silent, his expression neutral as he urged her towards the terrace.

The evening was only just beginning, he reminded himself. *They had plenty of time.*

CHAPTER SEVEN

MILLIE felt sicker and sicker. Wishing the baby would wake up and rescue her, she pushed the food from one side of her plate to the other, unable to face the thought of challenging her churning stomach by eating.

Candles flickered on the centre of the table and the silence of the warm evening was disturbed only by the insistent chirping of the cicadas and the occasional splash as birds skimmed the beautiful infinity pool, stealing water.

Across from her, Leandro said nothing. He lounged with masculine grace, his relaxed stance in direct contrast to her own mounting agitation. He wore a casual polo shirt, the simplicity of his clothing somehow accentuating his raw masculinity. *Whatever he wore, he looked spectacular,* she thought helplessly, putting her fork down and giving up the pretence of eating. The beauty was in the man himself, not in the way he presented himself. It didn't matter whether his powerful shoulders were showcased by an elegantly cut dinner jacket or a piece of simple cotton fabric, Leandro was all man. And that fact simply increased the churning in her stomach.

Or perhaps it was just because she was now more conscious than ever of the differences between her and the women he usually mixed with.

Had he had an affair?

The question played on her mind over and over again, a relentless torment fed by her own massive insecurities.

It was typical that he didn't try and put her at her ease, she thought desperately. He was so confident himself, he never thought that someone else might not be so comfortable in a situation.

'Alyssa must have been slaving all day,' she said, making polite conversation. 'The food is fantastic.'

'Then why aren't you eating any of it?'

'I'm not that hungry.'

Leandro leaned across and spooned some creamy *tzatsiki* onto her plate. 'When I first met you, you were always hungry. When I took you out to dinner, you ate three courses.'

'I had a very physical job,' Millie said defensively. 'I worked on a farm. If I didn't eat properly, I would have passed out.'

Leandro sat back in his chair, watching her across the table. 'Now I've upset you and I have no idea why.'

'You were criticising me.'

He tilted his head and she could see him rerunning the conversation through his brain. 'Exactly how and when did I criticise you?'

'You complained that I ate three courses, and—'

'It wasn't a complaint. It was a comment.'

'Same thing.'

'No, Millie,' he said gently, an ironic gleam in his eyes. 'It is *not* the same thing.'

'You mix with women who don't eat.' She ignored the food he'd put on her plate. 'In the circles you move in, eating is a bigger sin than adultery or wearing the wrong shade of pink.

All the women are thin. A visible rib cage is as much a status symbol as a pair of Jimmy Choos. So when you point out I ate three courses, what am I supposed to think?'

His gaze was thoughtful. 'You could think that the fact that you enjoy food and eating is one of the things I like about you.'

'Actually, I couldn't,' Millie said hotly, the defensive movement of her head sending her hair spilling around her face. 'Because I'm seeing no evidence to back it up. Apart from your momentary lapse with me, all the women you mix with clearly share DNA with stick insects. Take that actress—she's enough to give any normal woman a complex and a major eating disorder.'

He inhaled slowly. 'Your weight is clearly an issue.'

Millie played with her fork. 'You noticed that? I'm a woman,' she said sweetly. 'Of course my weight is an issue.'

'You have a fabulous body.'

'By fabulous, you mean fat.'

'I mean fabulous.' His eyes gleamed with lazy amusement and a trace of exasperation. 'Clearly I need a man-woman dictionary. Man says "fabulous", woman translates that into meaning "fat". Are there any other words in this unfathomable language I'm likely to need help with?'

'I'll let you know as we go along.'

'Thank you.' His tone dry, he leaned forward, and spooned some spicy sausage onto her plate next to the *tzatsiki*. 'Eat. Alyssa has spent all day in the kitchen in honour of your arrival. She remembered that you loved all Greek food, especially this. It was your favourite.'

'That was until someone told me how many calories were in each spoonful.'

'*Who* told you?'

'Oh, someone.' Millie felt the colour flood into her cheeks as she recalled that particular encounter. 'I expect she thought she was doing me a favour. Helping me fit into the strange world you live in.'

'I live in the same world as you, Millie.'

She glanced around her, looking at their privileged surroundings. 'If you think that, you're deluded. You move in a whole different world to most people, Leandro. It's no wonder I didn't fit.'

He was very still. 'Is that what you think?' His tone was soft. 'That you didn't fit?'

'It doesn't take a genius to see I wouldn't have had too much in common with some those waif-like celebrities you called your friends. My idea of a facial was splashing cold water to wake myself up at five in the morning during the harvest.'

He didn't answer immediately but she sensed a new tension about him and bit her lip, feeling suddenly guilty.

'Sorry,' she muttered. 'I didn't mean to criticise your friends. I'm sure they're lovely people. It wasn't their fault. If you drop a baby elephant into the middle of a flock of elegant swans, you've got to expect to startle them.'

Leandro's eyes glittered dark in the candlelight. 'And are you supposed to be the baby elephant in that analogy?' He sounded stunned. 'That's how you felt?'

Unsettled by his prolonged scrutiny, Millie shifted in her chair. 'How did you think I felt?'

A muscle flickered in his jaw and he toyed with the stem of his elegant wineglass. 'Honestly? I didn't think about it. Unlike you, I don't look for hidden meanings. Clearly I should have done.'

'Not all communication is verbal, Leandro.'

'Evidently not. But given your talent for reading me incorrectly, I think we'd better stick to the verbal sort for the time being. Tell me why you're not eating tonight.'

'My stomach is churning. I feel…sick.'

His dark brows met in a concerned frown. 'You're ill?'

'No. Just nervous.'

'Of what?'

'You, of course.'

His eyes held hers. 'I make you feel sick?' The incredulity in his tone made her wish she'd kept her mouth shut.

'Just a little bit.' Her cheeks turned pink. 'Well, quite a lot, actually.'

Leandro put the glass down on the table. 'Why?'

'I don't know. I'm not a psychologist. Maybe I'm seriously screwed up about you. But I think it's probably just the effect you have on me. Billionaire marries farm girl. It's pretty obvious that farm girl is going to have some major insecurities.'

'Billionaire marries farm girl,' he countered, 'and her insecurities vanish.'

'They double.'

'The way you think is a mystery to me.'

'Obviously.'

He rose to his feet and dropped his napkin onto the table. His mouth was set and determined, his eyes never once leaving her face as he stood next to her. 'Come.'

Millie looked at his outstretched hand. 'Why? Where are we going?'

'To put your insecurities to rest once and for all,' he purred, drawing her to her feet in a firm, decisive movement that brought her into contact with his hard, athletic frame. 'I intend to closely examine every curve of your fabulous body—and I mean fabulous, *not* fat,' he breathed, covering her lips with his fingers so that she couldn't interrupt, 'and by the time I've finished with you, your insecurities will be in a puddle on the floor along with your clothes.'

But that wasn't what was going to happen, was it? Millie's heart pounded. She thought of her body. *Thought of what he didn't know.* 'I really wanted an early night.'

'For once we agree on something.' His eyes gleamed with sexual promise. 'An early night followed by a lie-in. And another early night. The two might actually run together.'

Millie swallowed, her nerves almost snapping as she thought about the inevitable fallout of him taking her to bed. 'I can't— I just can't— I need some time.'

'I gave you time, Millie.' His voice was steady. 'I gave you space. And it was a mistake. All it did was widen the gulf between us. This time around we're doing things a different way. My way.'

'So I don't have a choice.'

His eyes shimmered with amusement. 'No, *agape mou,*' he murmured. 'There is no need to take on that martyred expression. I'm going to get to know you. Inside and out. In the past two days you have revealed more about yourself than you did in the entire time we were together. I am starting to realise that I didn't know you at all, but that is going to change from this moment onwards.' He trailed a finger over her flushed cheek. 'From now on I want to know everything in your head. And I won't let you shut me out.'

Standing in the bathroom, Millie pulled the robe tightly around her.

What was the best way to play this? Did she undress and walk into the bedroom naked? Or did she let him undress her?

Either way, it was going to be a disaster.

This was the moment she'd been dreading.

What was the point in putting it off any longer? Better to get it over with because the anticipation of what was to come was making her sick.

How would he react?

Forcing herself to move, she pushed open the door and stood for a moment, looking at him.

Leandro was sprawled on his back on the bed, eyes shut. His chest was bare and the light by the bed sent golden shadows across his sleek, bronzed shoulders.

In the year they'd been apart, he hadn't changed. Millie's gaze rested on the tangle of dark hair across the centre of his chest and then moved lower. He was naked, but he'd always been comfortable with his body, hadn't he? And no wonder. He was astonishingly fit, his physique strong and masculine.

His astonishing good looks had attracted the attention of the most beautiful women in the world.

Why did he want her? Was it just that he didn't believe in divorce? Was that the fragile bond that held them together?

Unable to see another possibility, she lost her confidence and would have slid back into the bathroom if his voice hadn't stopped her.

'If you run again, I'll come after you. And if you lock the door, I'll break it down. Your choice.'

Millie froze, her heart pounding frantically against her chest. But she moved forward, her legs stiff, as if they were trying to plead with her to take a different course of action. 'It isn't a choice, is it? You're not giving me a choice.'

'You made your choice when you decided to come back to me.' His eyes were open now, and he was watching her with that shimmering masculine gaze that always turned her stomach upside down. 'Come into the light where I can see you.'

Millie gripped the clasp of her robe tightly, wondering

whether she was actually going to have the courage to go through with this.

She stood there shivering and he frowned and sprang from the bed, prowling across to her with surprising grace for such a powerfully built man.

Leandro closed his fingers over her shoulders and forced her to look at him. 'I want to know what you're thinking.'

'Trust me, you don't.' Millie shook her head, the tears sitting in her throat like a brimming cup just waiting to overflow. She couldn't cry now. Later. *There'd be plenty of time for that later.*

With a growl of frustration, he scooped her face into his hands and lowered his head to kiss her. 'I don't understand why you are so insecure. You are a very beautiful woman.'

Her courage failed.

Maybe, just maybe, if he hadn't said those exact words she would have gone through with it.

'I'm not beautiful,' she croaked, dragging herself out of his arms. 'I'm *not* beautiful. And I can't do this. I just can't.'

'Why? Is this about what you think happened with your sister?'

'No, no, it isn't. It's about what happened to *me*. It's hopeless. I'm sorry, Leandro. I'm sorry.' Before he could stop her, Millie stumbled out of the room. Blinded by tears, she banged against the doorframe in her haste to get away from him, but the sudden pain in her arm was eclipsed by the far greater pain in her heart. She took refuge in one of the guest suites at the far end of the villa. Stumbling into the bathroom, she locked the door securely behind her and slid to the floor without bothering to switch on the lights.

It was impossible. The whole situation was impossible.

She should never have allowed him to blackmail her into

giving their marriage another try. She just should have stood there, told him what had happened and walked out while she still had some shred of dignity left. And she should have found another way of being close to her nephew. Visits. Letters. Photos. Anything other than this.

Why had she agreed to stay?

Had some small, stupid part of her hoped that this horrible situation could still have a happy ending?

In the pit of despair, she let the tears fall.

The door crashed open and she gave a jerk of shock.

Leandro stood there, a powerful figure silhouetted against the light of the bedroom. 'Every time you lock a door between us I'll break it down,' he vowed thickly, 'and every time you run I *will* find you.' With a soft curse, he flipped on the light and then sucked in a breath as it illuminated her ravaged features. His eyes fixed on her blotched, tear-stained face and his jaw tightened.

'Millie? What the *hell* is going on?' His voice was hoarse and he spread his hands in a gesture of helplessness. 'Why are you crying? *Maledizione*, I *never* wanted to upset you like this. Stop it, *agape mou*. Nothing is this bad.'

'Just leave me alone,' she choked, hugging her knees against her chest and burying her face in her arms. 'Please, leave me alone. Go and ring your actress.' She heard him swear under his breath.

'There is blood on your arm. You must have scraped it when you bumped into the doorframe. Let me look at it—'

'*Go away!*'

For a moment she thought he'd acceded to her request but then she heard the solid tread of his footsteps and he squatted down beside her, strong and calm, a man able to cope with any problem that came his way.

'You're going to make yourself ill. Enough.' Leandro slid his hands under her arms and lifted her to her feet and she looked up at him through eyes swollen with crying.

'Yes, it is enough.' Somehow she managed to get the words out. 'Enough pretending that our relationship can ever work. Enough pretending we can have any sort of marriage. It's over, Leandro. It's over.'

'You are *extremely* upset,' he breathed, holding her firmly so that she couldn't slide to the floor again, 'and it is never a good idea to make decisions when you're upset.'

'My decision is going to be the same whenever I make it. I mean it, it's over.' Her voice rose and he cupped her face in his hands, forcing her to look at him.

'Millie, I want you to take a deep breath.' His masculine voice was surprisingly gentle. 'Deep. That's right, and again. And now you are going to listen to me, yes? And you are going to trust me. Whatever is wrong—whatever has upset you this much—you will tell me and I will fix it. But for now I just want you to try and calm down.'

His unexpected kindness somehow made everything worse. 'Why won't you just leave me?'

'Because that option doesn't work for me,' he said grimly. 'I already told you, this time you are not walking away from our problems.' He drew her into his arms, but she shook him off and took a step backwards.

'Don't touch me. I can't bear you to touch me.' She heard the sharp intake of his breath and knew that her apparent rejection had hurt him.

'So you don't trust me.'

'This isn't about trust. This isn't about what happened with my sister. And it can't be fixed. Just—just—wait—and you'll see.' Her hands were shaking so much she couldn't untie the knot of silk holding together the edges of her robe and she almost screamed with frustration. Eventually the fabric loosened in her fingers and she bit her lip, trying to find the courage to do what she had to do. 'I don't know why you wanted me the first time, Leandro. You say I'm beautiful and—well, I never was. And even less so now.'

'I'm the best judge of that.'

'All right. Then judge.' Without giving herself any more time to think about it and change her mind, she allowed the dressing-gown to slip from her shoulders.

Naked, she faced him. Unprotected, she let him see. Vulnerable, she stayed silent and let him judge—*and saw his handsome face reflect everything she herself had felt over the past year.*

Shock, disbelief, distaste.

The emotions were all there.

'Now do you understand why I said this would never work? I wasn't beautiful enough for you before. How could I possibly be beautiful enough now?' Somehow the reality of exposing her damaged flesh was less traumatic than the thought of it had been. Now that she'd done it, she felt nothing but relief.

No more pretending.

He'd divorce her and she'd get on with her life. And it may not have been the life she'd dreamed off, but it would be all right. She'd make sure it was all right. She'd get over him, wouldn't she? It had only ever been a stupid dream.

Quietly sliding the robe back onto her shoulders, Millie cast one final look at his shocked face, reflecting on the fact she'd never actually seen him lost for words before.

'I'm sorry,' she muttered wearily. 'I'm sorry to do that to you—in that way. Perhaps it was cruel of me, but I honestly didn't...' Her pause was met with silence. 'I—just didn't know any other way.' Impulsively she lifted her hand to touch his arm and then realised that the best thing she could do for him was to just get out of his life.

Letting her hand drop, she walked past him towards the door feeling tired and completely drained of energy.

'God damn it, Millie, if you walk out on me one more time I won't be responsible for my actions.' His voice rasped across her sensitised nerve endings. 'You stay right there. I just need to—' He broke off and ran a hand over his face, clearly struggling with his emotions. 'Just give me a minute.'

She stopped walking. 'It doesn't matter. You don't need to work out what you're supposed to say or do. Nothing you say is going to make any difference.'

'Just *wait*.' Leandro pressed his fingers against the bridge of his nose and exhaled slowly. '*Maledezione*, you have no idea...'

'Yes, I do. I know what you're thinking. And I understand.'

'Do you?' His voice was harsh. 'Then you'll know that I'm asking myself what exactly I did to you that made you think you couldn't talk to me about this. Is this why you turned your back on me night after night?' He frowned and then shook his head, clearly angry with himself. 'No, of course. This...' He glanced towards her now concealed body. 'This didn't happen when we were together, did it? It couldn't have done. I would have known.'

Millie looked at him. 'It happened the day I left you.'

'*What* happened the day that you left me?' His hoarsely worded demand increased her tension.

'Can we talk about this tomorrow?' Seeing his face had been bad enough. She wasn't up to a conversation. She just wanted to hide.

Leandro gave a hollow laugh and his fingers closed around her wrist as he drew her firmly into the guest bedroom. 'No, *agape mou*. We're going to talk. Or perhaps I should say that *you're* going to talk. And you're going to do it now.'

CHAPTER EIGHT

KEEPING her hand in his, Leandro led her across the terrace to the pool. The evening was still stiflingly warm and the stylish curve of the swimming pool was illuminated by the tiny lights that gleamed under the water.

'I always loved sitting out here at night,' she said softly, sinking onto the edge of a sun lounger. 'It's so peaceful.'

'We made love out here. Do you remember?'

Millie didn't answer his question because she knew that the only way she was going to be able to deal with the present was if she didn't think about the past. 'So—what do you want to know?'

He sat down right next to her, the length of his powerful thigh brushing the length of hers. 'I want to know what happened to you. I want to know how you got those scars.' For once there was no mockery in his voice and she stared down at their linked hands with almost curious detachment.

'When I drove away that day I was...' She hesitated. 'Very upset. I didn't really think about where I was going. I drove south and found myself in a very rough part of London. I stopped at a set of lights—and three men took a fancy to the car I was driving.'

His fingers tightened their grip on hers. 'Tell me.'

'Are you sure you want to hear it?'

'Yes.' But the word sounded as though it had been dragged from him and she looked up at his hard, set profile dubiously.

'If you're just going to rant and rave and turn all macho, this is going to be hard.'

'I won't rant and rave.'

'You promise not to go and extract revenge?'

Leandro made a sound that was close to a snarl. 'No,' he said thickly, placing her hand on his thigh and holding it there, 'no, *agape mou,* I don't make that promise.'

'Then—'

'What caused the scars?' he asked harshly. 'Was it a knife?'

'Broken bottle.' Millie felt the horror of it burst into her brain. 'Carjacking. I stopped at a set of lights—they had the doors open before I even saw them coming.'

'They dragged you out of the car?'

'I refused to undo the seat belt—big mistake. I think I was in a state of shock. But that resistance got me the scar on my stomach.'

The breath hissed through his teeth. 'Why didn't you just give them the keys?'

'You gave me the car as a wedding present,' she mumbled. 'I liked it.'

'Cars are replaceable.'

'Spoken like a billionaire.'

'I would say the same thing if I was living on benefits and someone had just stolen your bicycle.' He spoke in a low, urgent tone. '*Nothing* is worth that sort of risk.'

'Well, I suppose you don't really think clearly when it happens. You just react by instinct.'

'And you were upset and that was my fault.'

She stilled. 'You told me that you didn't have an affair with my sister.'

'I didn't. I'm blaming myself because I was so blisteringly angry that you didn't trust me, I let you walk out instead of dragging you back and proving my innocence to you. If I'd done that, this wouldn't have happened.' The breath hissed through his teeth again. 'Normally I'm not a believer in wasting time on regret but believe me, *agape mou,* when I say that with you, my regrets are piling up. But we'll deal with that in a minute. Finish the story. You were very badly injured?'

'Yes. They dragged me out of the car, attacked me with the bottle a few more times just to make sure I'd got the message and then took the car and my bag. I was unconscious, lying on the road—so I had no identity with me. I woke up days later in hospital with everyone wondering who I was. Initially they thought I was the victim of a hit and run.'

'Did you have amnesia?'

'No.' Millie shook her head. 'I remembered everything. They told me they'd found the car ten miles away, burned out and abandoned. Because no one had reported it missing, they hadn't been able to identify the owner. I was so angry with myself.' She frowned. 'I should have noticed them waiting at the lights.'

'You're not exactly streetwise.' Leandro toyed with her fingers. 'You hadn't even lived in a city until you married me. And on top of that, you were upset. Because of me.'

'You're not responsible for the carjacking. That was my own stupid fault for not locking my doors. But I wasn't used to London. Where I come from we wind the windows down and offer people lifts. People leave their front doors open.' Her frank confession drew a groan of disbelief from him.

'You are ridiculously trusting. And I'm angry with myself for not teaching you to be more careful.'

'*Not* your fault,' Millie said gruffly. 'Just another example of how I'm the wrong woman for you.'

'How can you reach that conclusion? It's becoming increasingly obvious to me that I had absolutely no idea what was going on in your head at any point during our short marriage. But we'll come back to that later. First I want you to finish telling me what happened.'

'I've told you everything.' Millie shrugged. 'I was in hospital for a while, obviously.'

'Why didn't the hospital contact me?'

'At first because I had no identity. And later…' She paused. 'Because I asked them not to.'

Leandro greeted that confession with a hiss of disbelief. 'Why would you do that? No, don't answer that.' His tone was weary. 'You thought I was having an affair with your sister. You thought she was pregnant with my child.'

'I thought our marriage was over.'

'Millie, we'd been together for less than three months and I couldn't get enough of you! Until you started turning your back on me, we were constantly together and it was good, wasn't it?'

'It was incredible. At first.'

'At first?'

'You worked very long hours. You were always jetting off to New York or Tokyo and you didn't want me with you.'

'Because I had trouble concentrating when you were around,' he bit out, and Millie looked at him in surprise because that explanation hadn't ever occurred to her.

'Oh.'

'Oh? What did you think the reason was?'

'I…wondered if you had other women.'

His jaw tightened. 'When, before that incident with your

sister, did I *ever* give you cause to doubt me?' Leandro released his grip on her hand and rose to his feet in a fluid movement. *'When?'*

'I suppose I looked at the facts. When I met you, you were thirty-two, rich, good-looking and single. You'd never been committed to a woman, but you'd been involved with plenty.'

'Before I met you.'

'And they were all different to me.'

Leandro spread his hands wide, his expression expectant. 'And does that tell you anything?'

'Yes. It tells me that you made a mistake when you married me.'

He sank his fingers into his hair and said something in Greek. 'Always if there are two ways to interpret something, you choose the wrong one.' His usually fluent English suddenly showed traces of his Mediterranean heritage. 'Did no other reason come to mind?'

Millie gave a tiny shrug. 'You're Greek.' At the moment there was no mistaking that fact. 'I was a virgin and you're old-fashioned enough to like that.'

His laugh lacked humour. 'Yes. All right. I concede that point. But I took your virginity within hours of meeting you so that wasn't a reason to marry you.'

'Well. Everyone makes mistakes,' she said simply. 'Even you.'

'Why didn't you contact me after the accident?'

'What for? If I couldn't hold you before I was injured, I knew there was no chance afterwards.' Millie stared at the still surface of the pool. 'And I knew I could never be the sort of wife you needed. Lying there in hospital gave me the time to think about that.'

'The sort of wife I needed? What is that supposed to

mean?' His tone raw, Leandro sat back down next to her. His hand slid under her chin and he forced her to look at him. '*You* were the woman I married. *You* were the wife I needed.'

'No.' Millie shook her head, tears swimming in her eyes. 'I wasn't, Leandro. I was *never* the wife you needed. I learned that pretty soon after we were married. We came back from our honeymoon and I was plunged into the life you lead—and nothing about the time we'd spent together had prepared me for what was expected of me.'

'Nothing was expected of you.'

'Oh, yes, people expected a lot.' The tears still glistening in her eyes, Millie moved her head away from the comfort of his fingers. 'You're Leandro Demetrios—declared the sexiest man in the world. Everyone wanted to know who you'd married. And everyone wanted to comment.'

'Who is everyone? Are you talking about the media?'

'Them, too. But mostly your friends. The people you mixed with in your daily life. They used to give me these little sideways glances that showed what they thought of your choice.'

'You were *my* wife,' he gritted. 'I didn't care what anyone thought of you.'

'But I did,' she said simply. 'I'm not like you. When they said I was fat and that my hair was curly, I cared. When they said I didn't dress like any of your previous girlfriends, I worried. They made me realise that I was totally wrong for you.'

Leandro growled low in his throat. 'And you didn't think I might have been the best judge of that?'

'I met one of your previous girlfriends.' She gave a twisted smile. 'She took great pleasure in drawing comparisons between herself and me. And she made the very apt comment that if she hadn't been able to hold you, how could I?'

'*When* did you meet her?'

'At a charity ball, the first week we spent in London. We were standing in front of the mirror together.' Millie nibbled her lip. 'I looked at what I was wearing and I looked at what she was wearing—well, let's just say I could see what she was talking about. I thought to myself, OK, so I need to dress differently. I treated it like a project. When I joined you at our table, I started studying everyone. And I got home and bought magazines, went shopping…'

'And so began your obsession with clothes. I had no idea.' His tone flat, Leandro gently rubbed her fingers with his. 'Those hours you spent in your dressing room every evening, trying on this dress and that dress—I thought you'd suddenly discovered the joys of shopping.'

'Joys?' Millie gave a hollow laugh. 'I hated it. Not that it isn't fun to have nice clothes, don't misunderstand me, but when you know that everything you wear is going to be criticised… Have you any idea how many clothes there are out there? How was I supposed to know what to wear? All I knew was that every time I went out, people stared at me. I just never seemed to get it right.'

'Why didn't you say something to me?'

'I presumed you could see for yourself,' she said wearily. 'And the fact that you were getting so impatient with me seemed to confirm that I was getting it all wrong.'

Leandro muttered something in Greek and rubbed his forehead with his fingers. 'We were at cross-purposes,' he said gruffly. 'I didn't think you were getting it wrong. I had no idea you were feeling like this.'

'I didn't know what looked good. Every time I thought I liked myself in something, I'd remember how many times I'd been wrong before. Then my sister rang and told me she needed somewhere to crash in London. You were away all the time—I thought she'd be company and I thought she'd be a good person to give me advice. She'd always helped me before. By then I was a mess,' she confessed. 'My confidence was on the floor. Everything I put on I found myself thinking, What are they going to say about this?'

'Why didn't you ask me if I liked what you were wearing?'

'Why didn't you just tell me?' Millie defended herself. 'On our honeymoon you seemed crazy about me—everything I wore, you stripped it off and made love to me. And then we arrived home and…you changed. And it took me a while to understand what was going on.'

'And what did you think was going on?'

'It was obvious. Our relationship was fine when we were here.' She waved a hand. 'Sort of like a holiday romance. But when it came to living your life, well, that's when the cracks appeared. And I panicked. I tried every outfit, every style—but I could see I was different to every other woman you'd ever been with. Every time we went out was torture. Everyone looked at me, judged me.'

Leandro swore under his breath. 'They didn't.'

'They did. People do it all the time. You don't notice because you don't care what people think of you.' Millie sneaked a glance at him. 'And you're not very tolerant of weakness in others. I remember one evening I begged you not to leave me with that group of women and you just frowned and told me I'd be fine. There was some government dignitary you had to speak to so you just threw me to the wolves and let them devour me.'

He winced. 'Millie—'

'It's all right, you don't have to say anything. The truth is you shouldn't have *had* to hold my hand at events like that. I was pathetic, I realise that, but every time we went out I was hit with another ten reasons why you shouldn't have married me and I was shocked by how nasty people were.'

'Why didn't you talk to me?'

'You were too absorbed in your work to notice what was going on. And you were already starting to get irritated with me. Your favourite trick was to glance at your watch and narrow your eyes when I was fumbling about, getting dressed. So I started getting ready earlier and earlier until in the end it took me most of the day. And then I'd appear and you'd be pacing the room like a caged tiger plotting his way out of captivity.'

'Waiting isn't my forte.'

'I noticed that. But from my point of view the fact that you were so irritated made the whole thing even more stressful. I would have spent most of the day getting ready and you'd look at me in disbelief as if you couldn't quite believe that was what I'd chosen to wear and then you'd usher me out to the car.'

'That is *not* what I would have been thinking,' Leandro muttered. 'I was probably thinking how much you'd changed. When first I met you, you didn't do any of those things. You were straightforward and lacking in vanity.'

'I'm sorry! That's because I had never been to a charity ball in my life! The highlight of my social calendar was the village fete.'

He raked his hands through his hair and gave a groan of frustration. '*That was a compliment, Millie!* Don't you ever hear a compliment?'

Stunned by the force of his tone, she looked at him in confusion. 'But you said— I thought—I thought lacking in vanity meant that I didn't spend hours on myself.'

'Yes, but you didn't *need* to spend hours on yourself. I

liked you the way you were. I liked you the way you were that day I first met you.'

'I was working on the farm! You arrived, designer dressed from head to toe, to talk business and I was wearing a pair of torn, ancient shorts and a T-shirt that had belonged to my dad but had shrunk in the wash.'

'I don't remember the shorts,' Leandro growled, 'but I do remember your legs. And your smile. And how sweet you were crawling over that haystack, risking life and limb to rescue those kittens that were trapped. I remember thinking, *I want her in my bed.* I want her looking after our babies. And I remember deciding at that moment that I wanted to wake up every morning looking at that smile. Why do you think I stayed two days? It was supposed to be a two-hour meeting.'

'You invested in my dad's business.'

Leandro gave a wry smile. 'I'm going to be honest here, *agape mou,* and confess that your dad's business is the only investment I've ever made that has lost me money.'

Millie gave an astonished laugh. 'You made a mistake?'

'No. I knew it was going to be a disaster the minute he showed me the numbers. I wasn't investing in the business. I was investing in you.'

She thought of the changes her dad had made to the farm. How excited he'd been by his new venture.

'Oh. It was kind of you to do that for Dad.' For a moment she was too flustered to respond, then she frowned slightly. 'But it doesn't change the fact that you didn't stop to think how I'd cope with it all, did you?'

Leandro took her hand again. 'I assumed you'd love the lifestyle. I knew your parents were struggling with the farm and you were working inhuman hours for a pittance.'

'But I didn't marry you for your money or the lifestyle,'

she said in a small voice. 'I married you for *you*. And you were always away being the big tycoon. And when we went out, there were always millions of people around us and I couldn't relax because there were cameras stuck in my face and everyone wanted to criticise me. Yes, I was lacking in vanity, but someone like that can't survive in your world. I hadn't realised just how much was involved in being a billionaire's wife. And those awful celebrity magazines tore me to pieces. At the beginning they said I was fat—or "full figured" was the exact phrase— And then I was in this column about fashion mistakes. Don't even *start* me on that one.'

'Why did you read them?'

'I thought it might help me work out what was expected of me. I wanted to look like the perfect wife.' She bit her lip. 'I wanted you to be proud of me. I didn't want you to sit there at a charity event thinking, Why did I marry her?

'I *never* thought that.'

'Didn't you?' Her smile was wan. 'I don't know. I just know that it got worse and worse. Until I no longer had the confidence to undress in front of you—until I couldn't bear the thought of having sex with you because I imagined that you must be thinking, Yuck, all the time. I just felt so self-conscious.'

'*Theos mou.*' His tone raw with emotion, Leandro rose to his feet and stood facing the pool, the muscles of his powerful shoulders flexing as he struggled for control. 'And I didn't see any of this. Never before have I considered myself to be stupid and yet obviously I am.'

'No. You just move in different circles to me. You take it all for granted. The women you dated before know how to do their hair, what to wear, how to talk, what to eat, how much they're supposed to weigh.'

'Who makes these rules?'

'Society.'

'And do you never break rules?'

'Sometimes.' Millie looked at him cautiously. 'But I was desperate not to embarrass you or make you ashamed.'

'Suddenly everything is falling into place.' Leandro spun to face her, his voice harsh. 'Why didn't you tell me you felt this way? Why not just have a conversation?'

'Telling your husband that you feel out of place and unattractive isn't the easiest conversation to have. I suppose part of me thought that if I said it aloud, I'd draw attention to it.' *As if he hadn't already noticed.* 'We had fundamental problems that no amount of words could fix. And after the accident, well, I knew I was going to have bad scars. The break in my leg meant that I was in hospital for ages. There was no way you would want to be with someone like me.'

'You reached that conclusion by yourself?' His tone was tight and angry and she felt her own tension increase.

'Yes. You're a man who demands perfection in every part of his life,' she said quietly, 'and I was so far from perfect. I was already insecure about how I was—the accident just made it all worse. Can't you see that?'

'What I see is that we left too many things unsaid. I also finally understand why you were so quick to condemn me when you saw me with your sister.' His voice was low and rough in the semi-darkness. 'Your own confidence was at such a low point that it didn't occur to you that I could be faithful to you. It seems as though you were resigned to the fact that I'd have an affair. You seemed to regard it as inevitable. You assumed that I would prefer your sister.'

Had she been wrong about that? For the first time ever a significant rush of doubt seeped into her brain. 'You and my sister—that was a much more obvious relationship than you and me.' *But she was starting to wonder.* 'Even if that hadn't happened then—with her—it would have happened eventually. Sooner or later some woman would have come along and caught your attention. Maybe you *did* find me attractive—but the novelty would have worn off. We weren't meant to be together, Leandro.' Millie pulled her robe more tightly around her. 'My accident just brought that home to me.'

'You've just made a great number of assumptions.'

'Did you come after me, Leandro?' Gently withdrawing her hand from his, she stood up. The soft lap of water against the side of the pool mingled with the sounds of the Mediterranean. In the distance she could hear the hiss of the sea on the sand, the chirping of the cicadas as they sang their night-time chorus. 'If you'd wanted me, you would have tracked me down. You're that sort of man. You go after what you want. And you didn't go after me.' *Whatever doubts might be in her head, that, at least, she was sure about.* 'Not even when my sister sent the baby to you.' She managed to keep the emotion out of her voice. 'I'm going to go to bed now. We can talk about what you want to do in the morning. Can I ask you one favour?'

His jaw tightened. 'Ask.'

'Whatever happened before is irrelevant. What matters is how things are now. Who I am now. You'll want to divorce me, and I understand that.' She stumbled over the words. 'But will you let me have custody of Costas? Whatever the will said, you have good lawyers and I'm his blood relative. I can't afford to fight for him.' She glanced at his face and saw the tension etched there. 'Just think about it.' And then she turned and walked back into the villa.

CHAPTER NINE

LEANDRO stood in the doorway of the guest bedroom, staring at the slight figure under the silk sheet.

She reminded him of an animal that had crawled away to die. And he knew she wasn't asleep.

She was hurt.

Because of him.

His tension mounted. Wasn't he the one who had told her that there was always more going on in a picture than first appeared? And had he taken his own advice? No. He'd seen and he'd judged.

And he knew why. No matter how distasteful it was to admit it, his own past had coloured the present. When she'd walked out...

Guilt, an unfamiliar emotion, clawed at his body but he thrust it away, knowing that regret would do nothing to fix the current situation.

So many words unspoken, he thought grimly, closing the door quietly and walking towards her. His bare feet made no sound on the cool tiles but he knew she'd heard him because he saw the defensive movement of her shoulders.

'I have lost count of the number of times you've turned

your back on me in our short marriage, Millie,' he said softly, 'and I allowed you to do it. But I'm not allowing it any more. Those days are over.'

'Go away, Leandro.' Her voice was muffled by the pillow and he saw her curl up just a little bit tighter, as if trying to make herself as small as possible.

This less than flattering response to his presence sent new tension through his already rigid frame. 'I'm not good at apologies,' he confessed, and then frowned as she curled up smaller still. 'But I know I owe you a big one.'

'You honestly don't have anything to apologise for. No man in their right mind would find me attractive.'

She thought he was apologising because he didn't find her attractive?

Stunned by her interpretation of his remark, Leandro struggled to find a suitable response and decided that, whatever he said, she wasn't going to believe him.

Abandoning words, he lay down on the bed next to her. He felt her shrink and saw her try and shift away from him but he placed his hand firmly on her hip, halting her slide to freedom. Used to negotiating himself out of difficult situations, it was a struggle to stay silent, but he knew that the time for slick verbal patter was long past. She'd made up her mind about herself and the way he saw her. Words weren't going to make a difference.

Applying a different tactic, Leandro slid his arm round her, drawing her rigid, defensive body against his. Through the thin silk robe he could feel her shivering and he frowned because the evening was hot and the air-conditioning in the unoccupied guest bedroom had been switched off. She wasn't cold. She was afraid.

Of him? *Of rejection?*

Taking unfair advantage of the differences in their physical strength, Leandro rolled her onto her back and shifted himself on top of her, his body trapping hers against the silk sheets.

'Why won't you leave me alone, Leandro?' Her voice was a broken plea and he stroked her damp, tangled hair away from her face with a gentle hand.

'I tried that,' he said softly. 'It was my biggest mistake.' Although there was just enough light shining in from the pool area for him to be able to make out the outline of her body, what was going on in her eyes was a mystery to him. He contemplated turning on the bedside light and then decided that it wouldn't be a good move. Maybe, this time, the dark would be helpful.

She tried to wriggle away from him but he was too heavy for her. 'Leandro, please. Don't do this.'

Leandro curved his hand around her cheek and drew her face back to his. He wanted desperately to see her expression. He also knew that if he turned that light on, her distress would stop him in his tracks.

'Don't do this, Leandro,' she whispered, trying to move her head.

Leandro silenced her plea with the warmth of his mouth. And what had begun as an attempt to silence her objections quickly turned into a sensual feast. With a groan, he deepened the kiss, wondering how he could have forgotten how good she tasted. She was strawberries and summer sunshine, honey and green English pastures. But, most of all, she was innocence. And he took ruthless advantage of her lack of sophistication, pushing aside the niggling thought that perhaps it wasn't entirely fair of him to use every erotic skill at his disposal when she was this emotionally vulnerable. They were past being fair, he reasoned, feeling a rush of satisfaction as her mouth moved under his, allowing him the access he was demanding.

Without breaking the kiss, he eased the sheet down her body and untied her robe one handed, careful to keep his movements slow and subtle. But slow and subtle could only take him so far, and he identified the exact moment she realised that he'd undone the robe because she suddenly stiffened under him.

Her arm lifted, but he anticipated her urge to cover herself and closed his fingers around her wrist. Drawing her arm above her head, he restrained her gently, feeling her tug against his grip as she tried to free herself. She writhed under him, the unconsciously sensual movement sending his blood pressure soaring. Just to be on the safe side, he drew her other arm above her head, holding both with one hand, leaving the other free to explore her quivering frame.

Leandro dropped his mouth to her throat, feeling her pulse pumping against the hot probe of his tongue. Her soft groan was half encouragement, half denial, and he gently moved her robe aside, exposing the soft curve of her breast.

She tugged at her wrists and he tightened his hold, feeling her instant response as he closed his mouth over the jutting pink tip of one swollen breast. Millie arched in an involuntary movement that brought her into direct contact with the hard thrust of his erection. Denying her feminine invitation, Leandro pressed her down against the bed with the power of his body, suppressing her attempts to relieve the sexual ache he'd created.

Soon, he promised himself. *Soon, he'd give her what she wanted. And himself too. But first...*

Dragging his tongue over the rigid peak of her nipple, he stroked his free hand over the flat, trembling planes of her stomach, feeling the ridge of the scars under his seeking fingers. He lingered for a moment, infinitely gentle—*did it hurt?*—and then moved his hand lower still, this time to the tops of her thighs. *Another scar here,* and he explored it with the tips of his fingers and then shifted his weight to give himself the access he wanted.

His fingers rested at the top of her thigh and he felt the tiny movements of her pelvis as her body begged. Taking her mouth again, he moved his hand, encountering soft curls, damp now with the response he'd created. Stroking her gently, he felt her gasp against his mouth and then the gasp turned to a moan as he explored her intimately with sure, confident fingers. She was warm and slick, and he took his time, using all his skill and expertise to arouse her body past the point of inhibition. Her moan of desperation connected straight to his libido and suddenly it wasn't enough to touch. He wanted to taste—all of her.

Easing his mouth from hers, Leandro looked down at her, but he couldn't make out her features. Responding to her soft moans, he released her hands, and this time she didn't move them. She just kept them stretched above her head, like some pagan goddess preparing herself for sacrifice.

Leandro slid down her quivering, sensitised body and gently spread her thighs. He'd expected resistance, but her eyes were still closed, her body compliant as he arranged her as he wanted her and then lowered his head. The touch of his mouth drew a soft gasp from her and he closed his hands around her thighs, holding her still while he subjected her to the most extreme sexual torture, his touch so gentle and impossibly skilled that he turned her from doubtful to desperate within seconds. The air was filled with her cries and he continued his determined assault on her senses, sliding one finger deep inside her, the feel of her slick femininity challenging his own control. His libido bit and fought but he continued to touch, stroke, taste until the excitement was a screaming force inside him and she was mindless and compliant under him.

Like a man clinging to a ledge with the tips of his fingers, Leandro refused to allow himself to fall, and then he felt her hands in his hair and on his shoulders.

'Now—Leandro, please…' Her broken plea was all he needed and he shifted over her, sliding his hand under the deliciously rounded curve of her bottom and lifting her.

He wanted to speak—*he wanted to tell her what he was feeling*—but he was afraid of anything that might disturb this fragile connection he'd created between them, so he stayed silent, rejecting the words that flowed into his brain, reminding himself that there would be time enough for talking later.

Her damp core was slick against the tip of his erection and he gritted his teeth in an effort to hold back and do this gently.

'*Leandro…*' Her hips thrust against him, the movement sheathing him sufficiently to rack up the sexual torture a few more notches. Keeping his weight on his elbows, he eased into her slowly, the sweat beading on his brow as he forced himself to take it slowly. Her body gripped his like a hot, tight fist and his reacted by swelling still further, drawing a gasp from her parted lips.

'Leandro…'

'It's all right,' he breathed, 'just relax—your body knows how to do this. Relax, *agape mou*, and trust me.' He licked at her lips, nibbling gently, coaxing and teasing until he felt her respond. But he didn't move, holding himself still until she moved her hips in a tentative invitation.

By a supreme effort of will, Leandro held onto control,

keeping his own ravenous libido in check as he waited for her to reach the same point of desperation.

Millie groaned his name, arched and shifted, but still he didn't move, the muscles in his shoulders pumping up and hard under the effort of holding back. Only when she sobbed out a plea and rubbed her thigh along the length of his did he allow himself to move again, and this time her body drew him in deep, her slick delicate tissues welcoming the hard thrust of his manhood.

Trying to think clearly through the red mist that clouded his brain, Leandro slid one hand down her thigh, urging her to wind her legs around him, and then adjusted his own position in a decisive movement that drew a soft gasp from her.

Her soft moans increased with each rhythmic thrust and he was so aware of every movement she made that he felt the exact moment when her body tumbled out of control. The ecstatic tightening of her body stroked the length of his erection and he finally lost his own grip on control and fell with her, joining her in that scorching, exhilarating, terrifying rush to the very edges of extreme pleasure.

His mind blanked. In those few moments of exquisite perfection he forgot everything except the amazing chemistry that he created with this woman.

And as the sizzling, vicious response of his body finally calmed, he became aware of two things. One, that she was no longer fighting him and, two, that he was still hard.

Which gave him a choice.

He could either withdrew and allow her to sleep, or he could do what his body was urging him to do.

Allowing himself a half-smile in the safety of the darkness, Leandro made his choice.

* * *

Millie stared at herself in the bathroom mirror, seeing wild hair and flushed cheeks. And that was hardly surprising, was it? He'd made love to her until dawn.

Until dawn...

Trying to ignore the hurt that bloomed inside her, she pulled on a pair of loose trousers and a simple T-shirt and walked out onto the terrace.

A lizard lay basking in the heat of the sun and, nearby, one of the cats was stretched out, slowly licking his fur.

And as relaxed as any of them was Leandro, lounging at the breakfast table with his legs stretched out, his gaze focused on the financial pages of a newspaper. A coffee cup lay empty next to his lean, bronzed hand, his dark hair still damp from the shower.

Millie cleared her throat and he glanced up. His slow, sure smile made her want to hit him.

Leandro the conqueror, she thought miserably. *Man enough to bed a woman even when he didn't find her attractive.*

'*Kalimera.*' He greeted her in Greek. '*Te kanis?* How are you?'

'I'm fine, thank you.'

His eyes narrowed instantly and Millie quivered with suppressed emotion, so utterly humiliated that if she'd been able to leave the island without speaking to him, she would have.

She didn't want to have this conversation, but she knew that Leandro was far too quick not to pick up on her distress.

He folded the newspaper carefully and put it to one side. 'Obviously you're not feeling so good this morning.'

'I'm fine.'

'Fine?' His eyes rested on hers and then he said something in Greek to the staff who were hovering. They melted away, leaving the two of them alone on the terrace. 'All right.' His tone was even. 'We no longer have company. You can tell me what you think of me.'

'You don't want to know.'

'Yes,' he said softly, 'I do. No more secrets, remember?'

'All right.' Millie curved her hand over the back of the chair, too wound up and upset to contemplate joining him at the table. 'If you really want to know what I think—I think you are the most ruthless, insensitive man I've ever met.'

Stunned dark eyes met hers. 'Run that past me again?'

'You heard me.'

'I presume this interesting sentiment has hit you in the cold light of day. It certainly wasn't what was going through your mind last night when you were naked and sobbing in my bed.'

'Don't speak like that! I find it *really* embarrassing. It's bad enough that you do all those things to me and make me—you know…' Hot colour flooded her cheeks and she looked away from his hot gaze, unable to look him in the eye and maintain the conversation. 'It's as if you're sitting there smugly congratulating yourself on your amazing ability to turn any woman to jelly no matter what. What were you trying to prove?'

Leandro was unusually still, his gaze partially concealed by thick, black lashes. 'What makes you think I was trying to prove something?'

'Because why else would you have devoted your night to that whole…' Millie waved her hand wildly '…seduction routine. What? *What was it all about?*'

'They say actions speak louder than words—didn't last night say anything to you?'

'Yes. It said that you didn't know how to apologise, but you do know how to have sex.'

'You think that was apology sex?'

'I'd rather think that than the alternative.'

'Which is?'

'Pity sex. That's far worse than apology sex.'

'You think I made love to you because I felt sorry for you? I'm not sure the male anatomy would allow "pity sex", whatever that is.' His apparent lack of emotion somehow made everything worse.

'I'm sure yours would—you don't exactly have a problem with your sex drive, do you? Although I did notice that even you had to do it in the dark.'

'"Do it"?' He repeated her words with careful emphasis, the subtle lift of one eyebrow reminding her of just how unsophisticated she was compared to him.

Millie rubbed her damp palms on her loose trousers, wishing she hadn't started this conversation. 'It wasn't making love. Making your point would be closer to the mark. Why did you do it? Was it a challenge to your reputation as the ultimate lover? Or was it supposed to be a going-away present? You don't want me to feel bad about myself so you decided to give me a good night before you sent me packing, is that right?' Her emotions were in such a heightened state of turbulence that his calm, watchful gaze was even more infuriating. 'Aren't you going to say something?'

Leandro stirred and drew in a breath. 'I only realised yesterday how insecure you are, and clearly I've underestimated the depths of that insecurity.' Putting his napkin carefully down on the table, he stood up.

Something in the set of his powerful shoulders and the glint in his eye made her step backwards but he was too quick for her. His hand closed around her wrist and when she twisted it in an attempt to free herself he simply drew her closer.

Memories of the way he'd held her hands in the moonlight

deepened the flush on her cheeks. Hope warred with her feelings of inadequacy.

'Let me go. You're always grabbing me! What do you think you're doing?'

'You think last night was all about pity sex—you think I'm only capable of only "doing it" in the dark.' He swung her into his arms, strode a few paces across the terrace. 'Well, it's not dark now, *agape mou,* so let's test that theory, shall we?'

'Put me down, Leandro!'

He lowered her onto the nearest sun lounger. 'I've put you down.' His voice was a soft dangerous purr and he undid the clasp of her trousers with a practised flick of his fingers.

With a gasp of shock she clutched at her trousers but she was too late. They were already discarded on the floor and his hands were stripping off her T-shirt with the same decisive force. 'Stop it. Leandro, what are you *thinking?*'

'That you're incredibly sexy,' he growled, releasing the catch on her bra and stripping off her panties without pause or hesitation. It was easy for him, with his vastly superior strength, to keep her where he wanted her. 'And I'm thinking that being thoughtful wasn't the right approach. Apparently what a man sees as sensitive, a woman can see as insensitive.'

Horribly conscious of the sun blazing a spotlight onto her naked body, Millie tried to slither away from him but Leandro held her firmly, a dangerous gleam in his eyes. 'No more hiding, *agape mou.* No more robes, long trousers or dark rooms. We will do this in daylight and then you will know the truth, *hmm?* You will see how sorry I feel for you—how this injury of yours has affected me. You want to know if I'm aroused? If you still turn me on? Let's see, shall we?'

'Don't do this.' Millie drew her knees up, trying to cover

herself but he pushed her legs down with one hand and deftly dealt with the zip of his trousers with the other.

'Do I look as though I'm having a problem becoming aroused, *agape mou?* Do I look like a man doing you a favour?' His eyes glittered as he dispensed with his trousers, boldly unselfconscious as he stripped himself naked, exposing his lean, bronzed body. Lean, bronzed, *aroused* body.

With the flat of his hand Leandro pushed her gently back against the sun lounger and came over her in a fluid movement that was all dominant male.

His muscles were pumped up and hard and she felt the brush of his chest hair against the sensitised tips of her breasts.

When the blunt tip of his erection brushed against her exposed thigh she gave a gasp of shock that turned to a moan as he buried his face in her neck.

'Does that feel like pity?' He moved against her boldly and Millie groaned and turned her head away because the sudden explosion of excitement that consumed her was just too humiliating.

'Don't do this, Leandro…'

'Why? Because you're afraid I'm doing it because I feel sorry for you? I never do things for other people, *agape mou,* you should know that by now. I'm selfish. I do things for myself. Because it's what I want.' His tone rough, he took her hand and drew it down to that part of himself, and her mouth dried because he was velvety hard and she could barely circle him with her shaking fingers. 'I know you had no experience before I met you,' he purred, 'so let me spell out the facts, *pethi mou.* This isn't called pity. It's called chemistry. Hot, sexual chemistry. It isn't me "making my point", as you so eloquently put it, it's me making love.' He caught her face in his hands and lowered his mouth to hers. 'Making love,' he said against her lips. 'Have you got that?'

'Leandro—'

'I want you. I've always wanted you and that isn't going to change. Are you listening?' He slid his hand behind her neck and forced her to hold his gaze. 'Are you listening to me?'

Her hand was still holding him and she stared into the fierce heat of his eyes and forgot everything except the burning need in her pelvis.

His hand slid under her bottom, shifting her position. 'You have scars on your body, yes,' he said thickly, 'but it's still your body. One day, when you have my babies, you might have stretch marks or maybe other scars, but this will still be your body. And it's *your* body that I want. No other woman's.'

Babies?

Her head was spinning, her pulse racing out of control as she struggled to hold onto her thoughts before they slipped away. He'd said— Had he said…?

While she was struggling with his words, he entered her with a determined thrust, sliding deep, and Millie gave up on any thought of responding because the feel of him inside her drove every coherent thought from her brain. Unprepared for his invasion, she tried to make a sound but his mouth closed over hers and he held her hips as he drove deeper still, his virile thrust taking him straight to the heart of her. This time there was no gentle foreplay, no slow, clever strokes of his long fingers. Just an unapologetic demonstration of raw sexuality and male dominance.

His hand locked in her hair, Leandro lifted his head just enough to allow him to speak. 'Can you feel me, Millie?' He growled the words against her lips and ground deeper inside her. 'Can you feel me inside you?' He was big, hard and shockingly male, and she sobbed his name and dug her nails into his back, her body so sensitised by his invasion that she could hardly breathe. In that moment she'd never felt so wanted, truly desired.

His breathing unsteady, he gently bit her lower lip and then soothed it with his tongue. 'You feel incredible,' he murmured huskily, and he withdrew slightly and her eyes flew wide.

'No...'

'No what?' He gave a slow, wicked smile, withdrawing still further. 'No, don't stop—or, no, don't do this?'

'Leandro...'

He kept her on the edge for several agonising seconds and then slid deep again, the movement sending shock waves of excitement through her trembling frame.

'This isn't pity sex,' he breathed, lifting her hips to allow him even, 'it's hot sex, *agape mou*. It's what you and I share. Can you feel it?'

Millie was incapable of speech, her body rushing forward to meet the pleasure that he was creating with each skilled, fluid stroke. For a delicious moment her eyes met his. He held that look, the connection between them impossibly intimate. And then everything inside her splintered apart and she arched her back as her body was convulsed by an erotic explosion so intense that she couldn't catch her breath. The sensations devoured her, tearing through her body like a ravenous beast on the rampage, and she felt the sudden tension in his body and the increase in masculine thrust that brought him to the same dizzying peak of hot liquid pleasure.

Millie lay in dazed, breathless silence for a moment, her mind incapable of functioning. She was dimly aware of the hot sun burning her leg and the roughness of his thigh against her more sensitive flesh. And then she heard the distant buzz of a motorboat somewhere in the distance and was suddenly hideously conscious of the fact they were naked.

'Leandro...' She pushed against his bare shoulder, suddenly panicking that someone was going to see them. 'We have to move.'

'Why?' Typically relaxed, he raised himself onto his elbow and surveyed her from under thick, dark lashes. 'What's the hurry?'

'Your staff—'

'Don't venture near my private terrace,' he said smoothly, dropping a lingering kiss to her parted lips.

'But what if one of them comes to clear up the breakfast things?'

'I'll fire them.' He kissed her cheek. 'Relax.'

But she couldn't relax. 'I should check Costas.'

'He has a nanny, remember? And if he was awake you would have heard him through the baby alarm.'

'What if it isn't working? I need to get dressed, Leandro.'

'No. You don't. You just want to hide your body and I'm not going to let you.'

'You may be comfortable with nudity, but that's only because you look great.'

'Thank you.' Laughing, he caught her face in his hands. 'You have a great body, too. I thought I'd just proved that. You're *not* running away.'

Millie bit her lip and then gave a faltering smile. 'I really do want to see the baby. It's been such an upheaval for him, being passed around as if he's some sort of trophy. He needs stability and security. I want him to know I'm here. I need to take a shower and dress.'

He sighed and lowered his mouth to hers. 'You are quite extraordinary,' he murmured softly, stroking her hair back from her face. 'Go on, then. I'll see you in a minute.'

Her senses and emotions churning from what had happened between them, she drew away from him and walked awkwardly across the terrace and back into the bedroom.

Locking herself in the bathroom, she turned on the shower, wondering what exactly had it all meant to him. What had he been proving? Convinced that he'd made love to her in the night out of some misplaced sense of guilt, she was no longer sure of anything. Not even herself. Her body still ached and tingled from their lovemaking and she stepped under the shower and then changed into a long cotton skirt and a strap top.

She contemplated blow-drying her hair and decided against it, anxious in case Costas had woken and was upset.

Hurrying along to his room, she heard happy gurgles and cooing and walked in to find him lying in Leandro's arms.

Millie watched for a moment, her insides turning to mush as she saw how gentle he was with the baby. He was speaking in soft, lyrical Greek and then he looked up and saw her.

'And here is beautiful Millie.' He placed a kiss on top of the baby's head and handed him over. 'He seems quite happy.'

Millie took the baby, feeling his solid warmth in her arms. 'He needs his nappy changed.'

'Now, *that*,' Leandro drawled, 'is definitely outside my area of expertise. Do you want me to call the nanny?'

'Believe it or not, I'm capable of changing a nappy.' Millie laid Costas on a changing mat on the floor. Relieved to have a reason to avoid Leandro's disturbing gaze, she cooed at the baby who kicked his legs in delight. 'He thinks I can't change a nappy.'

'Why don't you put him on the bed?'

'Because he might roll off.' Millie deftly changed the nappy and scooped the baby against her. 'Time for breakfast.'

'Give him his bottle on the terrace,' Leandro instructed. 'There are things I want to say to you.'

She looked at him warily. 'Things that can be said in front of a baby?'

He looked amused. 'Absolutely. In the unlikely event that he files our conversation for future reference, it will do him good to know that adults can sort out their problems rather than giving up on their marriage. That is the example I would want to set for the younger generation. And you?'

Millie's heartbeat faltered. 'I— We— It isn't that simple, Leandro—you're unrealistic.'

He guided her towards the door that led to the vine covered terrace. 'The difference in our approach may be rooted in our cultures. Your divorce rate is higher than ours.'

Still holding Costas, Millie sighed as she walked towards the table that had been set for breakfast. 'I think cultural differences are the least of our problems at this point in our relationship.'

His response to that was to turn and deliver a slow, confident smile. 'Problems are merely there to test resolve. If you really want something, you can overcome the problems.' He stepped towards her, closing the gap until she drew in a breath. 'How much do you want our marriage to work, Millie?'

How much? Her heart was thudding and she was trapped by the unshakable confidence in his eyes. 'I—I want it, of course, but you don't—'

'Don't I?' He didn't even wait for her to finish the sentence. 'What do you think this morning was all about?'

'I have no idea. I'm assuming your caveman tendencies ran a little out of control.'

The look in his eyes sent her pulse racing again and she stepped backwards, grateful that she was holding the baby.

'I need to feed Costas.'

'If you think that's going to get you off the hook, you don't know me. We're going to talk about this, *agape mou*. I'm going to explore every last corner of...' His voice tailed off and her breathing quickened because the look in his eyes was unmistakably sexual.

'Of?'

His smile widened. 'Of our relationship,' he purred, and she knew he was perfectly aware that she'd been waiting for him to say 'your body.'

Millie gritted her teeth and was about to stalk towards the table when he closed his hand over her shoulder and bent his head so that his mouth was by her ear.

'That, too,' he murmured silkily, and the colour flooded into her cheeks.

'You've done enough exploring for one day.'

'I haven't even started.' Leandro pulled the chair out for her and made sure she had what she needed for the baby. Then he took the seat opposite her and poured her some coffee.

'What was it you wanted to say to me?' The anticipation of the conversation to come scraped at her insides like sandpaper, putting her off her food. Trying to distract herself, she slid the teat into the baby's mouth, her expression softening as he clamped his jaws and started to suck.

'Eat some food. This honey comes from a friend's bees. It's delicious.'

'I'm not hungry.'

'Eat, or I will feed you,' he said pleasantly, but his eyes glinted warningly across the table. 'I overlooked the fact that you didn't eat last night. You'd worked yourself up into a state about telling me what had happened to you, and you'd braced yourself for rejection. But that didn't happen, did it, Millie? You are still sitting at my table, having just climbed out of my bed—metaphorically at least—so there is no longer a reason for you to have lost your appetite.'

'Nothing's changed, Leandro.' She watched as he drizzled the thick, golden honey over the creamy yoghurt. 'The issues between us are still there.'

'All right—so let's address those issues because the worry is affecting you badly. First, can I get you anything? This sweet pastry is delicious.'

Millie shook her head, envying his calm. 'You're not stressed, are you?'

'What is there to be stressed about?' He drank his coffee and replaced the cup carefully in the saucer. 'I am relaxing on a beautiful island with a beautiful woman. If I found that stressful, I would be a fool, no?'

She closed her eyes briefly. 'So you're just going to pretend that sex solves everything.'

'No. I'm not going to pretend that. I want to make a few things clear to you. I made love to you in the dark last night because you were clearly very upset and I thought it was the sensitive thing to do, but…' he gave a self deprecating smile '…as I now know, a man's idea of what is sensitive isn't always the same as a woman's. As you keep pointing out, I'm not that good at the whole sensitive side of things, so I need to work on that.'

Millie gave a strangled laugh. 'What? You're suddenly going to turn into a modern man?'

'I wouldn't go that far.' There was humour in his tone and in the glance he sent in her direction. 'Tell me why you think I made love to you in the dark?'

'Isn't it obvious?' *Was he going to make her spell it out?*

Apparently he was, because he showed no inclination to let her off the hook. 'I think we've both accepted that what is obvious to me isn't obvious to you and vice versa. Guessing games haven't done much for the success of our relationship to date.'

Unable to argue with that, Millie grimaced. 'All right.' She adjusted the bottle in the baby's mouth. 'You made love to me in the dark because you didn't want to see my body. I thought being in the dark was the only way you could be sure you'd be able to—' She broke off and his eyes gleamed with sardonic humour as he challenged her unspoken assumption.

'Well, you were wrong about that, weren't you?'

Remembering just *how* wrong, her mouth dried. 'I suppose I was.'

His mind clearly lingering on the same memories, he gave a slow, masculine smile. 'It was fantastic, no?'

Millie looked away from him. 'It didn't solve anything.'

'Yes, it did.' His voice soft, Leandro leaned across the table and took her hand. 'It told me a great deal about you.'

'That I'm easy?'

'Easy?' He gave a hollow laugh. 'You're the most difficult woman I know. In every sense. You're complicated, contrary, you don't say what you think—and you put thoughts in other people's heads.' He paused. 'And that brings us to the most important part of this conversation.'

'Which is what?'

'Your insecurities. We married quickly, as you constantly remind me.' He pulled a face. 'And I didn't take the time to get to know you properly. That was my first mistake. The sex overwhelmed us both, I think.'

'Yes, it did. You can't build a marriage on…' she cast a

worried look at the baby and lowered her voice '…sex. Sex isn't communication.'

'Actually, I disagree.' His gaze was direct. 'I think sex is often a very honest form of communication. On our honeymoon you were insatiable—affectionate, uninhibited and spontaneous. When you turned your back on me, I should have made you talk. Instead, I gave you space.' Leandro leaned back in his chair. 'You assumed that I'd prefer your sister to you, isn't that right?'

'Yes.' Millie didn't lie. 'Becca was beautiful, elegant and witty. She wouldn't have had any difficulties knowing what to wear and what to say.'

'So you saw us together and instead of thinking, *He wouldn't,* you thought *I understand why he would.*'

'Sort of.'

'So would you agree that the whole incident said more about you than it did about me?'

Her heart was thumping. *Had she been unfair?* The doubt was slowly growing in her mind. 'Maybe. I don't know. She was my sister.' She bit her lip. 'I just want to put the whole thing behind us.'

His mouth tightened for a moment and then he lifted a padded envelope from the table and handed it to her. 'This is for you.'

'What is it?' Millie slid her hand into the packet and withdrew some discs. 'What are these?'

'It's the CCTV footage of what happened in the pool that day. Take it.' He leaned forward. 'It proves that I'm telling the truth.'

'You had proof?'

'I have a very sophisticated security system in the house.'

'But you didn't show me before?'

Leandro hesitated. 'Two reasons,' he said softly. 'Firstly,

because I had this idealistic wish for my wife to have unquestioning faith and trust in me. Secondly, I didn't want to be the one who exposed your sister for what she was. I'm doing it now because I realise how insecure you are and I don't want you to feel that way.'

Her heart lifted and sank and Millie looked at him helplessly. 'So this proves my husband is innocent and my sister is guilty.'

'Yes.'

Struggling with the truth, she fingered the CDs. 'When Becca came to stay, I thought she was helping me. But she was targeting you, wasn't she?'

'I think we have to assume that.'

Reflecting on that, Millie bit her lip and then put the CDs back in the envelope. 'Thanks,' she said gruffly, 'for giving me the chance to see them. Now I'm the one who owes you an apology.'

'Aren't you going to look at them?'

'No.' Millie rubbed her fingers over the envelope. 'I believe you. I think perhaps a small part of me always believed you, but believing you meant accepting that Becca—' She broke off and Leandro breathed out heavily.

'I know. I'm sorry.'

'She was my family. Someone I trusted.' Millie lifted her eyes to his and saw dark shadows there. 'What? You think I was stupid to trust her?'

'No.' His voice was rough. 'You should be able to trust family. It's just that sometimes…' He muttered something under his breath and stood up abruptly. 'Enough of this, Millie. It's in the past now.'

Millie looked at him, wondering what was going on in his mind. 'Leandro—'

'I want you to forget it,' he ordered. 'I want to put it behind us.'

'But it doesn't really change the facts! You need a wife who's able to stand by your side at glittering functions, someone who can hold her own with the elite of Hollywood, politicians, businessmen—'

'And I have a wife capable of all those things. The only thing she apparently isn't capable of is believing in herself.' Leandro reached for her hand across the table. 'But that is going to change.'

'I appreciate what you're trying to do, but you have to be realistic. That actress was right—I'm not your type.'

'She was trying to destroy your confidence.' His fingers tightened on hers. 'Are you going to let her?'

'Very possibly.' Millie gave a weak smile. 'You think I should look in the mirror and say I'm more beautiful than her? I'd have to be treated for hallucinations.'

Leandro gestured to a staff member who was hovering discreetly, and she hurried up and carefully lifted Costas from Millie's arms.

'I don't want him corrupted,' Leandro said silkily, 'so I didn't think he should be here for the next part.' He stood up and drew her against him intimately, a smile playing around his firm mouth. 'Are you aware of your own power yet?'

Feeling the hard thrust of his arousal, she looked at him in amused disbelief. 'You're insatiable.'

'With you, yes. You turn me on,' he breathed, lowering his mouth to hers, 'and on, and on. All the time. And I want you, all the time. So next time you don't feel beautiful, remind yourself of that.'

'So what happens now?'

'You learn to be yourself. No more dressing as you think

you are expected to dress—no more behaving as you are expected to behave. Just be you. Is that so hard?'

'And when I embarrass you?'

Leandro smiled. 'That won't happen. I find you beautiful, generous and kind and I intend to devote the next few weeks to making you believe in yourself.'

If they could have stayed in Greece forever, maybe their relationship would work, Millie thought. But his life was so much bigger than this one, idyllic island.

And what was going to happen then?

CHAPTER TEN

THE idyll lasted two more weeks.

'He loves his afternoon nap. He's sleeping really well now.' Millie tucked Costas into the cot and tiptoed towards Leandro, who was waiting in the doorway. He was dressed casually in shorts and a polo shirt and his dark hair gleamed in the sunshine.

'You are very good with him.' His eyes lingered on her face. 'And extremely generous to give so much of yourself to a child who isn't yours.'

Millie was horribly conscious of his scrutiny. 'He's part of my sister.'

Leandro took her hand and led her across the terrace and towards the narrow path that led down through a garden of tumbling Mediterranean plants to the beach. 'You are nothing like her.'

'I'm well aware of that. My parents were constantly reminding me of that.'

Leandro frowned down at her. 'Really?'

'I don't blame them. I never gave my parents anything to boast about. I was never top in maths, I was only ever picked for the netball team if everyone else was struck down by some vile virus or other, I didn't play a musical instrument,

I have a voice like a crow with a sore throat and I don't have the face and body of a model.'

'And is all that important?'

'Among you alpha high achievers, it is. My mum's face glowed with pride when she introduced Becca to anyone—"This is my daughter who works as a top model but she also has a maths degree from Cambridge, you know." And then she'd turn to me and say, "And this is our other daughter—Millie isn't academic, are you dear?" And I'd feel the same way I felt when I got my spelling wrong at school. The teachers would sigh and say, "You're nothing like your sister, are you?" as if that was a major disadvantage in life.'

'No wonder you have no confidence. But all that is going to change.' As they reached the bottom of the path, Leandro tightened his grip on her hand. 'You can't possibly still be feeling insecure,' he murmured, taking her face in his hands and kissing her. 'For the past two weeks we've done nothing but talk and make love.'

'Maybe I'm having problems believing that anyone can be this lucky,' Millie replied humbly, wrapping her arms around his neck. 'And I still can't believe you don't want someone who you can discuss the money markets with over breakfast.'

'I can't think of anything more guaranteed to put me off my food.' He dragged his thumb across her mouth in an unmistakably sensual gesture. 'I work in a very high-pressured, conflict-ridden environment—when I come home I don't want to discuss work. And I don't want conflict. I want a soft, warm woman who can challenge me in other ways. Which you do. So the answer to your unspoken question, *agape mou,* is no. I didn't ever want your sister. But I have told you that before.' He released her and took her hand, leading her towards the jetty.

Millie looked at the sleek motorboat. 'We're going out on that?'

'I feel in need of an adrenaline rush,' he drawled. 'In the absence of anyone to fire, bully or intimidate, I need to find alternative forms of excitement.'

Her eyes slid to his and he gave a slow grin. 'Yes, we'll be doing that, too,' he purred, helping her into the boat and loosening the rope. Lithe and agile, he followed her into the boat, taking the control with his usual cool confidence. 'Do you get seasick?'

'I don't know, but I'm probably about to find out.' Her nerve endings sizzling from the chemistry that constantly flared between them, she tried to concentrate. 'How fast are you going to go?'

His smile widened. 'Fast.'

And he did.

Having eased the boat skilfully out of the shallow bay, he pushed the throttle forwards and sent the boat flying across the waves at a speed that took her breath away.

Millie held tight to the seat, meeting his brief, questioning glance with an exaggerated smile of delight.

Men, she thought, relieved that she hadn't bothered with a hat. Her hair flew around her face and the spray from the waves stung her cheeks.

Leandro kept up the pace until they reached a neighbouring island, and then he cut the engine and dropped the anchor.

'Presumably you could have gone at half the pace.'

'And that would have taken twice the time.' Unapologetic, he leaned forward and kissed her hard. 'I don't like hanging around.'

'I'd noticed.' Millie looked towards the beach. 'Is that where we're going?'

'Later. If you want to. First I want to show you something. Put this on.' He handed her a slim, expensive-looking box with a discreet logo in the corner, which she recognised as that of a top fashion designer.

'If this is another swimming costume, you can forget it. In the last ten days all you've done is make me take my clothes off all the time.'

'That isn't quite all I've done, *agape mou*.'

She blushed. 'OK, so I wore a swimming costume on your island, but presumably this isn't private. Anyone could see me.'

"You have nothing to hide.'

'I still can't believe you got me into a swimming costume.'

'You looked fabulous.'

'From the back.'

'Yes, from the back. And from the front. And the side. From every angle,' Leandro said, sliding his shorts off to reveal the strong, flat stomach and hard thighs. 'You seem a little overdressed for a Greek beach. Open the box.'

'Where did this come from, anyway? You haven't been anywhere to buy me anything.'

He spread his hands in masculine apology. 'All right—I confess I didn't actually choose it. I made a call, gave someone a brief and it was delivered.'

'You made a call.' She mimicked him as she opened the box. Wrapped carefully inside layers of luxurious silken tissue paper was the sexiest bikini she'd ever seen. It was a shimmering gold and she could see that it was brief enough to be virtually non-existent. Her heart thudded uncomfortably. 'No *way*, Leandro!'

'Put it on.'

'I can't possibly wear this.'

'Trust me, you will look sensational in it.' Calm and unconcerned, he stripped off his T-shirt, revealing bronzed shoulders hard with muscle. 'I will enjoy watching you change into it.'

'Leandro.' Her tone was urgent and her fingers tightened on the slippery fabric. 'A swimming costume—well, I managed that. But I can't wear a bikini. I just can't. I have—'

'Scars—yes, I know.' He was as relaxed as she was agitated, and her fingers tightened on the silky fabric.

'You don't understand how self-conscious I feel.'

'I understand *exactly* how self-conscious you feel and I am trying to show you that I find you incredibly sexy in whatever you're wearing.' His voice was husky. 'Or *not* wearing. Get changed.'

Millie held the bikini in her hands. Looked at it. Then she saw the determination in his eyes. 'I can't wear a bikini.'

'You have ten seconds to change,' he warned in a silky tone, 'or I will put it on you myself.'

'You're not very sympathetic, are you?'

'Do you want my sympathy?'

'No. I just want to hide and you won't let me. For the past two weeks you've done nothing but expose me! You make love in daylight, you make me parade around in a swimming costume and now this.'

Leandro glanced pointedly at his watch. 'You're down to one second. Are you going to do it yourself or do I do it for you?'

Sending him a furious glare, Millie snatched up one of the neatly folded towels and retreated to the far side of the boat. Was he being intentionally cruel? Angry and upset, she wriggled into the minuscule bikini, snatched her clothes up from the baking leather of the seat and stalked back to him.

'Satisfied?'

'Not yet.' His smile was wickedly sexy as his eyes trailed down her body. 'But I will be. Remind me to thank the person who chose that. She followed my brief exactly. The emphasis being on the word "brief".'

Flustered by his lazy, masculine scrutiny, Millie stared down at the clear water. Shoals of tiny silvery fish darted beneath the surface and she watched them for a moment. 'I don't understand you.'

'Evidently not. But we're working to change that. You look fantastic in that bikini.'

She opened her mouth to argue with him but he walked across to her, wrapped his arms around her and kissed her. The heat he created with his mouth eclipsed anything produced by the sun, and Millie felt her body melt and her mind shut down. She forgot that she wanted to cover herself. She forgot to feel self-conscious. Instead, she felt beautiful and seductive.

When he finally lifted his head, she felt dizzy. 'How is your confidence now?'

Basking in the sexual appreciation, she gave a reluctant smile. 'Recovering.'

'Good. Because we are flying back to London tomorrow.'

Millie felt as though she'd been punched in the stomach. 'Why?'

'Because my business demands it,' he said dryly, stroking her hair away from her face. 'I have been absent for a long time—there are things that need my attention. And tomorrow night we have a gala evening to attend.'

'Tomorrow?' Millie tensed. 'You haven't given me any warning!'

'I didn't want you turning yourself into a nervous wreck.'

'Who will be there?'

'I will be there.' Leandro released his hold on her and stepped onto the side of the boat. 'And I am the only person that matters in your life.' With that arrogant statement, he executed a perfect dive, his lean, bronzed body slicing into the water with powerful grace.

Millie stared after him in frustration, realising that the only way she was going to be able to finish the conversation was if she followed him.

Knowing that a dive would definitely part her from the tiny bikini, she opted instead to use the ladder that hung from the back of the boat.

Sliding into the cooling water, she swam over to him.

Her confidence had increased a thousand times over the past few weeks, but was she really ready to go back to their old life?

She glanced up at the sky and, instead of being a perfect blue, it was grey and overcast.

And during the night the rain came.

Twenty-four hours later, Millie was back in London, reflecting on how much life could change in a few short weeks.

She looked in the mirror and for the first time ever she didn't wish that she could turn the lights down.

After two weeks alone with a flatteringly attentive Leandro, it was impossible not to feel beautiful.

Which was just as well because tonight they were going to be walking up the red carpet together. And there would be cameras.

To test her new confidence, Millie wore a dress of her own choosing, shoes that made her feel like a princess, and chose to leave her hair loose and curly.

Nestling against her throat was the heart-shaped diamond that Leandro had given her on their wedding day.

As she slipped her feet into her shoes, Leandro strolled into the dressing room.

He looked spectacular in a tailored dinner jacket and Millie felt a little pang as she realised that every woman in the room was going to be looking at him. For sheer visual impact there wasn't a man who came close to him, she thought weakly, and he caught her soft sigh and frowned.

'What are you thinking?'

'I'm wishing you weren't quite so attractive,' Millie said dryly. 'Then maybe women wouldn't all gape at you and I wouldn't feel so insecure.'

'After the past ten days I have no energy left,' he assured her in a silky tone, 'so you have no cause for concern.' He urged her out of the bedroom and down the stairs to the hallway. 'You look beautiful. You *know* you look beautiful.'

'I like hearing you say it.' Oblivious to the staff hovering, Millie wound her arms around his neck and he smiled and lowered his mouth to hers.

'Then I'll say it again,' Leandro murmured against her lips. 'You look beautiful.'

And she didn't argue because she saw it in his eyes when he looked at her.

'I didn't straighten my hair.'

'Good. I love your curls.'

'I've worn this dress before.'

'I know. I remember how good you looked in it the first time.'

'Do you think it makes my bottom look big?'

Leandro backed away from her, his hands spread in a defensive groan. '*Never* ask a man that question.' He laughed, but he turned her sideways and dutifully studied her rear view. 'It makes your bottom look like something out of a man's fantasy. And now I want to—'

'Don't you *dare* rumple me!' Wriggling away from the possessive slide of his hands, Millie couldn't help laughing. 'You're insatiable.'

'Yes. But unfortunately for me I am the guest of honour.' With a regretful sigh, he reached for his BlackBerry and made a quick call. 'Otherwise…' he returned the phone to his pocket '…I would feel the need to devote the rest of my evening examining the size of your bottom at close quarters. My driver is waiting outside for us.'

Millie walked towards the front door, but he stopped her.

'Wait—I have something for you.' His voice husky, Leandro reached into his pocket and retrieved a long black box. Opening it, he lifted out a slim, diamond bracelet.

Millie gasped and covered her mouth with her hands. 'Leandro, you can't—'

'I can.' He fastened it around her wrist and then stood back and narrowed his eyes. 'It suits you.'

'It matches my necklace.'

'Of course.' His hands firm on her shoulders, he turned her so that she could see her reflection in the hall mirror.

The diamonds sparkled against her creamy skin and she lifted a hand and touched them reverentially. 'I might get mugged.'

His jaw tightened and he drew her close. 'Never again,' he said gruffly. 'You're with me. And that's where you're staying. And I will protect you.'

As they stepped into the back of the luxurious car, Leandro spoke quietly to the driver and then turned to her. 'There will be media,' he warned her as they drew up outside the venue. 'Just smile.'

And she did.

Millie smiled her way up the red carpet, smiled at the cameras, smiled at the guests who gaped and jostled each other for an introduction, and she smiled at Leandro, who was as sexy as sin in his role of powerful tycoon. He slipped easily from one environment to another, she thought as she chatted casually to the man seated to her left.

She felt more confident, more at ease than she ever had before, and turned to Leandro with a grateful smile. 'I'm having a nice time.'

'Good.' His searing gaze rested on her cleavage. 'I'm not. All I want to do is take you home.'

Millie reached for her wineglass, enjoying the feeling of power that she had over him. The tension gradually mounted between them and by the time Leandro announced that they could leave, both of them were desperate.

They kissed in the car

As they approached the gates of his house, Millie noticed the hordes of press and her heart sank.

'What are they doing here? I thought they'd lost interest in us.'

'Ignore them.' A frown on his face, Leandro spoke to the driver in Greek and they were driven at speed through a network of roads which eventually brought them to the back of the house.

'I love this secret entrance.' Millie giggled, lifting the hem of her dress so that it didn't drag on the grass. 'It's so romantic. And I love the fact that the press haven't discovered it.'

'It's useful,' Leandro replied, but she sensed he was distracted by something. 'Come on. Let's go inside.'

They were greeted by the housekeeper, who was clearly agitated.

'I'm glad you're home—something terrible…' Nervously she rubbed her hands together and Millie felt her legs turn to jelly.

'Costas? Is he ill?' She stepped forward, panic making her legs shake. 'I shouldn't have gone out. Is something wrong with him?'

'The baby is fine, madam,' the housekeeper assured her, but the pity and embarrassment in her eyes made Millie drop back a few steps.

'Then what's wrong?'

'How anyone can write such stuff—do they have no shame?' Clearly distressed, the housekeeper blinked furiously. 'We've had all the papers put in the conservatory, Mr Demetrios, and I've instructed the staff that they're not to speak to anyone. The press have been knocking and calling, but we haven't answered. It's shameful, if you ask me, a man not being able to have peace in his own home.'

Without uttering a word, Leandro turned and strode towards the living room.

Feeling as though her shoes were lead weights, Millie followed him into the room and closed the door behind her. Even though she didn't know what was wrong, her heart was thudding and she felt sick with dread.

Even without looking, she knew that the newspapers would have done another hatchet job on her. But how? They'd only taken her photograph a few hours earlier.

Leandro picked up the first of the newspapers and scanned it briefly. The expression on his handsome face didn't alter as he threw it aside and picked up the next.

Almost afraid to look, Millie stooped and picked up one of the discarded copies. The Hollywood actress smiled seductively from the front page, and the caption read, 'Loving Leandro—my Unforgettable Night with my Greek Tycoon'.

Millie dropped the paper.

Her mouth was dry and her hands were shaking, but something made her pick up the next paper that he'd dropped. This time she read the copy.

'She's described your night together in minute detail.'

'She has a vivid imagination,' Leandro said flatly, picking up the last of the newspapers. 'They all say the same thing. Leave them. It's filth.' But as he scanned the final newspaper his expression did alter, as if something printed there was the final straw.

His mouth a flat, angry line, he quickly folded the paper but Millie reached forward and tugged it away from him, some masochistic part of her wanting to see what had upset him so much.

'Millie, no!' Leandro stepped forward to take it from her but not before she'd seen the pictures of herself in a bikini.

'Oh, my God.' Appalled and mortified, she felt like hiding under a rock. 'How did they—? We—'

'They must have had photographers near my island.' Leandro jabbed his fingers into his hair and cast her a shimmering glance of apology. 'This is *my* fault. I took you on that boat and I made you wear the bikini.'

'You didn't know there'd be a photographer nearby.' Millie gave a hysterical laugh. 'Where was he? On the back of a dolphin?'

Leandro undid his bow-tie and released his top button. 'I'm truly sorry.' He broke off and muttered something in Greek. 'I'll speak to my lawyers immediately. There may be something they can do.'

'It's already been done.' Her mouth dry, Millie stared at the photos and the close-up of her scars. Then she looked at the photographs of the actress taken from her latest film. The cruel positioning of the two photographs took her breath away. 'You can't undo this, Leandro. It's out there now. It will always be out there. And you can't blame them for making comparisons between me and the Hollywood actress—it's too good a story to miss, isn't it? The entire British public will now be asking themselves the same questions I asked myself—why would you choose me? And that's just going to keep on happening.' Her lips felt stiff and her brain numb as she stumbled towards the door. 'Excuse me. I need to check on Costas.'

'Millie—'

'I can't talk about this right now, I'm sorry. I need to be on my own. I need some time to get my head round it.' Without giving him time to intercept her, Millie shot from the room and took refuge in the nursery. She felt as though she'd been stripped naked and the sense of violation was worse than the vicious attack that had caused the scars in the first place.

Everyone across the country would be staring at those intimate photos and everyone would be making judgements.

As if in sympathy with her distress, Costas was screaming uncontrollably and Millie dismissed the nanny and lifted him out of his cot, holding him close, deriving comfort from his familiar warmth.

'There, angel. It's all right,' she whispered, 'I'm here now. It's all right. You're fine.'

'I'm so sorry,' the nanny apologised. 'I can't do anything with him. I think he's going down with something. He's been hot all evening and fretting.'

'It's OK, I'll sit with him,' Millie muttered, feeling the baby's forehead burning. 'You go to bed. There's no sense in everyone being awake.'

'Shall I stay while you get changed? I'd hate for him to ruin your dress.' The nanny looked at her pityingly and Millie realised that she knew about the papers.

Her face turned scarlet because she *hated* the thought of people pitying her. 'I don't care about the dress. You go to bed. Thanks.'

The girl hesitated and then quietly left the nursery.

Millie sat down in the chair, Costas in her lap, happy to hide away with the baby for a while. The alternative was facing Leandro, and she wasn't up to that at the moment.

She needed to get her thoughts straight.

'What a mess,' she murmured. 'You have no idea what a mess this is. Why can't people just mind their own business? Why do they love reading about trouble in other people's lives? I'm never buying a newspaper again on principle. I'm going to read gardening magazines. They don't hurt anyone.'

Exhausted by the demands of the conversation, Costas hiccoughed a few times and eventually drifted off to sleep on her shoulder.

As she laid him carefully in the cot, Millie stared down at him. She looked at the dark lashes and the dark hair and felt her stomach flip uncomfortably.

The gossip and speculation was endless.

It was always going to happen, wasn't it?

Maybe he wouldn't have affairs, but while she was with Leandro there was always going to be someone willing to sell him out for money, or point out her imperfections for an audience of millions to laugh at.

There would always be women willing to talk about their experiences in bed with him.

Millie dragged the chair next to the cot and flopped down into it, miserable, vulnerable and worried.

For half an hour she watched the baby sleep, checked his temperature and listened to his breathing.

* * *

Leandro stood in his study, his tension levels soaring into the stratosphere as he finished talking to his lawyers. The newspapers were strewn in front of him. Ordinarily he wouldn't have given any of them a first read, let alone a second, but this wasn't about him. It was about Millie. And he knew that today it was newspapers, but next week the celebrity magazines would pick up the story and it would run and run.

Thinking about Millie's fragile confidence, he wanted to punch something.

Being exposed to this wasn't fair on her, was it?

She was too sensitive.

He had no idea where she was now but, knowing Millie, he suspected she'd be curled up in an insecure heap somewhere, convinced that their relationship was never going to work.

His jaw tightened.

Perhaps she was right. Perhaps it never was going to work. Who on earth wanted to live with this?

Needing to do something to relieve his frustration, Leandro took the stairs to the top floor and pushed his way through the door that led to the secluded roof terrace.

Here, there were no cameras. No one watching.

Just the soothing rush of water from the fountain in the centre, the scent of plants, darkness and his thoughts.

He strolled to the balcony, from where he was able to see over the rooftops of London.

Up until this point in his life he'd been indifferent to the media intrusion. It hadn't bothered him. But now…

Millie was a living, breathing human being with feelings.

And those feelings had been badly hurt.

Leandro thought about those few seconds before they'd known what was wrong. Her thoughts had immediately been with the baby.

And when she'd seen those pictures of herself…

Guilt ripped through him, intense and unfamiliar as he dealt with the knowledge that he'd put her in a position that had allowed those pictures to be taken.

But the truth was that the media interest in his life was such that there would always be a photographer lurking, waiting to snap their picture. Even if he'd protected her from that one, he wouldn't necessarily have been able to protect her from the next.

And every time the press printed something nasty about her, another layer of her confidence would be shredded.

To be able to withstand the media you needed the hide of a rhinoceros, and Millie's flesh was as delicate as a rose petal.

She'd be torn, he thought grimly. *Ripped apart.*

And the decent thing would be to let her go—set her up somewhere new, where no one was interested in her.

From below in his courtyard he heard the roar of a car engine, but Leandro was too preoccupied to give it any thought.

Remembering that the last time he'd let Millie go had proved to be a mistake of gigantic proportions, Leandro strode back into the house and down the stairs, only to bump into the housekeeper, who was looking anxious and stressed.

'Don't tell me—more journalists?' Leandro spoke in a rough voice, a sinking feeling in the pit of his stomach. 'What's happened this time?'

'Millie has gone,' the woman told him. 'I heard her running through the house and then she said something like "No, don't do this to me" and then she took your car and drove like a maniac out of the drive. Gone. Just like that. She almost ran over the journalists waiting outside the gates.'

Gone. Crying.

Don't do this to me?

Remembering the roar of the car engine, Leandro's jaw tensed. 'Did any of the security staff follow her?' But he didn't need to see the appalled look on the housekeeper's face to know the answer to that one.

'It all happened so fast—'

Remembering what had happened the last time Millie had driven away from him upset, it took Leandro a moment to wrestle his emotions under control and think clearly.

He'd known she was upset but he'd given her the space she'd requested. And now he regretted it. He shouldn't have left her alone.

Leandro ran his fingers through his hair, his tension mounting as he thought of all the dangers she could now be facing. She was in London, alone and unprotected with a pack of press as hungry as hyenas. She was alone in his high-performance sports car in a cosmopolitan city where driving could be a life-threatening experience.

His expression grim, he strode into the house and walked straight to his study. Once there he contacted his head of security, gave him a brief and then proceeded to get slowly and methodically drunk.

After his third glass he discovered that there were some pains that alcohol couldn't numb, and he stopped drinking and closed his eyes.

How, he wondered, could he have made such a success of his life in every other area, and yet have made such a mess of his entire dealings with Millie?

Exhausted and anxious, Millie pushed the door open to Leandro's study.

Leandro lay sprawled in the chair, his dark hair rumpled, his shirt creased and his jaw shaded by stubble.

'Leandro?' Her voice was soft and tentative and he opened his eyes and looked at her.

Then he gave a hollow laugh. 'What did you forget?'

Thinking that it was a strange question, Millie gave him a rueful smile. 'Just about everything.' Not wanting to wake everyone else in the house, she closed the door quietly behind her. 'I was in such a state, I ran out of the house with nothing.'

'I know. The housekeeper heard you go.'

'You must have been a bit surprised.'

'Not really. Why would I be surprised? I know you were upset by everything. I understand that. What I don't understand is why you're back.'

Millie noticed the bottle and the empty glass by his hand. 'What are you talking about?' Confused, she took in his rumpled state and the lines of tiredness on his face. She'd never seen him anything other than immaculate before, neither had she seen him tired. He had endless energy and stamina. Only now he seemed spent. 'Why wouldn't I have come back?'

'I would have thought that was obvious.' Leandro growled. He lifted his glass to his lips and then realised that it was empty and put it down again.

Millie looked at him in exasperation. 'You're not making sense. And I don't know why you're getting drunk. I expect you're worried, but it's all going to be fine.'

'It is *not* going to be fine,' he said in a raw tone. 'This is going to keep happening.'

'No, they think it was just a one-off. It happens sometimes.'

'You're deluding yourself.'

Millie frowned, thinking that his comment was a little harsh. 'The doctor seemed to know what he was talking about.'

'Doctor?'

'That's where I took him. To the hospital.' She looked at

him defensively. 'Maybe I was overreacting, but I thought it might be life-threatening. I was so worried about him. What if I'd stayed here and he'd got worse? I looked for you and you'd disappeared. And after the stress and worry I've had this evening, I would have thought even you could be a little more sympathetic.' Hurt and not understanding his reaction, Millie turned away. 'I'm going to bed. I'm sleeping in Costas's nursery in case he needs me.'

'Wait a moment.' Leandro snapped out the words, his body still, his beautiful eyes narrowed to dark slits. 'What are you talking about? Why did you see a doctor? And why would Costas need you?'

'Because...' Millie was so tired that she couldn't even think straight and it took her a moment to absorb the implication of his question. 'Do you *honestly* not know what's been going on here? Where do you think I've been? Why do you think I dashed off?' She broke off and her breathing quickened as understanding dawned. 'Oh, my God, you thought I'd—'

'Yes,' he said softly. 'I did.'

Millie's heart started to pound. 'Why would you think that?'

'Do you really need to ask that question? The papers are full of my affair with that actress and extremely revealing pictures of you. Last time I saw you, you were upset.'

Millie walked across to him and stuck out her hand. 'Give me your phone.'

'I don't have it.' His voice was faintly mocking and a sardonic smile touched his mouth. 'Since you laid down your ground rules for our relationship I frequently lose track of where I've put it.'

'Well, isn't that typical of a man. The one time I need you to have your phone on you, you don't have it.' Bending over his desk, Millie shifted files and papers with scant regard for order and retrieved it from under a stack of papers. 'Here.' She thrust it towards him. 'I'm hopeless at technology. Switch it on.'

He switched it on.

Millie folded her arms. 'Now play back your messages. On speaker.'

Sending her a curious glance, Leandro played his messages.

Millie heard her own voice coming from the loudspeaker. *'Leandro, where are you? Costas is ill—I need to get him to a hospital. I'm taking your car. Call me when you get this message or meet me at the hospital.'*

Raising her eyebrows, Millie removed the phone from his hand. '*Now* I know why you didn't call. Really, you are going to have to be a bit more supportive when our own baby is born. If I'm going to have night-time panics, I want you with me. You're the one who is always calm in a crisis. I'm a mess. I'm never doing that again without you there to tell me that everything will be fine. What's the matter with you? I've never known you silent before. *Say* something.'

There was a long, tense silence during which Millie was sure she could hear her own heart beating.

When Leandro finally spoke, his voice was hoarse. '*Our* baby?'

'Yes. Our baby. I'm pregnant.' She gave a faint smile. 'Hardly surprising after all the sex we've had over the past few weeks.'

He inhaled sharply. 'Is that why you came back?'

'I never left,' Millie said softly, and Leandro held her gaze.

'Our baby.' He sounded stunned. 'All that stuff in the paper…'

Millie's heart missed a beat because everything she needed to know was in his voice and in his eyes. 'Well, I'm not pretending it wasn't upsetting. But I had plenty of time to think about it while I was watching over Costas in his cot. For a start, that actress is too thin for you. You hate women whose bones stick out. And you're forgetting, I was there that night. I could see that she was angry that you rejected her. The talk is that her latest film is rubbish. I expect she wanted to attract some different publicity—kick-start her career. And she wanted to hurt you.'

'It only hurts me if it hurts you,' Leandro said hoarsely, and then shook his head. 'I don't know why you're smiling. You like seeing me miserable?'

'No,' Millie said softly. 'I like seeing you in love.'

His eyes met hers. 'You're very confident all of a sudden.'

Millie shrugged and slid onto his lap. 'That happens when you're loved. And when you love back.' She leaned her head against his shoulder, feeling his strength. 'You should have known I wouldn't have left you.'

'Alexa said she saw you drive off, very upset.'

'I *was* very upset.' She sat up so that she could explain. 'I was sitting with Costas, just watching him, because I was worried about his temperature. And I was thinking about Becca—and us—and those awful pictures of me. Everything. And then Costas sort of went all floppy. I was terrified. I don't know. I'm not that experienced with children. He seemed so hot, and I was worried—'

'Why didn't you come and find me?'

'I did! You weren't here!' Millie was indignant. 'I ran around the house yelling your name but this house is so stupidly big and I couldn't find you. Neither could I find any of the staff.'

'I was up on the roof terrace. I needed fresh air.'

'Well, it's a shame you chose that particular moment because I was in desperate need of a serious dose of your decisive-macho-Viking-invader approach to life. Leandro?' She curled her hand into the front of his shirt. 'What is the *matter* with you? I've never seen you like this before. You look as though you have no idea what to do next, and you always know what to do.'

Leandro slid his hand into her hair. 'Not always. Tonight I thought I'd lost you forever and I had no idea what to do about it. My first instinct was to find you and haul you back, but I love you too much to involve you in the media circus that is my life. It's always like this, Millie. There's always someone wanting to sell me out to the media for money. And I blame myself for those photos of you,' he confessed in a raw tone, letting his hand drop so that she could see the look in his eyes. 'I should have known better than to expose you to that.'

'I don't care what they think,' Millie said softly. 'I only care what *you* think.'

Leandro wrapped his arms around her. 'When you left the first time, I was so angry. I'd thought you were the sort of woman who would stay by my side no matter what. I didn't understand how insecure you were and I didn't understand how much my behaviour had dented your confidence. When you were prepared to take on Costas, even though you still thought he was my child—' He broke off, his eyes bright. 'That was when I realised that I didn't know you at all.'

'I found it impossible to believe that a man like you could possibly want me.' Millie gave a wry smile. 'The media finds it hard to believe, too, so you can't exactly blame me.'

'The media don't know you,' he said roughly. 'And I understand now why you felt that way. I understand why you would have believed your sister.'

'I always just thought she was helping me.' Millie pulled a face, unable to disguise the hurt. 'Stupid me.'

'Not stupid. Generous. You don't see bad in people. And why would you? She was your sister. I see how growing up with her must have made it hard for you to see your own qualities. But those qualities shine from you, *agape mou*. And those qualities are the reason I love you. I love your smile and your values, I love the way you were prepared to care for a child that might have been mine, and I love the way you still treasure the good memories of your sister, despite everything.' He inhaled deeply. 'And you're right when you say that I love you. I do. I loved you the first moment I saw your legs in that haystack.'

'That was lust, not love.'

A sexy smile tugged at his mouth. 'Perhaps, but it was love soon after. That's why I was so upset when you walked out. I thought I'd found a woman who would be by my side always.' His hand tightened on hers. 'I should have come after you.'

'If you'd known me better, maybe you would have done. And if I'd known you better, maybe I wouldn't have left.'

'I understand now why you did.' His hand slid into her hair in a possessive gesture. 'But at the time I thought you were like my mother.'

Millie stilled. 'You've never talked about your mother. You've never talked about your family at all.'

'Because I try to keep that part of my life in the past, where it belongs. I built myself a new life.' His voice was husky. 'She left me. When I was six years old—old enough to understand rejection—she went out one day and left me with a friend of hers. And she never came back.'

'Leandro—'

'She was a single mother and life was tough.' He gave a weary shrug. 'I think she just woke up one day and thought life might be easier without the burden of a young child.'

Millie didn't know what to say so she just leaned forward and hugged him. 'Where did you go?'

'I was taken back to Greece and put into care. But I found it hard to attach myself to anyone after that. If your own mother can leave you, why wouldn't a stranger?'

'Why didn't you tell me this before?'

'I thought I'd put it all behind me, but scars don't always heal, do they?'

'But you can learn to live with scars,' Millie said softly, tasting her own salty tears as she pressed her mouth to his. 'If you can live with mine, I'll teach you to live with yours.'

His hand slid into her hair and tightened, as if he were holding on. 'You're sure you want this life?'

'I want to spend my life with you. You've given me so many things, Leandro. Diamonds, houses, cars, a lifestyle beyond my wildest dreams, but the most important thing you've given me is self-esteem. You make me feel special.'

'You *are* special.' He cupped her face in his hands. 'You took on your sister's child, despite everything.'

'So did you.' Millie's eyes filled. 'You took him on knowing that he wasn't yours. Knowing that everyone would make assumptions.'

'I didn't want Costas to go through what I went through.' He gave a twisted smile. 'The situation was different, I know, but for me it felt like a healing process. I was able to give this baby a home, a name—an identity. Everything I never had. Millie…' He was hesitant. 'This lifestyle isn't going to change. If you stay with me, there are always going to be people hunting you down, wanting to make you believe bad things about me.'

Millie leaned forward and kissed him. 'Is this a good moment to confess that I might need the services of your lawyer after all?'

'Why?'

She shrank slightly. 'I was in a panic when I put Costas in your car…'

'And…?'

'I think I might have accidentally damaged one of the motorcycles that the journalists had propped against your gate. It was in the way. I was also responsible for the fact that one of the journalists dropped his camera.'

'Sounds like you need driving lessons.' Laughter in his eyes, Leandro raised an eyebrow in mocking contemplation. 'Dare I enquire after the health of my Ferrari?'

Millie squirmed. 'It's nice to know where your priorities lie. It might need a teeny-weeny touch of paint.'

Leandro closed his eyes. 'I don't love you any more.'

Millie giggled and wound her arms round his neck. 'Yes, you do.'

'You're right, I do.' Leandro took her face in his hands and kissed her. 'I love you, *agape mou*. I will always love you, no matter how many Ferraris you get through or how many journalists sue me. You say that you're different to every other woman I've ever been with and that's true—you are. That's why I fell in love with you. I saw instantly that you were different. You weren't interested in my money and you had values that I admired and respected.'

'I can see why you were disappointed when you thought I'd turned into a shopaholic.'

'I didn't look for a reason for the change in your behaviour. I accused you of not trusting me, but I was guilty of that charge, not you. I assumed you'd suddenly discovered how much you enjoyed having the money.'

'Leandro, I *do* like the money,' Millie muttered. 'Anyone would be mad not to, wouldn't they? I love the fact that I don't have to queue for a bus in the rain. I'll never stop being thrilled when the lights turn on by themselves, but most of all I love the fact I'm going to be able to stay at home with Costas and our baby and not work.'

'Bab*ies*,' Leandro purred, his characteristic arrogance once more in evidence. 'I intend to keep you very busy in that department. I'd hate Costas to be lonely.'

Millie grinned. 'This one isn't cooked yet.'

He slid his hand over her flat stomach in a gesture that was both intimate and protective. 'You will be a fantastic mother.'

Millie kissed him, feeling the roughness of his jaw against her sensitive skin. 'What are we going to do about Costas? I can't bear to think of him growing up with this question of his parentage hanging over him.'

'My lawyers have started adoption proceedings,' Leandro told her. 'I can't pretend it's going to be a quick and simple process, but we'll get there, I promise you that. We're his parents.'

'And I think we should have a couple of dogs. Big dogs. Trained to bite journalists.'

Leandro laughed. 'I was so wrong about you. I used to think you were gentle and kind.'

'I am, most of the time. As long as no one upsets me.' Millie grinned. 'It's no good frowning. You don't scare me any more.'

'I'd noticed. In fact, I'm not sure I like the new, confident you,' he drawled. 'I'm not sure you know your place.'

Millie wound her arms round his neck. 'I know my place, Leandro Demetrios,' she said softly, and he lifted an eyebrow in question.

'So where is your place, *agape mou?*'

'By your side, bearing your children, loving you for the rest of my life. That's my place.'

And Leandro smiled his approval just moments before he kissed her.

The Diakos Baby Scandal

NATALIE RIVERS

Natalie Rivers grew up in the Sussex countryside. As a child she always loved to lose herself in a good book, or in games that gave free rein to her imagination. She went to Sheffield University, where she met her husband in the first week of term. It was love at first sight and they have been together ever since, moving to London after graduating, getting married and having two wonderful children.

After university Natalie worked in a lab at a medical research charity, and later retrained to be a primary school teacher. Now she is lucky enough to be able to combine her two favourite occupations—being a full-time mum and writing passionate romances.

CHAPTER ONE

KERRY was shaking as she looked down at the little white stick clutched in her hand—a plus sign was clearly visible in the window. The test was positive. A flutter of excitement rose up inside her—she was pregnant.

It wasn't planned, and she hadn't truly expected the test to come up positive—but she knew the discovery that she was pregnant would change her life for ever.

She pressed her teeth gently into her lower lip and stared at the test result for a moment longer. Her heart had instantly filled with joy at the prospect of having a baby—but her body had already started to tremble with nerves.

How would Theo react to the news that he was going to be a father? The thought of telling him sent a wave of apprehension rolling through her.

It was only six months since she'd become the live-in lover of Theo Diakos—one of Athens' richest, most powerful property tycoons. She'd shared his high-paced cosmopolitan lifestyle and spent night after glorious night in his bed. He'd treated her like a princess, and his close family members—his brother, Corban, and his wife, Hallie—had made her more than welcome.

But, although Kerry had fallen deeply in love with Theo, they had never discussed their feelings for each other. And they'd never talked about their future together.

She lifted her head, pushed her long blonde hair back from her face and walked out onto the roof garden. When she and Theo were staying in the city, this magical green and scented oasis was her favourite place. The warm fragrance of climbing roses wrapped around her and the gentle sound of trickling water filled the evening air. There was such an aura of tranquillity that it was hard to imagine the garden was right on top of one of the glitziest hotels in the city—the flagship property in Theo's empire.

Beneath her the city lights were starting to shine, and up high on the Acropolis Rock the floodlit columns of the Parthenon were glowing majestically against the darkening sky. It was an awe-inspiring sight, and one that would be forever linked in her mind with Theo. Being with him was wonderful. For the first time in twenty-three years she felt as if she was wanted—cherished, even.

At first she'd hardly been able to believe that he was interested in an ordinary girl like her, but the intensity of their whirlwind affair had swept her doubts away and she'd never been so happy.

The troubles that haunted her past had faded until they seemed almost to belong to another lifetime. It was wonderful, knowing that he valued her and wanted to be with her. It was something she'd never experienced before—but it was something that she was determined her baby would feel right from the start of its life.

She pressed her hand against her stomach. The knowledge that she was carrying Theo's child was still sinking in—but she knew one thing for sure. This baby would always feel wanted. Always feel loved.

Suddenly a rush of excitement bubbled through her body. Theo *would* be happy. She was certain of it. After all, he was a wonderful uncle—he clearly thought the world of his nephew, Nicco—and she knew he would be an amazing father.

All at once she was desperate to tell him the news immediately. She hurried back inside and dashed straight to Theo's study in their private apartments at the hotel, almost running in her enthusiasm. She couldn't wait to see the look on his face when she shared her wonderful secret.

She slid to a halt outside his study door as she realised he wasn't alone. He was with his brother, Corban, and from the sound of their voices they were discussing something important—something urgent. She paused to catch her breath, disappointed that her special news would have to wait.

Then, just as she turned to leave, the subject of their conversation suddenly became clear to her. She truly had not meant to eavesdrop, and her Greek was still far from perfect. But she knew enough to understand what Theo and Corban were discussing.

They were talking about taking little Nicco away from his mother.

A knot tightened in her stomach and her heart lurched horribly in her chest. She couldn't really have understood correctly. Could she? She stood frozen outside the study door—unable to tear herself away—listening to them talk.

'You *must* think about Nicco—it's your duty to protect him,' Theo said. 'He is your son, and his well-being must come first.'

'But Hallie is my wife—she trusts me,' Corban said. 'I don't think I can do this to her.'

'You must.' Theo's voice was emphatic. 'A Diakos child belongs with the Diakos family. And Hallie is not fit to take care of your son.'

'But it seems so drastic,' Corban said. 'Can't we at least let her see Nicco before we take him?'

'No. Absolutely not,' Theo said. 'This is the only way. If we do this right now—*tonight*—Nicco can be away by helicopter to the island before Hallie even notices he's gone. Then we can deal with her privately—get her out of the country without any fuss. No one outside the family ever needs to know.'

Kerry clamped her hand over her mouth in horror. Theo and his brother were plotting to take Hallie's child away from her.

She started shaking violently, suddenly revisiting all the pain and misery of her own childhood. She felt sick, remembering the heartbreak and despair—*the utter wretchedness*—of her own true mother, who had been unable to bear having her baby daughter taken from her.

Kerry could not stand by and let that happen to Hallie. She had to try and save her friend the anguish that her mother had suffered. Maybe if her mother had been allowed to keep her baby she would still be alive today.

Suddenly Kerry found herself backing unsteadily away from the study doorway. Her throat was tight, her stomach was knotted painfully and her mind was spinning with horrible memories that made it impossible to think straight. All she knew was that she couldn't let them take Hallie's child away from her.

She turned and ran to find her friend. She had to warn her.

She charged into the luxury apartment Hallie shared with Corban, stumbled through the huge open living space to the bedroom and found Hallie sitting in front of the mirror brushing her long brown hair.

'Kerry!' Hallie exclaimed, her cheeks flushed and her dark eyes wide with surprise. 'Is everything all right?'

'I'm sorry…' Kerry gasped for breath after her mad dash. 'It's Nicco. I heard Corban and Theo talking—they are going to take Nicco away tonight.'

'Why? What's wrong? Is he all right?' Hallie demanded, standing up so quickly that the stool she'd been sitting on crashed over.

'Yes, he's fine,' Kerry said. 'But listen—you don't understand. They said you're not fit to look after him. They're going to take Nicco away by helicopter without telling you.'

'No. They can't do that.' For a moment Hallie stood glued to the spot, her face blank with shock. Then her expression changed and she lurched into action, snatching her handbag from the dressing table so quickly that she sent a glass of wine flying. 'They won't take him. I won't let them,' she said, grabbing her car keys from a side table and hurrying unsteadily across the room in high heels. 'I'll take him away with me—somewhere they won't find us.'

'Wait,' Kerry said, automatically reaching for a handful of tissues to stem the spread of the red wine across Hallie's dressing table. 'I'll come with…'

Suddenly Kerry hesitated, looking down at the wine-soaked tissues. Hallie had been drinking. Remembering her flushed cheeks, and the way she'd swayed unevenly across the room, she'd obviously had quite a lot—way too much to be driving. But she'd just taken her car keys.

Kerry burst out of the room after her. But it was too late—the nursery door was open and Nicco's cot was empty. A glance at the lights above the family's private elevator told her that someone had already reached the underground car park.

Oh, God! What had she done? Hallie was drunk and she was about to drive out into the busy city traffic with her little boy in the car.

Kerry's heart was in her mouth as she hurtled back to Theo's study. She careered through the open door, making Theo and Corban look up in surprise.

'It's Hallie!' she cried, struggling to catch her breath to speak.

Theo was beside her in an instant. His strong hands closed reassuringly on her upper arms to keep her steady and his dark brown eyes held her secure in his powerful gaze.

'Take a deep breath.' His calm, assured voice cut through the panic that gripped her. 'That's it. Now, tell me what has happened.'

Kerry stared up at his handsome face, momentarily torn between the distress she'd felt when she heard him planning to take Nicco away from his mother and the comfort she instinctively felt simply from being close to him, from the feel of his strong hands on her arms.

'Hallie has taken Nicco in her car,' she blurted. 'She's been drinking.'

Corban cursed in Greek, then ran out the door, shouting urgently to Theo as he left. At the same time Theo spun away from Kerry to pick up the phone. She realised he was calling his security team to give orders that Hallie should not be allowed to leave.

Kerry folded her arms across her chest and hugged herself tightly. What had she done? Theo and Corban had no right to take Nicco away from his mother—but her impulsive reaction had put both mother and child in danger. She should never have acted without thinking things through.

'I'm going to help my brother,' Theo said, turning to leave. 'Hallie was away from the hotel before I warned Security, but Corban is right behind her.'

Kerry bit her quivering lip anxiously and felt her eyes burning with unshed tears. She wished she'd realised sooner that Hallie had been drinking—but it had never occurred to her that her friend would be in that state.

'It will be all right.' Suddenly Theo was back by her side, pulling her gently against his strong chest. He lifted his hands and slipped them under her hair, cradling the back of her head tenderly as he tipped her face up to his. 'You did the right thing—we'll take care of it now.'

Then, before she could reply, he was gone. But the warm, exotic fragrance of his cologne lingered in the air and the nape of her neck still tingled where his fingertips had brushed.

Theo was everything to her. Since the day she'd met him everything else in her life had faded into insignificance.

When her temporary job in Athens had finished she'd been overwhelmed with joy when he had asked her to stay with him. With his encouragement she had delayed looking for a new position, so that she would be free to travel with him wherever he went. He'd said that he wanted her with him always, so that they would be able to spend time together whenever his demanding schedule allowed.

Kerry closed her eyes, imagining the warm strength of Theo's arms around her. Being in his arms always felt so right. Just now, even when he was worried about his nephew and his sister-in-law, he had taken a moment to give her comfort and reassurance.

He had told her that she'd done the right thing—except he didn't know what had really happened. What she had really done.

She walked shakily across to the window and looked out at the city, which was now properly dark. Somewhere out there Corban was pursuing his wife and child. And Theo was helping him. She squeezed her eyes shut, feeling a tear escape to run down her cheek, and prayed that everyone would be all right.

Theo Diakos strode through the hotel with a face like thunder. Hallie and the child had been safely retrieved by his brother, but not before she had crashed her car on Syntagma Square.

Mercifully no one had been injured—but driving a sports car off the road on one of the busiest squares in Athens, right outside the parliament building, had attracted a deluge of unwanted attention, and a horde of paparazzi had appeared out of nowhere before Corban had been able to get his family away from prying eyes.

Theo swore under his breath. If only he had persuaded his brother to act sooner—to get Hallie out of the country and away from the family—then none of this would have happened. It had been becoming increasingly difficult to keep Hallie's drinking problem under wraps, and this fiasco would certainly blow it wide open.

Up until that evening almost no one had known about her difficulty with alcohol. Even Kerry—as far as he knew—had remained unaware. Corban had worked hard to keep it a secret—but now everyone would know.

Theo glanced at his watch. Only a few minutes had passed since he'd called Kerry to tell her that the situation was contained, but she had sounded so distressed by the whole event that he wanted to get back to her without delay. He was sorry that she'd been dragged into such an unpleasant family situation. Witnessing Hallie drunk and out of control, then putting Nicco at risk and creating an unsavoury public embarrassment, had obviously been upsetting for her.

Kerry would never behave like that. There wasn't a disagreeable bone in her body. She was gentle and graceful, and she hated drawing attention to herself. Theo valued every minute he spent in her enchanting company.

He'd first spotted her nearly a year earlier, talking to a group of tourists in the foyer of one of his hotels. Her long blonde hair, wide blue eyes and honeyed complexion had initially caught his attention, but once he'd spent an evening with her it had been her gentle charm that had utterly captivated him. After the cut and thrust of his high-paced business life, time with Kerry was the perfect refreshing antidote.

Now he was hurrying back to her, waiting for him on the roof garden. He knew how much she loved it there, and he hoped the pleasant surroundings would ease her distress. But if she was still upset when he reached her, he would pull her into his arms and make love to her until she forgot her worries.

He found her standing with her back to him, looking out over the city towards the Acropolis. The second he took another step towards her she seemed to sense his presence and spun round to face him, her hair bouncing about her shoulders as she moved.

'Is everyone all right?' she asked urgently. 'Hallie and Nicco? People on the street where she crashed?'

'Everyone is fine,' Theo said. He pulled her towards him, but her body was filled with tension and she didn't sway into his arms as he had expected. He leant closer, swept her silky hair away from her neck and pressed his lips to the sensitive skin below her ear. 'Forget about it now—it's all under control. Let me take your mind off your worries.'

'Where are they now?' Kerry asked, standing even straighter and stiffer than before. 'Are they all together?'

Theo stepped back and looked down at her. In the

time they'd been together Kerry had never once refused his lovemaking. She was so deliciously responsive to him that it made sex even more exciting and satisfying for him. Even thinking about the way she dissolved into a pool of desire at his slightest touch made him hot and ready for her.

Usually a simple look from him was enough to have her melting willingly into his arms. For her to be so immune to him she must be really concerned.

'Yes. Corban has everything under control. At any moment they will be flying out to the island—away from the press,' Theo said, skimming his hands up the bare skin of her arms with the lightest of touches. 'You can stop worrying about them now—and let me make you feel better.'

Kerry stood tall and drew in a deep breath. She had to talk to Theo—to tell him what she had done. And she had to ask about the conversation she'd overheard him having with Corban.

Then, after that, she still had to tell him she was pregnant. It was almost impossible to believe that only a couple of hours ago she had been running to tell Theo the amazing news that they were going to have a baby—and then everything suddenly seemed to become horribly confusing and wrong.

'Let me see if I can think of something new...something interesting,' Theo said, his voice deep and sexy, as he reached out to pluck a couple of beautiful pink roses from the trellis beside them.

Kerry drew in a wobbly breath and looked at the gorgeous blooms in Theo's large, sensual hands. Only last night he had carried her out to the roof garden from their bedroom, peeled off her lacy nightclothes and laid her naked under the stars. Then he'd scattered her body with rose petals before making long, slow, exquisite love to her.

Now the heady fragrance of roses was already filling her senses again, and her body was burning with the need to surrender to his lovemaking. She knew that she would soon forget everything in the bliss that he would give her.

But she couldn't surrender to her desires. It wasn't right when there were still so many concerns in her mind. She had to talk to him.

'Stop. I need to…' She hesitated, then pushed his hands away and took a step backwards. 'Earlier this evening I heard you talking to Corban. You said he was to take Nicco away from Hallie.'

'Yes. It's a shame I didn't give my brother that advice yesterday,' Theo replied. 'Then tonight's fiasco would have been avoided.'

'How can you be so cold?' Kerry gasped. 'Someone could have been seriously hurt tonight—or even killed!'

'Exactly,' Theo said. 'That could have been averted.'

'Not by depriving a mother of her child,' Kerry said.

For a moment she couldn't help thinking about her own mother—how she'd been utterly devastated to have had her baby taken away from her. Feeling like a worthless failure at only sixteen years old had made it impossible for her to get herself back on track. Her life had spiralled into depression and self-abuse. She'd turned to drink, then drugs—and eventually died alone of an overdose in squalid conditions.

For Kerry it was made worse by the fact that she hadn't even known who her mother was until it was too late to help her. Instead she'd been grudgingly looked after by her grandmother—the very person who had taken her away from her real mother. And for Kerry's entire childhood she'd made her feel unwanted and unloved.

'I know you are concerned about Hallie and Nicco.' Theo's clipped tones showed signs of tension. 'My brother and I are in your debt for raising the alarm—if you hadn't come to us so quickly things could have been much worse. But my conversation with Corban was private. How we choose to take care of our family is none of your concern.'

Kerry stared up at him. A muscle pulsed on his shadowed jawline. His eyes were dark and troubled. She had to tell him what she had done—but she was apprehensive about how he would react.

'Hallie is my friend,' she said. 'Of course I care about her. And Nicco.'

'You must trust me to do what is right for my family,' Theo said, studying her intently. Suddenly his eyes narrowed and the set of his expression hardened.

'You told her. Didn't you?' he demanded.

Kerry's heart jolted and her eyes widened with alarm.

'Yes.' Her voice was hardly more than a whisper—but she held her head up and met his gaze steadily.

'You had no business doing that.' Theo's expression was dark. 'It did not concern you.'

'Of course it concerned me!' Kerry responded, suddenly filled with anger on her friend's behalf—and on her own mother's behalf.

'No wonder you were so desperately worried—your actions put many people in danger tonight,' he said. 'Someone could have died. My nephew could have died!'

'I didn't realise she'd been drinking,' Kerry said. 'Not until—'

'Don't try to explain what you did.' Theo's voice cut through hers coldly. 'I'm not interested.'

'But—'

'I'm not interested in your excuses,' he said flatly. 'You put my nephew in danger.'

'I never meant to,' she said. 'That was the last thing I wanted.'

'You listened to a private conversation that did not concern you,' he said. 'Then you went behind my back and took the situation into your own hands.'

'Hallie is my friend,' she said.

'And what am *I* to you?' he demanded. 'You should have come to me first.'

'You... I...' She stumbled hesitantly, suddenly unsure of herself.

It was true that if she'd spoken to Theo about what she'd overheard then Hallie wouldn't have taken Nicco in the car. But that didn't change what she had heard. And Theo had made it clear that he saw nothing wrong with what he and his brother had been planning. They probably still intended to take Nicco away from his mother.

'I no longer want you here.' Theo spoke suddenly, his voice hard and controlled, his expression set in stone. 'Pack your bags and get out.'

'What? I don't understand...' Kerry's voice trailed

away and she stared at him in shock. But she did understand. Theo no longer wanted her.

He'd already turned his back on her and was walking away, as if from that moment she was dead to him. She was already out of his life.

'Wait,' she called. 'There is something I have to tell you. It's the reason I came to talk to you in your study in the first place.'

Theo spun on his heel and looked at her dispassionately. He was giving her a moment more of his time, and she knew she had to use it wisely.

'This evening I found out—'

Kerry stopped speaking abruptly and covered her mouth with her hand. Suddenly she was afraid to tell him that she was pregnant.

After the events of the evening, it was almost as if Theo was a different man. She would never have thought him capable of taking a child from his mother—but he had defended his intentions even when Kerry had challenged him.

And if they planned to do that to Hallie—who'd been married to Corban for several years—what would happen to *her* if they found out she was carrying a Diakos baby? Theo had made it plain he didn't want her. But would he want to take the baby?

'Get on with it,' Theo said, with undisguised impatience.

'I don't feel like I know you any more,' she said.

'The feeling is mutual,' he replied coldly. 'Now, get out.'

CHAPTER TWO

14 months later

'THANK you for inviting me to your home.' Theo held out his hand to the old man, who was sitting at a small wooden table drinking coffee under the shade of an ancient gnarled olive tree. 'Your island is charming—a very peaceful place to live.'

Drakon Notara ignored Theo's hand and snorted rudely, not looking up from his treacly Greek coffee. He was a moody and eccentric old man, but Theo had met him several times in Athens and was not fazed by his bad manners.

'Don't tell me you care about *peace*,' Drakon said. 'I know why you want to buy my island. You want to build one of your flashy hotels here—or maybe several. Bars, thumping music, people drunk and rowdy.' He paused, finally lifting his head and meeting Theo's eye. 'I can't have that happening here.'

Theo gritted his teeth and stared straight back, refusing to rise to the old man's provocation. No one spoke to Theo Diakos with such disrespect and got away with it—but he had a compelling reason to do business with Drakon Notara.

Theo *needed* to buy this island. It was his only chance to fulfil his mother's dying wish. And if he had to tread carefully to seal the deal, then that was what he would do.

He had not been invited to sit, nor offered any refreshment. The paving stones under the trees had not been swept before his arrival and were deep with browning piles of olive blossom. It was clear the old man was going to be as bloody-minded as usual, and was not going to make any transaction easy.

'That's not what I intend for the island at all,' Theo said smoothly. 'Perhaps if we talk—'

'No,' Drakon barked. 'Talk is cheap. And so are the scandal sheets. Don't think because I spend most of my time out here that I don't know what your family is like—rich and spoiled, caring only about money and excitement. Your brother...his drunken wife crashing her car with that child on board.'

'You have been misinformed.' Theo's tone was clipped as he suppressed the surge of anger that ripped through him. Whenever he thought about the night of the accident, which was over a year ago now, he felt his temper flare. 'My family is not as the media has portrayed it. The newspapers do not always report things exactly as they are.'

'Are you telling me it didn't happen?' the old man scoffed.

'I'm saying that my personal affairs are not relevant to our business,' Theo said. 'However, if you will allow me to set out my proposal, I believe we will be able to come to an arrangement we are both happy with.'

'I don't want to talk to you now—I don't want to hear the smooth and readymade business spiel you have prepared.' Drakon leant heavily on the table and levered himself up. 'If you're serious about buying my island, come and stay for a few days—so I can find out what kind of man you really are. Bring your pretty girlfriend—the one I met last year. I liked her—no airs and graces, which I found surprising in someone associated with you and your family.'

For a fraction of a second Theo did not reply. The wily old fellow had completely wrong-footed him. He searched his memory, trying to recall any occasions when Kerry and Drakon might have met—and realised there had been several charity events when they could have spoken.

Why did Drakon really want him to bring Kerry to the island? Did he know that she was no longer part of his life?

'Or have you broken it off with her? Moved on to someone new?' Drakon continued derisively. 'From the way she...' He paused, frowning as if he was irritated with himself. 'What was her name?'

'Kerry,' Theo supplied in a tight voice, not missing the fact that Drakon had used the past tense—as if he definitely *did* know the relationship was over. 'Her name *is* Kerry.'

Hearing himself say her name sounded strange and painfully familiar at the same time. He had not said it aloud since the night he threw her out—but that had not stopped her name, and the image of her face, pressing forward in his thoughts more often than he would have liked.

'Ah, yes. Kerry,' Drakon said. 'Utterly delightful young thing—reminded me of my dear wife when she was young. From the way she never left your side, I expected to see a wedding announcement in the press. But I suppose you're several women down the line by now.' He turned and started shuffling towards the house.

'As I said, my personal affairs are not relevant to our business,' Theo said, but a cold, fatalistic feeling had settled in his chest.

He realised that as far as Drakon Notara was concerned the way he conducted his private life was as important as the way he did business. The fact that not one single woman had caught his attention since Kerry would not impress the old man. He would simply judge Theo harshly for not making the relationship work in the first place.

And, to make matters worse, he seemed to have developed a real soft spot for Kerry.

'I'm a traditional old man,' Drakon said over his shoulder. 'I don't hold with the fast and wasteful way people live their lives these days. Fast cars polluting the air, fast relationships…everything is disposable.'

'If we talk, you'll discover that we share many of the same traditional values,' Theo said.

He wanted to follow Drakon and convince him that he did not plan to build hotels on the island. But his reasons for wanting the island were personal and he had no intention of sharing them with anyone—especially not a judgemental old man who thought it was his right to force his opinions on other people.

'Then come back and visit properly,' Drakon said, pausing on the threshold, as if to gather his strength before he disappeared inside. 'And bring Kerry with you.'

Theo watched him go. He might be physically frail, but his mind and his will were still as strong as ever.

'Allow me to escort you back to the helipad,' Drakon's assistant said, stepping out of the shadows at the edge of the paved area.

Theo nodded a curt acknowledgement, and turned to leave.

'I know the way,' he said, striding out of the shaded area into the bright Greek sunshine.

He frowned as he walked along the rutted ridge path, completely oblivious to the breathtaking view across the azure Aegean Sea.

He needed Kerry.

If he was to have any chance of buying this island as the first step in fulfilling his mother's dying wish, then he was going to need Kerry.

'Thank you so much for all your help,' the customer said, pushing open the glass door of the travel agent's and letting in a blast of cold, rainy air.

'I'm sure you'll have a wonderful holiday. I've only been to Crete once, but I'd love to go back there,' Kerry said, as the customer stepped out onto the wet street.

For a brief moment she let herself imagine how good it would feel to sit on a beautiful sandy beach, with nothing to do but rest and play with her six-month-old baby boy, Lucas. But that was a fantasy that wasn't likely to come true any time soon—not with all the bills she was struggling to pay on her own.

It was fourteen months since she'd returned from Athens—since the devastating night when Theo Diakos had brutally ripped out her heart and trampled it underfoot. Arriving back in London had been a nightmare. Trying to pick up the pieces of her broken heart—with no job, no money and nowhere to live—had been truly awful. And on top of everything else she'd been pregnant.

'It's nearly time for your break,' Carol said now, pulling her out of her thoughts. 'Are you sure you don't mind taking early lunch again?'

'When you've been up since five a.m., this doesn't seem early.' Kerry laughed. Lucas—as adorable as he was—had taken to waking with the rising sun.

At that moment the shop door opened again, and another blast of cold air whooshed in, making an icy shiver run through her.

'Ooh! I can't believe it's June already,' she said, as she pulled the collar of her uniform jacket more snugly across her throat and looked up to greet the customer who had just walked in. 'Good morning. Can I help—?'

Her heart skipped a beat and she felt herself go cold all over as she stared up into the face of Theo Diakos.

He was looking straight at her, with an expression of dispassionate assessment on his darkly handsome face. His black brows were drawn low, casting his eyes into shadow, but his penetrating eyes bored right into her.

Kerry drew in a shaky breath and felt her heart jolt painfully back into action. She knew she was staring—but she could not drag her eyes from him. If was as if she couldn't quite believe Theo Diakos was really standing there.

He was a tall and imposing figure. The size of his athletic body seemed to fill the entire doorway, and his magnetic presence seemed to fill the entire shop. He was wearing a dark suit, which was covered with a sheen of summer rain, and his black hair was damp and glistening with fine water droplets.

What was he doing here?

Had he found out about Lucas—his baby son?

'Can I offer you some assistance?' Carol asked, breaking the silence and walking around to the front of her desk. 'Would you like to see a particular brochure, or are you just at the ideas-collecting stage?'

A flash of almost feverish humour cut through Kerry like a sharp slap to knock her out of her stunned state. The idea of Theo Diakos—billionaire property tycoon—walking into a high street travel agency in a London backwater to book his next package holiday was laughable. Ludicrous, even.

No—he was here for a reason.

'I'm here to speak to Kerry,' Theo said, never taking his eyes off her for a second.

'Oh. You two know each other?' Carol paused, obviously surprised, and looked at Kerry questioningly.

She was still staring at Theo. He was so familiar, but at the same time like a total stranger.

She had been so utterly in love with him—but it had turned out she'd meant nothing to him. Nothing at all. In one horrifying evening she had discovered that his soul was made of stone, and that there was not even one ounce of compassion inside his hard, unyielding body.

He'd conspired with his brother to take a little child away from his mother. And when Kerry had made the mistake of getting involved he had not given her an opportunity to explain herself. It had been the first time in nearly a year that they'd had any sort of disagreement—but he'd simply thrown her out. Without a moment's hesitation.

'Carol, this is Theo. He is from Athens.' Kerry's natural politeness forced her to make at least some sort of introduction—but all her instincts told her not to say too much. No one at work knew anything about what had happened in Athens, and it paid to be as careful as possible. She didn't want any speculation about Lucas and who his father was.

'Why don't you go for your lunch break?' Carol suggested. 'You probably have lots to catch up on.'

Kerry's pulse was still racing and the palms of her hands suddenly felt damp. The last thing she wanted was to go off alone with Theo—but neither did she want to cause a stir at work. Her boss, Margaret, would be back from her emergency dental appointment soon, and chances were she would not be in a good mood. Kerry really needed her job, and she really did not want to give anyone fuel for gossip.

'All right. I'll get my bag.' She stood up and walked to the office at the back of the shop, desperately hoping that she didn't look as wobbly as she suddenly felt.

With every thump of her heart she felt Theo's gaze burning deeper and deeper into her—through the protective veneer of her uniform, piercing through all the emotional barricades she had tried to build up since that devastating night in Athens.

Why was he here?

The office door swung shut behind her, shielding her from his sight, and her legs buckled beneath her. She clung to the edge of the desk, gasping for air and shaking violently.

Had Theo come to try and take Lucas away from her?

She'd never let that happen—her gorgeous boy was everything to her. She loved him more than life itself, and she'd never, *never* let Theo take him.

She took a deep, steadying breath and looked back through the one-way mirror into the shop. Theo was still standing there, as inscrutable as an ancient Greek statue, and Carol was obviously trying to engage him in conversation.

The sudden, horrifying thought occurred to her that Carol might innocently mention Lucas. With another judder of her already painful heart she grabbed her bag and burst back through the door. She had to get Theo away from anyone who knew her as quickly as possible.

'Take as long as you want,' Carol said, trying to be helpful. 'I'll send you a sneaky text if Margaret gets back.'

'I won't be long,' Kerry said.

'Don't worry,' Carol said. 'Have fun. Enjoy your blast from the past.'

'Thanks.' Kerry slipped past Theo and pushed the heavy glass door open. She flashed her colleague a tight smile and walked away down the rainy street, leaving Theo to follow her.

Fun was the last thing she was expecting to have. And

as for Carol's unsuspecting use of the phrase *blast from the past*—all Kerry could think about was the more violent, destructive meaning of the word *blast*.

She desperately hoped Theo hadn't come to rip mercilessly through her life, laying everything to waste and destroying the tentative happiness she had finally found.

Suddenly she couldn't bear the agony of not knowing. She stopped abruptly and turned to face Theo.

'What are you doing here?' she demanded.

'I've come to take you back to Greece,' he said.

CHAPTER THREE

THEO stood still, watching Kerry's reaction to his announcement. For a second he hardly recognised her. Somehow she didn't seem like the woman he'd spent nearly a year of his life with.

There were the obvious differences—the unflattering navy blue uniform, and the new way she had done her blonde hair, twisting it up into a tight knot at the nape of her neck with a long fringe he didn't remember falling into her eyes. But the real differences seemed to be deeper, more profound than that. She looked older in some way, and the expression on her face was wary and troubled.

He frowned, momentarily disconcerted as he looked down into her eyes. He could have sworn that her eyes had been a soft clear blue, but now they appeared to be pale grey, as if they were reflecting the pastel colour of the rain-streaked sky.

'Why would you say that?' Kerry gasped. 'I'm not coming back to Greece with you.'

'Actually, you are,' Theo said.

'Why?' she demanded incredulously. 'Why do you want me to? And what makes you think I'd ever go anywhere with you ever again?'

'Because you owe me that,' he replied.

'I don't owe you anything!' Kerry exclaimed, anger suddenly flaring inside her. 'I gave up my career to be with you, and I never took any of the money you tried to give me. I used up all my savings while I was living with you, which made it really hard for me when I came back to London.'

She paused, racking her brain for any other possible reason he might think that she owed him. The very idea that he could want anything of her was ridiculous—he was one of the richest men in Athens.

'I left all the expensive jewellery you gave me behind,' she added, remembering how much that had hurt.

It wasn't because of the cost of the items—for Kerry their value had been entirely sentimental. She'd thought they were genuine tokens of Theo's affection for her. When he'd thrown her out so coldly, she'd realised that all the things she'd taken as meaningful in their relationship had obviously meant nothing at all to him.

'I'm not talking about trivial monetary matters,' Theo said flatly.

'Then what—?' Kerry's voice dried up in her throat. Did that mean he *had* found out about Lucas?

She bit her lip, desperately hoping that he hadn't discovered her secret. Surely he would have brought up something so important immediately? But perhaps he meant to string it out to torment her.

'You interfered with matters that did not concern you,' Theo said. 'The consequences could have been tragic.'

Kerry drew in a shaky breath, remembering the awful evening of the accident.

'No one was injured,' she said in a small voice.

She deeply regretted that her involvement had caused Hallie to drive off with Nicco when she'd been drinking. But that did not change the fact that Theo and Corban had been planning to take Nicco away from his mother.

'It's a miracle no one was killed,' Theo said. 'But that's not exactly the reason I'm here.'

Kerry stared up at him anxiously. What could be worse than causing a potential tragedy—something bad enough to bring Theo all the way from Athens to seek restitution from her?

'Your meddling stirred up a vicious media circus,' Theo said, as if that was on the same level as a tragedy. 'The paparazzi had a field-day. They hounded my family relentlessly—Hallie and Corban in particular. It made things very difficult.'

Relief that Theo had not come about Lucas poured through Kerry—making her bold. Was he *really* comparing the inconvenience of unwanted media interest with the possibility of someone dying in a car crash? How had she ever lived with this man—shared his home for six months—without realising what he was really like?

'You mean with the media watching everything you did it made it difficult for you to take your sister-in-law's child away from her?' she asked.

As soon as the words were out of her mouth she knew she should not have antagonised him. A change came over him that made goosebumps prickle across her skin. It was hard to pinpoint what was actually different about his expression or his body language, but something alerted her to danger.

'It would be better—*for you*—if you never mention what you overheard that night again.'

Theo's voice grated across her nerves, making her heart start to race once more. But then all of a sudden her hackles rose at the threat in his tone. How dared he tell her what to do? She wasn't in a relationship with him any more.

'Why not? Are you ashamed of yourself for contemplating something so horrible?' she demanded recklessly. 'Or are you simply lying low—intending to carry on with your plan once the heat is off?'

Theo glared down at her, his blood suddenly surging hot and angry through his veins. He'd had no idea that Kerry had it in her to behave like this. The woman who'd been his lover for nearly a year would never have been so hot-headed, never have challenged him so rashly.

'Be very careful,' he grated, stepping forward so that he towered over her, forcing her to crane her neck back to maintain eye contact.

'Why?' she demanded, planting her hands on her hips and refusing to back away. 'What are you going to do to me?'

Theo could almost feel the energy crackling between them. Despite the cool air of the wet summer day, there was real heat in the space around their bodies. It was the heat of anger—and it was far more than just that.

It was the heat of passion—emotional and sexual.

Suddenly he knew exactly what he wanted to do to

her, and it took every ounce of his self-control not to give in to his desires. The need to seize her in his arms and drag her hard against his body was almost overwhelming. He wanted to cover her angry mouth with his—to silence her in the most satisfying way he knew how.

He continued to stare down at her, letting the silence lengthen. His heart was pumping powerfully in his chest, and his body was thrumming with desire for her. Then he saw her eyes widen slightly, saw her lips part a little as her breathing deepened. And he knew she felt it too.

Pure physical attraction.

A few minutes earlier it had seemed as if he didn't know her any more—but now he knew precisely how her body was reacting to him. After all, they had been lovers for nearly a year. He recognised the heat suddenly dancing in her cheeks, and the way her pupils had grown large in her pale-coloured eyes.

She wanted him as much as he wanted her.

Suddenly he gripped her arms and pulled her towards him, up onto her tiptoes so that her lips were just below his. All he had to do was bend his head a fraction more and his mouth would come down over hers. He would take back what had once been his—reclaim her body in hot, hard retribution for what she had done.

But this wasn't what he had come to London for. He could not—*would* not—let his libido get in the way of fulfilling his mother's dying wish. He needed Kerry to convince Drakon to sell him the island.

'I didn't come here for this,' he said gruffly, letting go of her arms and stepping away from her.

'I don't know what you mean,' Kerry said, shaken by how husky her voice sounded.

How had she let herself fall under his sensual spell so easily? Why would she even respond to him at all, after the horrible way he had treated her?

'You know as well as I do,' he said. 'Let's not play any more games. I'll tell you what I came for.'

'Why don't you?' she said, pleased with how sassy she managed to sound, considering the way her body was still buzzing with unwanted desire for him. Even though her face was streaked with rain, she could feel her cheeks burning. 'It's taking you long enough to get round to it.'

The rain was coming down more heavily now, and she lifted her hand to brush her long wet fringe back from her face. She stared straight up into his eyes, determined not to let him see any weakness. She'd be ready next time, if he started looking at her like that again—as if he wanted to tear off her clothes and make love to her right there and then.

After everything that had happened she couldn't believe he'd had the audacity to come on to her like that. And she couldn't believe she'd let herself respond. She would not let it happen again.

'Do you want to go inside?' he asked, glancing around as if he was looking for a café. 'Sit out of the rain while we talk?'

'No. I'm already wet, and my break is nearly over,' she said. 'Just tell me what you want from me.'

She didn't relish the idea of continuing their conversation standing in the rain on a busy urban pavement—

but somehow she felt safer out in the open. The thought of being in a confined space with him, even a public café, sent a shiver of apprehension down her spine.

'I want to buy an island from an old man,' Theo said, getting straight to the point. 'I need *you* to help me secure the deal.'

Kerry frowned up at him. She felt slightly startled by the fact that he was finally being direct about his reason for coming to her, but she was also puzzled as to why he thought he needed *her* help.

'What have I got to do with it?' she asked, intrigued despite herself.

'It is because *you* meddled in my family's affairs—creating a situation that caused the media frenzy—that the old man is reluctant to do business with me,' Theo said. 'He wants to sell his island to someone with traditional values—someone he approves of.'

'I don't understand how you think I can help you—even if I wanted to,' Kerry said. 'What can *I* do to change the way this man thinks about you?'

'The old man in question is called Drakon Notara. He remembers meeting you. Apparently he liked you,' Theo replied, somehow making it sound as if he thought it highly unlikely that *anyone* would actually like her.

'I remember him.' Kerry frowned, irritated by Theo's tone. 'He told me all about the wildlife sanctuary he has on his island. He hates all these intensive modern developments and wants to keep somewhere natural.' She paused and looked at Theo quizzically. 'Why do *you* want to buy a wildlife sanctuary?'

For a long moment he didn't respond, and something made Kerry think that Theo hadn't even known about the sanctuary. He just wanted the island.

'No wonder Drakon doesn't want to sell to you,' she said. 'He doesn't want a hotel on his nature preserve.'

'It seemed to me that he was more concerned with my commitment to family values,' Theo said curtly. 'Therefore you will accompany me to his island tomorrow—travelling as my fiancée. At no point will you reveal that we have not been together since you met him.'

Kerry stared at him in shock.

'Fiancée?' she repeated.

For a moment she almost thought he was proposing to her. But that would be crazy. Almost as crazy as him expecting a woman he'd heartlessly cast aside for making one mistake to pose as his fiancée. Just so that he could buy an island from an old man who apparently did not approve of him.

'Yes,' Theo said. 'For the duration of the few days we are to spend on the island you are to act the perfect, adoring fiancée in every way.'

'I wasn't your fiancée when I met Drakon,' she said, saying the first thing that came into her mind. It seemed a ridiculous thing to say—but so was the charade Theo was suggesting.

'Time has passed since then,' Theo said. 'It would seem natural that our relationship has progressed.'

'Progressed!' Kerry exclaimed, finally coming to her senses. 'That's an interesting take on it. I thought it had ended—badly—the night you kicked me out without giving me a chance to defend myself.'

'There's no defence for what you did,' Theo said.

'So why would I listen to whatever spin you wanted to put on your meddling? Whatever excuse you were going to give me?'

'There's no way I'm going to help you persuade a dear old man to sell you his island,' she said.

'Yes, you are,' Theo said. 'I will collect you from your flat tomorrow morning.'

'You don't know where I live!' she exclaimed.

'Of course I do,' he replied scathingly. 'Be packed and ready by six-thirty.'

Biting panic suddenly flared within her—freezing her insides stone-cold with dread. He'd found out where she worked, which probably meant he *did* know where she lived. And if he knew that, what else had his people found out about her—what else would they find if they dug deeper?

She had to keep Lucas hidden from him.

She remembered his words—*a Diakos child belongs with the Diakos family*.

He'd had no qualms about taking Hallie's child from her, and she was married to his brother—a true member of the family. What chance did Kerry have against him if he wanted to take his son?

'Don't make me come for you at work tomorrow,' Theo said. 'I will find you if you try to hide from me. And if you give me the runaround I will not be pleased.'

Kerry stood on the pavement outside her block of flats at six o'clock the following morning. It was very early, but she could not risk Theo coming inside the building to look for her. The closer she let him come to her home, the more chance there was of him finding out about Lucas.

Half an hour later, when a smart black limousine pulled up beside her, she discovered that she'd be travelling alone. Theo had already returned to Athens the previous evening.

'Your ticket, Miss Martin,' his assistant said, handing her a white envelope. 'You are booked on a flight out of Heathrow airport this morning. You will be met when you arrive in Athens, and taken to join Mr Diakos. You will then fly out to the island together.'

'Thank you,' Kerry said automatically. Still slightly stunned by Theo's absence, she slipped into the limo and stared out through the tinted window.

Was Theo really so confident that she would meekly do as she was told? She'd never actually agreed to go with him. In fact she'd told him point-blank that she was not going. Had she always been so biddable that it just didn't occur to him that she might refuse to co-operate?

He didn't know the reason she'd had to go—the secret she could not risk him uncovering if she made him come looking for her. He must simply have expected her to do as she was told because that was what she had always done.

She closed her eyes and hugged herself, already missing Lucas although it was scarcely an hour since she'd left him with Bridget—the only person in the world she truly trusted. They'd been brought up together as sisters and, despite the fact that she had discovered later that Bridget was really her aunt, they still shared an incredibly close, sisterly bond.

Kerry knew Lucas would be safe with her. Bridget had her own little ones and was used to babies, but even so Kerry felt horrible leaving him. She knew she had no choice—to protect her son she had to leave him for a couple of nights—but somehow she felt she was letting him down.

Theo glanced across at Kerry as they climbed out of the helicopter on Drakon Notara's island. Her hair was whipping about in the wind, and as she put up her hands to hold it back from her face he saw that she was pale and shaky after the flight.

She'd never complained, even though he'd asked her to join him on many of his trips, but Theo knew she wasn't a good traveller. Chances were she hadn't slept much the night before, and the limo had picked her up very early that morning. Tiredness always made her travel sickness worse, and he guessed she was feeling pretty rough. But he wanted her bright and appealing, to convince Drakon to sell him the island.

'I know the way to the house,' he said, as the old man's quirky assistant came towards them. 'My fiancée needs a moment to recover from the journey—some fresh air and solid ground under her feet for a while will do the trick.'

He reached out, looped his arm around her waist and pulled her close to him. He felt a tremor pass through her as she tensed and tried to pull away from him.

'Lean on me till you get your strength back,' Theo said, tightening his hold on her. Then he dropped his voice and spoke quietly, for her ears alone. 'Don't forget why you are here. You are my fiancée and you will act like it.'

With a deliberate effort Kerry relaxed her body and allowed herself to lean against Theo. She was surprised that apparently he'd picked up on how she was feeling—he'd never shown any sign of noticing her tendency to motion sickness before. But this time it *was* particularly awful—probably almost anyone would have noticed if she looked even half as bad as she felt.

All she could do was concentrate on drawing calming breaths into her lungs and putting one foot in front of the other. Theo's arm was around her—a steady anchor and a welcome distraction from the nausea that rolled through her.

However, it didn't take long before her awareness shifted entirely onto the sensation of his hard body next to her. The stressful journey and the way it had made her feel so rotten slipped away, and she was simply conscious of how closely Theo was holding her.

His body was strong and athletic, and she could feel his muscles moving as they made their way along the rocky path together. They were walking in unison, and she suddenly realised that meant he had matched his stride to hers. For some reason that realisation sent a shiver skittering down her spine. Whether it had been intentional or instinctive, on some level Theo had been attuned to her body and the rhythm of her movements.

'Feeling better now?' he asked. His deep, masculine voice passed like a physical vibration right through her, setting her nerve-endings alight and making her even more conscious of his powerful male form beside her.

She turned to look up at him, suddenly convinced

that he had known the exact moment her attention had shifted onto the sensual experience of walking with him. Somehow the thought made her feel exposed and vulnerable.

She lifted her head and his eyes caught hers, holding them locked to his dark gaze. He was studying her intently, and all at once she got the feeling that he was probing—trying to read her mind. She didn't remember him looking at her like that before—as if he thought she was guilty of something.

Then she suddenly realised that she'd never had anything to hide from him before. Was she imagining his scrutiny because she had an enormous secret?

'The house is just over the brow of the hill,' he said, lifting his hands to cradle her face gently. 'Drakon may be old—but his mind is sharp. He'll be watching us, so never let the pretence that you are my fiancée slip.'

'I don't want to lie,' she said, pulling away from him slightly. She'd enjoyed meeting Drakon the previous year, and, despite his funny old ways, she had liked him. 'It doesn't feel right.'

'Then we'd better make our act convincing, so Drakon won't ask you any tricky questions,' Theo said. 'And, as they say, actions speak louder than words.'

Before she realised his intention, one strong arm had slipped around her back and pulled her hard against him. The other hand lifted to cup her chin and tip her face up to his.

She opened her lips to protest, and at that moment his mouth came down on hers.

CHAPTER FOUR

THEO'S kiss took Kerry completely by surprise, but her body responded instinctively. It seemed the most natural thing in the world for her to lean into him, pressing sensuously against his hard, athletic body, and part her lips in invitation.

His tongue swept into her mouth, hot and demanding, and she felt herself become molten with longing. There was nothing tender about his kiss—it was a fierce and passionate reminder of all the times they had made love. Of all the times he'd taken her to the point of ecstasy.

She lifted her own tongue to meet his, surrendering to the intense desire that suddenly stormed through her body, and kissed him back wildly. Her hands ran up to his shoulders, revelling in the hot, hard feel of his muscles, and she clung to him tightly—as if she never wanted to let go.

Then, without warning, Theo broke away from the kiss.

Kerry gasped in surprise, swaying unsteadily as he abruptly released his hold on her.

'Quite convincing,' he said, as he stepped away and stared down at her through narrowed eyes.

She held her breath as she looked up into his face, and for a moment the world stood still. She'd dreamed of Theo kissing her again for more than a year—but in her fantasy he had been kissing her because he had realised his mistake, realised that he loved her.

Her dream had never been like this—her kissing him desperately, with embarrassing eagerness. And with him appearing to be completely unmoved by the whole thing.

She felt the hot colour of humiliation staining her cheeks, and she looked down at the ground, mortified that she had given herself away so completely. Then a wave of anger rose through her, and her eyes snapped back up to meet his.

'It was my intention to be convincing,' she said. 'But there'll be no more free demonstrations. I'm here to help you with Drakon—not to be nice to you in private.'

Theo raised his straight black brows in surprise, but his lips quirked in amusement, and she had the feeling he'd seen right through her.

'Let's go and meet our host,' he said, sliding his arm around her waist and turning to continue along the path.

'I understand you weren't feeling too well when you arrived,' Drakon said, looking across the table at Kerry with sharp eyes. 'I trust you're feeling better now?'

'Yes, I'm fine,' she said. 'Thank you for asking.' She took a sip of her drink and smiled across at him. It was lovely sitting outside under the shade of the twisted old olive trees, enjoying the stunning view over the bay to the Adriatic. And making small talk with Drakon stopped her thinking about what had happened with Theo on the path from the helipad.

'Kerry suffers from travel sickness,' Theo said, taking her by surprise. She'd assumed he'd only guessed how she'd felt earlier because she had looked particularly rough. She'd never realised that he'd always known that she often felt ill on long journeys. 'After a short rest she's usually back to normal,' he added.

'What a nuisance travel sickness must be,' Drakon said. 'Especially when you travel such a lot.'

'Don't make me feel bad.' Theo's tone was wry. 'Even though I know she suffers, I ask her to come with me because I can't bear to be without her.'

'Love is selfish sometimes,' Drakon said, knocking back a huge swallow of ouzo.

'It can be.' Theo turned his piercing gaze onto Kerry.

A strange feeling washed over her as his dark eyes found hers, and suddenly she couldn't maintain eye contact with him. She took another sip of her drink, hoping to cover up how disconcerted she felt. The direction the conversation had taken had knocked her totally off balance.

When they'd been together Theo had told her the same thing—that he wanted her to travel with him because he couldn't bear to be without her. At the time his words had made her feel special—valued. Never before in her life had anyone shown so much desire to have her around.

She'd grown up feeling unwanted and unloved—and when she was eighteen years old she'd found out just how true that was. Her grandmother had not wanted to care for her, but had grudgingly become her guardian out of a twisted sense of duty, having refused to accept that her teenage daughter was capable of looking after her own baby.

But it had turned out that Theo hadn't genuinely valued her company either. She'd made one mistake—and then he couldn't get rid of her fast enough. Drakon's mention of love being selfish was just another cruel reminder of how little she'd meant to Theo. He'd never loved her and she knew he never would.

'I hope that tomorrow you will allow us to view the whole island,' Theo said to their host, pulling Kerry out of her thoughts.

'No business talk now.' Drakon waved away his request and looked at Kerry. 'My dear, I haven't seen you for such a long time. I know I don't leave the island much, but there were a couple of occasions in Athens when I was hoping to meet you again.'

'Oh, I'm sorry,' Kerry said, feeling a knot of tension tighten in her stomach as she found herself on the spot. She did not want to think about how Theo would react if she failed to convince Drakon that they were still together. 'Unfortunately I haven't been able to accompany Theo to every event lately,' she continued. 'I've been spending a lot of time in London—I've had family commitments.'

She pushed her long fringe out of her eyes and thought about Lucas. She was completely and utterly committed to her baby boy, and would do anything for him. Unlike her own mother—who had been too young and too weak when Kerry was born, and had not managed to stand up for herself or her baby.

'Nothing serious, I hope,' Drakon said, looking concerned. 'No one sick?'

'No, no...' Kerry's voice trailed away as a barb of guilt twisted inside her—as if somehow by hiding his existence she was betraying her son. 'Personal things...nothing important.'

She took a breath and smiled reassuringly at the old man, who still looked worried—all the time feeling like the very worst kind of mother. How could she imply— even though of course she didn't really mean it—that giving birth to Lucas had not been important?

'I'm glad to hear that,' Drakon said, as he pushed his chair back and levered himself up to standing. Theo was on his feet beside him in an instant, but Drakon waved his help aside impatiently. 'I'm going to rest before dinner. Take a look around the house if you're interested. Tomorrow you can see the island.'

Kerry stood up too, and waited quietly as Theo held the door into the house open for their elderly host.

'The door stays open on its own,' Drakon said tartly as he shuffled past. 'I don't need your help.'

A smile flashed across Kerry's lips as she saw Drakon roll his eyes irritably at Theo. She really did like the old man.

Then she realised Theo was staring at her, and the smile faded from her face as quickly as it had come. A shiver prickled down between her shoulderblades as their eyes met—it felt just as if his dark gaze was boring right into her.

'Something amusing?' he asked, closing the distance between them in two long strides.

'I like Drakon,' she said, turning away to escape his penetrating gaze. 'It's good to see him again.'

She tried to concentrate on the amazing view of the bay below the house—a gorgeous crescent of rocky shoreline, edged by wizened old trees that seemed to lean right out over the azure Aegean Sea. But all the time she was ultra-aware of just how close Theo was standing.

Suddenly his arm slid possessively around her waist from behind, and she couldn't help drawing in a sharp breath. She tried to ignore the tremor that ran through her as his fingers brushed against her skin, just under the hem of her top.

'It's good to see *you* again,' he said, letting his hand slip further up inside, so that he was caressing the sensitive skin of her midriff.

'You're not looking at me,' Kerry said, attempting to pull away, but he held her firmly against him.

'Then it's good to *touch* you.' He eased her closer, so that she was standing with her back pressed against his chest.

'Touching me wasn't part of the deal,' she protested, instinctively pulling in her stomach muscles as his other hand slipped around her waist on the opposite side.

'We never made any deal.' His voice was a murmur, so close to her neck that his lips brushed her skin and set off a whole new series of tremors within her. 'You came because I told you to. And because you wanted to.'

'No. I—' Kerry's voice caught in her throat as Theo pressed his open mouth against her neck and nibbled gently, making exquisite sensations ripple through her.

She couldn't hide the way her body was suddenly

trembling. Maybe it was because it was so long since she had felt Theo's touch, but suddenly the combination of his tongue moving across her skin and his warm breath feathering her neck felt like the most sensual thing she had ever experienced.

Her breath escaped her in a long, shuddery sigh, and he responded immediately by rocking his hips forward and pressing against her. The feel of his hard erection nudging into the soft curve of her bottom made a torrent of hot arousal cascade through her and her heart started to race.

'I've missed this,' Theo said. 'And I can tell you've missed it too.'

'No. I haven't.' Kerry's voice faltered as Theo ran his tongue lightly up the side of her neck and pulled on her earlobe with his lips. Another wave of tremors rolled through her—but she knew she had to put a stop to Theo's seduction.

If she let herself fall any further under his spell she wouldn't stand a chance—she knew she would end up in his bed. She could not let that happen. Not after the way he had treated her. And not with the huge secret she was keeping from him.

'I want to have a look around,' she said, taking a positive step forward and breaking away from his touch. 'Drakon said we could. I'm surprised you don't seem keen to take the opportunity to survey your potential acquisition.'

A smile spread slowly across Theo's face as Kerry pulled away from him, and he released his grip, letting her slip out of his arms. He burned to make love to her—hot, hard, passionate love—but he would wait until tonight.

He knew how much she still wanted him—it had

been impossible for her to hide the way he'd so easily set her body alight with desire. She might be playing hard to get, but that just made him want her even more.

He walked behind her as she headed for a gap in the trees at the edge of the paved area. The view of the shimmering sea stretching out from the bay beneath them was stunning, but he only had eyes for the sublime sway of Kerry's hips as she moved.

God, he'd missed her—missed losing himself in her beautiful, receptive body.

Theo would never forgive her for what she had done—she'd abused his trust to interfere with matters that did not concern her, and the consequences could have been tragic. She would never share his life again—but she would share his bed that night.

'Drakon doesn't like change.' Kerry turned back to speak, taking him by surprise. 'He doesn't believe in discarding old things on a whim—just to get something bigger, better or flashier.'

'He's not totally averse to progress,' Theo pointed out, pulling his thoughts back from erotic images of making love to Kerry. 'He has a nice new helipad, and travels to Athens by helicopter whenever the whim takes him.'

'I wonder where he plans to live after he sells the island,' she said.

Theo frowned. 'It's not going to be easy to persuade him. I think he'd like to end his days here. But he also wants to leave things in order for his daughter,' he said. 'She lives on the mainland with her family, but from what I understand she has her hands full looking after her husband, who was injured in an accident. She has no head for business and Drakon doesn't want to add to her burden.'

'He's a thoughtful man.' Kerry stopped and looked at him. Her silky-soft hair was blowing in the breeze coming off the sea and she put up her hand to hold her fringe out of her eyes. 'How do you know all that? I don't believe *he* told you. He seems to be quite a private person.'

'That's not your concern,' Theo said, lifting his hand to cover hers. Her fingers felt cool and slim beneath his. 'Why did you cut your hair?'

For a moment her eyes opened wide with surprise, and in the bright Greek sunlight Theo saw that they *were* the clear blue he had believed them to be—then she schooled her features into a blank expression and met his gaze steadily.

'I felt like a change,' she said. 'But now I'm growing the fringe out again—that's why it's always in my eyes.'

'I like to see your face.' He lifted his other hand and smoothed all the tendrils back from her forehead.

'You weren't there, so I didn't think you'd mind.' She shook her head with a touch of irritation and he let go. Her hair fell forward again, but not before he'd noticed the horizontal creases that had appeared across her forehead when she frowned. 'I'm going inside to get changed for dinner,' she added, turning away and heading for the house.

'You go on ahead,' he said. 'I'm going to look round a bit more.'

He watched her walk across the paved area and into the house, the bewitching movements of her body sending another surge of hot desire through his veins.

Her body seemed different somehow—slightly fuller, perhaps. Maybe it was his imagination, because he was so hot for her, but her breasts definitely seemed bigger than he remembered them. He pictured the way they'd look naked in his mind's eye—gorgeously ripe and full—and suddenly it was almost more than he could do not to follow her straight to the bedroom.

There was time to make love before dinner, but he wanted to make love to her properly, till he was utterly spent and all the tension had been burned out of him. That would take longer. A lot longer.

Kerry could feel Theo's eyes burning a hole in her back all the way across the patio. It was a relief to enter the cool interior of the house, but she was wound far too tightly to relax properly.

She hurried straight to their room, then showered and changed for dinner as quickly as she could. She was ready far too early—but she didn't want Theo to come back before she was dressed. From the way he'd been looking at her she knew exactly what he wanted to do—and that was the last thing she wanted. Or so she told herself.

She paced uneasily around the room for a few minutes, then decided to go out again. At least that way she could avoid being trapped in a confined space with him. Chances were that he wouldn't come on too strongly if they could be interrupted at any moment.

She closed the door quietly, then made her way along the corridor, admiring the many paintings that were hung along the simple whitewashed walls. She realised they were all different views of the island, and they were all painted by the same artist. There seemed to be something familiar about them, but she couldn't pinpoint what it was.

She was still looking at the paintings when Theo returned. Her heart skipped a beat as he paused beside her, and she could feel the heat radiating off his powerful body, smell his warm, musky scent. He was slightly flushed and looked as if he'd been hurrying.

'It took me longer to climb back up the cliff path than I expected,' he said. 'Drakon is waiting for us in the dining room. Go and join him—I'll be there very soon.'

She watched him stride away to their room, feeling her heart rate slowly subside once he was out of sight. She was happy to go and talk to Drakon. It was safer than spending time with Theo. And she was interested in finding out something about the paintings she had been admiring.

It wasn't long before Theo joined them and dinner was served. The meal that followed began much more easily than Kerry had anticipated. For the most part Theo carried the conversation, keeping the topics light and undemanding. She found herself starting to relax. It was almost possible to imagine that this was an ordinary social event like the many events she had attended with Theo in the past. Actually, it was more pleasant than many—she liked Drakon and enjoyed hearing his views on the world.

Theo was a charming and attentive companion. His manner seemed so natural and so familiar—so much like the way he had always behaved towards her when they were together. In fact there was nothing to distinguish the way he was treating her now from the way he had treated her during the year she'd been his lover.

She knew that tonight it was just an act—that he was simply playing the role of devoted lover—but it reminded her painfully of the past. Then suddenly, out of the blue, she found herself wondering if he had always been acting with her.

If he could turn on the charm now—even though she knew for sure that his feelings towards her were the complete opposite of those he was portraying—how could she know he'd ever been genuine? Had he ever really cared—or had she been nothing more than a suitably undemanding, biddable candidate who was willing to travel with him, to be at his beck and call for his personal convenience?

That thought felt like a slap in the face.

This evening showed that he was a master of deception. There was no way of knowing if he had ever been true to her—if his affection had ever been anything more than an act.

She stared at him across the table, unable to keep her expression neutral. After everything—what was she doing here with him?

She thought about Lucas. It made her chest ache, she missed him so much. She'd never been away from him overnight. By now Bridget would already have put him down to sleep. Had he settled quickly? Or had he cried because he missed his mother?

'Kerry?' Theo's voice cut into her thoughts, and she realised he had spoken to her more than once before she'd heard. 'Our host is saying goodnight.'

She quickly turned to Drakon, noticing how tired and drawn he was looking.

'That was a delicious meal,' she said quickly, hoping he hadn't noticed how distracted she'd become towards the end.

'Don't have the stamina I once had,' Drakon muttered as he heaved himself up on unsteady legs.

'Let me help,' Kerry said, rushing over to support him.

'I don't mind accepting help from a pretty young woman,' he replied.

She could tell he was trying to make his voice sound light, but the strain that he was trying to hide was clearly visible in his face. She helped him halfway across the room, then his assistant appeared with a wheelchair, which he gratefully sank into.

'Didn't want you to see this,' he mumbled. 'Don't really need it, but…'

'Thank you for a lovely evening,' she said, bending down to kiss him lightly on the cheek before his assistant wheeled him away.

She straightened her shoulders, already feeling Theo's eyes on her. For a moment she didn't want to turn and face him—but there was nothing else she could do.

'Alone at last.'

Theo's deep voice oozed with intent, and the sexual message in his tone tingled down her spine like a dark promise.

Kerry's feet felt as if they were glued to the floor, but she made herself turn on the spot until she was facing Theo. Their eyes met with a snap, and she felt a surge of emotion rush through her. It had been so easy for him to play the attentive lover that evening—but she *knew* he was just playing a role for the sake of their elderly host. Had it been that way all the time they were together?

'Was it always just an act?' she demanded.

CHAPTER FIVE

A GLIMMER of surprise flashed across Theo's face, but it was gone in an instant, to be replaced by a hard, shuttered expression. It was clear that he didn't intend to get into the discussion that she wanted—at least not in Drakon's dining room.

'I'm not sure I understand your meaning.' His voice sounded smooth and unhurried, but he closed the distance between them with a few rapid strides and wrapped his arm snugly around her. Although to an onlooker the gesture might have appeared affectionate, Kerry knew that was far from the truth. 'Let's go to our room, where we can talk quietly.'

'You know exactly what I mean,' she said curtly, attempting to pull away from him. But he tightened his hold on her and started walking out of the dining room. She had no choice but to go with him—not if she didn't wish to make a scene.

Reluctantly, she let him guide her back to their bedroom, clamped to his side by his powerful arm. She was acutely conscious of his firm, masculine body moving beside her. With every step they took she could feel his legs brushing against hers, feel his muscles working, feel the heat passing from his body to hers. It was as if there was a current flowing from him into her, making her more and more sensitive to him.

Her pulse-rate was rising and she was starting to feel slightly breathless. But it wasn't because of the strong emotions that had flared within her. Something else was building inside her now.

She tried desperately to ignore the way she was feeling physically—to call back the anger that had sparked in the dining room. But her mind and emotions were clouded simply from being so close to Theo.

'Let's not talk,' he said as he closed the door quietly behind them. He turned and pulled her towards him, face to face. 'I can think of things I'd far rather be doing with you.'

'No.' Kerry lifted her hands and pressed her palms flat against his chest to hold him away from her, although he was drawing her closer and closer with every second that passed. 'I want answers. I want to know if everything was always just an act. Did you never care for me at all?'

'An act?' Theo looked deep into her eyes in a way that sent a quiver of heat running right to her centre. 'You know this isn't an act. No one could fake sexual chemistry like this.'

'I'm not talking about the chemistry,' Kerry protested, trying not to be distracted by the heat of his chest through the fine fabric of his shirt. Her fingers twitched, longing to delve inside his clothing and feel his naked skin. 'There was more than that between—'

She hadn't finished speaking when Theo's mouth came down on hers, silencing her with a kiss. She gasped in surprise and he pushed his advantage home, plunging his tongue between her open lips.

It was a forceful possession of her mouth that she hadn't consciously invited—but her response was instant. An immediate rush of excitement tore through her body, making her tremble and moan with desire. It was as if her ability to resist him had evaporated in an explosion of pure physical arousal, and she arched towards him, moulding herself to his body.

His hands slid over her, touching and stroking through her dress. His tongue writhed erotically against hers, sending her pulse-rate soaring and making her head spin. It was impossible to think. Impossible to do anything other than surrender to Theo and kiss him back with equal passion.

Then, through the hot haze of sexual desire, she felt his hands moving on her hips. He was tugging at her dress, bunching the fabric up so that he could reach underneath.

A blast of feverish anticipation shot through her, making her legs buckle simply at the thought of what might happen next—of what she was suddenly desperate to experience again.

Theo's arms went around her, lifting her on to the bed, and for a moment she lay back breathlessly against the pillows, staring up into his flushed face. He was leaning over her, his black hair falling forward over his brow, filling her vision, blocking out everything but him.

His hand was on her leg, sliding quickly past her knee, along the inside of her thigh. Her whole being yearned for him, wanted to be one with him again.

But it would never happen—not truly. Not in the way her heart wanted.

He didn't love her. He'd never loved her.

'No.'

The word was hardly audible, but it was enough to make Theo stop completely still. His hand was resting just a few inches from the very top of her leg, right next to the most sensitive place on her body.

'Don't try to tell me you don't want this.' His tone was level, but Kerry could hear that he was breathing hard. She knew that he was fully aroused and expecting to make love to her.

'Not this,' she said, trying hard not to wriggle. The position of his hand was driving her to the point of distraction. If she rocked her hips it would move, slide intimately against her throbbing flesh. 'I want an answer to my question.'

'I told you—this is real,' he said, squeezing her inner thigh lightly. He didn't move his hand any higher, but the gentle pressure on her leg was enough to send waves of sensation rolling across the centre of her desire.

'Oh.' She couldn't help sighing in pleasure. She closed her eyes for a moment, drawing in a shaky breath.

'You want this,' Theo said. 'You want to make love.'

Kerry opened her eyes and looked at him.

'It's not love,' she said.

'No,' Theo replied, studying her through narrowed eyes. 'No one ever said it was.'

'But I thought that you had feelings for me,' Kerry said shakily, finally finding the will to push his hand away and sit up against the pillows. 'I thought that we had feelings for each other. At least that's how it seemed.'

'Feelings?'

Theo pulled away abruptly and stared at her in disgust. How dared she bring up the subject of their feelings?

She was the one who'd betrayed his trust—gone behind his back and stirred up trouble, almost causing a family tragedy.

'Don't even think of trying that one,' he bit out, standing up beside the bed. 'What kind of fool do you take me for? I can't be manipulated so easily.'

Her face was flushed and he could see the rapid rise and fall of her breasts as she breathed. She was just as turned on as he was—yet she was tormenting them both, trying to make him say something unguarded in the heat of passion.

He saw her shrink back a little, and her eyes widened with surprise, as if she was startled by his sudden change of temper. But then her expression hardened and her brow creased with annoyance. He knew she was about to challenge him.

'You have always been the one controlling our relationship. You still are—even though it's more than a year since you kicked me out,' she said, sliding off the opposite side of the bed and turning to face him. 'So don't talk to me about manipulation—I've always done everything you ever asked of me.'

'We *have* no relationship,' Theo grated. 'It ended the night you betrayed the trust I'd placed in you.'

He was shocked to hear her use the present tense—surely she knew the score as well as he did? This was just sex—nothing more. Why would she make it sound as if their affair was ongoing?

'You threw me out without a second thought,' she said. 'And now it suits your purpose you want me back.'

'I don't want you back,' he said through gritted teeth.

'But you still made me come here with you,' Kerry said. 'And you're deliberately messing with my head—acting like a devoted lover and trying to seduce me.'

'You understood the situation when you came here,' he said. 'So don't act surprised by the way I've treated you in public. And in private you want me just as much as you ever did.'

Kerry bit her lip and stared at Theo, feeling lost and utterly humiliated.

He was right. She did still want him. Despite everything, she *did* still want him.

'I never meant anything to you,' she said, hearing her voice crack with emotion. 'You've never even had the slightest respect for me.'

'Respect?' he repeated incredulously. 'After everything, how can you even *mention* respect?'

It was the confirmation she'd been dreading—proof that she'd never meant anything to him at all. That was why it had been so easy for him to discard her when she did something foolish.

She felt her heart breaking all over again. Tears pricked her eyes, but she blinked them away, refusing to let him see her cry. He didn't respect her—but she had to show some respect for herself.

'Get away from me,' she said. 'I don't want to be in the same room as you.'

'I'm not leaving,' he said. 'I'm not asking our host for separate rooms. That would defeat the point of you being here.'

'Then I will,' Kerry said. She turned and stepped quickly towards the door.

Theo moved like lightning. In an instant he had circled the bed, and caught up with her just as she reached for the door handle.

His fingers closed like a vice around her wrist and he flipped her round, pinning her to the wall.

'Don't do something you'll regret.' His voice was deep and rough, as if he was only just holding his temper in check, and she could feel the tension in his muscular frame as he pushed up against her.

'It's too late for that,' she whispered miserably. 'I should never have come here with you in the first place.'

He pressed her back to wall with one hard thigh thrust between her legs and stared straight into her eyes. His gaze held her trapped as securely as the strength in his large, powerful body, and she could feel the angry energy emanating from him.

Then he released her with such abruptness that she stumbled forward into the room.

She was still finding her balance when she realised he had gone. He'd moved so quickly and shut the door so silently that it was almost as if he'd simply vanished.

She staggered over to the bed, breathing in jerky, painful gasps. Her eyes were swimming with tears, but she wouldn't let them fall. She would *not* let them fall. She could not let him win any more.

But she knew it wasn't over. No matter how many times she cried, or how hard she tried to hide the pain, it would never be over—because she was the mother of his son.

The following morning Kerry woke to the sound of the shower running in the *en suite* bathroom—Theo must have come back, but she had no idea when. It had taken her hours to fall asleep, but he hadn't disturbed her when he came into the room.

She frowned, wondering when he'd returned—and if he'd slept elsewhere and just come back to shower, or if he'd slipped into the bed during the night while she was sleeping.

She got up quickly, collected some fresh clothes from her case and sat at the table flicking through a magazine, intending to dash straight into the bathroom as soon as he appeared. After their argument she was not looking forward to the day, and she wanted to be washed and dressed before she had to talk to him again. She had the feeling he was going to make her pay for not meekly complying with his wishes the night before.

A minute later she heard the door to the bathroom open.

'Good morning.' Theo's voice seemed deeper than usual, and for a second Kerry wondered how much sleep he'd had—not much, if his gruff tone was anything to go by. But most importantly she realised his tone was neutral—he didn't sound angry any more. A ripple of relief ran through her and she turned to reply.

'Good morn...' She faltered, staring at him standing

in the doorway—naked apart from a small white towel wrapped around his hips—and all coherent thought flew out of her head.

He looked absolutely magnificent, and she could not drag her eyes off him. His skin was still glistening with water droplets and his wet hair was sexily dishevelled, as if he'd just roughly towel-dried it.

He started walking towards her across the room, and she swallowed reflexively, simply staring at him in awe. The movement of his muscles rippling beneath his taut bronzed skin was totally mesmerising. And totally arousing.

Her gaze slid easily over the contours of his broad chest, down to the sculptured beauty of his lean stomach muscles. A sprinkling of black hair arrowed downwards, drawing her gaze lower still.

Her eyes widened as she found herself staring at his towel. Her attention was having a powerful effect on him, and he was making no attempt to hide it. She pressed her teeth into her lower lip, feeling an answering heat flood through her own veins.

She jumped up awkwardly, clutching the bundle of fresh clothes to her chest, suddenly desperate to get out of there. She couldn't bear a repeat of last night's humiliation.

'There's no need for you to hurry,' Theo said, blocking her access to the *en suite* bathroom with his large, virtually naked body. 'Unfortunately Drakon cannot see us yet. We'll have to occupy ourselves for a while.'

'Oh,' she said, forcing herself to meet his gaze, but hardly registering his words as he lifted his hand to brush her hair back from her face. She knew exactly how he wanted to occupy himself—and, despite everything, her treacherous body felt the same way.

She shivered as his fingers made contact, knowing he was watching her reaction. She was certain he was aware how much she still wanted him—even after she had pushed him away the night before—but she would not give in to the desire that was rapidly taking her over.

She felt her cheeks flare even hotter and she stepped quickly to the side. His hand dropped slowly from her face, skimming lightly down the side of her body, but he didn't try to stop her as she fled into the bathroom.

When she emerged some time later she discovered that she was on her own again. A delicious breakfast had been laid out on their private balcony, but only one place had been set. She was to eat alone.

Like many Greeks, Theo rarely bothered with breakfast. Kerry felt light-headed if she skipped a meal—she couldn't imagine how Theo, six foot two inches of solid muscle, powered his body and made vital business decisions fuelled by nothing more than the occasional coffee.

She sat down, realising it was a welcome relief to be able to eat alone in the morning sunshine, enjoying the stunning view across the island to the Adriatic. The land sloped away from the house, down to olive groves shimmering silvery green, and beyond that the sea was a beautiful pale turquoise, wreathed with a slight sea mist that she knew would soon burn off as the day heated up.

She was just finishing her meal when Theo returned.

'I have some disappointing news,' he said, stepping out to join her on the balcony. 'Drakon is not well, and there is no chance we will be able to meet with him this morning. However, we do have his permission to walk up to the highest point on the island.'

'Oh, no—I hope it's nothing serious,' Kerry said.

'I don't know,' Theo said dispassionately, moving over to the edge of the balcony and leaning out to get a better view of the hill beside the house. 'His health is poor—which I believe is what prompted him to consider selling the island. Do you have suitable footwear? I'm not sure how rough the path will be.'

Kerry frowned, staring crossly at Theo's impassive expression. He didn't care at all that the poor old man was unwell—he just viewed it as a business opportunity.

'Give me a moment to change,' she said shortly, heading back inside without looking at Theo again.

'The island is small—only a few kilometres across—and there are no good roads or transport,' Theo said as they left the house. 'But we should be able to get a good view from the top of the hill.'

He watched Kerry step through the doorway ahead of him, letting his gaze run down her body appreciatively. She was wearing light cotton trousers that pulled snug over the gorgeous curves of her bottom as she walked, and a loose-fitting top that rippled against her in the slight breeze that was blowing in from the sea.

'Poor Drakon,' she said, as if the sight of the table under the trees where the old man had entertained them had suddenly made her think of him. 'I hope he feels better soon.'

'I know his staff are taking good care of him,' Theo replied.

He glanced down at the paving stones, noticing for the first time that the drifts of dead leaves and old olive blossom had been swept up. A wry smile flashed momentarily across his face as he realised it had been done for Kerry's benefit, but not for *his* initial visit, when he'd been on his own.

It was interesting that Drakon had made a concession to his inflexible 'take me as I am' persona for Kerry's sake. The old man really liked her, and Theo knew that bringing her here had been a wise move. Her presence had brought him one step closer to fulfilling his mother's dying wish.

They left the house and headed up the hill through olive groves that seemed almost as ancient as the land itself. It wasn't long before they were out from the shelter of the trees and looking at the final steep climb to the top of the hill.

'Do you want to rest for a moment?' Theo turned to look at Kerry and spoke for the first time since they'd left the house. His tone was neutral, but somehow Kerry got the feeling he didn't want her to take him up on his offer of rest.

'No, I'm fine,' she said quickly. She felt uneasy at the thought of sitting still with Theo anyway—especially as it was clear that he was keen to keep moving.

The silence between them was deafening, but all the time they were walking the atmosphere had been tolerable. Concentrating on keeping her footing and admiring the stunning scenery had distracted her from Theo's taciturn brooding.

He looked straight ahead and kept on walking without breaking his stride. It was still a fair hike to reach the top of the hill, and from the way Kerry's muscles were already aching it felt more like a mountain.

By the time they reached the summit she was breathing heavily, and her legs felt like jelly. She sat down on a large boulder to catch her breath, and gazed at the beautiful scenery. The mist had cleared to reveal an amazing view of the nearest neighbouring island. It was many times larger than Drakon's island, and he had told her that it had a reasonable population for its size.

'When you've rested for a moment we'll head back down,' Theo said, staring out across the glittering sea.

'We only just got here!' she gasped in surprise. 'Don't you want to look around or something?'

'I've seen all I need to see—and in any case nothing will alter my intention to buy the island.' Theo turned to look down at her and a flash of surprise showed on his face as he registered how heavily she was breathing. 'Now I want to get back, in case Drakon feels well enough to see us. I don't intend to miss an opportunity to move my negotiations with him forward.'

'He's sick!' Kerry exclaimed. 'Can't you leave him in peace?'

'I wouldn't dream of disturbing his peace.' Theo studied her through narrowed eyes. 'But this is business—and Drakon is looking for a buyer. Are you ready to get going?'

Kerry stared up at him crossly. She'd barely caught her breath, and her muscles were still burning from the effort of climbing the steep hill—but Theo hadn't even really needed to come up here!

She might have felt differently if they'd climbed slowly, enjoying the sunshine and the scenery, possibly even chatted a bit. But he'd just marched her up to the top of the hill in stony silence, to prove something to Drakon—perhaps to show that his interest in the island was genuine. Or maybe that he appreciated the privilege the old man had granted him when he'd allowed him to roam unaccompanied on his land.

Whatever his reasons, he had shown Kerry very little consideration—he'd been driven purely by his own agenda. Suddenly their conversation from the previous day, when they'd first arrived on the island, flashed into her mind. Even back when she'd thought he cared about her Theo really had done everything for his own personal convenience.

'If you always knew I got travel sick, why did you never say anything about it?' she demanded.

'I didn't think you wanted me to,' Theo replied, without missing a beat, although her comment must have seemed completely out of the blue. 'I thought you preferred not to think about it too much.'

She paused, staring at him through narrowed eyes. In a way he was right—she did try not to dwell on it. And any distraction, apart from reading, was usually a good way to feel better. But that didn't excuse him for never showing her any concern.

'How did you even know I didn't feel well?' she asked.

'It seemed fairly obvious—to me at least,' he replied. 'You went pale and shaky. And very quiet. But you usually seemed to recover pretty quickly once you were back on firm ground.'

'If you knew how I felt why did you make me travel so much?' she asked accusingly.

'I assumed you didn't want to let it interfere with your life,' he said. 'You never liked admitting any weakness. Like just now—apparently the climb was too much for you, but you haven't said anything.'

'It wasn't too much for me,' she said, infuriated by his patronising tone. 'Come on. Let's get going again.'

She sprang up to her feet, but her legs still felt like jelly. For a moment she wobbled slightly, and he was beside her in an instant, wrapping his arm around her waist.

'Your legs are shaking.' His voice was suddenly deep and sensually loaded. 'But—as you insist the climb wasn't too much for you—maybe it's me making you tremble.' He hugged her tightly to him with one arm and lifted his other hand to brush her hair off her face. 'In fact I can remember many different ways I used to make you tremble and shake.'

'Let go of me!' Kerry snapped, despite the fire that suddenly burned through her veins at the images he conjured in her mind. 'I don't want you to touch me again. Not ever.'

'Really? I don't think that is completely honest.' Theo stepped away from her. 'But it seems that honesty was never a central part of our relationship.'

'I was always honest with you,' she said defensively.

'Maybe you never lied to me directly,' Theo said.

'But you lied by omission. Neither of us discussed your travel sickness—but we both knew about it.'

'And what does *that* say about our relationship?' Kerry asked, thinking that they'd never really talked about anything important.

'I hardly think *that* was the defining point of our relationship,' Theo said derisively. 'Another moment stands out far more clearly in my memory—the moment you went behind my back and betrayed me.'

'No. It wasn't meant like that,' Kerry replied automatically, but as the words left her mouth she knew the past didn't matter. Whatever had happened between them in the past was completely irrelevant.

She was guilty of dishonesty now.

She was keeping his son a secret.

A wave of emotion washed over her, squeezing her heart and making her throat tight. Baby Lucas was thousands of miles away, being looked after by someone else, and she was here, with Theo, and the secret she was keeping seemed to be growing more awful with every passing minute.

CHAPTER SIX

THEO started striding down the steep path back towards the house. Kerry followed behind, struggling to keep up. He was a very tall, athletic man, with a lengthy stride, and it seemed his bad temper was making him walk even faster than normal.

It was typical arrogant behaviour, she thought bitterly. He was making no concession to her naturally slower pace, but there was no way she was going to ask him to slow down. Her legs were still shaky, but so was the whole of her body—inside and out. She flicked her fringe back from her damp forehead and kept walking.

All she could think about was Lucas.

She'd kept him secret because she was scared of what might happen—of what Theo might do. She'd seen for herself that he'd been so protective of his brother's son that he'd wanted to take him away from Hallie.

Kerry had not been able to stand by and watch that happen. For personal reasons she couldn't bear to see a child forcibly taken from its mother. But her own background had also taught her that lies and deception led to heartache and tragedy—and by keeping Lucas a secret she was guilty of that herself.

Without warning her eyes blurred with tears. She wanted to do what was right for everyone—but she was too scared of the possible consequences if she told Theo.

Suddenly her foot hit a rut, and she staggered forward on the steep path, letting out a sharp cry of alarm.

Theo shot back up the slope and was beside her almost before she'd realised that she was lying headlong on the ground, her face pressed against the loose dirt path, pebbles digging into the palms of her hands.

'Kerry? Are you all right?' His deep voice sounded genuinely troubled, and for a moment she was startled by how familiar it sounded.

Only a moment ago she'd been convinced Theo had never shown any concern for her—but now she realised she'd been mistaken. The tender tone of his voice was achingly familiar, and made fresh tears swim in her eyes.

'Are you injured?' he asked, his hand gently cupping her shoulder.

'No—I'm fine.' She pushed her hands against the path to lever herself up, but it was hard with her head down and the stones jabbing into her palms.

Theo reached for her immediately, helping her into a sitting position, and stared into her face. His expression was so intense that for a moment she was glad she was wearing her sunglasses. She didn't want him to see her tear-filled eyes.

'My legs were wobbly,' she said, feeling her cheeks

flare at the thought of how she'd been sprawled so humiliatingly on the ground in front of him. 'I'm not used to climbing up mountains.'

'Then you should have asked for a longer break,' he said sharply. 'It's not responsible to push yourself too hard out here—you know how isolated we are.'

She gasped, stung by his harsh tone of voice.

'You just want to avoid the expense of calling a helicopter if I sprain my ankle,' she retorted. She hadn't been deliberately careless—*he* was the one who'd been walking so fast.

'If you're foolish enough to sprain your ankle I'll carry you back myself,' he said. 'Over my shoulder,' he added, letting his eyes run across her as if he was assessing how easy she would be to carry.

Kerry glared at Theo, suddenly furious with him for being so heartless. What if she really hadn't been fit enough to keep up with him? She hadn't exactly had much time to keep herself in shape lately. Looking after Lucas and working in the travel agency took up every minute of her time. She wasn't Theo's adoring lover any more—with nothing better to do than run around after him.

'Thankfully, that won't be necessary,' she said coldly, ignoring the flush of embarrassment that heated her face at the thought of being carried over his shoulder. 'Let's get going—I thought you were keen to get back.'

Theo studied her from beneath dark brows as she pushed herself up to her feet—she was still a little unsteady, but she looked all right.

'We'll go a little slower on the way down,' he said. 'But first you need to wipe your face—it's covered with dirt.'

Kerry drew in a startled breath and rubbed her fingers across her face.

'Lucky for me you are trying to impress Drakon,' she said, looking down at her dirt-streaked fingertips before lifting her eyes to meet his gaze straight on. 'Or you might never have bothered to tell me I've got half the path stuck to my face.'

The rest of the day passed slowly for Kerry. They'd arrived back at Drakon's house before lunch, but he'd still not been feeling well enough to receive visitors, so Theo had spent the afternoon working on his laptop, and Kerry had sat in the shade of the wizened old olive trees on the paved area, trying to read.

It was a wonderful place to sit, but despite her lovely surroundings she found it impossible to relax. She kept thinking about Lucas, and questioning whether she was making a terrible mistake.

It was one thing to hide her pregnancy and then her child from Theo when he was in another country—after all, at the time she'd had very good reasons for keeping her secret. But now that she was back in Greece with Theo everything seemed different.

That morning, when he'd accused her of dishonesty, his comment had cut her deeply—because she knew he was right. She wasn't being honest with anyone. Not with Theo. And most importantly not with Lucas.

She knew from personal experience just how devastating it was to discover that everything you believed to be true was actually false. Deception ruined lives—and she could not let her son's life be blighted by secrets and dishonesty.

By the time she went inside to get ready for dinner she had made an enormous decision. She would tell Theo about Lucas. She knew that he would want to be part of his son's life—but she also knew that she would *never* let him take Lucas away from her.

She wasn't like Hallie. Theo had told Corban that Hallie was not fit to be a mother, but Kerry would never give him reason to doubt her devotion and suitability as a mother. It was her right to take care of her son, and no one could take that away from her. But she *was* prepared to make changes. She would move to Athens, find a job and somewhere to live. Then Theo could have regular access to his son.

'Drakon is still too ill to join us for dinner,' Theo said, knocking her out of her thoughts as he came into their room.

'I do hope he will be okay,' Kerry said, worried about the old man again.

'The doctor is due to visit tomorrow,' Theo said. 'Meanwhile, we will be eating alone tonight. Why don't you shower first? I still have a few calls to make.'

'All right.' Kerry picked up a change of clothes and headed into the *en suite* bathroom. It was strangely familiar—getting ready for dinner first while Theo talked on his phone. She showered and dressed, and was just about to come out of the bathroom when Theo knocked sharply on the door.

'Kerry! Are you nearly done?'

'I'm here,' she said, opening the door. 'What is it?' Somehow the urgency of Theo's voice had sent an icy chill down her spine.

'Your sister, Bridget, called,' he said. 'I answered your mobile because she was calling repeatedly and I thought it might be important.'

'What is it?' Kerry's heart lurched with fear and her throat closed with panic.

Oh, God—don't let it be Lucas! Don't let something bad have happened to Lucas!

'Lucas has fallen,' Theo said. 'Down the stairs, I think. Your sister sounded pretty upset. I think it best if you go to her.'

'Oh, my God!' Kerry clamped her hand over her mouth and slumped back against the doorframe in an agony of distress.

All coherent thought flew out of her mind. All she could do was imagine her poor, sweet baby boy falling down the stairs.

Oh, God—she should never have left him. It was all her fault. Lucas had come to harm and she wasn't there with him. She would never forgive herself—she should never have left him.

Theo stared at her, momentarily shocked at the strength of her reaction to the news about her nephew. She had gone as white as a sheet, and she was shaking so violently that he could see it from across the room. He swore under his breath in Greek, cursing himself for not breaking the news to her gently.

'I think it's all right,' he said, taking hold of her upper arms and shaking her slightly to get her to look at him. 'They've taken him to the hospital—but they think he's okay.'

'He's only six months old.'

She stared up him, her eyes drowning in tears, and he wasn't entirely sure she'd understood what he'd said. His chest contracted as he saw her distress, and he knew he had to find a way to comfort her.

'A helicopter is on the way,' he told her. 'And my jet is waiting in Athens to take us to London.'

'You're taking me there?' she asked, as if she was finally starting to come out of her state of shock.

'Yes. I'll come with you.' Theo guided her across the room to a chair and gently pushed her down into it. He could tell it would be pointless to try to make her eat or drink anything—hopefully she'd be able to have something on the plane. He knew that travelling on an empty stomach was the worst thing possible for her. And she'd need to be in a fit state to help her sister when they reached London.

He moved around the room swiftly, collecting up their belongings and packing them into small cases. It wouldn't be long before the helicopter was here.

Kerry sat in Theo's private plane, staring out of the window at the inky black night. Lucas should be tucked up in his own cot by now, with her to watch over him, not waiting to be seen by a doctor in a strange accident and emergency department—if that was where he even was. She didn't actually know for sure.

She'd made a frantic phone call before they'd left Athens, but Steve, Bridget's partner, hadn't heard anything. Mobile phones weren't allowed in hospital, and he was at home with their children, waiting for his mother to come and babysit. Then he would join Bridget at the hospital. When he knew anything—anything at all—he would call Kerry.

'We'll be there soon,' Theo said, coming to sit beside her. He smelled freshly showered, and when she glanced at him she saw his black hair was still damp. 'I have a car waiting for us at the airport.'

'Thank you,' Kerry said. 'It would have been a nightmare trying to get home by regular transport.'

'How are you feeling?' Theo asked, glancing at the half-eaten sandwich on the table in front of her.

'All right,' she lied, feeling her stomach roll over with nausea—but whether it was travel sickness or fear for Lucas she couldn't say.

'I'll get you some more iced water,' Theo said, standing up and going to fetch it from the bar himself.

Kerry watched him, realising that he'd done that for her a hundred times before when they were travelling. He'd always shown her little kindnesses—but in her distress over the brutal way he had ended their relationship she had blotted out so many of the good things.

'Lucas will be all right,' he said as he sat beside her once more. 'If it was bad news I'm sure Steve would've heard something.'

'Thank you for being so kind,' Kerry said.

'Family is everything,' he replied, his voice full of genuine feeling. 'You know how much my own nephew means to me. Of course you feel the same about yours.'

Kerry drew her lower lip into her mouth and turned to

look at him. She'd guessed he'd made the assumption that Lucas was Bridget's baby. She didn't know what her sister had told him—but from what Theo had said she'd been pretty upset. It would be natural for him to think that.

If she was ever going to confess her secret to him, then the moment was here.

'Lucas is not my nephew.' Her voice was quiet, but her heart was beating so loudly it almost deafened her. 'He is my son.'

'What?'

Theo stared at her in shock—not sure he had heard her correctly.

'Lucas is my son,' Kerry repeated.

She looked pale and sick, but she was meeting his gaze straight on—and he knew she was utterly serious. Then, almost as if his mind was working in slow motion, his thoughts pulled together to reach another obvious conclusion.

Kerry had said that Lucas was six months old. That meant six months...plus nine months...

'He is *my* son.'

The words sliced through the air like a knife—like a giant blade slicing through the reality of Theo's tightly disciplined and controlled world.

He had a son.

How could that be true? It didn't seem possible that such a monumental fact could have been kept hidden from him. Kerry had kept his son—his own flesh and blood—a secret from him.

Why hadn't she told him? The question flashed through his mind, but then he pushed it aside. *Why* didn't matter.

'You will regret this.'

'Having your son?' Her voice was thin and tremulous, as if she could sense the anger that was starting to build within him after the initial shock had sunk in.

'The fact that you kept him from me,' he said.

He stared at her pale face, feeling the violent thud of his heart beneath his ribs and the escalating fury surging around his body.

He had a son. He was a father. And Kerry had tried to stop him from knowing about it.

If it hadn't been for Drakon Notara's island Theo would never have gone looking for Kerry, and he would never have found out that he was a father. Even after they'd been together for more than a day it had taken this emergency for Kerry to confess to her deception. And that was probably because she knew she wouldn't be able to keep up the pretence at the hospital.

'You will not keep my son from me any longer.'

His voice throbbed with dangerous intent and his dark eyes bored into her like a weapon. Then he turned and walked away.

Kerry stared after him, shaking so hard that she had to grip on to the armrests. She knew trouble was coming.

Theo did not speak to her again apart from to confirm the details of which hospital Lucas had been taken to. They sat in his limousine silently. Kerry was dimly aware of the tension simmering within him, but mostly she was overwhelmed with anxiety about Lucas.

They arrived at the hospital and she spotted Bridget and Steve almost immediately. They were waiting for her in the hospital entrance hall with baby Lucas. The doctors had already discharged him.

'Oh, my little one,' Kerry said, holding her baby tightly to her. 'Oh, my little angel.'

Her lips were trembling and her throat felt tight—then suddenly she burst into tears. Bridget was there with her, her arms around both of them.

'He's all right,' Bridget said, hugging her reassuringly. 'They said he's all right. I overreacted when he fell—but I just felt so terrible.'

Kerry looked down at her baby through a film of tears. His bright blue eyes fixed on her just as sharply as ever, and then he broke out into one of his most engaging smiles, with dimples dancing in his cute little cheeks.

Her eyes blurred once again as fresh tears formed, and all she could see was his thick black curly hair. Then she heard him giggle, and her relief and joy at their reunion was complete.

She blinked away her tears and held him tight—determined never to let him out of her sight again.

Theo stood to the side, watching events unfold through narrowed eyes. He understood that everything was all right. That Lucas was safe and sound. Lucas—his baby son—was safe and sound.

Kerry was crying and hugging the baby, and suddenly Theo caught a glimpse of curly black hair as she turned slightly to the side. His son had curly black hair. Somehow that detail surprised him. In the couple of hours since he'd discovered he was a father he had never even wondered what his baby looked like. All babies looked alike, didn't they?

Suddenly he wanted to see his son properly, and he took a step closer. At that moment he heard a sound he couldn't immediately recognise. Then he realised what it was—Lucas was giggling.

It was a beautiful, pure sound—the sound of his baby son's happiness at being back in his mother's arms. Something inside Theo contracted. That was *his* baby. And no one was ever going to deprive him of even one more moment of his son's life.

The next few minutes passed for Kerry in a daze of overwhelming relief while Bridget tried to explain everything that had happened. But all Kerry could focus on was the fact that Lucas was all right. Apart from a few bruises he had survived his fall intact. It wasn't as bad as Bridget—in her state of guilty panic—had originally made it sound.

Kerry had imagined him falling from top to bottom of a flight of stairs, when in fact he had just tumbled down the short flight of steps that led from Bridget's kitchen to her utility room. Lucas wasn't crawling yet, but he could roll, and she had only turned her back for a second.

Theo had barely spoken. He had been perfectly polite to everyone at the hospital, but Kerry knew him well enough to know something was going on behind those dark, assessing eyes.

'Thank you for bringing Kerry so quickly,' Bridget suddenly gushed, throwing her arms around him and hugging him tightly.

'You are welcome,' he said, standing as still and unyielding as a rock until she stepped back awkwardly.

'Thank *you* for contacting us earlier this evening,' Theo continued. 'I want you to know that I appreciate all you have done for Lucas—but now you and Steve should leave us and return home to your own children.'

'I...' Bridget paused, and looked at Kerry in confusion.

'He knows,' Kerry managed to say.

'Yes. I know that Lucas is my son,' Theo said. 'And now that I know I will take my responsibility as his father seriously.'

'What do you mean?' Bridget asked, looking worriedly from Kerry to Theo to Lucas, who was now dozing peacefully in Kerry's arms.

'I mean that from this point onwards I will take charge of his care,' Theo said.

'Hang on a minute,' Bridget said, rising to her sister's defence. 'You chucked Kerry out. You're the one who finished it—you didn't want to know her.'

'That was before I knew about my son,' Theo said. 'Everything is different now.'

'But you can't just waltz in here and—'

'It's all right, Bridget,' Kerry said. She knew Bridget was trying to protect her, and Kerry loved her sister dearly for it. Bridget was just a few years older than her—not old enough to have been involved in the conspiracy to keep Kerry in the dark about her mother. 'You go home now. This is something Theo and I have to sort out.'

'But—'

'Come on, love. You heard her,' said Steve, looking exhausted.

Kerry tried to smile at her sister reassuringly as Steve

led her away. Inside she was a horrible mess of churning emotions, but at least she had Lucas back in her arms again. She bent forward and brushed her cheek against his soft curls, feeling a wave of love for her baby son. Lucas was all that mattered. And as long as she had him everything would be all right.

'We will go to a hotel for what remains of the night,' Theo said. 'Then tomorrow we will discuss the future.'

They travelled in the limousine in silence once more. But this time Lucas was secured in his car seat next to Kerry. The atmosphere between them had changed somehow—and not for the better.

Earlier she'd known Theo was furious with her, and she'd understood why. Even though his temper had been building, and sometimes he had seemed on the verge of exploding, she'd felt as if she'd known where she stood with him.

Now everything seemed different. She had no idea what he was feeling or thinking, because his expression had become as cold and impenetrable as ice.

She looked up and found him studying her. His eyes glinted in the dark. They bored into her like lucid black ice—freezing the blood in her veins and delivering a dreadful premonition of the storm that was brewing.

She shivered and looked away. She knew the freezing-cold fury that Theo was holding battened down under tight control was just as lethal as anything he'd been feeling earlier.

The limousine pulled up by the grand entrance of a top London hotel, and Kerry unfastened Lucas from his safety belt. She carried him inside and they were shown immediately up to a massive luxury suite. But if she'd expected separate rooms she'd been mistaken, because Theo insisted they all share one room.

'We are a family now,' he said, as he oversaw the arrival of a cot for Lucas. 'Because of his fall we will have our son in our room with us for a few days. Then he will have his own room.'

Theo's words sent a prickle of warning running down Kerry's spine—but she was totally exhausted and not entirely sure that she had heard him correctly when he'd said *our room*.

She bent over the cot to lay Lucas carefully inside, and as she straightened up she felt every muscle in her aching body protest. The last couple of days had been tough—physically and emotionally. And the last few hours had been overwhelming. She'd known that telling Theo about Lucas would change things—but even so she wasn't prepared for what happened next.

'In our room with us?' she repeated, feeling a shiver of anxiety as she straightened her shoulders and turned to face him. 'I don't understand what you are saying.'

'We are a family now,' Theo repeated.

Kerry drew in a shaky breath and lifted her eyes to meet his gaze. It was as hard and impenetrable as ever—but Kerry knew he meant business. A frozen wedge of ice settled in her stomach, and suddenly she was dreading what he would say next.

'Let me make myself clear,' Theo said. 'We will be married immediately.'

CHAPTER SEVEN

'MARRIED? You want me to marry you?' Kerry gasped.

This time she knew what Theo had said—she just couldn't believe it. After everything that had happened, how could he want to *marry* her? And why would he assume that she would accept?

'No—it's not what I *want*,' Theo said. 'But the situation has forced my hand.'

'I'm not *forcing* you to marry me,' Kerry said in shock, staring at him with wide eyes. He was making it sound as if she had done this deliberately—had his baby to coerce him in some way. 'It's not what I want either!'

'That much is clear,' Theo said flatly. 'Considering you took my son and hid him from me.'

'Then why are you telling me this?' Kerry said, raking her hands through her hair in frustration as the long fringe kept falling in her eyes.

'Because it is what's best for my son,' Theo said, walking across the room and looking down at the baby where he was lying in the cot. He was awake—looking sleepily at the lights moving across the ceiling from the city outside.

'*Our* son,' Kerry said automatically, feeling a shiver of foreboding as she saw just how intensely Theo was staring at Lucas. Already he seemed as possessively protective of him as he'd been of his nephew, Nicco. 'How is it best for our son to be brought up in a loveless marriage?'

'What do *you* think is best for him?' Theo asked harshly. 'To live in poverty in an inner-city studio flat, being looked after by strangers while his mother works?'

'It's not as bad as you make it sound,' Kerry said defensively, not even wondering how Theo knew exactly what kind of flat she lived in. 'I'm still getting myself back on my feet. Soon I'll be able to move—then he can have his own room.'

'*Then* he can have his own room?' Theo bit out incredulously. 'Stop being ridiculous. Now that I know I have a son he will never live like that—but that is not what's important.'

'You're right—material things don't matter,' Kerry said, hating the way Theo was tying her up in knots. 'I love him—that's all that matters. That's all he needs.'

'He needs his father,' Theo grated.

Kerry bit her lip and looked up at him. His eyes were narrowed dangerously, and he was staring at her with an expression of pure dislike. It cut her to the core. She'd never meant any of this to happen the way it had—but when he'd thrown her out she hadn't felt she had a choice. She'd been so scared that he would take her baby—just as he'd told his brother to take Nicco from Hallie.

'I'll move to Athens. Find a job.' Her voice was quiet but she managed to keep it steady—to show him she was serious about meeting him halfway. 'You can see him whenever you want. You can be part of his life.'

'This isn't a discussion,' Theo said coldly. 'We're not doing a deal here. I have told you that we will be married. That is the only option open to you.'

'I can't marry you,' Kerry said. 'You don't love me. It would be a sham. How would that be good for Lucas?' *Or for her*, a little voice inside her wept.

'Let me make it simple for you.' Theo took a step closer, so that he was looming over her. 'I realise I don't know much about your background—about the way you were brought up. But obviously you are close to Bridget, so you understand *something* about the importance of family.'

'Don't patronise me,' Kerry said, horrified that he was referring to her past. As far as she was aware he knew nothing about the awful truth of her upbringing. 'My past isn't relevant.'

'It is if you don't understand the importance of a father in a child's life,' Theo said. 'My son will not grow up under a different roof from his father. He will always know that I love him unequivocally and unconditionally. He will never, ever doubt my love for a single second of his life.'

Kerry stared up at him, feeling the passion in his voice rumbling through to her very soul. She knew that he meant every word that he said. He'd only known his son for an hour but already his love for him was burning brightly, shining out like a beacon.

Out of nowhere she felt tears welling in her eyes, and she turned away so that Theo wouldn't see them. How could she deny her son such powerful love?

She didn't even know who *her* father was. She had never felt love as all-encompassing as the love Theo was expressing for her son. How could she deny Lucas that?

'Lucas needs both his mother and his father,' Theo said. 'Despite the fact that you have tried to keep me out of his life, I can see how much you love him. I love him too, and want what's best for him. That means we must marry.'

Kerry blinked to clear her eyes, then turned back to face Theo.

'All right,' she said. 'I will marry you.'

The following day they flew back to Greece. Theo took them to the family's private island residence, saying that the peaceful isolation would be ideal for father and son to get to know each other.

Kerry could see the benefit of staying somewhere quiet, because Theo was always busy when they were staying in one of his many hotels. But it would mean that he was free to spend every minute with them, making it impossible for her to relax and let down her guard.

The only respite for Kerry that day was the time he spent on the telephone, enquiring after Drakon's health. He was still determined to acquire the old man's island, and did not intend to let the slightest window of opportunity pass him by.

The next day, despite his good intentions to spend time with Lucas, Theo found he had to return to Athens on business. Kerry was secretly pleased. As she watched the helicopter take off she felt the knot of tension in her stomach start to ease. They'd spent most of the previous day travelling, and she was exhausted. And on top of that the atmosphere between them had become increasingly strained, making her feel that more trouble was brewing.

It was a welcome relief to spend the day playing with Lucas on her own. In the afternoon she decided to take him swimming. The huge infinity pool, where Theo habitually pounded through length after length, seemed far too big for them. But there was a smaller, child-friendly pool, shaded by an awning on one side. It seemed much more suitable for splashing about in with the six-month-old.

Kerry looked at the choice of swimwear that the housekeeper, Sara, had laid out on the bed for her—there was nothing but bikinis. At home, when she took Lucas to the local pool, she always wore a one-piece costume, but she had forgotten to bring it. Pregnancy had taken its toll on her body, and she wasn't completely back to her previous shape. And, to make matters worse, the lower part of her stomach was covered with red stretch marks.

Being on her own, she hadn't thought about them much. She'd always been too busy taking care of Lucas or working. Now, even though Theo was away in Athens, she was reluctant to leave her stomach uncovered. But she didn't want Lucas to miss out, so she slipped on a bikini, wrapped a towel around herself and carried him outside.

The water was gorgeous—just the right temperature and crystal-clear.

'Do you like that?' She laughed as Lucas giggled and splashed while she walked around the pool, pulling him through the water. He was already kicking his legs strongly, and she had a feeling that he would grow up to be a powerful swimmer—like his father.

After a while she took him over to the wide shallow steps that led into the pool and set him down on the top step, up to his waist in water. She sat on the step below, holding him up so that he could play safely with the little boats and balls she had found.

She knew the toys must belong to Nicco, and that made her think about Hallie and Corban. She deeply regretted what had happened on her last night in Athens, and she was nervous about seeing them again. But as they were away, travelling around Europe, she wouldn't have to face them for some time.

'Here's the little boat,' she said, floating the toy Lucas was playing with back towards him. He squealed with delight and batted it again, making a big splash. 'It's blue,' she said. 'A blue boat.'

She found herself thinking about her decision to marry Theo. It was always there, in the back of her mind, and it had been weighing on her constantly.

She was worried that she was taking a risk—that their marriage might be part of Theo's plan to get Lucas away from her. Once he'd established himself firmly as Lucas's father, maybe he intended to cut her out of his life. She *knew* that he'd encouraged Corban to take Nicco away from Hallie.

But, from the impassioned way he'd talked about a child needing both his parents, she didn't truly think that he would do that to Lucas and her.

The situation with Hallie had been different. Theo

had been concerned that she was not a fit mother. Even though in Kerry's eyes that didn't justify his intended actions, she could understand his motivation. It also meant that she knew that she must never give Theo any grounds to doubt her own ability as a mother.

Suddenly, the unmistakable sound of a helicopter caught her attention. She looked up and saw that it was leaving the island—she must have been so lost in her thoughts that she hadn't heard it arrive. Theo was back on the island.

'I managed to get away earlier than I expected.' His voice right behind her nearly made her jump out of her skin.

'Hello.' She twisted round and looked up at him. He loomed over her, dressed in a dark business suit, with dark sunglasses hiding his eyes. His hair was ruffled from the helicopter's downdraft, and he had loosened his tie, but he didn't look remotely approachable. In fact he looked even more steely than usual, and the knot of tension started to tighten inside her again.

'I'll change, then come and join you in the water,' he said.

'No!' Kerry's voice squeaked unnaturally high in response to Theo's words. The idea of being seminaked with him in the pool sent a wave of panic through her. 'No—I mean, we're coming out now. Lucas is getting tired.'

Then, as soon as the words were out of her mouth, she remembered her stretch marks. She didn't want Theo to see them. They were unattractive, and she was already self-conscious of the way her body had changed after her pregnancy. She couldn't get out with him standing there—she'd left the only towel on the sun lounger a couple of metres away.

'Would you pass me that towel?' she asked, thinking that she could hold Lucas against her shoulder as she stood up and let the towel drape across his body and down past her stomach. She looked up at Theo expectantly—there was no reason he shouldn't do as she'd asked—but she got the impression that he wasn't really listening. The expression on his face seemed intense, but she had no idea what he was thinking or feeling. 'The towel?' she repeated hopefully.

Theo took off his sunglasses and looked at Kerry, sitting on the second step, with the water lapping gently at her waist. His eyes followed the alluring shape of her hips below the surface, ran along her long slender legs down to her feet. Then his gaze tracked back up, roaming instinctively over her top half. She was wearing a pale blue bikini, which looked good next to her creamy skin. It seemed like a lifetime since he'd seen so much of her naked body, and a familiar surge of arousal powered through him.

On Drakon's island he had thought that her breasts seemed fuller than he remembered, and now he could see that it was true. She was breathing quickly, and the rapid rise and fall of her chest made him want to reach down and slip his hands inside the pale blue cups of the bikini, caress her luscious breasts and tease her pert nipples. He'd done that many times before, and she had always responded by melting in his arms. In fact it had been very rare that they had swum together and not ended up making love.

But right now he knew that Kerry was *not* pleased to see him. His arrival had startled her, and he'd seen her body language become defensive. She'd been like that with him ever since they took Lucas from the hospital—in fact her standoffishness seemed to be getting more pronounced.

It bothered him. He didn't like coming into a room and seeing her whole body become tense and hunched inwards. Even though he knew that the changes in her behaviour were barely perceptible—that no one else would notice—it was an affront to his masculine dignity. She'd used to tremble like a kitten when he approached her, and look up at him with sultry eyes that had let him know just how much she desired him. It had made him feel as powerful as a lion—and he'd swept her up into his embrace knowing that she was burning for him to make love to her.

Now everything was different. On Drakon's island the chemistry between them had still been there, but she'd held back—presumably because she'd been worried he might find out about Lucas. However, since he'd brought her back to Greece the atmosphere between them had been increasingly cold and difficult.

He knew that she didn't want to marry him. If she had any feelings for him at all, or any desire to share his life, she would not have kept Lucas a secret from him. That knowledge was demeaning—like a vicious slap round the face.

The sound of splashing and giggling pulled him out of his thoughts. He looked down, letting his eyes skim past Kerry to his baby son.

His bright blue eyes were twinkling merrily, his curly

black hair was glistening with water and he was splashing and chuckling energetically. To Theo's untutored eyes he didn't seem all that tired, but he didn't know much about babies. If Kerry said he was tired then he probably was.

'Let me take him while you get out,' he said, putting his sunglasses into his pocket and reaching down to the baby.

He closed his large hands around Lucas's warm little body and lifted him straight up and out of the water. Lucas gave a high-pitched squeal and Theo felt an answering bolt of alarm shoot through him—he'd moved too abruptly and frightened his son.

He held him up in front of his face and looked at him worriedly. But then Lucas squealed again, and suddenly Theo realised he wasn't crying. He was excited. He'd enjoyed being flown straight up.

He found himself smiling as he gazed into his son's face, and as they made eye contact he felt an unexpected wave of emotion roll through him. This extraordinary little person was his son—his own flesh and blood.

Then, at that moment, he realised he was dangling Lucas in front of him in what seemed an entirely unnatural position. Perhaps he should wrap him in a towel and hold him against his shoulder. He had to do something—but suddenly he felt awkward, and didn't know how to manoeuvre the baby.

He turned to look at Kerry, but she was still sitting in the pool on the steps, hugging her knees up to her chest. Why wasn't she helping him? Was she trying to prove something by letting him struggle alone?

'Pass me that towel,' he said.

Kerry bit her lip and stared up at Theo. Seeing him hold her son—*their* son—for the first time made a strange feeling run through her. She'd seen an expression of love pass across Theo's face as he met his son's eyes, and it had filled her with an uncomfortable mixture of emotions.

She was profoundly happy that Lucas would grow up in the warmth of such powerful paternal love—but at the same time it left her feeling unsettled and hollow. At one time she'd dreamed of Theo gazing at *her* with love in his eyes—now she felt confused and adrift.

Suddenly she realised that Theo was looking awkward—as if he was also finding the first time he held Lucas strange. To be fair, holding a squirming and wet six-month-old wasn't the best way to start, and she should help him. But he had taken her by surprise when he'd swooped in and plucked Lucas from out of her grasp.

She pushed herself up out of the pool, trying to keep her back to Theo and her stomach hidden as much as possible, and stepped over to the sun lounger. She held the towel up, letting it unroll so that it was covering her stretch marks, and moved closer to Theo and Lucas.

'I can take him,' she said, reaching for the baby.

'It's all right,' he said, holding on tight to Lucas. 'I've got him. Just help me get that towel round him.'

Kerry hesitated. She needed the towel to hide her stretch marks—not to mention the extra weight she was still carrying on her tummy. But she couldn't very well wrestle Lucas out of Theo's grasp.

'You can relax—I won't drop him,' Theo said caustically, obviously having misinterpreted her hesitation.

'It's not that—' Kerry started, then realised there was nothing she could say that wouldn't draw more attention to her situation.

She pressed her lips together and eased the towel around Lucas, helping Theo to get a better grip on him up against his shoulder. Then she let her hands drop and crossed her wrists self-consciously over her stomach, hoping that Theo would keep his eyes on his son.

It was a vain hope. A moment later he'd lifted his head and was looking at her over the top of Lucas's black curls. His eyes ran appreciatively down her body, just as they had done so many times before, but then suddenly they stopped, locking on to her stomach.

A slight flash of surprise lifted his black brows for a moment. Then his eyes narrowed and his face became as dark as thunder as he continued to stare at her stretch marks.

Before she could react—turn away to hide, or pick up something to hold in front of her—she watched his expression change for the second time. From anger to disgust.

Then he spun on his heel and strode away, carrying Lucas with him.

CHAPTER EIGHT

KERRY stared after Theo, startled and hurt by what had happened. She knew her stretch marks weren't attractive, and that she hadn't completely regained her figure. But she hadn't thought she was disgusting.

Yet as she pictured Theo's face before he'd turned away, that was clearly what *he* thought about the changed appearance of her body.

Dismay welled up inside her, and she felt her cheeks grow red with shame. He'd used to look at her as if he adored her body. She knew how much pleasure he'd found in it—and had given her in return. The knowledge that he found her repulsive now that pregnancy had left its marks on her cut her to the quick.

She started following him back towards the house, feeling her heart thumping miserably.

Then, out of nowhere, a blaze of anger flared up inside her.

How *dared* he look at her like that and make her feel so horrible about herself? She'd never asked him to bring her here. She'd never asked for any of this. If life had carried on the way she'd planned she would never have laid eyes on Theo Diakos again—and *he* would never have laid his hateful, judgemental eyes on *her*.

She stormed up the grand staircase and marched through to the bedroom. The housekeeper was just carrying Lucas out of the room, chattering to him about what a lovely bathtime they would have. She watched them leaving—torn between the desire to call Sara back, so that she could bathe her son herself, and the burning need to have it out with Theo.

The door closed, leaving them completely alone for the first time since they'd come back to Greece, and she turned to face him. He was staring at her in open hostility, his eyes cutting into her like knives. Then, to add insult to injury, he deliberately let his gaze drop to her stomach and linger mercilessly on the red stretch marks.

'How *dare* you look at me like that?' she demanded, planting her hands on her hips and making no attempt to cover herself. 'How dare you try to make me feel bad over the perfectly natural way pregnancy has marked my body?'

'Just how vain and self-centred is it possible for you to be?' Theo threw up his hands in an uncharacteristically dramatic gesture, then shrugged his jacket off and tossed it angrily on the bed.

'I'm not vain!' Kerry responded hotly. 'I barely even thought about my stretch marks until you kept staring at them in disgust.'

'You think I'm disgusted with your *body*?' Theo demanded, letting his gaze sear a trail all over her, from top to toe.

'I *know* you are,' Kerry insisted. 'I saw the expression of revulsion on your face. Well, I'm pleased—I hope you never touch me again.'

'Really?' Theo grated. He grabbed hold of her and pulled her hard up against him. 'I know that's what you want me to think—why you've been giving me the cold shoulder since we came back to Greece.'

'It's true!' Kerry gasped as he tightened his hold on her, making the breath shudder out of her body. 'I don't want you near me.'

'Let's put that to the test,' Theo taunted, suddenly sweeping her up into his arms and dumping her on the bed. 'I think you *want* me to touch you. And I don't believe you'll try to stop me, however—*wherever*—I touch you.'

'No! Let me up!' she cried, but Theo was already leaning over her, pressing her down with his hard body. His words had caused an explosion of panic inside her, but despite everything they had also started a river of molten desire running through her veins.

Lying on the bed beneath Theo, in the exact place where he had brought her to the point of rapture so many times when they were lovers, had set off a whole realm of remembered responses and feelings rocketing through her mind and body. So far he'd hardly touched her—but just the idea of him touching her was turning her on.

She stared up into his face, and the raw sexual intent she saw blazing in his dark brown eyes started her trembling deep inside. At that moment she knew that whatever common sense her mind was trying to exert, her treacherous body yearned for Theo—just as much as it always had.

'When I first saw you sitting in the pool I wanted to touch you,' Theo said. 'I wanted to slip my hands inside your bikini top and feel your nipples against my palm as I caressed your breasts.'

A hot, delicious wave of anticipation rolled through Kerry's body—but at the back of her mind warning bells were ringing. He was just playing with her—trying to humiliate her. She'd seen the way he looked at her, and heard the scornful taunts in his voice.

She reared up against him, trying to push him away and swing her legs off the bed at the same time. But Theo was ready for her, and turned her movements to his own advantage. She ended up sitting on the edge of the bed in between his legs, with her back pressed against his chest. His arm was wrapped right around her, circling her from behind, and he was leaning forward over her shoulder, with his head beside hers.

'Don't try and tell me you don't want to feel my hands on you,' he murmured, feathering the side of her neck with his hot breath.

She looked down and saw his arm around her waist, holding her securely. But his other hand was moving, brushing backwards and forwards across her midriff, getting higher and higher with each sweep. As his fingertips skimmed across her skin she felt herself shaking—awash with conflicting thoughts and emotions.

He was right—so right. She wanted to feel his hands on her. She wanted him to lie over her, possessing her, making love to her like he used to. Her pulse was racing and she was breathing erratically just from the lightest touch of his fingertips. But she didn't want it to be like this—him taunting her with her desire for him.

'You feel so good,' he breathed against her ear, sending renewed shivers quivering through her. Then his fingers slipped under the blue fabric of the bikini top and he held her breast cupped in his hand.

An involuntary sigh of delight escaped her and she arched her back, lifting her breast in subconscious invitation. His fingers moved and he gently massaged her in the way that he knew would bring her exquisite sensual pleasure.

She was hardly aware as he released his tight hold on her waist and laid her back on the bed. She didn't fight him—her eyes were closed and she was lost on a rising tide of desire. Then, when his mouth closed over her other nipple, she went rocketing into another level of arousal.

'Oh,' she breathed, momentarily forgetting everything as magical sensations spiralled out from where his tongue worked her aching nipple. 'Oh, Theo.'

Suddenly her eyes snapped open and her hands were on his shoulders, pushing him roughly away.

It was as if by saying his name out loud she had broken the spell. For a few dizzy moments she'd been in thrall to him, had lost all strength to resist—but now she was plummeting back to earth, remembering her determination to keep him at arm's length.

She stared up at him, dragging her scattered thoughts back together. Then, like a drenching with cold water, she pictured the look of disgust on his face as he stared at her stretch marks.

'You don't truly want me!' she cried, springing to her

feet and staring down at him, still kneeling on the bed. 'Why are you doing this? I saw how you looked at my stretch marks.'

'You really think I care what your stretch marks look like?' Theo's voice was incredulous as he stood up next to her. 'In all the time we were together I never realised how vain and shallow you are.'

'I saw the expression on your face,' Kerry said. 'So don't try to tell me that you don't think they are horrible and ugly.'

'They're nothing!' Theo grated. 'Skin-deep, superficial lines that will soon fade. They are the marks of being a mother—you should be proud of them, not cringing and trying to hide them.'

'You don't mean that!' Kerry exclaimed. 'I saw how disgusted you looked when you saw them.'

'I was disgusted at what they represent,' Theo barked. 'Disgusted with you! With what you took from me.'

He spun away, scrubbing his hands roughly over his face as if he was in the grip of strong emotion. Then he turned back, fixing her with his piercing gaze.

'They are the marks of your pregnancy—the marks that formed because *my* son was growing inside you.' Theo's voice was dangerously calm, but Kerry could see the fury glinting in his eyes. 'You took that from me— denied me the chance to be part of that.'

Kerry stared at him, stunned that he felt so strongly about missing out on her pregnancy. She'd never guessed it would mean so much to him.

'You should have told me,' Theo said. 'You should have told me you were pregnant.'

'I tried,' Kerry said. 'But you wouldn't listen.'

'I don't believe you,' he said. 'You never tried to contact me.'

'No, I mean...' She hesitated, suddenly realising that Theo had assumed she'd discovered her pregnancy *after* he threw her out.

Theo cursed savagely in Greek, then stormed across the room and seized her by the arms.

'You already knew!' he accused. 'You knew *before* you left Athens!'

'I tried to tell you,' she insisted. 'You wouldn't listen to me. You just told me to get out.'

'You should have made me listen,' he said. 'My God! To think you walked out of my home with my son already growing inside you!' He swore again. 'How long had you known?'

'I found out that evening,' Kerry said shakily, staring up at him nervously. It was as if a violent storm was building, towering up into a wild sky, crackling with electricity that was waiting to strike. 'I was on my way to tell you when I overheard you talking to Corban.'

Theo's eyes flared dangerously again and she realised it had been a mistake to mention Corban, reminding Theo about the events of that awful night. Then she remembered him accusing her of dishonesty—of never being open and of deliberately keeping things from him.

There and then she vowed that he would never be able to justifiably challenge her on that score again. If this forced relationship between Theo and herself had any chance of working she could never again give him grounds to call her out on her honesty—or lack of it.

'I didn't keep on trying to tell you after the first time because I was scared,' she whispered. 'Scared of what you might do. I'd just heard you telling your brother to kidnap Nicco from his mother. I was frightened you would try to take *my* baby from *me*.'

Theo stared down at her, a muscle pulsing in his jawline and his eyes narrowed intimidatingly. The moment lengthened, and Kerry shifted her weight uneasily from one foot to the other.

'I will never try to take Lucas from you,' Theo said at last. 'In return, I expect you to be a perfect mother to him—and to the other children we will have.'

'Other children?' she gasped. 'Surely it's too early to be talking about more children?'

'Why?' he demanded. 'Do you want Lucas to be an only child? Are you not fully committed to this marriage?'

'No…it's not that.' She paused, suddenly feeling under even more pressure.

Everything had happened so quickly that she didn't know *what* to think.

'Let me assure you that *I* am fully committed to this family,' Theo said. 'And I expect you to give me more children.'

His words rolled through her like a command, and his gaze seemed to penetrate to the centre of her being. She pressed her teeth into her lower lip and stared at him, knowing unequivocally that he was deadly serious.

'You will also be a perfect wife to me,' he added. 'In the bedroom or anywhere else I want you.' His voice was loaded with sexual intent, and his eyes skimmed meaningfully over her semi-naked body. Then he turned and walked out of the room.

Kerry swallowed reflexively and started to tremble all over again. Because she knew exactly what he meant—what he wanted from her.

A sweet dark river of anticipation began to flow along her veins, spreading out and filling every inch of her entire being with renewed desire for him. She longed to surrender her body to him again. Completely.

Later that evening, after Lucas had been put down for the night in his new nursery, Kerry strolled through the house feeling very unsettled. Theo was in his study, catching up on some work, but he'd told her he would join her for dinner. She'd showered and dressed carefully, choosing a dark blue halterneck dress and high-heeled sandals. The soft silky fabric was gathered below the bust and fell in gentle folds to just above her knees.

She wandered from room to room, thinking about everything that had happened. But it was almost impossible for her to take on board just how much her life had changed over the last few days. All she knew was that for Lucas's sake she had to find a way to make her marriage to Theo work. She knew they were compatible in the bedroom—but there was more to married life than making love and looking after children.

She was walking through the hallway when she found herself drawn to a series of paintings on the wall. Something about them seemed really familiar. Of course she knew she'd seen them lots of times before, but it was more than that.

Suddenly it came to her. They reminded her of the watercolours she had admired at Drakon's house. She tucked her hair behind her ear and looked even closer. The more she studied them, the more certain she became that they were by the same artist—and they were all of locations on Drakon's island. There was more to Theo's interest in the old man's island than he was letting on.

A few moments later she heard the door of Theo's study open. She looked up to see him coming along the corridor, rolling his shoulders as he often did when he became tense working at his computer.

A little frisson ran through her as she watched him walking towards her. He was so utterly good-looking that simply gazing at him took her breath away. He had changed out of his business suit and was dressed casually in dark jeans and a T-shirt that fitted him like a second skin. Even from that distance she could see the magnetic movement of his sculpted muscles as he walked towards her.

She realised that she had missed just looking at him and admiring his athletic physique—marvelling in the fact that such a gorgeous man shared her bed at night.

'Ready for dinner?' he asked as he came up beside her.

'Yes,' she said, matching his mild tone. 'I'm starving. Lunch seems a long time ago.'

A little jolt shot through her as he slipped his arm around her waist, but she forced herself to relax. He clearly intended that they should put their earlier argument behind them and act like a normal couple—and she wasn't going to give him any cause for complaint.

He turned her away from the paintings and started

walking towards the dining room. But at that moment she made a decision—if they were to act like a normal couple, then she ought to feel free to discuss things openly with him.

'Before we go,' she said quickly, 'I was wondering about these paintings. I'm intrigued as to why you and Drakon both have paintings by the same artist.'

Theo stopped in his tracks, and she felt him grow tense beside her.

'I'd thought that by now you would understand that I don't like people meddling or sticking their nose in where it doesn't belong,' he said. His voice was level, but she could feel displeasure emanating off him.

She turned towards him, determined that he would not over-awe her with the steely force of his personality.

'I'm not meddling,' she said, shaking her head slightly. 'I'm asking a perfectly natural question. Presumably you want Lucas to grow up with a mother who is able to have a proper conversation with his father?'

Theo looked down at her upturned face, into her wide blue eyes, surprised to realise that she was right. His response had been automatic—a knee-jerk reaction to unwanted interest in his family's difficult past. Now she was going to be part of his family, bringing up his son as a Diakos, it made sense for her to know a little about his family background—if not all of it.

In the past they had never really talked about anything personal, and now he understood that it had not turned out to be a very good basis for a relationship. If they had been more open with each other then it would not have been so easy for Kerry to keep her pregnancy from him. Trust was vital in any relationship—and he did not want her keeping secrets from him in the future.

'The paintings are the work of my uncle,' Theo said.

'Your uncle was an artist—how wonderful!' Kerry exclaimed—then she paused, her expression quizzical. 'But that means your uncle used to live on Drakon's island!' she gasped. 'Why didn't you tell me?'

'Who told you that?' Theo asked, disconcerted by how much she already seemed to know.

'No one,' Kerry said. 'I just worked it out this minute. I asked Drakon about the paintings in his house the first evening at dinner—you were late joining us because of your long walk. He told me that the artist who painted them used to live on the island.'

'That is correct,' Theo replied, unsettled to discover how close to sensitive information Kerry had strayed during her conversation with Drakon. He wondered how much the old man actually knew about the paintings and their artist.

Kerry went on. 'He said that they came with the house when he bought the island twenty-five years ago, from a property developer who'd run into financial difficulties—luckily before he'd started any building on the island.'

Theo nodded. 'That failed property developer left quite a mess when he went bankrupt—half-finished projects all over the place.'

'How fascinating,' Kerry said enthusiastically, as if her imagination was well and truly captured. 'So does that mean your uncle once owned the island?'

'Not exactly.' Theo pushed his hands through his hair and turned to walk away from the paintings, out onto the terrace that overlooked the infinity pool. 'It belonged to my mother's family. Her twin sister, my Aunt Dacia, was married to the artist.'

'What made them sell it?' Kerry asked. 'It's such a beautiful place.'

Theo frowned and looked away. He was out of his comfort zone—taken aback by how quickly Kerry was delving deeper into the story, peeling back layers that would soon reveal more than he wanted.

An ironic smile flashed across his face. His first foray into openness with his soon-to-be wife and he was already getting cold feet. It wasn't as if information about what had happened wasn't already out there in the public domain—in fact it was of very little interest to anyone but his immediate family. But it was something he preferred not to talk about—he felt shamed by association. Shamed to be his father's son.

'You don't have to tell me,' Kerry said. 'Not if you don't want to.'

She looked up at him. His black hair was spiky from where he had dragged his fingers through it and she could tell he was feeling uncomfortable. She didn't want to put him in a position he would regret later. She knew the tentative understanding they seemed to have reached could be easily broken.

She turned away, to show that she wasn't badgering him for information, and looked towards the sun going down in the western sky. They were standing overlooking the infinity pool, and in the fading light the sun-bronzed water really did seem to stretch on for ever, in a seamless sweep right out across the Aegean Sea.

This island, with its tasteful buildings and luxury swimming pools, was beautiful. But if she was completely honest it didn't have the same magic as Drakon's island. Perhaps it was the untamed wildness of that place, with its unkempt ancient olive groves and the tumbledown buildings made of natural materials. Something about that place made it truly special.

'It must have been hard for your mother and her sister to leave the island,' she said.

'My mother left by choice,' Theo replied. 'She wanted the excitement and opportunities that the mainland could offer. My aunt loved the place. She was still relatively young when her parents—my grandparents—died. But she managed to keep the place going, continuing the small business they had established making olive oil. Then she started to open her home as a retreat for painters and artists. That's how she met my uncle, Demos.'

'What made them leave?' Kerry asked. She didn't want it to seem as if she was prying, but she was genuinely interested.

'My father.' Theo's voice changed, becoming hard and unforgiving.

Kerry drew her lower lip into her mouth and looked at him apprehensively, knowing that their discussion had stumbled into hazardous territory. Now she understood why Theo had been reluctant to talk about the island—she knew he was estranged from his father, although she didn't know why.

'My father has an insatiable appetite for meddling with other people's lives,' Theo said bitterly. 'Because of his interference, my aunt and uncle lost their island. My uncle died penniless, feeling he'd failed my aunt. She was left alone, utterly broken-hearted, having lost the love of her life *and* her island home.'

'How terrible,' Kerry gasped. 'Is your aunt still alive? I've never heard you or Corban mention her.'

'That's because she won't see us,' Theo said. 'She won't have anything to do with us because of my father.'

'But it's not your fault! You aren't responsible for things your father did when you were a child,' Kerry said indignantly. 'You don't even see him any more.'

'Aunt Dacia was too badly hurt by what happened to see things rationally,' Theo said. 'For years my mother tried to help her, but she kept refusing because ultimately the money she was offering came from my father—the man she hated.'

He paused, pushing his hands through his hair once more, revealing just how unsettling he found the subject. Kerry wanted to reach out to him—to offer comfort and support. But she was scared of upsetting the fine balance they had reached.

'My father made my uncle feel inadequate because he was content to live a simple life,' Theo continued. 'He persuaded Demos and Dacia to mortgage the island and invest the money. But they weren't cut out for it. Demos was a gentle fellow, with no head for business. They lost everything.'

He turned back and looked down at her, his expression unguarded.

'My father is a dominating, powerful man,' Theo said. 'They had no chance against him. It was my mother's dying wish that her sister should have her island back.'

'And now you are trying to fulfil that wish to get back what they lost because of your father?' Kerry said quietly. 'Your aunt will be so grateful.'

'I don't know,' Theo said, with a simple shrug of his shoulders that said so much about his uncharacteristic uncertainty that Kerry felt her heart turn over in sympathy.

'Of course she will,' she said, reaching out instinctively and taking Theo's hand.

He looked down at their hands. For a moment Kerry thought that he would pull his away, that she had overstepped the mark. But then he rotated his palm against hers and threaded her fingers through his, so that they were interlocked in the way they'd always used to hold hands when they were together.

'I know how my aunt feels about my father and his money—because I feel the same way,' he said. 'All my life he interfered with my choices, tried to control me in every way. By the time I was grown up I had to get out—be my own man. I built my business up myself from scratch. I never took a single cent of his money.'

'That's amazing,' Kerry said simply. 'Lucas will be so proud that you are his father.'

Theo turned and looked down at her, feeling an unexpected ripple of emotion spread through him at her words. She had touched on a sensitive and deeply felt desire within him—that he would share the kind of relationship with his son that he had never experienced with his own father.

He wanted Lucas to grow up to love him and be proud of him. And Kerry's vote of confidence meant more to him that he would have guessed.

Her face was tilted up towards his, and she was gazing into his eyes with an open expression that took him back to a time when things had been simple between them. When they'd always seemed to be in perfect accord.

The last rays of the setting sun bathed her skin with golden light and her hair shone like satin.

'You look beautiful,' he murmured, lifting his hands to cup her face tenderly. Then he bent forward and touched his lips to hers in the lightest of kisses.

He felt a sigh of delight escape her and deepened his kiss, easing his body closer to hers and letting his hands slide into her soft silken hair. He saw her eyelids glide down and he closed his own eyes, giving himself over to the pure sensual pleasure of kissing Kerry.

Her lips were soft and yielding beneath his, and he felt her tongue lift tentatively to caress his. A rush of red-hot desire stormed through him, setting his heart thumping and the blood surging through his veins.

He needed to make love to her—right now. And this time he knew that nothing was going to stop him.

In one fluid movement he swept her up into his arms and carried her back into the house.

CHAPTER NINE

THEO strode across the hallway, carrying Kerry towards the staircase. She was as light as a feather in his arms, and felt as sexy as hell curled against his body, with one arm wrapped sensuously around his shoulder and her other hand stroking his chest.

His heart was pounding powerfully beneath her fingers and his ardour was making him feel unstoppable. He wanted to bound up the stairs to the bedroom—but at the same time he wanted the moment to last.

It felt so good to be taking Kerry to his bed, and somehow it reminded him of the first night they'd ever made love. It had been her very first time, but she'd given herself to him freely. The pure and gentle way she'd offered him her body had touched him deeply, and had made their lovemaking a thing of beauty. It felt the same way now—as if all the mistrust and anger they had been feeling towards each other was forgotten for the moment. Their desire was uncomplicated and entirely mutual.

He paused at the foot of the stairs and looked into her

wide blue eyes. Her long fringe had fallen back, away from her face, and he saw that her brow was clear and smooth. She was giving herself completely to the moment—she wanted this as much as he did.

Another surge of desire crashed through him and he bent his head to kiss her again. She reacted instantly, parting her lips to welcome his tongue into her mouth, and pulling herself up to meet him with her arms linked behind his neck.

He kissed her fiercely, revelling in the fervency of her response. She was clinging to him passionately, arching her back and thrusting her breasts against his chest. He heard her moan and felt her trembling—and he knew it was time to get to the privacy of the bedroom. Or he wouldn't be able to stop himself from making love to her right there in the hall.

He took the stairs two at a time and strode into the bedroom, kicking the door shut with his foot. For a moment his eyes settled on the king-sized bed across the room. Ever since Kerry had left the bedroom had seemed empty and cold. But now he had brought her back, to make this room into a place of vibrancy and life. A place of hot, hard passion.

He felt her flex impatiently in his arms, asking with her body to be put down. Then she was standing face to face with him—only inches away, but far enough so that he could look down into her lovely face.

He could see that her colour was high, her breathing was rapid and her blue eyes were almost black with the power of her desire for him. His own body was throbbing with his need, and he pulled her roughly towards him once more, plundering her mouth with his and letting his hands run wild over her supple body. What had started with a gentle kiss in the glow of the sunset had rapidly accelerated into a vortex of unbridled passion. He couldn't stop now even if he wanted to.

Kerry gasped for breath and pulled back from Theo's kiss, staring up into his flushed face through a haze of feverish excitement. Her entire body was trembling, yearning for him to make love to her. She could tell how much he wanted her, and that knowledge had unleashed an answering torrent of desire within her.

When he'd swept her up the stairs and into the bedroom she'd felt like a new bride being carried over the threshold. At the back of her mind she knew that things weren't like that. But she pushed those thoughts aside and gave in to the sheer happiness of being back in Theo's arms.

It was so long since they'd made love that she almost felt like a virgin again. All her memories of how wonderful it had been seemed too good to be true, as if they were simply wild fantasies. But now she was going to experience Theo's physical love once more.

'You look so good,' Theo said, letting his eyes roam over her as she stood in front of him, wearing a backless dress that skimmed over her curves.

His words sent a wave of confidence running through her, and she reached up to unfasten the halterneck. The fine midnight-blue fabric slipped through her fingers, and a moment later the garment was pooled in a circle around her feet.

'Now you look even better.'

From the way his deep voice caught in his throat, Kerry

knew that he liked what he saw. Feeling even bolder, she walked towards him in her high-heeled sandals, just wearing a lacy bra and matching French knickers.

'You are wearing too many clothes,' she said huskily, pulling his T-shirt up and over his head. As his bronzed torso came into view she sucked in a shuddering breath of pure appreciation. He was mouth-wateringly well formed, with perfect satiny skin that made her want to lean forward and run her tongue across his muscled chest, to put her face as close as possible to his beating heart.

She stared at him, feeling her breathing growing faster again. Rampant desire was rushing through her, and suddenly she needed to feel his hands on her again.

As if he had read her mind, he reached out to her and pulled her into his arms. Then his hands were skimming down her back, curving over her bottom, running back up between her shoulderblades to her bra clasp.

With one expert flick he undid the flimsy garment, then cast it aside and pulled her to him. Skin on skin. Hot, hard muscle pressed to tingling, sensitive breasts. With every heaving breath she took her nipples moved against him. The delicious friction of his chest hair rubbing across their throbbing points was driving her to distraction.

She curved sinuously against him, needing to feel more of him. His hands were moving downwards again, and this time he hooked his thumbs into her French knickers. He tugged them past her hips, and then her last remaining item of clothing fell to the floor.

With a deep breath of pent-up excitement she stepped out of her knickers and slipped off her sandals at the same time. She was completely naked.

Theo's dark eyes swept over her, leaving a trail of tingling anticipation prickling over her skin. But she wanted more—she needed more.

'Touch me,' she pleaded. 'Put your hands on me.'

He needed no further encouragement, and in an instant he was standing behind her, skimming his hands around the sensitive skin of her midriff. His chest was pressed against her back, warm and solid behind her, but all she could think about was the wonderful way he was touching her.

As she felt his hands sliding upwards over her ribs, she instinctively looked down at herself. The sight of her own naked breasts, jiggling slightly with the trembling of her body and the rapid rate of her breathing, startled her. Her nipples were jutting forward, taut and throbbing with the need for his attention, and even looking at them herself seemed to make them ache even more.

Suddenly his hands curved up and over her breasts, and a shuddering sigh escaped her. He massaged her tender flesh, sending waves of sensual pleasure rolling through her. Then he teased her nipples gently between his fingers and thumbs, and the pleasure intensified.

Her head fell back against his shoulder and she closed her eyes. It felt so perfect standing there, feeling the skin of her back pressed against his solid chest while his hands created marvellous sensations, spiralling out from her breasts.

Then he lifted one hand to sweep her hair to the side, baring her neck so that he could lean forward and kiss the sensitive skin below her ear. He nuzzled her and she wriggled against him, as a ticklish shower of sexually charged sensations feathered through her, sending her pulse-rate soaring.

She was breathing rapidly, and every gasping breath renewed her awareness of his hand on her breast—of the glorious pleasure he was creating with his touch. But his other hand was moving again, sliding downwards, towards the most sensitive part of her body.

She parted her legs slightly, instinctively rocking her pelvis forward as his hand slipped between her thighs, seeking the throbbing core of her arousal.

'Oh, Theo!' His name burst out of her as his fingers made contact, and as his fingertips caressed her pulsing centre the pleasure was almost too great. She bucked against him, aware only of the blood singing in her ears and the impossibly intense sensations shooting out from where he stroked her.

Her legs turned to jelly and she started to sink downwards, but he swept her up into his arms just in time and carried her to the bed.

Suddenly she couldn't wait any longer to feel him lying over her, thrusting into her, taking her out of her body and into the heavens beyond. She reached feverishly for his belt, and with shaky, uncoordinated movements pulled the supple black leather through the loops on his jeans, then unfastened the buckle.

She moaned—a low, almost feral sound—and struggled desperately with the button, then the zipper. She could feel his erection thrusting powerfully against the fabric of his jeans and she wanted, *needed* him to be totally naked—but her hands were trembling too much for her to manage.

Theo pushed her hands aside with movements that betrayed a sense of urgency that matched Kerry's. Then he rolled from the bed to kick his jeans off himself.

For a moment he stood looking down at her. The sexual hunger that shone from his dark eyes made her quiver with anticipation. She couldn't lie still—the overwhelming need she felt for him was too great.

She pushed herself up on her elbows, aware of every part of her body, from her tingling nipples to her trembling legs, and looked up into his handsome face, knowing that her desire for him must be written all over her features.

Then he came towards her, moving across her body with power and grace. She reached up and looped her arms around him, delighting in the broad, masculine strength of his back. Her thighs fell apart and her hips tilted upwards, ready to welcome his intimate possession of her willing body.

'Oh!' She cried out as he pressed forward and she felt his hard length sliding smoothly inside her. A wave of pleasure washed over her and she lifted her legs, wrapping them tightly round his hips, pulling him deeper still. He paused for a moment, driving her almost wild with unfulfilled need, and then he started to move.

She clung to him, flying higher and higher. Every masterful thrust of his hips brought a surge of wonderful sensation powering through her that quickly blocked out everything but the present.

All those long lonely nights when she'd wondered if Theo's lovemaking could possibly be as amazing as she remembered were forgotten. The only thing that existed for her now was the all-consuming pleasure of being one with him.

She could hear his breathing getting harder, and her own breath was coming in shallow, moaning gasps.

The pleasure within her was tightening, growing more and more focussed. Suddenly her shoulders lifted off the bed, her back arched and her inner muscles clenched tight around his hardness. She had reached the pinnacle of delight and she gasped for breath, her world exploding into a rapturous kaleidoscope of colours.

A second later, from deep within the glow of her climax, she heard Theo shout as he stormed towards his zenith. He reared up above her and gave a mighty shudder as he reached his moment of release.

A shaft of silvery moonlight shone across the room as Kerry lay quietly on the bed, listening to the sound of Theo breathing. Even in sleep his presence seemed to fill the room. But now, for the first time since he'd come back into her life, Kerry was basking in it. She just wanted to lie there and soak up the warmth radiating off the magnificent man next to her.

The embers of her orgasm were still glimmering inside her, diffusing an amazing sense of fulfilment throughout her body. And, even more wonderfully, she felt hopeful for her future with Theo.

She knew that the conversation they'd had right before Theo had swept her upstairs had helped to change the atmosphere between them. He'd been so candid and it had touched her deeply. It was a change in him that she hoped would continue. Not that they'd been dishonest in their communication before—but they'd both held back too much.

She knew that she'd been reserved and guarded—too worried by what Theo would think if she was completely open with him.

But she'd been hurt so many times throughout her childhood, culminating in the most horrible shock when she was eighteen. So she'd taught herself not to expect too much from other people. Not to ask for anything because it would inevitably lead to disappointment.

She had continued to live by that philosophy when she first met Theo—being grateful for their time together but never asking for more. And never burdening him with anything that was troubling her.

But that was going to change. Now she was going to follow Theo's lead and take down her protective barriers. He had done it, and it had made them closer. But she knew they could be closer still.

Very early the following morning Kerry brought Lucas downstairs to give him a drink of milk. He'd always woken up at the crack of dawn, and nothing seemed to be changing about that since they'd arrived in Greece.

As she walked outside onto the terrace she saw that Theo was swimming. She sat at the table with Lucas on her lap as Theo powered through the water beside them. She never tired of watching him—he was a natural swimmer, and he seemed to glide at super-speed through the water with the effortless strength of a dolphin.

It was a beautiful morning—still so early that the sea was a shimmering silver-blue and the sky was tinged pale apricot from the recent sunrise. Kerry felt good—genuinely happy that Theo had brought her back here with him.

He finished his lengths and lifted his head, noticing her for the first time. She lifted her hand to wave at him as he swam over to the steps—just as she had done so many times in the past.

A strange feeling washed over her. Maybe it was still the afterglow of their lovemaking—or the positive effect of their conversation the evening before. But she felt as if she was home. As if she belonged here.

Theo reached the steps and surged out of the pool, water pouring off the hard planes of his muscled body. He looked like a Greek god emerging from the sea, and Kerry felt a renewed kick of desire deep inside.

'Good morning.' Her voice sounded huskier than normal, and she smiled up at him, suddenly feeling shy.

'Hello,' he said, towelling himself off roughly and coming to stand beside the table. 'How are you this morning? And Lucas?'

'We're very well, thank you,' she said.

She drew in a shaky breath as she looked up at his magnificent masculine body, wondering what he was planning for the day—whether or not he had to fly to Athens again. She felt so different from yesterday, when she'd been glad that he'd had to leave the island.

'I'm going to shower,' he said. 'And then I'd like to spend some time with you and Lucas—if that suits you.'

'That would be lovely,' Kerry said, feeling a warm glow of expectation spreading through her.

* * *

Theo emerged from the shower feeling fully energised, thinking about making love with Kerry the night before. It had been good. Incredible, actually. If their marriage was going to work, that was the way they should always make love. Openly and honestly. Untainted by their troubles outside the bedroom.

When they'd arrived on the island Kerry had been so withdrawn—moody, even, although she'd barely spoken—he'd started to have serious concerns for their future. But now she seemed to have snapped out of it, and their situation seemed to be more manageable.

The sound of his phone ringing cut into his thoughts.

'Diakos,' he barked, annoyed with his PA for calling him so early. It had better be important…

Two minutes later he stormed through the house in a black temper. He strode out of the terrace doors and nearly collided with Kerry coming the other way, not looking where she was going because she was chattering away to the baby.

'Oh!' Kerry gasped, clutching Lucas tightly as she wobbled, grateful for Theo's steadying hold on her arm.

'All right?' Theo asked, slowly releasing his grip.

'Yes. Thank you,' Kerry replied, looking up into his face. His dark expression made her catch her breath. 'Are *you* all right? You look like you've had bad news.'

'I'm fine,' Theo replied shortly. 'But I *have* had some bad news.'

He looked at her sharply for a moment, then led her into the living room and sat with her on the sofa.

'It's Drakon,' he said. 'I'm afraid he's taken a turn for the worse. He's in hospital in Athens.'

'Oh, no—poor Drakon!' Kerry gasped. 'How serious is it?'

'I'm not sure,' Theo replied. 'My PA is trying to find out more information. I'll let you know when I hear anything.'

'We must send something,' Kerry said, feeling tears prick her eyes. Drakon loved his island home so much that the thought of him lying in a city hospital was awful. 'Can we visit him?'

'I'll try to find out,' Theo said.

Later that day they heard the good news that Drakon's condition was improved. In fact he had asked for Theo to visit him in hospital, to discuss the sale of the island.

'He must be feeling better,' Kerry said, a smile of relief spreading across her pale face.

'Yes,' Theo agreed, although he wasn't so hopeful as Kerry.

He leafed through the documents he had just thrust into his briefcase, trying to keep his expression bland. Kerry seemed to have become so attached to the old man that he didn't want to risk her getting in a state. He had to leave for Athens as soon as possible.

He wasn't as naive as Kerry. He had the feeling that Drakon was putting his affairs in order. That he wanted the sale to go through quickly so that his daughter was not left vulnerable to property sharks after his death.

'You should tell Drakon why you want the island,' Kerry said suddenly. 'Then he would definitely sell to you.'

'He *is* going to sell to me,' Theo replied flatly, feeling

a nasty jab of irritation at Kerry's unexpected comment. 'Mine is the best offer he's received.'

'But it's not about the money,' Kerry insisted. 'You told me that. He cares about the island.'

'Don't give me business advice.' Theo's voice was bitingly cold. 'Don't think that because I took you to his island you are in any way qualified to offer me your opinion.'

He stared at her angrily. Why had she become so bold all of a sudden? The girl who'd shared his life before would never have started trying to tell him how to manage his business affairs.

'I'm thinking about Drakon,' Kerry said crossly.

She met his hostile stare square-on, unable to believe how cold he was being. Her eyes flashed over him, standing tall and stiff in his dark business suit, and once again she felt as distant from him as she'd ever been.

She'd never got involved in his work before, even when she'd been present at business dinners or overheard him discussing work matters. She'd always known that it was not her concern and that Theo would not welcome her input.

But that timid young girl had changed. Maybe it was the fact that she was a mother now, and had spent the last six months fending for herself and her baby, making decisions that impacted on another little person's life as well as her own.

Or maybe it was because a year ago Theo had heartlessly severed their relationship and thrown her out onto the streets, making her realise how little respect he had for her.

Whatever the reason, she found she couldn't stand by silently any more.

'An old man is lying sick in a hospital bed,' she said passionately. 'And you have the power to make him feel good about the one thing that really matters to him—his island.'

'It's none of his business *why* I want the island,' Theo replied.

'He has devoted the last twenty-five years of his life to preserving that island,' Kerry snapped. 'If he knew that you wanted it for your aunt—so she could live simply, in harmony with the place—think how much that would mean to him.'

'That's not the way I do business,' Theo snapped. 'With rose-coloured idealistic drivel. I deal with hard financial business plans.'

'Don't be so hypocritical,' she said hotly. 'This isn't *normal* business for you. You're not looking for a profit. You told me yourself that you want the island to fulfil your mother's dying wish—so that your aunt can have her home back.'

'I'm not about to share my family's past shame with a stranger,' Theo snapped. 'We don't air our dirty linen in public.'

'You don't have to tell him everything,' Kerry said in exasperation. 'Just say your aunt wishes to live there quietly.'

'I didn't have to tell *you* everything—and I'm already regretting that I did,' Theo said bitterly, slamming his briefcase shut and striding angrily towards the door. 'By now, after everything that has happened, *you* of all people should understand that in this family we keep our personal problems private. We keep things in the family.'

Kerry stared at him as he stood in the doorway, glaring back at her. Suddenly the unmistakable sound of a helicopter approaching the island caught her attention—and her memory flashed back to the conversation she'd overheard on the night Theo had thrown her out.

He had told Corban to take Nicco away to the island by helicopter, without his mother's knowledge. Then he'd said they'd deal with Hallie privately—no one outside the family needed to know.

'Like Hallie,' Kerry cried. 'Hallie was a problem. So you planned to take her son and deal with her in private.'

'It would have been better for everyone if that had happened,' Theo bit out. He raked his hand roughly through his hair and came back into the room, shutting the door behind him.

Kerry felt a wave of anxiety roll through her as she looked up at his livid expression. What had made him close the door, even though the helicopter was waiting for him outside?

'Hallie is an alcoholic,' Theo said. 'And Corban was desperate to take care of her. But instead of accepting the best care in a private facility abroad she crashed her car, with Nicco in it, on the busiest square in Athens, narrowly missing a souvenir stall surrounded by tourists. There was quite an audience when the ambulance men pulled her from the car, crying that her husband planned to steal her child from her.'

'Is that what stopped you taking Nicco?' Kerry gasped.

'No,' Theo grated. 'It stopped Corban putting her

quietly in rehab, which was where she needed to be—for her own sake and for Nicco's sake. With all the media attention her recovery was much slower than it should have been. Your interference nearly broke up their marriage—not to mention causing what might have been a tragic accident.'

Kerry stared up at him, suddenly speechless. Was he telling the truth? That Hallie was an alcoholic? That he and Corban had simply been planning the best way to help her? Had she jumped to the wrong conclusions—putting everyone at risk and causing a whole barrage of problems for the family?

'Because you are the mother of my son, you will soon be part of this family,' Theo said. 'But if you want to stay—be part of Lucas's life—never interfere again.'

'Don't threaten me,' Kerry said shakily. 'You can't take Lucas from me.'

'Yes, I can.' Theo said coldly. 'And if you cross me I will. Never doubt that for a second.'

He turned and strode out of the door, leaving Kerry staring after him in shock.

CHAPTER TEN

THE heavy aroma of flowering jasmine hung in the air as Kerry pushed Lucas's buggy through the streets near Kolonaki Square, passing designer stores and chic cafés filled with elegant Athenian ladies and well-heeled businessmen.

The floral fragrance was typical of Athens, and it reminded Kerry painfully of her first summer in the city—when Theo had swept her off her feet and she'd fallen head over heels in love with him.

She'd never stood a chance. His charm, his amazing good-looks and the irresistible force of his personality had totally overwhelmed her. At the time she'd believed she was blissfully happy with him—but she'd been living in a dream world. Now she knew their relationship had been harmonious simply because she'd gone along with everything he wanted, never doing anything to upset the balance. Never asking for anything.

As she looked back on that summer, Kerry realised a more confident, experienced woman might not have been so in awe of him—might have realised that the relationship was completely superficial. But Kerry had been too in love to see beyond the joy she'd felt just being with Theo.

She knew that some people wanted to spend their lives enjoying the present, with no thought for the future—but she wasn't one of them. As a child she'd longed to be part of a warm, loving family, and that was what she so desperately wished to give Lucas. But now it seemed to be an impossible hope—every day Theo seemed to become even more distant from her.

They'd returned to Athens, and preparations were underway for a quiet family wedding, but communication between them was limited to brief, impersonal exchanges about Lucas. She longed to talk to him properly, to try and improve the atmosphere between them. But their last argument had been so terrible that she was afraid to disturb the uneasy equilibrium they'd reached.

At least she now understood why Theo had been so blindingly furious with her the night Hallie had crashed her car—but the reason made her feel dejected and guilt-ridden. It wasn't just that she'd interfered—questioning Theo's intentions and challenging his command—it was because he truly believed that he'd been doing the right thing for the people he loved. He couldn't even begin to understand why she had gone against him.

But Kerry had never guessed Hallie was an alcoholic. Looking back on it, she realised the signs had been there. But as she'd usually only seen her friend on social occasions it had never occurred to her that Hallie drank a lot—and she knew that sometimes alcoholics became very good at concealing their problem. It was also likely that Theo and Corban had done their best to hide it, thinking that by keeping it in the family they were doing the right thing—but if Kerry had known she would never have made such a terrible mistake.

She returned to the hotel with a heavy heart. She felt so sorry for what had happened—*for what she had done*—but she didn't know how to talk to Theo about it. However, she did know that the problem was not going to go away on its own. It was always going to be there, creating a chasm between them.

She took the elevator up to the family's luxury apartments and got Lucas ready for his nap.

'Time for a sleep, my little angel,' she said, laying him carefully in his cot.

He settled almost immediately, and she wandered out onto the balcony, drawn by the sounds of splashing and laughing floating up to her. She looked down to the private terrace of Corban's apartment and saw Corban, Hallie and Nicco, all playing in the pool. They were back from their trip.

A wave of emotion rolled through her. They all looked so joyful. Nicco had grown so much, Hallie was pregnant again and the love and pride Corban felt for his family shone out of his face.

They were all together, having fun, enjoying each other's company. It was the perfect family moment. And because of her that moment might never have been able to happen.

Suddenly her throat felt tight and her eyes filled with moisture. The next second she burst into tears.

* * *

Theo strode through the hotel on his way up to see Kerry. His staff had informed him—as they always did—that she'd returned to the hotel, and he wanted to tell her that Corban and Hallie had arrived home from their travels.

He did not want her to stumble across them inadvertently, possibly creating an awkward situation. It was his intention to be present the first time they encountered each other, so that a potentially tricky moment would be under his control.

He walked through their apartment quietly, in case Lucas was asleep, and found Kerry standing on the balcony looking down at the terrace below. Something about her body language pricked his attention immediately. Her shoulders were drawn in and she was shaking.

Suddenly he realised she was weeping.

'Kerry?' He spoke her name quietly, but she spun round at once, her face an open book of remorse.

'I'm sorry,' she sobbed. 'Oh, Theo—I'm so sorry for what I did that night.'

The pure emotion in her voice cut into him disconcertingly—but he told himself it didn't matter what she said, how she tried to defend her actions. He knew he would never forgive her for what she'd done. She'd deliberately betrayed his plans—putting both his sister-in-law and his nephew in danger.

'I did something inexcusable—something terrible.' Her voice rose urgently. 'But I never meant harm to come to anyone. You have to know that wasn't my intention.'

'I have no idea what you intended,' Theo said honestly. He'd racked his brain repeatedly—wondering what had possessed her to go running to Hallie. Surely she'd known him well enough to realise that he only ever wanted what was best for his family. 'What in God's name were you thinking?'

He stared at her, feeling all the anger he'd tried to put aside for Lucas's sake rising up within him once more.

'I was thinking about my mother,' Kerry suddenly blurted. 'I was thinking about how it killed her!' She dragged in a tortured breath and turned away from him, covering her face with her hands.

Theo stared at her in shock. What was she talking about? What did the death of Kerry's mother have to do with what had happened the night Hallie crashed the car?

'They took my mother's baby away.' Kerry's words were muffled, but Theo could just about hear what she was saying. 'They took *me* away from my mother—and it destroyed her.'

She scrubbed her palms over her face, then turned round to look at him again. He could see just how badly talking about—even *thinking* about—her mother was affecting Kerry. Her face was pale and her eyes wide, and her whole body was shaking violently.

'Come inside and sit down,' he said, reaching out towards her.

She curled in on herself and shrank away from him—as if at that moment she couldn't bear to be touched. But then she edged past him and walked unevenly to the sofa.

For a moment Theo hesitated, then he poured her a glass of cold water and sat down next to her.

Kerry picked up the water automatically with a trembling hand and took a sip. It was the first time she had ever spoken about her mother to anyone. Her heart was thumping and her palms felt damp and clammy.

She didn't want to say anything else—what would Theo think when he knew the truth about her?—but now she had started she knew she had to finish.

'My mother was very young when she had me,' Kerry said. 'Only sixteen.'

She paused, glancing at him to see if he seemed shocked—but his expression was unreadable.

'My grandmother was horrified. She forced my mother to hand me over to her, so she could bring me up alongside Bridget, her other, much younger daughter,' Kerry said. 'But it was a disaster for everyone. She never really wanted me, and always resented having an extra child to take care of. But even worse, her decision to take me destroyed my mother's life. It made her feel like a failure and she never managed to get her life on track.'

She paused again, and took another sip of water to steady her nerves. Now she was telling Theo she felt really strange—almost as if she was watching someone else telling their life story.

'So Bridget is really your aunt,' Theo said. 'But you were brought up together, by the same person.'

'I *think* of her as my sister,' she replied. 'We grew up with each other and there's not much age difference between us.' She rubbed her hands over her face and took a few steadying breaths. Now she had started, she had to tell the final, most awful piece of the story.

'Maybe if my mother had had her child to look after, she would've had a purpose in life—a reason to sort herself out,' Kerry continued. 'As it was, she turned to drink and then started taking drugs. She died of an overdose in the end.'

'I'm sorry,' Theo said. 'That must have been very hard for you.'

'At the time I thought she was my much older sister,' Kerry said. 'I didn't even know her because Mum—I mean my grandmother—threw her out after I was born and wouldn't let her back in the house. I met her once or twice when I was little, but I barely remember it.'

For the first time Kerry detected a response in Theo—and she lifted her eyes to see a look of shock on his face.

'She didn't tell you who your mother was? She lied to you?' he asked incredulously.

'My grandmother said it was in everyone's best interests,' Kerry said bitterly. 'Really she was covering up the shame she felt because her teenage daughter had had a baby. I only found out when I was eighteen years old. I needed my birth certificate to apply for a passport when I got a job in the travel agency.'

She shuddered, hugging herself as she remembered the utter shock she'd felt as she'd looked at the birth certificate, staring in disbelief and confusion at her older sister's name, written clearly in the section for her mother's name.

By then she'd already been dead. It hadn't been possible for Kerry to get to know her. Her grandmother, an embittered, mean-spirited woman, who hadn't even wanted to look after her in the first place, had denied her the right to get to know her mother.

It was only when her eyes blurred with tears that

Kerry realised she was weeping again. Theo was beside her in an instant, this time pulling her into his arms and holding her to his broad chest.

She leant into his embrace, taking comfort from the strong, regular heartbeat below her cheek. It meant so much that he hadn't pulled away from her in disgust when he'd heard her story. She knew it was a lot for anyone to take in—and now he had discovered that the mother of his son came from a truly messed-up family.

'I'm sorry,' she said. 'I'm sorry that I haven't given Lucas a better background.'

'Don't apologise for things that are not your fault. I would never blame you or think less of you because of your background,' Theo said, stroking her hair gently away from her tear-streaked face. 'Things like that mean nothing to me. I only care that our son has what he needs—love from both his parents.' He paused, cupping her chin softly and tipping her head back so he could look down into her eyes. 'Lucas will never be short of love.'

A wave of warmth washed through her at his words. She knew he was speaking sincerely—and she knew that he really did not judge her for her troubled background.

It felt as if an enormous weight had been lifted off her shoulders, and for the first time she felt that Theo was looking at her and seeing the whole truth about the person she really was. Until that moment she had never realised what a heavy burden the secret of her background had been.

'I'm glad you told me,' Theo said, sliding his fingers through her hair to the nape of her neck.

He looked down at her, finally understanding what had driven her to react so recklessly to the conversation she had overheard the night of the accident. He meant what he had said—he would never judge anyone according to their background. After all, he would hate to be judged on the basis of being his father's son.

But it was terrible to think about Kerry growing up in such difficult circumstances. It was no wonder she'd never talked about her past.

'I can't face seeing Hallie and Corban again,' Kerry said. Then she bit her lip, realising how cowardly that sounded. She couldn't hide from her mistake for ever. She had to face up to it and take responsibility for what she had done.

'I'll be with you,' Theo said, drawing her towards him with his hand behind her head.

'Thank you.' Kerry looked up at him, wondering if that meant he thought there would be trouble. Theo had been angry with her—surely Corban would be too? It was his wife and child that Kerry had endangered.

'Don't think about it now,' Theo said, bending his head and pressing his mouth to her cheek with the lightest of touches. 'Don't think about anything.'

A ripple of pleasure ran through her and she closed her eyes, feeling him kissing her again and again. The touch of his lips was as light as a shower of raindrops, scattering over her face to wash away her tears.

It felt wonderful—just knowing there were no more secrets between them. For the first time ever she could truly let down her guard. Theo knew all about her—and yet he was still here with her, kissing her, caressing her…starting to make love to her.

She sighed with delight and leant into his embrace, opening her lips as he finally kissed her on the mouth. Her pulse rate leapt up as his tongue slid inside, setting off a cascade of feelings surging through her body.

Suddenly she was burning with desire for him. She was hot and desperate to feel his body moving against hers, to feel his hands on her bare skin.

She grappled with his clothing urgently, pulling and tugging—and he was undressing her at the same time. Then all at once they were both standing naked, devouring each other with their eyes.

'You look so good,' she murmured, startled by how husky her voice sounded. For a second she didn't move, just stood there letting her eyes roam freely over his magnificent body. He was fully aroused and ready for her, and his erection drew her gaze like a magnet. Her breathing was becoming ragged just from looking at him—but she wanted the moment to last.

His eyes were on her too, searing a tingling trail over the peaks of her breasts, down across her stomach to the soft curls at the apex of her legs—and the expression of erotic hunger on his face was turning her on even more.

Then suddenly he stepped towards her, as if he was unable to keep his hands off her a moment longer, and her world exploded into a wild, sexual tangle of entwined limbs and kissing mouths.

Hot, liquid arousal sang through her veins and rang

in her ears, blotting out everything but her growing need to feel Theo lying over her, thrusting long and hard into her body. But suddenly she found herself leaning back on the sofa, with him kneeling between her legs.

She barely had time to anticipate the exquisite rapture he was about to deliver, when his mouth came down on her. She let out a shuddering cry as his tongue and lips caressed her most sensitive, intimate place, setting wave after wave of pure sexual sensation rolling through her. Her whole body was suffused with pulsing pleasure and she felt herself rocketing upwards, straight towards a shattering, all-encompassing climax.

She cried out as she reached a moment of release, but before she had a chance to drift back down Theo had lifted himself over her and thrust his hard, masculine length deep into her body.

Her trembling, sensitised flesh clamped around him, and she shot back up into the heavens immediately. She hadn't known it was possible to feel such intense sensual pleasure—but Theo drove her higher and higher. Thrusting deeper and deeper into her willing body, he carried her up and up until she was lost in a whirling vortex of pure sexual excitement.

Then, as the final crescendo of delirious ecstasy crashed through her, she heard Theo shout as he reached his own explosive climax.

Kerry smiled tenderly as she looked at Theo lying beside her. Her body was still glowing from their lovemaking, and her heart felt a gladness she could never remember feeling before. She had told Theo about her past—about all the sordid details of her dysfunctional family—and he still wanted to be with her.

She knew it was for Lucas's sake, but she finally felt as if she and Theo were growing closer. She didn't think that he had fully forgiven her for what she had done, but at least now he understood *why* she had not been thinking clearly the night of the accident.

She lifted her hand and traced her fingers gently over the contours of his gorgeous face—across his high cheekbones and down to his strong, angular jaw. He opened his dark brown eyes and looked at her, his sensual lips curving into a lazy smile as his gaze held hers, filling her with another wave of warmth.

'You look beautiful,' he said, his voice low and husky.

She smiled, feeling the flutter of butterflies deep inside her. Just looking at him made her feel good—joyful and excited at the same time. Her blood tingled through her veins like champagne. She was so happy to be there with him—so happy that he was the father of her child.

Suddenly her heart turned over and she realised something—something wonderful and terrible at the same time.

She loved him. She had fallen in love with Theo all over again.

Later that day Theo took Kerry to meet Hallie and Corban. Her legs felt weak with nerves, but she knew she had to overcome them. Not just for the sake of her future in the Diakos family—but because it was the right thing to do.

'I'm so sorry for what I did.' Kerry rushed the words out the moment they were all together.

They seemed to jar uncomfortably around the room, as if she'd just said something out of place, and she felt her stomach crunch with nervous agitation. But in her heart she knew there was no point waiting, working awkwardly through small talk, with such a big issue still hanging in the air between them.

'It's all right,' Hallie said suddenly, throwing her arms around Kerry impulsively. 'Everyone is all right.'

'But…but when I think what might have happened…' Kerry stammered, feeling her eyes brimming with tears of remorse. She'd thought that after her afternoon of confession with Theo she was all cried out—but as the tears ran down her cheeks she knew that she wasn't.

'Honestly, I can't remember much about it,' Hallie said. 'But I know you—I know you didn't mean to harm anyone. Maybe you even helped me, in a way.'

'I don't understand,' Kerry said, gratefully taking the tissue Hallie offered her and dabbing her eyes.

'I don't think I was ready to accept that I needed help,' Hallie said. 'I know it wasn't the best way to realise that I did—but at least crashing the car made me stop and think.'

'But…but…' Kerry wasn't ready to believe that anything good could have come of that night.

'You didn't put the car keys in my hand,' Hallie said. 'But you did try to stop me—and you went straight for help.'

She turned and reached out her arm for her husband, drew him closer to them.

'We forgive you,' Hallie said. 'And we are pleased that you will be part of the family again.'

Kerry smiled tremulously as she looked at Hallie. She was such a kind, generous soul, and Kerry felt so grateful. Hallie's friendship had always meant a lot to her, and she knew that it would enrich her life now that she was to be married to Theo.

'Theo has told me what happened.' Corban's deep voice rumbled beside her and she turned to look up at him. He was so like his brother that when his dark eyes met hers she felt a rush of nervousness. 'I accept that you did not mean for any harm to come to my family.'

Despite his words of assurance there was no warmth in his eyes. Kerry knew that he was still protective towards his wife and child—and she understood why. The fact that Hallie had forgiven her so freely was more than enough. She knew she would have to earn Corban's trust again, but for his brother's sake he was prepared to accept her into the family.

'Thank you.' Kerry spoke sincerely.

'Let's go for dinner.' Hallie's voice was bright and breezy, and Kerry knew she was determined to lighten the atmosphere, to put the past behind them. 'You can tell me all about the wedding plans.'

Theo fell into step with his brother as they walked through into the dining room, but his eyes were on Kerry. She was clearly relieved that seeing Hallie and Corban again had gone so well—and Theo shared that relief.

He wasn't in the habit of worrying about what other people thought, but he realised he'd been ill at ease, waiting for this meeting to take place.

Perhaps it was because up until this afternoon Kerry had never truly apologised for what had happened. He'd only known that she regretted the outcome—rather than the fact that she had interfered in the first place. But now he believed that she was genuinely sorry. And he'd been impressed by the open honesty she had shown Hallie and Corban.

As he looked at her a strange sensation passed through him. He frowned, momentarily disconcerted as he couldn't identify what he was feeling. Then he realised what it was—pride. He was proud of how she had taken responsibility and given such a heartfelt apology to Hallie and Corban.

CHAPTER ELEVEN

OVER the next few weeks Kerry re-established her friendship with Hallie. They'd always got along well, and it was wonderful to have someone to pass the time with while Theo was working. It was good for the children to play together too. Lucas, who had just started crawling, had great fun following his older cousin Nicco around.

The wedding came and went with the minimum of fuss. It was a small ceremony, just for immediate family, and afterwards Theo took Kerry and Lucas to the island for a couple of days. She was a little disappointed that he'd only taken such a small amount of time out of his busy schedule for them. Not that she'd wanted a big fancy honeymoon, but she would have liked the chance to spend more time with Theo. She finally felt as if they were starting to get to know each other again, but it was slow progress because he was always working.

When they returned to Athens, Corban and Hallie had already left to continue the trip they had interrupted to attend the wedding. Kerry and Lucas were alone during the day once again, and life settled into a quiet pattern.

One day, about a week later, Kerry received a message from Drakon, asking her to come and see him at the hospital. She was surprised because Theo had told her that he wasn't well enough for visitors—and hadn't been for some time. In fact the afternoon that Theo had flown from the island to meet Drakon at the hospital the old man had taken another turn for the worse. Theo had been refused access and the situation with the sale of the island was still unresolved.

Kerry looked at the handwritten note that Drakon had sent to her. She had the feeling that Theo would not be pleased if she went to see the old man alone—but he'd flown to Paris that morning and wouldn't be back till late. She didn't want to keep Drakon waiting. His health seemed so precarious that he might not be fit to see her if she delayed her visit.

So she left Lucas with the housekeeper and went to the hospital alone.

'Thank you for coming,' Drakon said, struggling to sit up straighter against the starched white hospital pillows. 'I wasn't sure if you'd be able to.'

'Of course I came,' Kerry said, crossing the room to kiss Drakon lightly on the cheek. She was startled by how changed he seemed—he looked so frail that she'd hardly recognised him at first.

'There are a few things I want to ask you,' he said, getting straight down to business. 'Forgive me for not worrying about the social niceties—but I tire easily.'

Kerry looked at the old man, suddenly feeling wary. She had a feeling that she wasn't going to want to answer his questions…

Theo signed the last of the documents securing his purchase of Drakon's island and stepped back, away from the old man's hospital bed.

'You take care of my island,' Drakon instructed him testily. 'And take care of that pretty wife of yours. You've got a gem there—although I think you're too pig-headed to realise it.'

Theo looked down at the old man, biting back the cutting retort that had come into his mind. The island was his now—he did not have to answer to anybody about what he chose to do with it. And—unfortunately—he was well aware of what kind of woman he had married.

'Trust me—I know my wife,' he replied smoothly. She was a woman who still had not learnt her lesson about meddling in his affairs. A woman who had gone behind his back *yet again* and betrayed his confidence.

Drakon snorted derisively, as if he was far from convinced by Theo's words, then held out his hand to shake on their deal.

'We're finished here,' he said. 'Don't let me keep you from your other business.'

Theo shook his hand firmly, a wry lift of his brow the only indication of what he thought about Drakon's clumsy dismissal.

He left the hospital and headed straight back to the hotel. He could not believe what had happened. He had finally acquired the island for his aunt—but all he could think about was how Kerry had betrayed him. Again.

Kerry looked down at Lucas, already sleeping soundly. She walked out of the nursery and closed the door quietly, biting her lip distractedly.

She'd been in a permanent state of agitation since Drakon had called her to the hospital the previous day. She'd been determined not to do or say anything that would displease Theo, but it hadn't made any difference—because Drakon already knew everything.

He'd told Kerry the story of Theo's aunt and uncle, and how they'd lost the island. And then he'd simply watched her response as he'd quizzed her about Theo's plans. When he'd suggested that Theo might be buying the island in order to give it back to his aunt, her reaction had confirmed his guess was correct.

She felt awful for inadvertently giving Drakon the verification he was looking for—but short of telling him an outright lie she hadn't been able to hide the truth.

Although she knew Theo would be furious with her, she had decided to tell him what had happened as soon as possible. But he never seemed to be around. She'd tried to call him, but he was always in meetings. And in any case it wasn't the kind of conversation she wanted to have over the telephone.

She walked out onto the roof garden, hoping to calm her nerves, but somehow the heavy fragrance of jasmine seemed too overpowering, and the trickle of the fountain didn't soothe her as usual.

Suddenly she realised that she was thinking about the

last time she'd waited for Theo on the roof garden, knowing that she was about to confess something that would make him angry. That time she *had* made a terrible mistake—and Theo had reacted by kicking her out of his life. This time she had not done anything wrong except *not* tell Drakon a barefaced lie to protect Theo's privacy. But she knew he would still be angry.

She turned to go back inside, but at that moment Theo appeared in the doorway.

'I'm glad you're home,' she said right away, pleased at how steady she kept her voice, despite the unease that filled her. 'There's something I need to tell you—something that happened yesterday.'

'You went to see Drakon,' Theo said, pre-empting her confession.

Kerry looked up at his face and felt herself tremble. Whether he'd meant to or not, Drakon had put her in a terrible position. And now she had to try to explain it to Theo.

'He sent me a message,' Kerry said. 'I felt I had to go right away—he's been so unwell that I didn't think I should delay.'

'I've also been to see him. In fact I've just come from the hospital now,' Theo said, partially drawing a sheaf of papers out of his briefcase. 'The island is now mine.'

'Oh!' Kerry gasped, relief running through her as she watched Theo return the documents to the safety of his case. 'Oh, that's wonderful.'

Then she looked back at his face, and a bundle of nerves tightened inside her as she realised her relief had been misplaced. Despite the fact he'd finally bought the island he was furious.

'Why aren't you pleased?' she asked. 'You've got what you wanted.'

'I wanted a wife who understood not to meddle in my affairs,' he grated.

'I didn't meddle!' she said incredulously, a spike of annoyance stabbing into her.

'You told Drakon things that I'd told you in confidence,' he said.

'No, I didn't!' Kerry exclaimed. 'Drakon already knew. He just wanted confirmation.'

'So you gave it to him,' Theo said stonily.

'No, it wasn't like that. He told me what he knew—which was everything,' Kerry insisted. 'I didn't say anything—but I couldn't deny what *he'd* said. Short of lying, there was nothing I could have done.'

'You went against my wishes,' Theo said. 'Even though I made myself absolutely clear to you.'

'Did you want me to lie to a sick old man—tell him he was wrong about something he already knew to be true?' Kerry demanded.

'Don't try to turn this around,' Theo grated. 'You're not the martyr here.'

'And neither are you!' Kerry threw back at him, suddenly furious with the way he was treating her. 'You're acting like I deliberately set out to defy you!' she cried. 'Nothing bad has happened. You should be pleased—you've finally bought the island you've wanted for years.'

'Drakon would have sold to me sooner or later. That

is not the issue,' Theo said, stepping closer so that he was looming over her—a menacing physical presence. 'The point is I cannot have a wife that I don't trust.' He moved closer. 'And I don't trust you.'

Kerry did not miss the threat in Theo's words. But rather than make her nervous they sent a wave of anger rolling through her.

'This isn't about *trust*,' she accused him. 'This is about what kind of wife you want—someone who is quiet and biddable, someone who never expresses her own opinion.' She paused for breath, still glaring up at him. 'In fact you don't want a wife at all. You want another employee—someone who'll happily jump to do your bidding and never challenge you in any way!'

Theo was staring down at her, his dark eyes glinting dangerously. She could see a vein throbbing at his temple and a muscle pulsing in his jaw.

'Whatever accusations you make—whatever defence you plead,' he said coldly, 'understand that I will not tolerate your continued interference in my affairs—private or business.'

'Don't try to intimidate me,' Kerry said, placing her hands on her hips and standing her ground as he loomed over her. 'A lot has happened since the night you threw me out—I'm not the same timid girl I was then.'

'Really? Then why are we right back to square one—arguing about how you betrayed me?' Theo demanded savagely.

'I didn't betray you—that's just how you've chosen to interpret what happened,' Kerry said. 'It's impossible for you to accept that anybody else can ever have a valid opinion or be well motivated.'

She turned to the side for a moment, dashing away the foolish tears that sprang into her eyes as she realised it didn't matter what she said—Theo had already judged her. Whatever she did, he always construed it harshly. She drew in a steadying breath, lifted her head and looked him straight in the eye once more.

'You are a control freak,' she said. 'Everything always has to be on your terms. No matter what, you're always convinced that you know best—that your way is the right way.'

Theo glared at her, his heart thumping angrily in his chest. How dared she make such an accusation?

'Demanding respect from the people around me and taking charge of my life does not make me a control freak,' he said angrily.

'Never accepting that anyone else can ever have a valid point of view, always insisting that everything happens in exactly the way you envision it—even when the outcome is the same—*that* makes you a control freak,' she said.

'However you try to turn this around—to point the blame at me—I will never tolerate your interference in my affairs,' Theo bit out.

'Don't you realise how hypocritical you are being?' Kerry asked, her voice rising with exasperation. 'By wanting to control everything all the time *you* are the one guilty of interfering with other people's lives. *You* told Corban to put Hallie in rehab. *You* bought the island for your aunt with the aim of totally changing her life. And *you* forced me to come to Greece to marry you.'

'I want what is best for my family,' Theo said. 'There is nothing wrong with that.'

He'd only ever tried to do the right thing—for Hallie, for his aunt. And most importantly for Lucas. He would *not* permit Kerry to twist his good intentions.

'It's the way you go about it—refusing to see anything from anyone else's perspective,' she said. 'You told me how you couldn't stand your father meddling in your life. But I think you've put so much energy into single-handedly taking control, that you can never accept anyone else might have something to contribute.'

'Don't compare me to my father,' Theo grated.

'Why not?' Kerry demanded recklessly. 'You behave in the same way—riding roughshod over other people's lives.'

'You don't know what you are talking about,' he said, his voice throbbing dangerously.

She stared up at his furious face, and suddenly all the anger drained out of her. She couldn't bear to continue arguing with him.

'I can't do this any more—it won't make any difference.' She felt her shoulders slump with defeat. 'I feel like I'm constantly walking on eggshells. However hard I try I can't help making you angry with me.'

'If you kept your nose out of my affairs we wouldn't have this problem,' Theo said.

She lifted her head and met his gaze straight on. She loved him—but she didn't know how they could ever make their marriage work.

'I just can't talk to you. It's pointless,' she said, feeling her heart breaking all over again. 'You'll never really hear what I'm saying. Whatever I do you'll just interpret it negatively.'

She turned to leave—there was nothing else she could do.

'Don't walk away from me.' He spoke through gritted teeth. 'I'm not finished with you yet.'

She stopped and looked up at him, feeling a wave of despair rising up through her.

'I know,' she said, her voice breaking with emotion. 'You never will be. Because we have Lucas you'll never be finished with me.'

Theo stood rooted to the spot, staring down at her with hostile eyes. But as she turned to leave he didn't try to stop her.

Kerry hardly slept that night. It was a welcome relief when morning came and she heard Lucas stirring in the nursery. She slipped out of bed quietly, although she suspected Theo wasn't asleep either, and went through to get him up and dressed for the day.

After their argument she couldn't face seeing Theo. And apparently he felt the same way, because he began working in his study very soon afterwards. Although it was a large apartment, she started to feel claustrophobic. Simply knowing that Theo was behind the closed door of his study, a dangerously brooding presence like a volcano waiting to erupt, made her feel uneasy.

So as soon as it seemed a reasonable time she put

Lucas in his pushchair and went out for a walk. After the air-conditioned hotel it felt very hot and heavy outside—even though it was barely eight o'clock in the morning. The weather had been unsettled for a few days, so she'd put the rain cover on Lucas's buggy—something that was rarely necessary in the Athens summer.

She set off away from the bustling business district of the city, towards the winding medieval alleyways around the Acropolis. But she'd forgotten that the tourist area was slower to wake up in the morning and found the streets disconcertingly deserted, apart from a few shopkeepers mopping the marble pavements outside their small stores.

Eventually she found an open café and sat down to give Lucas a drink. She ordered cappuccino and baklava for herself, hoping the combination of caffeine and sugar might give her a boost. The air was so muggy that her sleepless night was really catching up with her.

But as she sat there, looking distractedly at the reflections in the shiny wet marble in front of the trinket store across the alleyway, she felt increasingly weary. And all she could think about was how much she loved Theo—and how he would never, ever love her. He'd broken her heart into a million jagged fragments once more. And this time she didn't know how she'd ever find the strength to pick the pieces up.

Theo watched his Aunt Dacia's face as the helicopter approached the island. He'd met her properly for the first time in his life that morning, and he couldn't quite get over how like his mother she was. It wasn't really the way she looked—it was more to do with the way she moved, her gestures, and particularly the sound of her voice.

It was a strange feeling, finally bringing her back to the island where she'd grown up with his mother. He'd been amazed and pleased that she had agreed to come with him so readily. After the way she'd refused to have anything to do with him—even slamming the door in his face once or twice, before he'd given up on direct personal contact—he'd been prepared for a lengthy process of persuasion.

She didn't speak as they walked along the ridge from the helipad, but as he glanced sideways at her he could see her eyes were shining brightly, and he knew coming back to the island was an emotional experience for her.

'I can't believe I'm really here,' Dacia said eventually, as they followed Drakon's assistant into the house.

'Does it seem very different?' Theo asked, as he held the door for his aunt. A wry smile flashed across his face as he remembered Drakon's terse comment that he didn't need help because the door stayed open on its own.

A lot had happened since that evening when he'd first brought Kerry to the island. His well-ordered life had been completely turned upside down. He was here, properly meeting his aunt for the first time, and fulfilling his mother's dying wish that he find a way to help her. And back in Athens he had a wife and son.

An unpleasant ripple of emotion went through him as he remembered the argument they'd had the previous evening. The look of desperation in her eyes when she'd said she knew he'd never be finished with her had cut him deeply—unexpectedly so. As had the way she'd curled away from him all night, on the very edge of their large bed.

'The outside hardly seems to have changed,' Dacia said. 'And even the inside seems the same, apart from the furniture.'

'There are some maintenance issues—mainly with the olive groves and the traditional press that was used to make the oil,' Theo said, pulling his thoughts back to the present. 'But I've already made contact with several experts we could employ to get things back on track—if that's what you decide to do with the place.'

'These are the paintings I was asked to point out to you,' Drakon's assistant said, leading them into the whitewashed corridor. 'Now, if you'll excuse me, I'll go and check on the refreshments.'

'Oh!' Dacia gave a little cry and lifted both hands up to her cheeks.

Theo could see how much she was trembling as she walked closer, to look at the paintings that had been done by her late husband—the love of her life. Her head was tipped to the side as she gazed at them, and suddenly he saw that tears were running down her face.

A strange lump tightened in his throat and he reached into his jacket pocket automatically for a clean handkerchief. He stepped nearer and offered it to her, and then, without thinking what he was doing—maybe because she was so like his mother—he put his arm around her thin shoulders and gave her a reassuring hug.

She jumped slightly, and turned to look up at him with startled eyes.

Theo cleared his throat gruffly and dropped his arm stiffly by his side.

'Please excuse me,' he said, stepping back awkwardly. 'That was too forward of me.'

'No. You must excuse *me*.' Dacia looked up at him with sparkling eyes, shaking her head from side to side. 'Thank you so much for doing this for me.'

'It's nothing.' Theo brushed her thanks aside.

'It is everything,' Dacia said with feeling. 'After the way I turned my back on you and refused all your offers of help I don't deserve this.'

'I am pleased to have found a way to put things right,' Theo said. 'It was because of my father that you lost so much.'

'Because of your *father*—not because of you,' Dacia said. 'But I was so foolish I turned my back on my sister and on her boys. And now you've grown up to be such a wonderful, handsome man—I'm sorry that I missed so much of your life. That I threw my sister's good intentions back in her face.'

Theo looked down at her, completely lost for words. He knew that Dacia and his mother had never been particularly close. They'd been very different people—Dacia had liked to lead a simple life, and his mother had relished the high-paced, fashion-orientated life that marriage to his father had brought her. But it was sad that they hadn't overcome their differences before his mother had died.

'I'm sorry that I never accepted all your offers of help,' she said. 'Especially the paintings I returned unopened—that was unforgivably small-minded of me after the trouble you must have gone through to get them. I was so determined not to accept anything from your family that I hurt myself—denied myself the chance to have something that would have brought me comfort.'

'What made you change your mind now?' Theo asked. 'I was absolutely delighted when you accepted my call and agreed to come out here with me. But I must admit I was a little surprised to find you so willing.'

'I'm sorry,' Dacia said again. 'I'm ashamed to say that if it hadn't been for the elderly man who used to own this island contacting me and asking me to visit him in hospital, the chances are I still wouldn't have come to my senses.'

'What happened?' Theo asked.

'I went to see Drakon Notara. He told me that you were trying to buy his island so that I would be able to return to my old home,' Dacia said. 'I was shocked, and I think I would have walked away—but he is such an engaging old fellow. Once he started talking I found I didn't want to leave any more.'

Theo looked at his aunt, feeling a touch of irritation towards Drakon. He'd been busy—he'd seen Kerry in the morning, then his aunt that afternoon, and then finally Theo on the following day.

'What did he tell you?' Theo asked, uncharacteristically uneasy about what Drakon might have told his aunt.

'More or less his whole life story, I think.' Dacia smiled. 'About his dear wife and their love of nature. About how his greatest concern was to preserve the island as it was. He couldn't bear the idea of modern development ruining it—and that was where his interest in me came in.'

She paused and smiled apologetically at Theo, as if to soften what she was about to say. 'He wanted my assurances that I would keep you in check—make sure you kept to your word and didn't start building hotels here.'

Theo raised his brows, startled to feel a burst of ironic humour rip through him. Drakon was such a character. The idea that his aunt, a woman Theo had never even met properly before, would be able to hold sway over him was absurd. He'd build a concrete jungle on the island if he wanted to—*no one* told Theo Diakos what to do.

But then he found himself feeling an unexpected amount of respect for Drakon. That cunning old man was no fool. In fact he had completely got Theo's measure. He knew he had bought the island to mend bridges with his aunt, and that he *would* listen to what she had to say.

'I won't build any hotels,' he said. 'But you will have to decide what you want to do with the island. There are plenty of possibilities—from restarting the olive oil production to running small painting retreats like you used to.' He paused, suddenly realising that suggesting something that would inevitably bring memories of her late husband might be too painful.

'You don't have to decide immediately,' he continued. 'Take as long as you need to think about it. And if you feel that the island is not the right home for you now—that's all right too. We can still find a way to preserve what Drakon has started here.'

Dacia smiled, and turned to look back at the paintings hanging on the whitewashed wall.

'I'd like to send you the other paintings now,' Theo said, thinking about how they had caught Kerry's eye and spiked her curiosity. It had taken him years to find and then acquire work by his uncle. Most of his paintings were in private collections, and it was very rare that they came onto the market.

'Thank you.' Dacia smiled up at him warmly. 'But, you know, after all this time I realise that what I would love is the chance to get to know the people I foolishly shut out of my life.'

'Of course,' Theo said. 'I know Corban would be delighted to introduce you to his family.'

'And I would love to meet your wife,' Dacia said. 'Drakon clearly thinks the world of her. I got the impression that she was instrumental in his decision to sell the island.'

'Yes, Drakon's always been very taken with Kerry. I believe she reminds him of his late wife, back when he first met her,' Theo replied without missing a beat—but inside he felt an unexpected jolt.

He'd always known that Kerry would play a part in the old man's willingness to do business with him—which was why he'd followed Drakon's request and brought her out to the island to meet him. But suddenly he was thinking about what she'd said the night before—that he was a control freak. That he always judged her negatively, never believing her involvement could be well motivated.

'The refreshments are ready.' Drakon's assistant spoke politely, interrupting his thoughts.

'How lovely,' Dacia said. 'Thank you.'

Theo turned to escort his aunt out to the paved area overlooking the Adriatic. Despite everything he had said the night before, he did acknowledge that Dacia was here now, with the minimum of persuasion, because of Kerry and Drakon's involvement. And he knew that if he'd done things his own way it might have been a much longer, more painful process.

'I've kept on all of Drakon's staff,' Theo said. 'It should make the transition of ownership easier. But of course you will be free to make your own decisions about staffing in due course.'

'You've turned my world upside down,' Dacia said, reaching out and squeezing Theo's hand. 'You can't even begin to imagine what this means to me. Thank you—thank you so much for doing such a marvellous thing.'

Theo smiled. He was about to say that it was nothing when suddenly he realised that might diminish how much it meant to Dacia to return to her island home. 'I can't take all the credit,' he found himself saying.

'I can't wait to meet your wife,' Dacia said. 'She must be a wonderful person to have in your life.'

'She is.' Theo smiled at his aunt politely, thinking about Kerry again.

Back when they'd first been together, he'd used to think of her as the perfect antidote to his fast-paced, pressurised lifestyle. She had been exactly what he was looking for in a lover—calm, beautiful and receptive to his wishes. Like an oasis of serenity amidst the cut and thrust of his life.

But Kerry had changed. She'd once been his perfect lover—but she was very far from being his perfect wife. She'd gone against his wishes. And she'd stood up to him, calling him a control freak.

His life had been so well ordered and organised, with everything under his control and nothing unexpected. That was how he liked it.

Did that make him a control freak? Suddenly he wasn't sure.

All he knew was that Kerry and Lucas had exploded into his world and nothing was the same. Nothing was predictable.

He was used to demanding immediate obedience from everyone in his life—but Kerry wasn't an employee. She was his wife. Did he really want the kind of biddable, spineless creature she had described?

Ever since he'd found out about Lucas he'd only ever done what was best for his son—he hadn't thought about what might be best for Kerry or for himself.

He remembered the look in her eyes when she'd said she knew he would never be finished with her. The thought of spending her future with him had obviously filled her with despair—and for some reason that made him feel cold inside.

CHAPTER TWELVE

THE sound of thunder rumbled through the city, and Kerry realised with a sinking feeling that a storm was coming. The air was heavy and humid, and it seemed to press down on her as she trudged along the pedestrianway beneath the Acropolis. She was tired and, despite the atmosphere between herself and Theo, she wanted to get Lucas back to the hotel as soon as possible. But what seemed like a reasonable walk on an ordinary day suddenly seemed like a marathon.

The first raindrops fell as she turned out of the small backstreets onto the busy main road that lead to Syntagma Square. She'd always thought of it as a horrible wide thoroughfare, with what seemed like all the traffic in Athens speeding along it—but it was the most direct route to the hotel, and the place where she thought she stood the best chance of flagging down a taxi.

Then suddenly, with a monstrously loud crack of thunder and a flash of lightning right above her, the skies opened and the rain poured down.

Lucas howled as she hauled his rain cover over him.

He was keeping dry—but he wasn't used to being enclosed by the plastic cover, or to the horrendous noise of the rain pelting down onto it. Kerry was drenched to the skin in a second, but she kept on pushing the buggy towards home.

The rain was so heavy that the huge towering columns of the Olympian Temple of Zeus were almost invisible, even though they were only across the road from her. And within minutes wide torrents of rainwater were surging along the gutters—turbid and brown from a whole summer's dirt being washed off the streets in one go.

Lucas was howling so loudly that she could hear him even over the sound of the storm. It was impossible to flag down a taxi because she was too scared to get the buggy close to the gushing deluge of run-off water along the roadside. So she bowed her head into the rain and kept pushing towards home.

Theo was already back at the hotel when the storm hit the city. It was just a summer thunderstorm—but when he discovered Kerry and Lucas were out in it he felt a sharp kick of concern. He paced up and down his study, looking out at the torrential rain, wondering where they were.

Suddenly the sound of his mobile phone made him jump—it was Kerry.

'Where are you?' he barked.

'The National Gardens... Lucas is upset... I broke the rain cover and he won't stay under it...' It was impossible to hear her clearly over the crackling connection and the sound of the storm, but he just about managed to make out the location she described. 'I can't get Lucas home. Please...will you help me?'

The sound of her distress raked across his consciousness, setting his heart thumping urgently. She must be in trouble to call *him*—as far as he could remember in all the time they had been together she had never once asked for his help.

He seized a giant golfing umbrella and bolted from his study. A car could pick them up at the entrance to the gardens and bring them back to the hotel—but he could get there quicker on foot. He didn't want to leave Kerry alone for a second longer than he had to.

The rain stung his face as he ran, carrying the umbrella unopened in his hand, dodging pedestrians and jumping the rivers of water sluicing along the gutters. It didn't take long to reach the National Gardens, and he sprinted along the deserted paths towards the place where she'd said she was waiting.

At last he saw her—crouched down by the pushchair in the pouring rain, attempting to keep the torn cover over the howling baby at the same time as trying to comfort him. Theo's heart was in his mouth and he felt a powerful rush of protectiveness.

She looked up as he approached, and the forlorn look on her face cut him to the quick. An overwhelming urge to reach out to her and haul her up into his arms seized him. He wanted to kiss away her misery and make her forget her worries. But then a cold wave of bitterness washed over him as he remembered *he* was the one making her miserable.

He stopped abruptly beside her and hesitated. Suddenly, for the first time in his life, he didn't know what to do.

'It's all right—Daddy's here,' Kerry said to Lucas. 'I can pick you up now. We can hide under the umbrella together.'

Her words galvanised Theo into action. He opened the umbrella and held it over all three of them, then he reached out with one strong arm, supporting them as she stood up.

Apparently being in his mother's arms was all that Lucas needed, because as soon as he was cradled against her shoulder he quietened down. Theo saw the tension across Kerry's shoulders visibly ease, then she lifted her face to him.

'I ripped the cover,' Kerry said, trying to look at Theo across the top of Lucas's black curls. Her long fringe was sopping wet and plastered over her eyes. 'I folded it back for a moment, to try and calm him down, but somehow it got caught and tore. I couldn't keep the rain off him and walk at the same time.'

She lifted a hand to push her hair back, expecting to see an expression of displeasure on Theo's face— annoyance that she hadn't taken better care of his son. But the look of concern she saw in his eyes made an unexpected ripple of emotion run through her. His gaze was fixed on *her*—not on Lucas. And she had the strangest feeling that he did care for her, maybe just a little.

'I'm sorry—I took a shortcut through the gardens,' she rushed on, trying to ignore the foolish feeling. She knew what Theo thought of her, and it wouldn't do any good to let herself get carried away by pointless wishful thinking. 'It was a silly thing to do. I should have taken shelter in a shop or café, not kept on walking in the rain—but I just wanted to get home.'

'You couldn't have known the cover would break,' Theo said, lifting his hand and brushing a long wet lock of hair back from her face. His touch was gentle, and something about it made Kerry's heart skip a beat. 'You made a wise decision, putting it on the buggy today. I didn't even know there *was* a rain cover.'

Kerry gazed up at him, struggling to concentrate on what he was saying. The tender touch of his fingers and the concerned expression on his face were making her feel oddly light-headed.

It was completely unnerving. She *knew* what he thought of her—he'd made it painfully clear. But the way he was looking at her now made her long to give in to the fantasy that they could be happy together. That one day he might come to love her—the way she loved him.

Suddenly she felt her eyes burning with tears. She dropped her gaze, flustered by the unexpected surge of confusing emotions within her. She should not let herself pine for something that could never be. She was just setting herself up for a lifetime of disappointment and heartache.

'I'm sorry.' The words were jerked awkwardly from Theo's lips as he gazed into Kerry's misery-stricken face. The haunted look in her eyes reminded him agonisingly of the previous night—when staring into her future as his wife had filled her with despair. 'This isn't what you wanted.'

Suddenly he couldn't bear the thought that being with him was making her miserable—she deserved so much more.

He felt ashamed that he hadn't realised the truth sooner. It had taken his aunt's comment that Kerry must be a wonderful person to make him see what had been right in front of him all the time. She *was* wonderful.

She was gentle and compassionate, yet ready to stand up for what she believed to be right. She was overflowing with love for Lucas, and had showed unwavering loyalty to the people she cared about. She should not have to live her life in misery.

It was his fault she was unhappy. He'd brought her back to Greece in anger, expecting her to meekly do as she was told. He'd never given her any respect. He'd never considered the possibility that she meant well when she showed an interest in his life.

'It's stopped raining,' Kerry said, startling him out of his thoughts. She was looking at him with an expression of confusion. 'I'm sorry I called you—disturbed your work. If I'd lasted out a couple more minutes the storm would have been over.'

Theo looked around them in surprise and saw that she was right—the rain had stopped. A rich, earthy smell filled the air as the ground around them soaked up much needed water, and the heavy atmosphere that had pressed down on the city before the storm eased.

He folded the umbrella away and felt the sun on his face. But its warmth didn't reach through to his cold soul. *He* was the cause of Kerry's misery, and that thought cut him deeper than he would have expected.

'Don't apologise for calling me,' he said. 'I want you to feel you can always come to me—but I know I haven't done anything to make you feel that you can. After everything that has happened I can't blame you for not trusting me.'

Before this she'd never turned to him for help. And now he realised just how much that had hurt him. The fact that she had never contacted him about Lucas—had never wanted him to be in her life—had felt like a slap in the face. But he'd pushed it to the back of his mind, refusing to consider why it had wounded him.

'I do trust you,' Kerry said, looking at him earnestly. 'I'm ashamed that I didn't trust you enough to come to you the night Hallie crashed the car. I wasn't thinking straight. If I'd stopped for just one moment I would have realised I'd got it wrong.'

Theo stared down at her, suddenly realising the terrible truth. If she had come to him that night, the outcome for their relationship would have been the same. Even then, when their affair had been completely harmonious, he would not have been able to stand her challenging his actions.

'You were right when you called me a control freak,' he said unevenly, raking his fingers through his own wet hair. 'I didn't know. I take my need to be in charge of my life, of my business, too far—and I can never forgive myself for hurting you.'

As soon as the words were out of his mouth he knew it was true. But, even more importantly, another realisation was forming. It was as if the storm clouds in his head were clearing—leaving the truth standing bold and undaunted in his mind.

'I love you,' he said, his voice full of confidence and amazement at the same time.

Kerry stared at him in shock.

The thread of his conversation had already been disconcerting. She'd never expected to hear Theo admit that he had been controlling. And now to hear him tell her that he loved her was just too much to take in.

'I'm sorry,' Theo said, lifting his hand and cupping her cheek gently. 'I shouldn't have just come out with that—it wasn't fair of me.'

Kerry frowned, gazing at him in confusion. He was being kind to her. He'd said he loved her. But after everything that had happened between them—after their argument the night before—how could he be telling the truth? And why had he just apologised for saying he loved her? Nothing made sense.

'When I first met you I was drawn to your beauty,' Theo said, slipping his fingers beneath her wet hair to caress the nape of her neck. 'Then I discovered what a gentle, sweet-natured person you are. I think I started to fall in love with the woman I believed you to be—but I wasn't prepared for what happened next.'

'I let you down.' The words caught in Kerry's throat as she thought about the terrible thing she had done. It wasn't surprising Theo had realised the mistake he'd made in sharing his life with her.

'No—I let *you* down.' Theo's voice was deep and resonant, and Kerry stared at his handsome face, transfixed. 'I wasn't prepared to realise that you were not just the beautiful, angelic creature I imagined you to be.' He paused. 'You are so much more than that—more than I ever deserved.'

'I...I don't understand,' Kerry stammered, finding it impossible to make sense of what he was saying.

'I controlled everything and everyone that came into my orbit,' Theo said. 'That was how I liked it—or so I thought—but I was so focussed on taking command that I never realised I was standing still.'

He drew her close and locked his eyes with hers, so that she could see the naked truth illuminated in their depths.

'But then you and Lucas exploded into my life—setting my cold, unchanging world in motion,' he said. 'I never knew what I'd been missing until I realised what you'd given me.'

Kerry stared at him, feeling her heart start to patter inside her. A warm feeling was spreading slowly through her body—but still she hardly dared to hope. What he was saying seemed too incredible to be true.

'I love you, Kerry,' Theo said.

Suddenly the pure, simple truth of his words wrapped around Kerry's heart like a tender embrace. She knew he meant what he said—and at that moment all her doubts disappeared.

'I love you too,' she said, her voice quavering with intense feeling.

She saw a flash of emotion pass across his face, but then he frowned, shaking his head in denial.

'How can you, after the way I've treated you?' Theo said. 'I've made you so unhappy.'

'It was partly my fault,' Kerry said. 'I was wrong not

to tell you about Lucas. I should never have kept him a secret from you for so long.'

'But I'd thrown you out,' Theo said. 'It's no wonder you didn't contact me. I'd never done anything to make you feel it was safe to confide in me, or to ask me for help.'

Kerry hesitated, suddenly feeling unsure of herself. Growing up unwanted in her grandmother's house, she'd learnt not to ask for anything, never to expect too much. It had been the best defence against inevitable disappointment. But Theo wasn't like her grandmother. He'd been generous from the day she'd met him—and he'd never given her reason to doubt his willingness to help.

'I should have had more faith in you—and in myself,' Kerry said. 'Right from the start I never wanted to make myself vulnerable by asking for anything—but now I realise I was shutting you out.'

'Knowing you didn't want me hurt my pride,' Theo admitted, a wry smile playing on his lips.

'But I did want you—I always wanted you,' Kerry said. 'I was afraid of you rejecting me.'

She gazed into his eyes, feeling the love inside her growing, knowing it was real. This magical moment with Theo was real.

'I love you,' she said. 'I've always loved you.'

Suddenly his lips found hers, and he kissed her in the gentlest, most tender way she could imagine. She felt her happiness growing alongside the blossoming love she felt for him.

'We've wasted so much time,' Theo said, drawing back and looking down at her, his eyes burning with emotion.

'We've been on a journey,' Kerry replied, thinking

how much they'd both learnt on the way. How much they'd both grown. 'But now we're finally together.'

'You are the centre of my universe,' Theo said. 'Without you my world stops turning. Please believe that I'm never going to let you go again.'

Kerry smiled and eased the sleeping baby away from her shoulder before placing him gently in the pushchair.

'I'm not going anywhere,' she said, reaching up and drawing Theo towards her with newfound boldness. 'But first, please take me home—and get me out of these wet clothes.'

* * * * *

Special Offers
Hot Nights With... Collection

Jet-set getaways with the world's most gorgeous alpha males

Hot nights with an AUSTRALIAN
On sale 6th July

Hot nights with a SPANIARD
On sale 3rd August

Hot nights with a GREEK
On sale 7th September

Hot nights with an ITALIAN
On sale 5th October

Indulge in four exotic adventures courtesy of Mills & Boon® Modern™ romance's most popular authors!

Save 20%
on all Special Releases

Find out more at
www.millsandboon.co.uk/specialreleases

Visit us Online

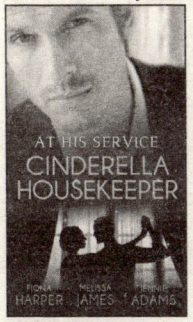

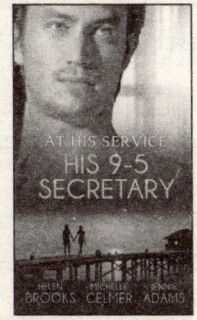

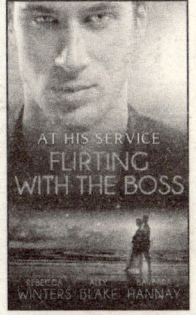

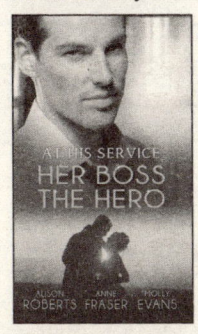

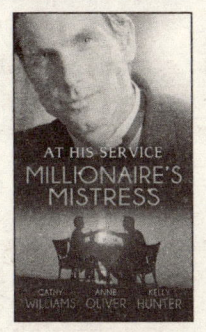

The World of Mills & Boon®

There's a Mills & Boon® series that's perfect for you. We publish ten series and, with new titles every month, you never have to wait long for your favourite to come along.

Blaze
Scorching hot, sexy reads
4 new stories every month

By Request
Relive the romance with the best of the best
9 new stories every month

Cherish
Romance to melt the heart every time
12 new stories every month

Desire
Passionate and dramatic love stories
8 new stories every month

Visit us Online
Try something new with our Book Club offer
www.millsandboon.co.uk/freebookoffer

What will you treat yourself to next?

HISTORICAL
Ignite your imagination, step into the past...
6 new stories every month

INTRIGUE...
Breathtaking romantic suspense
Up to 8 new stories every month

Medical Romance
Captivating medical drama – with heart
6 new stories every month

MODERN™
International affairs, seduction & passion guaranteed
9 new stories every month

nocturne™
Deliciously wicked paranormal romance
Up to 4 new stories every month

RIVA™
Live life to the full – give in to temptation
3 new stories every month available exclusively via our Book Club

You can also buy Mills & Boon eBooks at
www.millsandboon.co.uk

Visit us Online

M&B/WORLD2

Mills & Boon® Online

Discover more romance at
www.millsandboon.co.uk

- **FREE** online reads
- **Books** up to one month before shops
- **Browse our books** before you buy

...and much more!

For exclusive competitions and instant updates:

Like us on **facebook.com/romancehq**

Follow us on **twitter.com/millsandboonuk**

Join us on **community.millsandboon.co.uk**

Visit us Online — Sign up for our FREE eNewsletter at **www.millsandboon.co.uk**

Have Your Say

You've just finished your book. So what did you think?

We'd love to hear your thoughts on our 'Have your say' online panel
www.millsandboon.co.uk/haveyoursay

- Easy to use
- Short questionnaire
- Chance to win Mills & Boon® goodies

Visit us Online

Tell us what you thought of this book now at
www.millsandboon.co.uk/haveyoursay